★

California Dreaming

THE BROWNS

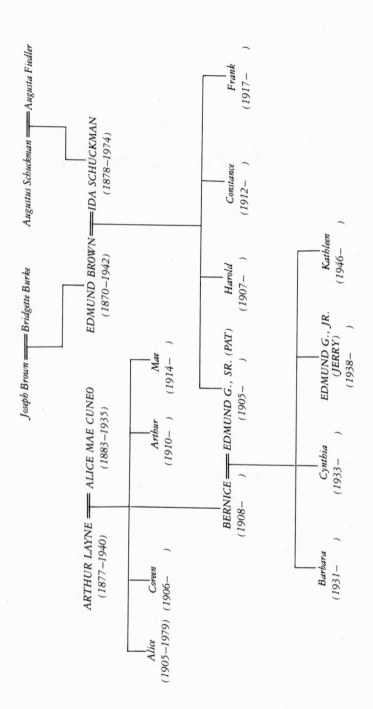

THE POLITICAL ODYSSEY_____
_____OF PAT & JERRY BROWN

1927 – Pat Brown registers as a Republican

1928 – Twenty-two-year-old Pat Brown loses state assembly race in San Francisco under the slogan "Twenty-two years in the District."

1934 – Pat Brown influenced by Matthew Tobriner and others converts to the New Deal and re-registers as a Democrat.

1939 – Pat Brown runs against veteran San Francisco district attorney Matthew Brady, using slogan "Pick a New and Competent D.A." and loses.

1943 – Running under the banner, "Crack Down on Crime, Pick Brown this Time," Pat beats Brady and becomes District Attorney of San Francisco.

1946 – Pat Brown loses campaign against state Attorney General, Frederick Howser, who is carried into office as part of an Earl Warren-led sweep.

1950 – Brown, with a hand from Republican Governor Earl Warren wins Attorney General Race on the strength of a "Pick Brown and Warren" campaign. He is the only Democrat elected to statewide office that year.

1952 – Pat Brown, along with Alan Cranston, Richard Richards, and George Miller form the California Democratic Council (CDC).

1954 – Brown re-elected as Attorney General, emphasizing law-and-order and high moral standards, often concludes his speeches saying "As for me, let me walk humbly with the Lord."

1958 – Republican Senator William Knowland, who owns the *Oakland Tribune,* and Governor Goodwin Knight agree to run for each other's jobs. Exploiting this "big fix," Pat Brown becomes California's second Democratic governor since the turn of the century.

1962 – Pat Brown wins re-election, trampling former vice-president Richard Nixon who concedes defeat to the Governor telling the press "You won't have Nixon to kick around anymore because, Gentlemen, this is my last press conference."

1966 – Prominent screen actor Ronald Reagan prevents Pat Brown from joining Earl Warren as the only three-term California governor. Pat is handicapped by U.C. campus and Watts riots which occurred during his second term.

1969 – Jerry Brown emerges from crowded field to win seat on Los Angeles Junior College Board of Trustees. Jerry makes news with budget slashing proposals.

1970 – Jerry Brown, promising to "take the price tag off public office," wins Secretary of State race.

1974 – Assuring voters he "disagrees" with his "father on many things," Jerry Brown is elected Governor, beating Republican Houston Flournoy.

1976 – Jerry Brown makes last minute entry into presidential primaries, wins a series of stunning victories but is unable to catch up with Carter, who has been collecting delegates for a year. Jerry is easily beaten at the Democratic Convention.

1978 – Promising to open up an "Era of Possibilities," Jerry Brown changes his mind, supports Proposition 13 and easily wins re-election as Governor over Attorney General Evelle Younger.

1980 – Jerry's offer to "Protect the Earth, Serve the People and Explore the Universe," is declined by Democratic voters who force an early end to his Presidential Primary Campaign.

1982 – Suggesting the Three R's must be changed to the Three C's — Computing, Calculating, and Communicating, Jerry runs for the U.S. Senate.

California Dreaming:

THE POLITICAL ODYSSEY OF PAT & JERRY BROWN

BY ROGER RAPOPORT

Editors: Stephanie Harolde
Ralph Warner

NOLO PRESS · 950 Parker St.· Berkeley, CA 94710

Front cover photo:
Governor Edmund Brown awards his son Jerry a Bachelor of Arts degree at
commencement exercises, University of California, Berkeley, June 1961.

Back cover photo:
The Brown family — Pat, Bernice, Barbara, Cynthia, Kathleen and
Jerry, arriving in Los Angeles during Pat's 1950 campaign for Attorney
General.

ISBN 0-917316-48-7

Library of Congress Catalog Card Number: 82-081858

For Margot, Jonathan and Elizabeth

ACKNOWLEDGMENTS

California Dreaming is based on two principle sources. First, the Brown family and more than two-hundred of their friends, co-workers or acquaintances contributed their own recollections. Second is archival material and oral history at the University of California's Bancroft Library, the state archives and the governor's office. The Bancroft Library allowed me to make generous use of their extensive collections on Pat Brown and Earl Warren. That library's Regional Oral History Project was also a valued resource. Governor Pat Brown was kind enough to release a portion of his own oral history not yet available to the public. In addition, Governor Jerry Brown's office provided me with several hundred recordings of his speeches, as well as transcripts of numerous talks, press conferences and other appearances. Extensive use was also made of government documents, periodicals, magazines, newspapers, manuscripts and other transcripts.

Both Pat and Jerry Brown generously made time available for this project on a formal and informal basis. I was able to join Jerry Brown on several long trips and spoke at length with Pat Brown on several occasions. In addition, Bernice Brown, Kathleen Brown, Cynthia Brown Kelly, Frank Brown and Harold Brown made significant contributions. From the beginning it was clear that I would be free to evaluate information supplied by the family without any manuscript review or editing by the Browns. No one connected with the family or their friends would see this unauthorized book until after it was published.

One of the pleasures of a book of this kind is the generosity an author encounters along the way. During the nearly five years spent on the project, I was the beneficiary of many large and small kindnesses. As soon as a friend or acquaintance learned what the book was about they seemed to know something or someone familiar with the subject. Others contributed their own files or unpublished manuscripts dealing with various parts of the story. The result was an abundance of new material which found its way into this book.

These friends include Peter Collier, Peter Sussman, Gerald Hill, Per Manson, Robert Fairbanks, Lynn Ludlow, David Johnston, John Vasconcellos, John Cummins, Gray Davis, Jacques Barzaghi, Wilson Clark, Elisabeth Coleman, Francis Boyd, Betty Singer, Claudia Ayers, Estelle Rebec and Amelia Fry. I also want to thank Lana Beckett for turning the Governor's research office upside down in behalf of this book.

Smoothing the road to publication were the Sterling Lord Agency and my friends at Nolo Press, Charlotte Johnson, Amy Ihara, John O'Donnell and Barbara Hodovan. Special thanks go to Carol Pladsen, who supported this book from the beginning, Toni Ihara and Keija Kimura. Two talented editors, Ralph Warner and Stephanie Harolde worked to make this a better manuscript. It was my good fortune to publish with them.

Roger Rapoport
Berkeley, California
April 15, 1982

PROLOGUE

Jerry Brown had been governor of California for two years and seven months, when he heard about a man proposing answers to the most difficult problems of the late twentieth century. He was Dr. Gerard O'Neill, a fifty-year-old Princeton physicist who some people were calling the Werner Von Braun of space colonization.

The Governor met the scientist on a warm July morning at a basement Sunnyvale, California conference room stacked with pink cardboard lunch boxes full of ham sandwiches, pears, Granny Goose potato chips and hardboiled eggs. O'Neill jumped up from his seat when Brown arrived with an entourage, including Apollo 9 astronaut Rusty Schweickart—the first man to walk in space without an umbilical. Here at the National Aeronautics and Space Administration's Ames Laboratory, O'Neill had just concluded a summer seminar on how America could sponsor mass emigration into space for only $100 billion. And according to his calculations, even this initial expense would be promptly reimbursed by beaming unlimited cheap energy back to Earth. Not since the dawn of the atomic age, when scientists were promising nuclear energy "so cheap you won't even have to meter it," had the technical community come up with a more promising scenario. No longer would our presidents have to kowtow to OPEC, supertankers break up off our coasts, and thousands of Americans contract black lung disease in Appalachian coal mines. By simply adopting Dr. O'Neill's space colonization plan, the energy crisis would go the way of the button-shoe before the dawn of the twenty-first century.

Perhaps even more beneficial than energy savings, O'Neill explained, space migrations would break down "planetary chauvinism," man's pre-occupation with life on terra firma, as the new society evolved. With an infinitely large, heavenly frontier to conquer, people could abandon seemingly insoluble terrestrial problems and learn to live in tropical space communities, where everyone — even the Palestinians — was guaranteed a low-gravity swimming pool. Best of all, space colonization would go a long way toward ending the possibility of nuclear war on Earth by giving men and nations vast new opportunities to accumulate steller real estate. Even the minor pestilences of Earth would be absent — no need for mosquito repellent or snake bite kits in space. The extraterrestrial colonies would abound with squirrels, deer, otter, birds, and butterflies, while rats, cockroaches, fleas and medflies stayed home. Heart patients and the elderly could live comfortably in a low-gravity, low-stress environment where people either walked or rode bicycles and had no harsh noises, congestion or pollution to contend with. Giant television screens would provide entertainment and it would be simple to communicate with relatives on Earth via low-cost videophones.

Projecting an eventual space population of 7.3 billion (nearly double that on earth), O'Neill pointed out that one of the most significant benefits of implementing his vision would be the reduced occupancy on the mother planet. "A non-industrial Earth with a population of perhaps one billion would be far more beautiful than it is now. Tourism from space could be a major industry and would serve as a strong incentive to enlarge existing parks, create new ones and restore historical sights. The tourists coming from a nearly pollution-free environment, would be rather intolerant of Earth's dirt and noise and that would encourage cleaning up the remaining sources of pollution. The vision of an industry-free, pastoral Earth, with many of its spectacular scenic areas reverting to wilderness, with bird and animal populations increasing in number, and with a relatively small affluent human population, is far more attractive to me than the alternative of a rigidly-controlled world whose people tread precariously the narrow path of a steady-state society."

A non-industrial earth with a population of perhaps one billion would be far more beautiful than it is now. Tourism from space could be a major industry and would serve as a strong incentive to enlarge existing parks, create new ones and restore historical sights. The tourists coming from a nearly pollution-free environment, would be rather intolerant of Earth's dirt and noise and that would encourage cleaning up the remaining sources of pollution. The vision of an industry-free, pastoral earth, with many of its spectacular scenic areas reverting to wilderness with bird and animal populations increasing in number, and with a relatively small affluent human population, is far more attractive to me than the alternative of a rigidly-controlled world whose people tread precariously the narrow path of a steady-state society.

NASA scientists who had already heard O'Neill's vision of stellar nirvana calmly munched their corn chips as the speaker finished chalking an outline of his plan for evacuating most of spaceship Earth. But the Governor of California's ham sandwich lay before him, untouched, on the formica table. Here, in this California basement, Jerry Brown understood how Enrico Fermi's colleagues must have felt when the Italian-born scientist set off his first chain reaction beneath the University of Chicago football stadium. Brown believed that like Fermi, O'Neill had shattered technical boundaries and presented a thesis of revolutionary impact. Here was a solution that, if it worked, promised not only to end the world's problems of hunger and disease, but also to do away with war and overpopulation. And amazingly O'Neill's answer to the doomsday crowd could be in the black in a generation.

In O'Neill's view, California was in a good position to become the launching pad for this new civilization where $300,000 annual incomes, superb recreation and fresh vegetables would be the norm. Yes, there would be a touch of culture shock at first, but soon everyone would come to love the hidden benefits of space colonization — like climbing the path to the North Pole and biking out along the zero gravity axis to view what Rusty Schweickart characterized as the "most beautiful sight in orbit—a urine dump at sunset."

The Governor promptly invited O'Neill to shop Sacramento for seed money, announcing happily that California would have its own space program. This disturbed Resources Secretary Huey Johnson, who challenged the physicist.

"You want to take $100 billion," said Brown's newest cabinet member, "when I as a resource manager can't get people to type, let alone reforest the state. I see this as a tremendous cost. I realize this may sound irrational, but spending all this money on space projects will never be right as long as the Potomac River is a stinking mess. I want to clean up our cities first. I want to be able to walk safely on the streets of Oakland and Newark."

"Would it have been better if Queen Isabella had cleaned up the slums of Spain instead of grubstaking Columbus?" asked O'Neill as his NASA friends chuckled to themselves.

"You realize," said Jerry Brown's Whole Earth talent scout Stewart Brand, "there are some people who would say yes."

On August 11, 1977, the dream of colonizing space brought more than 2,000 people to the Los Angeles Museum of Science and Industry for Jerry Brown's California Space Day. Corporate sponsors joined hands with the Governor's office, state agencies and sci fi enthusiasts to salute the high frontier. The first free flight of NASA's space shuttle, scheduled for the following morning over Mojave desert wilderness, was characterized as the golden spike in America's reach for the stars. Visionary speakers suggested the agency's pioneering venture into the long haul freight business amounted to nothing less than the declaration of a galactic Manifest Destiny.

Among the space fans attracted to this vision were oceanographer Jacques Cousteau, poet Michael McClure and Whole Earth Catalogue publisher Stewart Brand. But in the rear, other guests, including members of Brown's staff, were not amused. "This," said his thirty-year-old special assistant for energy matters Wilson Clark, "is disgusting. It's a technology worship session." And conspicuously absent were some of Jerry's closest advisors, like state architect Sim Van Der Ryn. The planner, who had just completed a book on ecologically sound disposal of human wastes entitled *The Toilet Paper,* bluntly rejected the Governor's invitation to celebrate this special day with senior staff. "Space colonization is total bull. I refuse to discuss it seriously. I'm not going."

Yet another Ph.D. standing in the rear of the museum begged to differ. "Like the Governor says," he explained with a grand gesture at the booster rockets, lunar landers and re-entry vehicles hanging from the rafters, "this is a merger of the practical and spiritual. Earth is the cradle of man. But man can't live in the cradle forever."

The Governor echoed this theme when his turn came to address the enthusiastic audience. "I don't think the frontier is closed. It's just opening up in space. That opening up, that exploration, is first and foremost a discovery of the unknown, a breaking out of the egocentric, man-dominated perceptions that still tie us down here below. As we break out of that narrow perception . . . we concentrate the creative energies of the best and most talented of those among us."

A few minutes later, he ducked out of a Carl Sagan slide show to answer reporters' questions alongside a solar collection unit heating coffee for the delegates inside.

"Governor," said a TV reporter as he jabbed a microphone in the politician's face, "some people say that your new advocacy of space exploration contradicts your philosophy of lowered expectations and that government would be better off investing its money in urban problems than the heavens."

"Oh, I don't know," said Jerry Brown. "If Christopher Columbus had taken the attitude that he should worry about what's happening in Spain and didn't care about exploring the New World, where would we be today?"

INTRODUCTION

"California politics are peculiar and dangerous," Lord Bryce wrote nearly a century ago in *The American Commonwealth*. Although the thirty-first state's population and influence now give it more economic power than most nations, the political peculiarities remain. The phenomenon of California politics, little more than a curiosity in Bryce's day, is now of world-wide significance. Political analysts who have never been to Lansing, Jefferson City, or Olympia, know every Sacramento hang-out from Frank Fats to the Torch Club. And when California governors travel abroad, they are received like heads-of-state.

In the early days of the American republic, Virginia and Massachusetts gave us most of our presidents. Then, during the years from the Civil War to World War II, as farming and trading gave way to the Industrial Age, New York and Ohio combined to provide nine chief executives. More recently, political power has drifted south and west, with California alone giving us two presidents since 1968.

This power shift and resultant focus on Golden State politics has unearthed a political tradition that differs from the rest of the country in a number of respects. Party organizations and ward-type machines, once so powerful in states like New Jersey, Massachusetts and Illinois have never been as important in California. Indeed, along America's Pacific shore, even the traditional parties mean less than they do elsewhere, as illustrated by Ronald Reagan's switch from the Democratic to the Republican Party in the 1950's and Earl Warren's winning the gubernatorial nominations of both in 1946.

California's long history of political candidates loosely tied to ideologically-based parties goes back at least as far as the days of Hiram Johnson. This young progressive who successfully fought to make the initiative, referendum and recall provisions of the state constitution a reality in 1911, had earlier split with his father, Grove Johnson, on the issue of the Southern Pacific Railroad. While Grove championed the railroad's interests in Congress and the state legislature, Hiram fought for, and ultimately won, the governorship, under the slogan "Get the Southern Pacific out of politics." Once elected, Johnson pushed for reforms that were to lead to a new generation of nonpartisan candidates.

In 1913, Johnson's Progressive wing of the Republican party was preparing to form its own party. To protect themselves they replaced a primary law requiring office seekers to run only for the nomination of their registered party with a provision allowing cross-filing. The new law meant politicians were now free to pursue the nomination of all parties. Of prime interest to Johnson, Progressives could now run in both the Republican and Progressive primaries. If they won both, fine, but if they failed in the GOP primary, they had a second chance in the general election campaign under the Progressive banner. The immediate effect of everyone running in all primaries was to undercut the power of traditional political organizations. In particular, Democrats could no longer count on a clean shot because cross-filing meant that their candidates could lose in their own primary. And even if they didn't, the Progressives and Republicans could unite to beat them in the general election. As if this wasn't confusing enough, new rules also prohibited primary candidates from listing their party affiliation on the ballot.

In the years after Hiram Johnson gave up the governorship, moving on to the U.S. Senate where he served until 1945, the Republicans—who were then the majority party—were able to use this cross-filing advantage so effectively they won ten of the subsequent eleven gubernatorial races. And no one used it more skillfully than Oakland district attorney Earl Warren. Warren, who won three terms as governor under the banner "Leadership—Not Politics," masterfully exploited voter antipathy toward professional politicians and their party organizations.

2

Earl Warren is particularly important to this story because of his profound influence on the career of Edmund G. Brown. Not only did Pat model his "law-and-order" career as district attorney of San Francisco on Warren's earlier success in Alameda County, he managed to get the Republican governor's backing for his first successful campaign for state-wide office in 1950.

Pat's career prospered and his legend grew largely because he, among all politicians of his generation, best understood the great lesson of California politics—never allow yourself to become trapped in a ideological box. In spite of the ridicule it sometimes brought him, he also mastered the crucial corollary to this first principal — don't be afraid to change your mind. This flexibility was augmented by an instinctive grasp of what it took to be a political survivor in California: liberal rhetoric on human rights issues, assistance to the poor, and protection of the environment, balanced by a tough stance on crime and the willingness to pipe Northern California water to the corporate farms of the arid south.

Perhaps Pat Brown was such an artful dodger because of a history of contention in his own family. Reaching back almost as far as statehood, there were disputes between Republicans and Democrats, Catholics and non-Catholics, teetotallers and drinkers, and bookies and police captains. In more recent times there were confrontations over schools, the war in Vietnam, political candidates and campaign strategies.

And then there is Edmund G. Brown, Jr., who is often portrayed by the national media as if he had just dropped from the outer space he advocates exploring. Important influences on his personality include his father's lengthy career in politics, the independent-progressive tradition of California politics in general, and the pessimistic altruism of the Jesuit Order. These ingredients, leavened by an almost manic curiosity and need to understand everything going on around him, cause the younger Brown to surround himself with a remarkable group of intellectuals, and to doggedly pursue the answers to many important questions himself. It has often been accurately observed that Jerry Brown is the only major politician in America who does much of his own research.

Jerry's diverse brain trust seems to offer something for almost everyone. There are space visionaries, solar power advocates, traditional good government reformers, poets, mass transit enthusiasts, a fast food franchise pioneer turned economic guru, spiritual seekers and Green Berets, as well as a covey of environmentalists striving to save the rafting rivers, reforest the over-logged land and stop nuclear power, to name just a few. While the thinkers and dreamers who contribute to the Governor's vast repertoire of interests influence him in a number of ways, it's easy to overemphasize their importance in his scheme of things. Indeed, it is

3

not uncommon for single-issue crusaders to be drawn to him, and then come away disappointed when he doesn't adopt their entire point of view. Just as Kennedy and Roosevelt were surrounded by extraordinary people but were never controlled by them, Jerry Brown is remarkably adept at gathering a large, talented band and then marching to the beat of his own drum.

Writing about populist Louisiana Governor Huey Long, historian T. Harry Williams suggested "the politician who wishes to do good may have to do some evil to achieve his goal." Certainly political survival in California has meant periodically spurning one's closest allies and embracing the ideology of long-time enemies. Better than many politicians, Jerry Brown understands and exploits this truth. It is the essence of the political lesson that has served his family well since his father's first victory as district attorney of San Francisco in 1943.

Jerry Brown's ability to change, as well as his personal delight in trying to synthesize opposing views, opens him to charges of opportunism and inconsistency, just as Pat Brown was called a Tower of Jello when he vacillated on major issues like the execution of Caryl Chessman. While Jerry has enjoyed some success balancing seemingly incompatible view points on major issues—such as the compromise he orchestrated between large farming interests and their workers—on other occasions— such as his attempt to get the Sierra Club and the Southern California land corporations to compromise on peripheral canal legislation—he ended up angering everyone. It is this commitment to reconciling antagonists—which Jerry found in the writings of the maverick Jesuit Teilhard de Chardin—that so often causes him difficulty. More than once, Jerry has been credited for the accomplishments of others and blamed for problems that were not his fault.

But above all, Edmund G. Brown, Jr. remembers one bitter political lesson. This was the occasion of the greatest Brown family defeat—his father's personal high noon—when a lightly regarded film actor shot down Pat's bid to become only the second California governor to be elected to a third term. In 1958, Pat Brown easily portrayed Republican senate leader William Knowland as an enemy of the working man, and beat him handily in the gubernatorial race. Again in 1962, Pat's middle of the road views helped him humiliate a powerful Republican—former Vice-President Richard Nixon. It was only in 1966, after the University of California disturbance and Watts riots, that Pat lost his sure eye for the middle-of-the-road. Allowing himself to be portrayed as a big spender, soft on crime, students and revolutionary minorities, the elder Brown was finally beaten.

While some political observers wrote that the electorate turned Pat out because they were tired of his many flipflops, Jerry read the defeat to mean just the opposite—Pat's footwork wasn't fancy enough. Despite all his famed flexibility, Jerry felt Pat had paid the price for tarrying too long at one end of the political spectrum. Indeed, Jerry actually campaigned for governor in 1974 by promising not to resume his father's expensive, liberal programs.

As soon as he was installed in the executive chamber, the younger Brown demonstrated the same political agility that served his father so well for most of his career. Particularly on one issue, parallels were hard to miss. As attorney general, Pat won the Ivanhoe case, a landmark decision beneficial to small farmers, which upheld the 160-acre limitation on federally-irrigated farms. Answering to a larger constituency as Governor, this flexible politician then put through an expensive state water plan favorable to large agricultural interests. Similarly, after testifying in favor of enforcement of the 160-acre limitation in 1976, Jerry waffled in 1977. Then in 1978 he decided to avoid flaunting the law by limiting a personal Nevada County purchase to 160 acres. But far from apologizing for changing his mind, as Pat sometimes did, Jerry offered this ability to reverse himself as a role model for the politician of the future, who would have to be, above all things, flexible.

Jerry Brown's willingness to change his mind is complemented by his "hands off" attitude concerning many major issues, such as new programs to alleviate social ills. He has limited faith in government's ability to solve problems and, in his darker moods, suggests government intervention is likely to make things worse. As a result Jerry has a remarkable ability to refuse to take any action at all. This commitment to slowing the political process down by not throwing money at the symptoms of social disorder has saved California taxpayers billions of dollars. It has also gotten Jerry into trouble. A case in point was California's 1981 buzzword, the medfly. While Jerry laboriously consulted experts all over the world on the best and safest way to kill it, the pesky fly refused to slow down its mating ritual. Indeed, Jerry was still trying to harmonize vastly conflicting advice as the medfly emerged from its egg and threatened to gobble up the state.

But Jerry has proved he can move fast when his political survival is at stake. A lightning 1978 decision to recant his opposition to Jarvis-Gann's property tax roll-back demonstrated a survival instinct superior to his father's. Even Jerry's adversaries concede no politician in the modern history of California has been better at getting out from under losing issues quickly than Governor Jerry Brown. Thus, while Jerry took his lumps over the medfly, when he finally moved he authorized a paramilitary-type operation sufficient to subdue a small nation.

5

While Edmund G. Brown, Jr. has governed far more in the mainstream tradition of his family and state than is generally recognized, it is undeniable that he has developed a leadership style all his own. Thus, this governor who preached the "era of limits" and a return to "smallness" and "simplicity," at the beginning of his tenure, saw nothing inconsistent about reversing his field and proposing to underwrite America's only state-sponsored space program. Even when the Governor's favorite Buddhist economist, the late E.F. Schumacher, gagged at the idea of space colonization and immediately sent word from London that he would purchase one-way tickets into the heavens for proponents of this grandiose scheme, Jerry held fast. "Contradiction is the essence of life," he explained. "Everything is contradiction. You want one thing and the opposite at the same time."

It has been more than half a century since Pat Brown began his rise in California's volatile political climate. In those fifty years, many successful politicians have tried to put a stop to what is now seen as the American West's only modern political dynasty. As of the middle of 1982, all but Ronald Reagan have failed. During the lives of most Californians, few things have been more predictable than a Brown in high state office.

All this is somewhat baffling to those unfamiliar with California politics. For unlike dynastic political families in other parts of the nation, such as the LaFollettes, Tafts, Kennedys and Longs, who owed at least their initial success to powerful political organizations, Pat and Jerry Brown have taken pains to gather support across party lines. Indeed, Pat not only switched from being a Coolidge Republican to a Roosevelt Democrat after losing his first campaign in 1928, but later succeeded in winning the attorney generalship with the support of Republican Governor Earl Warren. And Jerry—an activist on humanitarian issues, a lover of new age technologies and a fiscal conservative—has always prided himself on being a maverick's maverick.

During the years of Brown leadership, California's economy has eclipsed that of all but half a dozen nations. While it may be an exaggeration to say Pat and Jerry Brown have wielded the kind of power usually reserved for heads of state, their influence has been formidable. The governor of California, for example, now appoints more judges than anyone in the world, including the President of the United States.

As Jerry moves his sights from Sacramento to the Potomac, other Browns wait in the wings. His sister, Kathleen Brown Rice, has already made an impressive debut with a term on the Los Angeles school board. Now married to the president of CBS News and living in New York, she talks of returning to political life soon. And cousin Jeff Brown, San Francisco's public defender, frankly acknowledges his plan to eventually try for higher office.

The story of this family, long overdue in the telling, is particularly timely now. Cut adrift from the mainstream and outside the traditional liberal Democratic establishment, Jerry Brown continues to astonish, confuse and confound the electorate. With little hope of ever realizing consensus, this unusual son of a remarkable father continues to work for it in unconventional ways. In the process, the Brown family remains central to the political evolution of California and the dream it represents.

PART I

The Age of
Responsible Liberalism

"I kept my mouth shut and no one knew where I stood"

CHAPTER I

I t's quiet in the hallways of power. The security officers monitoring the closed circuit TV network installed by Ronald Reagan try to look busy. But now that the late show has ended, there is nothing to watch but empty divans, silent photocopiers and dormant push-button phones. The only visible faces hang from wood frames on the wall of the corridor outside the men's room. Here thirty-three governors eye one another from opposite walls. Dominating this portrait gallery are big men who proudly display ballooning waistcoats in an era when girth was equated with prosperity. Although beards dropping to sternums partially obscure many of the Anglo-Saxon faces, students of California history can easily recognize the memorable leaders.

There is California's first governor, Peter Burnett, who believed a "war of extermination will continue to be waged until the Indian race becomes extinct" because it was "beyond the power or wisdom of man to avert the inevitable destiny of this race." Standing in for the plutocracy is Governor Leland Stanford, who persuaded state geologists to re-map the Sierra's western base to the flat Sacramento suburbs, thus enabling his Central Pacific railroad to win increased federal subsidies during construction of the transcontinental link. Nearby rests the portrait of Friend W. Richardson who was so obsessed with reducing government extravagance that he ordered press releases typed single-spaced on onionskin stock. To his right is the man who collapsed from exhaustion at his own inaugural barbecue at the state fair grounds, Culbert L. Olson. Further down the corridor hangs the likeness of chubby Jim Rolph, who applauded the work of a vigilante mob that broke into the San Jose County jail in November 1933 to hang two men for allegedly kidnapping and murdering a local businessman. "This is the best lesson California has ever given the country," thundered Rolph, who was nicknamed Governor Lynch. After promising to pardon anyone indicted for the "good job," he suggested releasing all California's convicted kidnappers to the custody of "those fine patriotic San Jose citizens with pioneer blood in their veins." Close by is the portrait of Goodwin J. Knight that replaced the earlier version which was not to the Republican's liking. Alongside Knight is a more familiar face; Edmund G. Brown, Sr., looking serious, flanks the American flag, papers in hand. He proclaimed the portrait an "excellent likeness" at the 1967 unveiling, but asked for a replacement eight years later. "It's so somber," he complained, "and I was a fun-loving governor." His request was denied by the administration of Edmund G. Brown, Jr.

The man who was unwilling to upgrade his father's gubernatorial image never wanted Attorney General Brown to run for the job in the first place. While Pat deliberated entering that campaign, his son wrote from the seminary that the United States Senate was the place to "seek and to find." Dismissing state government as small potatoes, the novice argued that Pat could do far more for the cause of world peace in Washington than in Sacramento. Bernice Brown also had reservations about leaving her native San Francisco, the temperate city air-conditioned by God, for the state's hot and boring capitol. "I'm not going to Sacramento," she warned her husband of twenty-seven years not long before he filed.

Her efforts to persuade Pat to run for re-election to his San Francisco-based job as Attorney General were supported by the conventional wisdom that Governor Knight couldn't lose. Culbert Olson was the only Democrat to win the top spot since 1899 and he only lasted for one disastrous term. The Attorney General remained undecided until Senator Knowland and Governor Knight announced what was to become a political suicide pact. Both men looked like shoo-ins for re-election in 1958. But Knowland, whose staunch defense of Chiang Kai Shek's China lobby had led opponents to dub him "the Senator from Formosa," decided state leadership would do more to better his presidential prospects than returning to the U.S. Senate. Knowland was first appointed by Earl Warren in 1945 to repay a political debt to Joseph Knowland, the publisher of the then powerful *Oakland Tribune*. It was the *Tribune* that sped the Oakland D.A.'s career along, helping him become attorney general in 1938 and governor in 1942. After filling the unexpired term of the late Senator Hiram Johnson, Knowland was re-elected, served as Majority and Minority leader in the Senate and became a regular at Taiwan embassy dinners where he delighted his hosts by toasting "Back to the Mainland."

Unfortunately for Knowland, the road back to office in his home state turned out to be as difficult as Chiang's attempt to return to the mainland. Governor Knight, who was looking forward to leading his state into the sixties, denounced Knowland for trying to use California as a stepping stone to the presidency. When the Senator's party allies and the *Los Angeles Times* suggested that California's chief executive reconsider, he instead stepped up his attack. Only after his gubernatorial campaign financing began to dwindle did Knight reluctantly accept Eisenhower and Nixon's suggestion that he run for Knowland's senate seat as a consolation prize. "I had no other choice," confided the humiliated leader. "I was like a man in the middle of the ocean, standing on the deck of a burning ship."

As the Republican yacht began to founder, Democrats gleefully rowed alongside to help sink it. Native son and state Attorney General Pat Brown was one of the first into the Democrat attack boats, realizing Knowland was badly hurt and perhaps even doomed by opportunism. Suddenly an office that seemed unattainable a few months earlier was within Democratic reach.

For more than a century, utopians had dreamed of a chance to turn California into a blueprint for progressive government, where human needs took first priority. Now, suddenly, the opportunity was there. While the San Franciscan knew there would be obstacles to major progress in welfare, water resource development, law enforcement, education, civil rights and dozens of other areas, he was confident he could put his state on the right path. Suddenly Pat had a real chance to make good on some of the promises that had drawn his ancestors to California a century before. Pivotal man at a watershed moment, he announced his candidacy for governor on October 30, 1957.

Hungry for victory, Brown's party rushed to capitalize on the "cynical Knowland-Knight switch", which they branded "the big fix." The Attorney General, who was now beginning to line up Southern California financial support with the aid of millionaire duck hunting partners like oilman Edwin Pauley, went on the offensive against this "package deal" that deprived party voters of the opportunity to freely choose candidates. Wealthy contributors, seeing that Pat really did have a good shot at the governor's mansion, began writing checks for the jubilant Democrat who now openly boasted of financing his successful 1942 San Francisco district attorney campaign by betting on himself at five to one against super lobbyist Arthur Samish. "It's a felony now," he admitted, "and it may be a little out of line for the Attorney General to be talking about it." But the story only enhanced the Horatio Alger image of the man who was determined to send the Senator from Formosa back to the city room.

"I know," the Democrat told an audience in Marysville, "that the people are deeply disturbed at seeing our democratic processes made the victim of a transparent political pressure operation and the governorship and a United States Senate seat irresponsibly regarded as only a game of juvenile musical chairs."

Ignoring the advice of his eighty-four year old father, Nixon's chief strategist, Murray Chotiner, and party leaders, Knowland compounded his problems by making the "right to work" a major campaign plank. The conservative Republican figured that moderate Governor Knight and liberal Pat Brown would split the pro-labor vote. That would allow him to cross-file in both primaries and duplicate Earl Warren's 1946 feat of winning the Republican and Democratic nominations. But before Knowland could embark on the dream of winning the governorship at the primary level, Knight switched to the senate race. This allowed labor to focus their support on Brown as the progressive advocate of workers' organizing rights. The Attorney General was now the one man who could save them from the conservative senator who was out to ruin the trade union movement.

Like a man who had just shot himself in the foot, Knowland seemed disoriented. Besides running an anti-union campaign in a strong labor state, the Republican insisted on remaining in Washington during the spring 1975 primary campaign. He deputized his wife and daughters to ride around the state in an effort to sell his bipartisan image from the back of a trailer. After playing tapes of Billy's speeches, the Knowland-ettes passed out leaflets crammed with encomiums from Democrats like Majority Leader Lyndon Johnson ("I know of no finer man than the senior Senator from California") and Senator Hubert Humphrey ("No greater patriot ever served his country").

Knowland did pick up endorsements from conservative columnists like Newsweek's Raymond Moley, who dismissed Brown as "an ordinary, run-of-the-mill politician, fairly well-known around county courthouses, who has not taken much of a stand on any issue except on right to work, in line with the union bosses whose votes he needs to win." But he was hurt when conservative papers like Hearst's *San Francisco Examiner* bannered Knight's charges that the Senator merely saw Sacramento as a stepping stone to the White House. Stubbornly refusing to return home to campaign until two weeks before the June primaries he had hoped to sweep, Knowland performed badly at the polls. For the first time, a Democratic gubernatorial candidate received more cross-over votes than his Republican opponent. While 313,385 Democrats voted for Knowland, 374,879 registered Republicans went for Brown.

After the returns came in, several theories were advanced to explain why traditionally loyal Republicans broke ranks. The Attorney General's explanation was characteristically straightforward: "I kept my mouth shut (on controversial issues) and no one knew where I stood." *The Reporter* magazine suggested the key to Brown's breakthrough was "his extraordinary ability to reverse himself. He is often accused of announcing two positions on the same subject in less than an hour. A former member of his office once said, 'The last man to speak to Pat Brown knows his mind.'"

While this sort of perpetual uncertainty may have been a liability in states like New York or Massachusetts, where politicians ran on carefully defined platforms, it proved an asset in diverse California. The widening gap between northern and southern interests almost necessitated that aspiring officials develop contradictory platforms. Supporting wild rivers at a San Francisco campaign breakfast and then telling an afternoon Los Angeles crowd you want a multi-billion dollar California water plan to siphon Sierra water south might sound confusing to some, but this was no problem for a politician like Pat Brown, since at best the two constituencies saw only spotty coverage from the rival area.

From the sidelines, Democratic liberals marveled at the new campaign style pioneered by their main man. Flying around the state, the Attorney General boasted to liberal audiences about how he was working to end unfair subsidy of Central Valley agribusiness. Back in 1902, Congress passed a law stipulating that land owners were only allowed to purchase enough water from a federal reclamation project to irrigate 160 acres. But expensive lawyers helped rich corporations like Kern County Land, Standard Oil, DiGiorgio Fruit Farm, Inc., Southern Pacific Railroad and the Chandler family (owners of the *Los Angeles Times*) circumvent the limit and buy water from the federal government's Central Valley Project at less than half the going rate charged by other districts. For years big growers had been getting around the statute through a variety of loopholes. But they feared that one day vigorous enforcement of the 1902 statute would force them to sell off federally irrigated holdings which exceeded the 160-acre limit. Determined to repeal the acreage limitation that threatened their profits, major landowners in the Ivanhoe Irrigation District brought a test case against "All Persons." Reversing the position of his predecessor, Fred Howser, Brown announced he would fight the insatiable agribusiness interests, including his Magellan Street neighbor, Robert DiGiorgio, all the way to Washington. But after a circuit court rejected the acreage limitation, Brown adroitly ducked the honor of arguing his own case before Earl Warren's Supreme Court. Anxious to avoid antagonizing potential agribusiness supporters, this fighter for the little guy kept his distance from Washington by letting subordinates handle the appeal.

When the Supreme Court ruled in Brown's favor during his 1958 campaign against Knowland and frightened big valley farmers, the Democratic candidate really demonstrated what an adroit fence straddler he could be. Flying into valley airports, Pat told big growers that validation of the 160-acre limitation did not mean they had to call up realtors and begin subdividing. Standing on the tarmac, Pat assured wealthy farmers that once elected he would put through a monumental water plan which was capable of irrigating all the acreage they could realistically plant. He explained that the 160-acre federal limit wouldn't apply to water distributed by a state-financed water system.

Friend of the common and uncommon man, Pat Brown quickened his pace as Knowland compounded his ill-advised support of right-to-work laws by delivering the sort of anti-communist sermons that had worked well in the Senate during the McCarthy years. This meant characterizing the United Auto Workers as second only to Red China in its subversive intent. When the Republican troops failed to respond to the Senator's anti-union, anti-red pleas and continued snickering over the Knowland-Knight "big switch," Knowland's wife drafted a seven-page letter to set the record straight. Knowland killed the first draft, but after three of the states four traditionally Republican Hearst papers unexpectedly backed Brown at the eleventh hour, Mrs. Knowland released it to two hundred party leaders on her own authority. "I may end up without a husband," she admitted, "but as he says, so be it. Our country is at stake."

The release read:

> The real story of Billy's reason for running for governor has not only *not* been properly understood, but the exact opposite of the truth has been skillfully manufactured and successfully sold.
>
> Billy has said: "I do not intend to sit complacently by and allow California to become another satellite of Walter Reuther's labor-political empire!"

14

And he has said: "There is a job to be done in California."

And he has warned us against the new, big tax-free Labor Trust aborning between one James Hoffa and one Harry Bridges.

He's also said that he's been away for a long time and would like to be nearer to his family, always mentioning his five grandchildren which he has "accumulated," and his 84-year-old father.

All four statements are true, but the first three statements reveal his stark-naked, ungarnished motivation. But the people don't know what he is talking about! And, apparently, that is as far as he intends to go . . . because to spell it out labels a man by the name of Goodwin Knight for what he is, a tool of the labor bosses. . . .

Now, you and I realize that the Labor bosses were perfectly happy with Knight as governor, and if "Patsy" Brown had chosen to run against him, which I doubt, these bosses wouldn't have particularly cared which of them won. But they would have preferred Brown to remain Attorney General, a very nice spot in which to have one of their men. And Knowland was conveniently outvoted in the United States Senate, so, until Knowland decided to run for governor, he did not concern them in 1958. Probably Knowland and Knight, as incumbents, each running for re-election to his own office, would have both won re-election in the primaries.

But when Knowland got in the governorship race, it was a different kettle of fish! My goodness gracious sakes alive, what a stew this cooked up. . . .

On the face of it, it is ridiculous for anyone to think that Billy would have been a party to a deal to get Knight out of the race (Billy is not a stupid man), to say nothing of the fact that he is incapable of doing such a despicable thing, his character and principles being what they are.

You may not be aware of the great damage this did to Billy, for he is no ordinary man but was held on such a high pedestal by the people of California that this cleverly created apparition of a major flaw in his integrity shocked to the very core and literally took the heat out of hundreds of thousands of people in this state. To draw a comparison, though in a different field (although not so different basically), can you imagine what would happen to people's faith were people to believe that Billy Graham had been caught with his fingers in the cookie jar?

On November 4, 1958, Patsy Brown won 54 of the state's 58 counties defeating Billy Knowland by more than a million votes. Democratic Congressman Clair Engle returned Knight to private life, thanks to a 723,000 vote plurality. For the first time since 1878, the Democrats controlled both houses of the state legislature. All Republican candidates for constitutional office lost except veteran Secretary of State Frank

Jordan. The lone miss made no difference to the new Governor. Everyone in California knew the Secretary of State never did anything besides polish the Great Seal.

"You run your life and I'll run mine"

CHAPTER 2

I da Schuckman Brown was in the front row on January 4, 1959, as her eldest son placed his hand on the New Testament and took his solemn oath: "I, Edmund Brown, do solemnly swear . . ." Pat was taking over a town that only faintly resembled the Sacramento she first visited sixty-three years earlier. Either demolished or malled, much of the old downtown had given way to utilitarian office buildings, overpasses, and parking lots. Except for the gold-domed capitol and a few Victorians scattered nearby, it was hard to find much that had been here during her first visit to Sacramento in 1896. That occasion had been a brief stop during the move from her native Venado, Colusa County, to San Francisco.

The first leg of her journey had begun with a stage ride to the county seat of Williams. From their vantage point in nearby fields, her Venado neighbors watched Ida's carriage disappear down the serpentine dirt trail. These German-born hay and barley farmers loved this dark-haired, baby-faced young postmistress in spite of her bothersome habit of steaming open everyone's mail before they collected it. Everyone felt naked as she handed over the letters from her booth at the Mountain House, a stage stop complete with a store, bar, post office, and overnight lodging built by her father, Augustus. Yet no one ever had the courage to protest this well-informed young woman's persistent invasion of their privacy.

One reason Augustus chose this farming country was its secure location one hundred and fifty miles northeast of the violent San Francisco metròpolis where, in an average week, no less than sixteen people were murdered. The German immigrant had arrived here in the fall of 1852, after a six-month covered wagon trek from St. Louis. His diary of that overland trip reflected some of the many nightmares lived by pioneers rushing to California in the wake of John Sutter's lucky gold strike:

> On the 20th of June, we came to the first sand desert — it was 41 miles. We went there at night and rode nineteen hours in it.
>
> Here we came to a river as large as the Weser and had to cross it immediately... after that we had awful mountains which we ascended and had to come down on the other side risking our lives.
>
> On the 26th of July, we came to the second large plain —also 40 miles long. Here we lost 7 oxen which died of thirst. We also had to leave a wagon here. Thousands of cows, horses and mules were lying about dead. This took 22 hours.
>
> The discarded wagons by the hundreds were driven together and burned. We saw wagons standing that would never be taken out again, and more than 1,000 guns that had been broken up. Here on this 40 miles are treasures that can never be taken out again.

When he arrived with fellow German immigrants, Augustus Schuckman felt like he had never left his native Westphalia, so similar were these rolling foothills to the land he had left behind. Assured of the promise of California's rich soil, he homesteaded a new farm. Then the newcomer retraced his steps to Soest, Germany, where he met, and married, Augusta Fiedler. Although this handsome, cultured woman felt no enthusiasm for rural life in the uncertain west, she agreed to return to Venado with her new husband. After the inevitably difficult ride across the plains in a covered wagon, Augusta Fiedler Schuckman arrived in California with no knowledge of the English language. Her fellow German immigrants took time away from their wheat and barley fields to tutor her intensively, but it was months before she was able to communicate in anything but German.

Unlike the forty-niners mining the other side of the Sacramento Valley, there were no instant millionaires at Venado. The influx of fortune hunters from all over the world had increased the state's population more than fifteen-fold to nearly 225,000 between 1848 and 1852, but only a handful of these newcomers trickled into western Colusa County, where the soil turned out to be less fertile than the German pioneers were led to expect. Nevertheless, these settlers were able to grow enough to feed themselves and have a little left over at harvest's end for the Williams market twenty miles away in the Valley. Gradually, the farmers began supplementing the income derived from the fields by raising turkeys, hogs and chickens. This is when Augustus Schuckman decided to build the Mountain House.

Like her seven brothers and sisters, this Schuckman child handled her Mountain House duties between classes at the community's one-room school house. Three of her siblings had died in childhood at this settlement that was five hours by horseback from the nearest doctor. And in 1890, when Ida was twelve, her mother, Augusta, passed away. She was buried in the Pioneer Cemetery in Williams, and most of the inhabitants of Venado rode stage and horseback to attend the funeral.

On her trip in 1896, Ida and a friend had done little more than change trains in Sacramento. The steam locomotive pulled them along the Sacramento River with its dozens of small islands, past the grain warehouses of Port Costa and finally to the terminal in Oakland. There she transferred to a ferry for the short trip across the bay to the west coast's dominant commercial center, San Francisco. This fabled city of nearly 300,000 was the eighth largest in America, with only New York having more trade volume.

Back in Venado, Ida Schuckman had heard tales of new ten- and fifteen-story steel-frame buildings rising over the city. Now she could take in the skyline crowned by the monumental nineteen-story Claus Spreckels Building at Market and Third. Apparently anything was possible in the fog-bound bohemia named for ascetic St. Francis of Assisi, patron saint of the Franciscan order. A child of the mines, San Francisco was now home to leaders like Stanford, Hearst, and Crocker who honored themselves by building turreted mansions big enough to accommodate all of Venado.

Walking downtown, Ida Schuckman encountered splendid evidence of the riches amassed by this advancing California civilization. In the hotels, businessmen who dominated the Pacific trade dined in garden courts where glass roofs allowed the sun to shine in all day. Theaters, with their gold ceilings, offered seats of plush velvet and soft leather. And in the offices along Montgomery Street, she saw Persian carpets stretching between tapestried walls.

But riding the cable cars out to the residential districts, Ida found that the prosperous boulevards quickly gave way to muddy lanes. Nob Hill, Pacific Heights, and a few other wealthy districts might exhibit riches beyond anything she had imagined, but outlying neighborhoods looked shabby. Most of the pioneers drawn to California by dreams of gold they never found had not ended up in Victorian splendor but here in an attached row house — if they were lucky enough to find a home at all.

Out in these neighborhoods most parks were knee-deep in weeds, schools were largely unfurnished so children had to learn their lessons standing up, and litter and broken glass accumulated in uneven piles outside the storefronts. Numerous bond issues had been put forward to improve these neglected facilities, but all had been voted down, thanks to the "Keep the $1 Limit" campaign of San Francisco's blind boss, Chris Buckley. This Irish politician, who broke into American politics at Tammany Hall in New York, had such poor vision that he couldn't read or write. But voters believed their white-caned leader (whose prosperity derived from a lucrative side business of selling protection from the police to gamblers, brothel keepers and opium dens) when he told them on three separate occasions to vote down a new city charter because it would void the $1 per $100 limit on taxes.

This position, which neatly served blind boss Buckley's business-criminal interests and demonstrated a total absence of concern for the deplorable condition of city services, was not hard to sell to an electorate that preferred a tight lid on taxes to decent schools, roads, parks and landscaping. For this reason, municipal jobs were hard to come by. One of the newcomers fortunate enough to land such a position was Golden Gate Park gardener Joseph Brown. He had come to the West coast from Tipperary, County Cork, Ireland in 1852 with his wife Bridgette, a distant relative of Sir Edmund Burke.

The new city employee's work habits proved somewhat irregular. He was known to take occasional unauthorized leaves and go off on three or four-day benders. After sobering up, he would solemnly pledge to maintain sobriety for six months. As soon as the moratorium ended, he went off on another four-day drinking spree.

Brown's son, Edmund Joseph, decided not to follow in his father's modest footsteps. Inspired by the success of self-made San Franciscans like Mark Hopkins, the younger Brown plunged into a business career by renting a cigar store on Market Street. By the time a mutual friend introduced Ida Schuckman to this sandy-haired, twenty-six year old entrepreneur, he was branching out into the laundry business and looking over numerous other hot commercial enterprises.

The country girl was charmed by young Brown, who resembled Jim Corbett and talked optimistically of his future in the theater business.

Not long after they were introduced, the couple married and moved in with his parents. Edmund was nervous about Ida's reaction to the spectacle of his father's hard drinking ways, but she accepted his handicap with quiet grace. After all, the new bride conceded with a wink to Edmund, her own father had been going off on similar binges for years.

Only after her Catholic wedding did Protestant Ida Schuckman Brown learn that her jaunty husband, who favored derbys and custom-tailored suits, was busy making book in the rear of his cigar store. But Edmund was never a man to stand still. He soon decided to diversify his fledgling empire into the theater business with one of the city's first motion picture houses, the Musee on Fillmore Street, which opened in 1905. With profits from this new venture, he and Ida were able to lease an apartment out on Central Street. Their first child was born the same year and christened Edmund Gerald. Following the great earthquake and fire the following year, the Brown family moved to Oakland for a brief period. But as rebuilding got underway, they returned home, with Edmund promptly resuming both his licit and illicit enterprises.

By the time the Brown's second son, Harold, arrived in early 1907, Edmund was desperately trying to make a go of the Liberty, a Market Street movie theater and successor to the Musee. While the store, laundry and theater remained marginal operations, Brown increasingly looked to bookmaking to meet living expenses. Finally one day in 1911, he collected on a bet big enough to finance construction of three flats on Grove Street in the Western Addition. Ever the pragmatist, Ida vetoed the architect, who believed cars were merely a passing fancy, and insisted all units include garages.

Not long after the family moved into their new home, a theater across the street from the Liberty burned down and was replaced with a stylish new structure that opened for business complete with a brass band parked on the sidewalk. Unable to compete, and physically beaten because he didn't employ enough union help, Edmund was forced to abandon Hollywood's silent productions for a mixture of vaudeville and burlesque. Neither offering caught on, and in 1912, the Liberty closed. Determined to quickly reverse his sinking fortunes, Brown rashly covered a series of bets without laying off enough on other bookies around town, and lost heavily. As a result, family income plunged and they were forced to live off the meager earnings from the cigar store, laundry, penny arcades, and the photo studios he opened along Market Street in subsequent years.

The income from these and other ventures barely met the subsistence needs of Ida and their four children (a daughter, Constance, in 1912, followed by a third son, Frank, born in 1917). Money was so tight that every night when he returned home to the flat at 1572 Grove, Ida watched her husband empty his back pockets onto a kitchen plate. By carefully allocating the few dollars he brought home each evening, she was able to feed and clothe the family. Fortunately the mortgage was covered by income from upstairs and downstairs tenants.

Edmund Brown continued to work seven days a week, obsessed by the notion that he could recoup his losses with a repeat of his 1911 windfall. While the brass ring continued to elude him, he had high hopes for his children and insisted that a good Catholic upbringing was important to their future success. Although he was too busy to attend church himself, the workaholic demanded that Ida take the children to Mass. She agreed on the condition that they could also attend Protestant services. As a result, the children of Edmund Joseph Brown and Ida Schuckman embraced two faiths every Sunday. Ida always had her doubts about the notion of purgatory and detested the way Catholics built opulent churches in colonies like Mexico while doing nothing for the starving masses. Curious about religion, she systematically dragged her children in and out of nearly every major San Francisco church. Interested in more than just ecumenicism, Ida Brown also took them to various synagogues. She was determined that they should have both knowledge of and respect for all faiths.

Although the children attended Catholic confirmation classes, young Edmund proved to be something of a disciplinary problem at St. Agnes' Church. Just before the all important ceremony, he struck a classmate who had insulted his younger brother Harold. In turn, one of the church sisters slapped Edmund on the hand and told him not to return. When confirmation time arrived, the two boys left the family's Fillmore district flat together. Harold went in to church, while Edmund waited outside, heeding the sister's warning. Afterwards the boys returned home without ever telling their parents that only one of them had been confirmed.

By now, Edmund, Jr. was known as "Pat," short for "Patrick Henry," a nickname he had acquired after he delivered a fiery "Give me liberty or give me death" World War I liberty bond sales pitch in the seventh grade at Fremont Grammar School. At Lowell High, this yell leader, basketball player and debating club leader was the only non-Jewish member of Sigma Delta Kappa. Among his fraternity brothers was a bright young man named Norton Simon.

Watching his children grow up, Edmund Brown worried that they were beginning to drift away from the Catholic Church. He blamed this on his wife, who had come to loathe being lectured to by her Irish in-laws about her obligation to raise the youngsters under the Holy See. Although Ida tried to keep an open mind, she was beginning to hate Catholicism. She could no longer follow Edmund's instructions to take the younger children to Mass. The Catholic Church hierarchy was simply too materialistic and other-worldly; the congregation would be better served, Ida believed, by child care centers than opulent new sanctuaries.

The couple argued endlessly over theological matters until Ida finally decided to affiliate with the Unitarians. Edmund, who now employed his sons Pat and Harold to work at his cigar stores, penny arcades and photo studios, apparently saw nothing inconsistent about professing his devotion to the Church, while skipping Mass and establishing a series of downtown cardrooms. During the late twenties, however, it was his eldest son who unintentionally caused the senior Brown great concern. Pat became enamoured of Bernice Layne, the precocious teenage daughter of San Francisco police captain Arthur Layne, one of the few honest officers on the notoriously corrupt force. After meeting the thirteen-year-old in a history class, Pat asked her to go out with him. Although Bernice had been told she was too young to date, she thought she could change her mother's mind. After three weeks, the teenager conceded her case, but she never told Pat exactly why she wouldn't see him. "I just said I couldn't go, and didn't elaborate," she recalled sixty years later. Undaunted, Pat continued to pursue the policeman's daughter. A couple years later, he gave her a bloodstone ring, and the couple began going steady. He never told Bernice the ring was actually a gift from an old girlfriend. Fortunately for the Brown's illicit poker parlors, Layne's district did not overlap theirs.

Working days at his father's store, Pat learned firsthand about the difficulties of underfinanced capitalists. Although he put in a seven-day week at the various family enterprises, he too frequently came home with only spare change for Ida's dinner plate. Always praised by teachers for his mental agility, Pat saw little future in merchandising and began casting about for a profession that would allow him to live by his wits. Before long he started taking night courses at San Francisco College of Law while working days for a blind attorney named Milton Schmitt. Every morning he escorted his boss to the office by streetcar; each evening he guided him home.

In 1927, twenty-two year old Brown received his L.L.B. and passed the bar. That same year, Bernice, then eighteen, graduated from the University of California. While she sought a teaching job, Pat went to work full-time for Schmitt. The following year, the young lawyer's mentor died. When Pat inherited the practice, he invited his brother Harold and two other partners to help him form a new firm. With legal business flourishing at their Russ Building office, Pat announced his candidacy for the state assembly on the Republican ticket. Friends suggested he needed more experience before launching a political career, but the impatient young bookie's son simply shrugged and began campaigning from dawn to midnight.

Thanks to his experience as a youth running for junior and senior high school offices, Pat moved through the wards like a veteran politician. Nothing and nobody could persuade this high-spirited candidate that he wasn't old enough to pick up and carry the banner of the great Calvin Coolidge. "I'll never believe," he told campaign workers after voters greeted his youthful promises with skepticism, "that I can't get everyone to like me."

Pat's modest campaign staff genuinely liked this thoughtful politician who was perpetually in good cheer. By Model A, public coach and on foot they spread from Telegraph Hill to Land's End attempting to ignite the political bonfire necessary to light their candidate's path to Sacramento. The entire family was involved — with Ida working the Western Addition, Edmund handling the downtown district, Harold in the Fillmore, and Bernice Layne coordinating the Avenues.

Despite all the Brown's energy, Pat was soundly defeated. Undaunted, he turned his attention back to an expanding law practice and became one of the town's most prosperous young lawyers. The following year he and the twenty-one year old Bernice eloped to Reno. To protect her probationary teaching job limited to single women, the couple decided to keep their marriage secret. Unfortunately, by the time they returned home from Nevada, their secret was spread across the society page of the *San Francisco Chronicle*. Bernice lost her position but didn't suffer unduly. Even in the depression, there was strong demand for the legal services of her competent, hard-working husband.

Although he had no doubts about his future at the bar, Pat began reassessing his GOP philosophy. The year was 1931, Franklin Roosevelt's star was ascending, and heirs to the great Coolidge were presiding over one of the greatest economic debacles in the history of the Republic. Already some of his closest Republican friends, like Matthew Tobriner, a labor lawyer who worked down the hall on the Russ Building's twelfth floor, had actually gone over to the New Deal.

During their periodic encounters in the men's room, Brown's fellow Lowell High alumni tried to make him see how the Republicans fronted for a monied few while the Democrats were the people's party. As the young lawyers addressed adjoining porcelain urinals, Tobriner explained that Roosevelt's election was not just the changing of the guard from Tweedle Dum to Tweedle Dee, but the dawn of a new American politics. The second generation quasi-Irishman listened thoughtfully. He knew most of the depression-bound nation lived like his father, scrambling all day to put food on the dinner table. But what about industrious men like himself, who had found a way out of that vicious cycle of poverty? How could you say the American dream was not still intact when through thrift, hard work, and the knack of luring in new clients, a young lawyer could get ahead?

Democratic evangelist Tobriner replied it was not enough that the system allowed a lucky few like Pat Brown to speedily ascend the ladder to success. For every success like Pat's, there were a hundred hardworking families, like the Schuckmans, whose precarious livelihood was held hostage by the great depression. And just as farmers were easily wiped out by a single frost, and sole proprietors like his father couldn't hope to compete with well-financed corporations, most wage earners were at the mercy of their employer's whim. The common man didn't have a prayer, Tobriner continued, as he reached into his back pocket and brought out a copy of Bruce Bliven's latest *New Republic* article and handed it to Pat.

Pat took the magazine back to his office and read the article. He remained unconvinced. True, Roosevelt had mass appeal in hard times, but as soon as economic conditions righted themselves, the Republicans would regain control. Not so, countered Tobriner in yet another twelfth floor, men's room encounter. He went on to quote Walter Lippman:

Scientific invention and blind social currents have made the old authority impossible in fact, the artillery fire of the iconoclasts has shattered its prestige. We inherit a rebel tradition. The dominant forces in our world are not the sacredness of property, nor the intellectual leadership of the priest; they are not the divinity of the constitution, the glory of industrial push, Victorian sentiment, New England respectability, the Republican past or John D. Rockefeller. Our time, of course, believes in change. The adjective 'progressive' is what we like. The conservatives are more lonely than the pioneers, for almost any prophet today can have disciples. The leading thought of our world has ceased to regard commercialism either as permanent or desirable, and the only real question among intelligent people is how business methods are to be altered, not whether they are to be altered. For no one unafflicted with invincible ignorance, desires to preserve our economic system in its existing form.

For several years, Tobriner hammered away at his stubborn friend. Finally, one morning in 1934, Pat Brown announced he was joining the New Deal. Appropriately enough, he made his announcement in the men's room, where his unrelenting colleague whooped for joy. But back in the law office, brother Harold was skeptical of Pat's claim that he was changing his affiliation to the Democratic Party because it stood for people rather than profits. Indeed, Pat's younger brother believed that the switch was more a matter of political expediency than conviction. "I was a Republican and stayed one. He changed but it didn't make any difference. I don't think my politics were any more conservative than Pat's." The new Democrat, genuinely offended, dismissed the suggestion that his change of heart was merely an effort to bolster business by giving the Brown brothers San Francisco's first important bipartisan law office. Nevertheless, it was true that new Democratic clients were drawn to Pat, while Republicans continued to seek out Harold.

It didn't take Pat long to rise in the organization of his new party. Soon after switching over, he was elected to the San Francisco Democratic Party's central committee. But covering himself in a style which must have made his gambler father smile, Pat also assumed the presidency of the Order of Cincinnatus, a bipartisan group plugging for "clean government."

"Clean" was to be a key word in Babylon by the Bay in the next few years. Since pioneer days, when residents of California's largest city were murdering one another at the rate of three hundred per year, San Francisco had become synonymous with violence, graft racketeering and the vigilantism it spawned. By the turn of the century, the *San Francisco Call* was accurately editorializing that "to hold one of the principal city offices for two years is equivalent to obtaining a large fortune." The bag man at the center of these schemes was Republican boss Abraham Ruef, who handed out huge pay-offs to supervisors at the behest of utilities and rail companies who were prowling about for municipal freebies. Although this manipulator was ultimately convicted of bribery on behalf of a local trolley company and sent off to San Quentin in 1908, new white collar thieves moved in promptly to replace him.

San Franciscans were initially shocked by the sensational turn-of-the-century revelations from muckrakers like Lincoln Steffens, but gradually, they came to see political corruption as an inevitable component of municipal growth. When people turned on their faucets, for example, they knew the water was coming from Hetch Hetchy reservoir, which had sunk one of the most breathtaking valleys in Yosemite National Park. Initially, conservationists like John Muir managed to thwart the project in a legal grudge match. Then, in 1913, dam forces got a key break when San Francisco city attorney Franklin K. Lane, the man who had submitted many of the key city briefs in the legal battle to flood Hetch Hetchy, was appointed Secretary of the Interior by Woodrow Wilson. In Washington, Lane quickly passed out the patronage necessary to persuade Congress to pass the Raker Act, which authorized damming what Muir called "one of nature's rarest and most precious mountain temples."

While this kind of politics may have had its place in the city's formative years, Pat Brown and his Order of Cincinnatus brethren wanted an end to boss rule. In particular, they were out to end influence peddling by millionaire lobbyists like Artie Samish, who by the middle nineteen thirties fronted for the distilleries, breweries, railroads, race tracks, tobacco manufacturers, banks and insurance companies from his suite in Sacramento's Senator Hotel. But their vision of reform fell short of the radical political upheaval espoused by muckraker Upton Sinclair and his End Poverty in California (EPIC) party.

The author of *The Jungle,* a 1906 expose that unmasked unsafe and unsanitary conditions of the meat packing industry and converted many readers to vegetarianism overnight, championed a utopian Socialist solution to the nightmare of the Great Depression. In his 1933 novel, *I, Governor of California and How I Ended Poverty: A True Story of the Future,* Sinclair outlined his plan to have the state buy up idle factories and bankrupt farms and reopen them as cooperatives. The acquisitions would be financed by municipal bond issues, while co-op members exchanged script for goods and services. Collectives could also barter surplus produce from their fields for factory wares.

This grassroots plan, which featured tax code changes designed to redistribute the wealth, led Sinclair to a landslide victory in the Democratic gubernatorial primary in 1934. It also revitalized several of the utopian organizations that had flourished throughout California at the end of the nineteenth century, including the Bellamy clubs, formed to spread the Socialist dream of Edward Bellamy's evangelical novel *Looking Backward.* With the help of sister organizations like the Utopian Society of America, as well as leaders from the ranks of the unemployed, Sinclair's followers organized thousands of EPIC clubs across the state.

Newspapers, railroads, and state and federal governments promptly banded together to smash this threat to their profits. As the 1934 general campaign moved ahead, red-baiting became the main tactic to discredit Sinclair. Conservative forces dipped into the prolific author's iconoclastic thirty-three volume oeuvres to find language that could be quoted to portray him as a Godless, amoral lackey of Marx, Lenin and Engels. Metro-Goldwyn-Mayer's Louis B. Mayer put his documentary makers to work on a phony newsreel that showed the first trainload of East Coast tramps arriving in the Golden State to claim spoils that would be theirs after Sinclair was elected. The churches circulated hate literature characterizing the Democratic candidate as a "slanderer of all Christian institutions." And phony "Sinclair [sic] Dollars, Good Only in California or Russia" were labeled "redeemable, if ever, at the cost of future generations." Heeding the funny money's admonition that "a vote for Sinclair will put California on the bum and the bums on California," the electorate sent Republican Frank Merriam to the Governor's office in November.

With Sinclair safely returned to his typewriter, Pat Brown reflected on the failed campaign. He concluded no politician would ever reach Sacramento by running against the ruling class. Lord Bryce had correctly pointed out that Californians were impatient "with the slow approach of the milennium." But their eagerness "to try instant, even if perilous, remedies for present evils," led to sloppy campaigns which inevitably failed. For instance, down in Long Beach, an unemployed physician named Francis Townsend started an old age revolving pension movement that would give everyone over sixty years of age $200 a month, the money to be generated by a federal sales tax. Pensioners would be required to spend all they received within a month, which in Townsend's view would both help the poor and revitalize the economy. Eventually 1.5 million elderly joined Townsend clubs around the country, gathered in state and national conventions and even wrote a theme song: "Onward Townsend Soldiers." The plan itself eventually lost out to the more modest benefits of the 1935 Social Security Act.

In the meantime, Pat began to search out another cause with which citizens might identify. In time he realized that the answer was not to be found in Roosevelt's Washington, Huey Long's Louisiana, or even Francis Townsend's Long Beach, but just a ferryboat ride away, in neighboring Oakland. There, a young, broad-shouldered district attorney named Earl Warren was building a marketable reputation by relentlessly prosecuting con men and women, bunko artists, prostitutes, bookies and racketeers. Hailed by the U.S. Criminal Justice Administration for running the best D.A.'s office in America, the prosecutor frequently found his courtroom heroism on the front page of Joseph R. Knowland's *Oakland Tribune*. By the time Pat Brown assumed the presidency of the Order of Cincinnatus in 1936, Republican leaders were urging Earl Warren to run for statewide office.

Inspired by the Oakland politician's rapid rise, Pat began to think about challenging veteran San Francisco District Attorney Matthew Brady. Bernice didn't want her husband to run because victory would substantially reduce his salary. A thrifty woman, who had persuaded Pat to stop smoking by keeping a chart on the cumulative expense of his tobacco habit, she was not anxious to lower the family's living standard. After all, Bernice pointed out, she and Pat now had their two little girls, Barbara and Cynthia, to raise. But the aspiring prosecutor was quick to point out how he could help honest cops like her father, Arthur Layne, who struggled to keep the peace on a subsistence salary. What was needed, Pat claimed, was vigorous law enforcement calculated to drive the crooks out of town.

Pat's bookie father, who had recently separated from Ida and moved into a downtown hotel, also had reservations about his son's solemn pledge to wipe out the gambling parlors. What was so bad, he wanted to know, about running a little card room where lonely old men could play a friendly game of Pan? Would the elderly be better off sitting in their depressing, paint-chipped rooms, drinking Old Crow and listening to "Amos and Andy"? A lifelong Republican, who had been part of the powerful Tom Finn machine, Edmund Joseph Brown believed his son should reaffiliate with the GOP.

Pat, however, was convinced that his future was with the reform Democrats, and late in 1937 he began mapping his campaign against Brady. Mindful of Bernice's economic anxieties, he accepted an invitation to move his family to father-in-law Arthur Layne's Schrader Street house. The police captain, who had recently lost his wife, was delighted to share his home with the growing Brown family. One of his first grandfatherly duties was to help his daughter select a name for the child she and Pat were expecting the following spring.

In April 1938, Bernice gave birth to a son at St. Mary's Hospital, and Pat happily agreed to the proposal that the baby be named Edmund Gerald, Jr. The baby's grandmother, Ida, helped tend the child during the day, while her daughter-in-law regained sleep lost at night. Although he was recuperating from a recent stroke, Pat's father also visited frequently. The entrepreneur's doctor had assured him of rapid recovery, provided he gave up the hard drinking that contributed to the break-up of his marriage.

During his card games, Edmund limited himself to tea and soda, and bored friends with photographs of his new grandchild, who closely resembled Bernice. He also boasted about his son, Pat, who was now out hustling support at fund-raising dinners, as part of his campaign for Matt Brady's office at City Hall. One of the first orders of business was to visit his dad's Padre Club down in the Tenderloin. As the gamblers played illegal poker, Pat turned to Edmund and his cronies and said, "Just think of what it would look like if there was a police raid on this place while I was running to clean up this city."

"You run your life," Edmund Joseph Brown told his eldest son as he beckoned to the dealer for another hit, "and I'll run mine."

Brown's fears about being hurt by his father turned out to be imaginary. Brady demolished him at the polls without ever bothering to bring up the Padre Club issue.

Following the campaign, a tired Pat accepted a friend's suggestion that he renew himself spiritually through a weekend church retreat at El Retiro, in suburban Palo Alto. Here the lapsed Catholic reconsidered his mother's antipathy toward the church of Rome. Yes, there was something unnerving about the notion of purgatory. And perhaps congregations would be better served with child care centers than grandiose sanctuaries. But as he read Cardinal Newman and thought about Walter Lippman's *A Preface to Morals,* Pat found himself being drawn back toward his father's faith. One day in 1940 he told Bernice he would like to have a second wedding ceremony in the Catholic Church. Although she had been a lifelong Episcopal and was certainly not persuaded by the papal view of birth control, she agreed to the ceremony. Soon they were up on the St. Agnes altar reiterating their marital vows in front of their three children.

Pat's parents, who had not been invited to the original wedding, missed this ceremony too. Ida wasn't about to enter the Catholic Church and Edmund's worsening health had recently forced him into a nursing home. Although incapacitated by a series of strokes, he remained in high spirits and always had a few pennies for his visiting grandchildren. Edmund was hospitalized in the summer of 1942, and one day in early July his doctor suggested it was time to call in a priest. When the man of cloth arrived, Pat's younger brother Frank tried to shoo him off: "He hasn't gone to church in years. You'll only frighten him." But the priest, who insisted he was well-versed in delicate situations of this kind, walked into the dying man's room, placed a hand on his shoulder and asked if he would like to make a confession.

"Oh, Father," sighed the dying Irishman, "it would take too long."

"Let me walk humbly with the Lord"

CHAPTER 3

Shortly after his father's burial at Holy Cross Cemetery, Pat Brown made the down payment on a five-bedroom Mediterranean home in San Francisco's Forest Hill district. A white, stucco structure perched over a first-story garage, this Magellan Street residence, like others in the neighborhood, was built close to the street and had a small backyard. Nevertheless, Pat and Bernice were pleased that Barbara, Cynthia and Jerry, as the third child was called, could play with children from some of the community's leading families. A few doors away was the home of Robert DiGiorgio, director of California's pre-eminent corporate farming firm.

Although the new home had little land, Pat enjoyed walking out back at night to glance up at the great illuminated crucifix on nearby Mount Davidson. This site never failed to inspire the born-again Catholic. But if Pat had recently found God, he hadn't lost politics. Indeed, he was soon out proselytizing precincts from Nob Hill to the Mission in his second bid for Matthew Brady's seat. Campaigning beneath the banner "Crack Down on Crime. Pick Brown this Time," the Democratic candidate told the electorate in 1943: "There is no organized crime in San Francisco; the crime is all organized by the police department." He explained how officers simply winked at favored abortionists, bookmakers, gambling parlors and two-dollar whorehouses.

At first, few experienced politicians in the city believed Brown had a chance against an incumbent who had been D.A. for twenty-four years. Artie Samish, the heavyweight lobbyist, shared this view and turned down Pat's request for a campaign contribution. Later, Samish drove downtown wearing his trademarks — a tropical blue suit and straw hat — and pulled up at a popular gambling parlor. Inside, the three-hundred pound influence peddler once described as "Falstaff, Little Boy Blue and Machiavelli, crossed with an eel," offered $5,000 at five-to-one odds for Brady. In this pre-Gallup era, when political odds were determined by how much a man would bet, Pat decided to meet the offer with $1,000 of his own money. Determined to emphasize how much of a long shot he considered Brown, Samish put up another $5,000, at five-to-one. The aspiring D.A. again matched him.

Pat's second campaign against Brady went well from the start. When he picked up the endorsements of both the *Chronicle* and the *News,* the betting odds began to drop. Heartened by this vote of confidence from the gamblers, Pat campaigned eighteen hours a day, shook the hands of over 100,000 voters and stepped up his verbal assault on Brady via the radio. Just before the election he was near exhaustion. Even so, the candidate's campaign workers, who were used to Pat's scorching pace, couldn't believe it when a fifteen-minute talk suddenly ended four minutes ahead of schedule. Brady argued the Democrat had many limitations, but no one ever suggested he was a man of few words. When Brown's aides worriedly pressed up against the studio door to see what had happened, they saw him staring silently at the microphone as if in a trance. But just as they were about to tell the announcer to plead technical difficulties, Pat roused himself, shook his head and resumed his familiar baritone.

With the posted odds now showing the race a dead heat, Brady raised an eleventh-hour charge! Attorney Edmund Brown had filed incorporation papers for two social clubs which were actually notorious gambling dens. Unruffled, the Democratic challenger immediately replied: "If these clubs carried on illegal activities (over the past ten years), why didn't the

District Attorney stop them — and why doesn't he stop them right now?"

It was a good question, for which Brady had no good answer. The Republican, who looked so unbeatable only a few months earlier, had lost the credibility contest and Pat Brown won easily. He used winnings from his Samish wagering to pay off campaign debts and moved into public office a happy man. Everyone in the Brown family was delighted except Bernice. She didn't know how she was going to manage a family of five now that her husband's income was skidding from the $25,000 a year he made as a lawyer to $9,000 as D.A. And down in the Tenderloin, Edmund Brown's old gambling friends asked one another if the new D.A. was really going to make good on his pledge to wipe out betting parlors as they anted up for another hand.

Although Brown specialized in defense work for over sixteen years, he walked into his office determined to prosecute in the Earl Warren tradition. His initial efforts were handicapped by the fact that he inherited a staff that did not include even one full-time attorney. All of Brady's twenty-four assistant D.A.'s worked part-time. Two secretaries took care of all the city's legal affairs in longhand — the office didn't even have a typewriter.

Anxious to learn how to be an effective prosecutor firsthand, Pat headed over to Oakland to study the Alameda County system which Earl Warren had developed. Brown learned fast, and within months the San Francisco Police Department was relieved of their time-honored right to indict suspects, thus putting an end to a notorious system whereby defense attorneys actually plea-bargained with police officers. Henceforth, all complaints would be filed by Brown's staff.

Thanks to these and other Alameda County-inspired changes, San Francisco's arrest rate began soaring. Honest policemen knew that their arrests now had a good chance of resulting in convictions. This dismayed Edmund's old friends, particularly when the bookie's son began prosecuting bookmaking as a felony. "The philosophy of a district attorney is to get convictions," explained Pat. The first bookie he indicted went to jail for a year. So did the second and third. Card players all over town suddenly found their favorite poker parlors padlocked. Even the prestigious Menlo Club, that had been doing almost $500,000 worth of wagering monthly, was forced out of business.

In Sacramento, the state's new governor, Earl Warren, read stories of Brown's exploits with amusement. They reminded him of his own career. In fact, this San Francisco D.A., who characterized himself as "a mean little bastard," continued to study the techniques pioneered by his Oakland mentor in his quest to clean up San Francisco. If a train called "reform" could carry Earl Warren to Sacramento, Pat reasoned, he might as well buy a ticket on the same line.

Closing down card games, brothels and abortionists was only the beginning. Pat needed more causes to keep his eager young staff busy and, of course, to keep his name in the headlines. Walking down Market Street, past block after block of suggestive movie ads, this proponent of strict law enforcement, who believed in wire tapping and capital punishment, decided that the time was right to wage a war on pornography. Back at the office, he ordered the staff to file a complaint against *The Outlaw,* a Howard Hughes film featuring full-figure girl, Jane Russell. After enjoying a private peek at the picture's big nude scene, where the actress climbed in bed with a shivering Billy the Kid, the court ruled against Pat. The bench also rejected the D.A.'s petition to ban *Memoirs of Hecate County.*

Undaunted, the D.A. put pornography on the back burner and began crusading against juvenile delinquency. His office widely distributed "Don't be a Chump" and "Advice to Youth" booklets to teenagers, while Pat, himself, characterized California as "the most lawless country in the world." He pointed out that one-third of the nation's three million crimes are committed by people under twenty-five. "The most dangerous age for boys is seventeen," explained Pat. "For girls it's anywhere from eighteen to twenty-two." This crusade against young criminals added to Pat's popularity with the city's parents. "If I can get these kids of San Francisco to see how important it is to play the game of life according to the rules," explained the Democratic leader, "they are going to be a lot happier."

But by the time Brown announced his 1946 campaign for Attorney General of California, his relatives and friends were getting a good chuckle over precinct literature which characterized him as a leader in the war against juvenile delinquency. Apparently, they joked, the candidate was so preoccupied trying to beat incumbent Frederick Howser that he was unaware of his own son's reign of terror on Magellan Street. Known colloquially among family and friends as "the little bastard," eight-year-old Jerry was beginning to look like a good prospect for the honor farm. Uncontrolled and uncontrollable, the wiry youngster, who sported a fat upper lip from the time he was shoved into a drinking fountain by playmates, exhausted both Bernice and his grandmother Ida. The latter's decades of experience as a mother and grandmother didn't prepare her for keeping track of Pat and Bernice's youngest. "That child," she would cry at the end of a trying day, "I've never seen anything like it."

Neither had other residents of Magellan Street, who complained vociferously when this third grader tied a playmate to a tree, lit a fire beneath him and then whooped his way around the trunk. On another occasion, one of the youngster's teachers became particularly furious when she

34

found him trying to shoot her dog with a B.B. gun. And neighbors were continually upset that Jerry had become the ringleader of a grade school gang that delighted in harassing the entire block. It got to the point where some parents would sweep their children indoors the moment they heard the noisy Brown boy coming up the street.

Jerry's behavior persuaded at least two of the Brown's Magellan Street neighbors to go all out for Fred Howser in the 1946 Attorney General campaign. Determined to defeat the little monster's father, they passed out leaflets and plastered big signs for Pat's Republican opponent in their front windows. Although the D.A. hated to lose votes in his own backyard, he wasn't about to make Jerry the target of his "get tough on juveniles" stance. The sensible solution, Pat thought, was to find a constructive outlet for the child's seemingly endless energy. Finally, Pat came up with an idea that worked. He drove his tough eight-year-old over to the Olympic Club gym, where retired pro, Spider Roach, outfitted him with a shiny pair of crimson Everlasts.

After Jerry learned how to hook, jab, and feint, Pat drove him up to Weed, a small community in that extreme Northern Calfornia region politicians referred to as Baja Oregon. There he faced the reigning juvenile boxing champion at a Siskiyou County political picnic. Here in the shadow of Mt. Shasta, the San Francisco challenger scored an easy T.K.O. After the match, his father rose to assure the gathered crowd they could count on the same kind of no-holds-barred law enforcement from Attorney General Brown.

Sensing that his son had become a political asset, the Democratic candidate began dragging Jerry to clambakes, parades, testimonial dinners and rallies. Soon, however, the child tired of Earl Warren-style campaign pitches delivered by his old man. It was boring to travel around the state and have to listen to his father repeat the same speeches as if they were Latin exercises. Pat's performance was nearly always the same. First he would compliment himself for transforming decadent San Francisco into a fitting subject for a Norman Rockwell cover on the Saturday Evening Post. Then he echoed his successful 1943 campaign against District Attorney Brady by linking Republican candidate Fred Howser to unwholesome gambling interests. Finally, he assured voters that following his victory, Californians would no longer have to put Artie Samish on the payroll to accomplish something in Sacramento.

Of course, Samish, who Pat had beaten out of $10,000 in his famous bet on the 1943 campaign, knew the Brown family fairly well. His daughter, Joanne, attended Convent of the Sacred Heart with Pat's eldest child, Barbara. But connections like these had no impact on the Democrat, who assured voters in communities from Chico to Chula Vista that he didn't want or need the services of power brokers, influence peddlers and thieves wearing secular white collars. Other politicians could have these apostles of special interests; "As for me," Pat declared, raising his eyes skyward in a benediction that ended every campaign speech, "let me walk humbly with the Lord."

The San Francisco archdiocese's favorite politician remained optimistic about his prospects right up to election day. Particularly encouraging to Pat was the way Earl Warren avoided speaking from the same rostrum as Fred Howser. The Republican attorney general candidate campaigned on the strength of his record as Los Angeles D.A. But unlike Brown, he had not been elected. His appointment had been slipped through the Los Angeles County Board of Supervisors almost before the last rites were completed for his predecessor. And the word in Sacramento was that Artie Samish had nominated Howser for the job. When the new Los Angeles prosecutor gained the Republican nomination in 1946, Warren immediate proposed a Commission on Organized Crime to report on underworld bookmaking and slot machine wars independent of the Attorney General's Office. During the campaign he brought up the Los Angeles D.A.'s name as seldom as possible. But even without this crucial endorsement, Howser won in November, thanks to a Warren-led Republican sweep.

In the fall of 1947, while Pat was running a successful campaign for re-election in San Francisco, Jerry enrolled at a new Catholic grammar school named St. Brendan's. This parochial institution, founded by the Jesuits and run by nuns, taught children from some of San Francisco's best families. Watching Jerry amble down the street each morning in his new school uniform, some Magellan Street neighbors speculated that the boy would probably not last through the semester. But they underestimated the Jesuits, who had been shaping up incorrigible children of ruling class families for over four centuries.

Founded in the sixteenth century by a minor Spanish aristocrat named Ignatius of Loyola, the Society of Jesus had become the largest religious order in the world, and probably the most controversial. St. Ignatius had put the paramilitary organization together following his religious conversion. Leaders of the counter-reformation, the black-robed Jesuits operated unconditionally at the service of the Pope. And what distinguished these Catholic militants from earlier orders was their determination to carry the church's word beyond the monastery walls to the far corners of Europe, Asia, Africa and the Americas.

Something of a mystic, Ignatius wrote *The Spiritual Exercises,* which helped Jesuit novices mortify the intellect so it could be replenished with knowledge from Renaissance times. Under the doctrine of Ignatius, students strived to re-educate themselves, beginning with the study of the natural arts and concluding with the esoteric, or supernatural. In the process they learned to approach spiritual goals through strict exercise of will. After swearing their indifference to material wealth, and pledging chastity and obedience, the new Jesuits were encouraged to move out into the world to spread Papal doctrine and eliminate Protestantism. In many lands they founded excellent schools for sons and daughters of the elite and served as confessors in many sovereign courts. Jesuits soon became leaders in European education, as well as successful businessmen and important scientists.

Advocates of the counter-reformation across Europe, the Far East and the New World, these black-robed priests took control of Baja California for the Spanish in 1697. But the first half dozen leaders of the Jesuits in Mexico never even ventured into the northern portion of their territory, known as Alta California. In the meantime, the Jesuits began to fall on hard times at home in the European Catholic states. Jesuits abroad were accused of master-minding sedition, exploiting the poor in business enterprises, conning the Pope into giving them spiritual privileges, and establishing secret female lay affiliates. Even the order's inquisitive spirit was called into question by critics ranging from Bourbon monarchs to Voltaire. The Jesuit dialectic, which encouraged seminarians to challenge sacred religious ideals, was now characterized as blasphemy. Jesuits were even accused of being sworn to a secret doctrine — "the end justifies the means." Their superiors were sometimes referred to as the Black Pope.

Indeed, in *Japan: An Interpretation,* Lafcadio Hearn devotes an entire chapter to "The Jesuit Peril," which chronicles the history and influence of the Jesuits in Japan.

Yet this religion, for which thousands vainly died, had brought to Japan nothing but evil: disorders, persecutions, revolts, political troubles, and war. Even those virtues of the people which had been evolved at unutterable cost for the protection and conservation of society — their self-denial, their faith, their loyalty, their constancy and courage — were by this black creed distorted, diverted, and transformed into forces directed to the destruction of that society. Could that destruction have been accomplished, and a new Roman Catholic empire have been founded upon the ruins, the forces of that empire would have been used for the further extension of priestly tyranny, the spread of the Inquisition, the perpetual Jesuit warfare against freedom of conscience and human progress. Well may we pity the victims of this pitiless faith, and justly admire their useless courage: yet who can regret that their cause was lost? . . . Viewed from another standpoint than that of religious bias, and simply judged by its results, the Jesuit effort to Christianize Japan must be regarded as a crime against humanity, a labor of devastation, a calamity comparable only — by reason of the misery and destruction which it wrought — to an earthquake, a tidal-wave, a volcanic eruption.

Although the Society fought back, members found their once well-respected name being widely profaned. "Jesuitical" became a disparaging adjective applied to a coy, intriguing or equivocating individual. The Society's methods were increasingly characterized as casuistry — fallacious application of ethical principles. By 1759, the Jesuits were persona non grata. Five years later, they were suppressed throughout France. Then, in 1767, Spain's Charles II responded to charges that the Jesuits were ignoring their vows of poverty in favor of conspicuous consumption by expelling the order from all Spanish dominions.

Captain Gaspar de Portola arrived at Loreto, Baja California, in December of that year and handed over Jesuit missions to the Franciscans. Considered more loyal to the crown and less materialistic than the Society of Jesus, these Franciscan friars began exploring the New World alongside Columbus.

Under the direction of General Jose de Galvez, the Spanish troops initiated a land and sea campaign to colonize Alta California. But Indians blocked the ground route, driving the military leader into a frenzy. Convinced he was The Lord incarnate, Galvez mapped plans to crush the native Americans by inducting six hundred Guatemalan soldiers as combat troops.

Meanwhile, under Father Junipero Serra, the Franciscans marched on to settle Alta California in 1769. These explorers established missions at both San Diego and Monterey and eventually colonized the Indians through a chain of twenty-three religious outposts spreading north to Sonoma. It would be more than two centuries before the Jesuits regained any influence in this land, which was named for an imaginary Amazon island called California in an obscure Portuguese novel.

Their comeback was not an easy one. In 1773 Pope Clement XIV, under pressure from European monarchs and a number of his own cardinals, dissolved the Society of Jesus. But efforts at deprogramming the disciples of St. Ignatius failed. The Jesuits survived underground until 1814, when Pope Pius VII renewed diplomatic relations with the order. Soon the Society resumed its educational and missionary activities throughout the world. In California, the region they had lost to the Franciscans, Jesuits took over the mission at Santa Clara, where they established a university.

By the time Jerry Brown started at St. Brendan's, the order had provincial headquarters in San Francisco, colleges throughout the state, and a novitiate at Los Gatos. The Jesuit elementary school Pat selected for his son was first-rate. The insatiably curious child, who had unnerved first grade teachers at West Portal elementary school with endless questions, admired the nuns. And instead of avoiding Jerry, they spent long hours with him discussing aspects of Catholic theology that troubled him.

Jerry chattered enthusiastically about theological matters over dinner. His mother and sisters were interested, and happily joined in, but it was harder for his father to sustain interest, especially when he was strategizing a campaign. He frequently shifted the conversation to political questions, such as whether the Republican leadership was stymieing California's progressive spirit. Pat wanted a rematch against Attorney General Howser in 1950, but local Democratic leaders, like his old labor friend Matthew Tobriner, were not encouraging. Thanks to cross-filing, Earl Warren received the nomination of both parties in 1946 and ran unopposed in the general election. This strong showing made it difficult for the Democrats to find anyone to challenge the distinguished Republican leader in 1950.

Brown knew the incumbent governor was unbeatable. While he couldn't switch back to his original party, the District Attorney hoped that Warren could help him indirectly. The Governor had already let it be known that he was unhappy with Fred Howser. When the new Attorney General refused to run his office in Warren's tough, good-guy image, California's chief executive lobbied intensively for his proposed Commission on Organized Crime. After the unit was approved by the 1947 legislature, Howser was slow in providing staff support. But other state officials were more cooperative, and soon the agency's well-publicized underworld investigation began to get results. Warren was delighted; he had fathered another model law-and-order project, one that even won praise in the U.S. Senate.

Inspired by Warren's latest program, Pat drafted an ordinance to block rumored racketeers' plans to flood San Francisco with one-ball pin games and free-play slot machines. And while this crackdown was on the front page, Pat got the benefit of an even larger media splash by supplying muckraking columnist, Drew Pearson, with verification of corruption charges against the Attorney General. A former Howser associate told the Washington columnist that the politician took a $1,200 bribe from a Long Beach bookmaker during the 1946 campaign. The journalist promptly checked out this rumor with Brown, who characterized it as merely the tip of the iceberg. San Francisco's D.A. said that when the truth surfaced, all America would be scandalized. Personally committed to exposing Howser, Pat offered to talk to any newsman who was interested.

After getting verification from Brown, Pearson broadcast the story on his coast-to-coast radio show. Howser promptly sued Pearson for libel, but court proceedings failed to salvage his career. In 1949, the embarrassed Republican Attorney General announced he would not be a candidate for re-election. Now the San Francisco prosecutor enjoyed a chance to unite the broad-based coalition he had been building for more than two decades. Pat knew he could count on regular Democrats, law-and-order enthusiasts, and union members cultivated in past campaigns. His intelligent defense of civil rights and liberties also helped with the left and minorities who, with justification, admired this founder and former president of San Francisco's National Lawyers Guild chapter.

When the federal government tried to deport longshoremen union leader Harry Bridges during World War II because of Communist affiliations, the D.A. had come to his aid. And while Earl Warren took the easy political course and eagerly supported President Roosevelt's decision to evacuate the state's 93,000 Japanese-Americans to remote internment camps, Pat was opposed. Not only did the D.A. courageously denounce this incarceration, he also implemented special measures to protect his city's Japanese from racist attacks when they returned home following the armistice.

All this, plus Brown's crusade to do something about the miserable housing conditions of the blacks who had come from the South to work in San Francisco's busy wartime shipyards, helped broaden his political base. The Catholic politician also got financial support from old Jewish fraternity brothers like Norton Simon, who had joined the gentry in Southern California.

Like many other campaign contributions, Simon's $10,000 check was spent on one of the most remarkable bipartisan advertising campaigns in state history. As they motored up and down the highways of California in the summer of 1950, voters passed a procession of billboards urging them to elect Warren and Brown. Furious over Republican Attorney General nominee Ed Shattuck's charges that he was a regal, power-hungry kingmaker, the incumbent chief executive sanctioned the San Francisco D.A.'s request to use his name in campaign literature and newspaper ads. Republicans also slipped Brown copies of Shattuck's poison pen letters about Warren. Determined to sign his opponent's political death warrant, Pat leaked the hate mail to his favorite columnist, Drew Pearson.

With his campaign secure in familiar Northern California precincts, Pat concentrated his attention on the flourishing Los Angeles region. For the first time he went on television to show off his handsome wife and four children (a third daughter, Kathleen, had been born to the Browns in 1946). Anxious to highlight his law enforcement experience, the D.A. sought out local crime fighters for publicity opportunities. He even posed soberly by the bed of a skid row drunk to publicize inventor Haig K. Bonaparte's mineral compound that supposedly sobered up alcoholics in just twenty-five minutes. On platforms in Santa Monica, Pomona and Riverside, Pat announced his plan to crack down on domestic and foreign subversives. "Eastern hoodlums must not be permitted to gain a beachhead in California," declared the Democrat who occasionally gave lip service to the anti-Bolshevik plank made popular by the Republican U.S. Senate candidate from Whittier, Richard Nixon. "The Communists in our midst," warned Pat Brown, "are no different from Communists abroad. Both are dedicated to a single purpose, the destruction of representative government and the abolition of the democratic institutions that we hold so dear." When a wiseacre in the back of the auditorium inquired how a man of this persuasion could defend pinkos like Harry Bridges, Pat Brown recalled the controversial labor leader's wartime patriotism.

At one of his last fundraisers in the palm-gardened Ambassador Hotel, Pat listened to Jose Iturbi play the Steinway. He realized how prudent he'd been to withhold support from Democratic gubernatorial candidate Jimmy Roosevelt. Watching the donkey ice sculpture on the head table melt into a bipartisan puddle, Pat felt he was making political history. There was no doubt in the mind of this former Republican, now advertising his Democratic candidacy with the state's ranking Republican leader, that he would win.

He did just that in November 1950, becoming the only Democratic candidate for statewide office to survive the Republican landslide. Riding Warren's coattails to a 225,000-vote victory, the new Attorney General confirmed an old California tradition and demonstrated unequivocally that there was a future in bipartisan politics. To the extent that he could cater to the special interests of both parties, Brown knew he had a promising future.

By the time the new Attorney General had moved across San Francisco's Civic Center Plaza to his new office in the state building, his son Jerry, had memorized the Latin mass, become an altar boy, and begun the first of the three paper routes that would take him through the foggy hills of the city on a bicycle each morning. His younger sister, Kathy, sat by the window in pajamas and watched her crew-cut thirteen-year-old brother get off to his usual late start. How long, she wondered, would it be until she got her two-wheeler? Neither Bernice nor Pat lavished extravagant gifts on their children. They took their vacations in the Sierra rather than Europe or Hawaii, and the children were each expected to attend a public university, preferably on a scholarship. When the Browns finally bought a bicycle for Kathy, they shopped carefully before purchasing a second-hand model from the parents of one of her Magellan

Street friends. After cleaning and oiling the bicycle, Pat placed it under the family tree for Kathy to find Christmas morning.

Ida, who by this time had sold the Grove Street flats and moved into a Sunset district apartment, was impressed by this fiscal conservatism. She gave most of the credit to Bernice, who was far more disciplined than her politician husband. With a glance at her journal, Bernice could name her bridge partners on a given day in 1942, as well as how much she spent on school tuition for any given year. Characteristically, when Bernice decided to take up golf, she practiced for a year before setting foot on a course.

Both Bernice and Pat encouraged their children to be independent thinkers. At the dinner table, the family continued to have lively discussions. And no one enjoyed this more than Jerry, who took nothing for granted. When a sister at St. Brendan's blamed Dean Acheson for losing China to the Communists, Jerry disagreed. He also refused to swallow established notions about the church's omnipotence. While his classmates sat passively at their writing desks, Jerry kept hammering out questions. Why is the Pope infallible? Why do some rosaries have fifty-five beads while others have fifty-nine? If you don't go to hell, when does a venal sin become immoral? Why can't Catholics eat meat on Friday?

Ida was delighted that Jerry, like his mother, did not accept the Catholic liturgy unquestioningly. He raised exactly the kind of questions she used to throw at her husband. How could the church be so doctrinaire? Shouldn't sanctuaries be converted to child care centers? Why did Jerry's Boy Scout troop do as much public service work as the entire St. Brendan's parish? When was the church going to do something about the desperate, jobless men who loitered in the streets of the Tenderloin where her husband used to work? Why were there more derelicts cluttering the Emporium's sidewalk than she'd seen during the Depression?

Pat shared many of these concerns, and now, as Attorney General, he was in a position to address them statewide. At Sacramento's Del Paseo Country Club, Brown turned to his mentor for guidance. For several hours the chief executive spoke excitedly of his star pupil's progress. Then, moving closer to Pat to prevent other diners from hearing, he suggested nothing would stop Pat's progress provided he learned the virtue of silence. "Play your cards right up here like this," said the broad-shouldered Republican, cupping a hand to his face. "Don't lay them down on the table where everybody can see them. You can't play poker that way."

When Warren decided to keep his crime commission going for another year, Pat asked him to reconsider. "I wish you would give me a chance to enforce the law without any overriding body. I think you would resent the governor trespassing on your constitutional functions if you were Attorney General. I want all the credit or all the blame. I don't want to share it with anybody if I do a good job as Attorney General."

"Pat, I understand how you feel. Now let me tell you something. I've been around here for a long time and you're new here. Do you want to walk outside here at the beginning of your career and have the press — the headlines — talking to ten million people in this state — saying 'Attorney General Breaks with Governor'?"

"Governor, we *shall* have a crime commission," Brown responded.

Some time after this conversation, Warren invited Brown to go bird hunting with him at the ranch of his friend, Wally Lynn, in Colusa County. Enroute, Warren had his driver detour so that he could visit an elderly friend who helped his career in Alameda County and was now in a rest home. Pat waited in the car and was genuinely touched by Warren's act of kindness.

At the ranch, Warren's friend, Lynn, served his famished guests cracked crab. Up the next morning at dawn, Warren and Brown each took their positions in the marsh, a few miles from the Mountain House built by Ida's immigrant parents. Pat shivered in the early morning air with the man many politicians believed could be the next president of the United States.

Brown's thoughts were suddenly interrupted by an unmistakable sound overhead. He and Warren jumped up to spot a splendid pair of Canadian honkers coming toward them. A terrible shot, Pat decided to wait as long as he could and fire his rounds alongside Warren, so it wouldn't be certain who hit the birds. Finally with the birds just overhead, Pat fired, thinking Warren had fired at the same instant. As the two geese fell from the sky, the San Franciscan turned to congratulate his mentor on a fine display of marksmanship. But the Governor was sitting on a bench with a fully loaded gun and Pat realized that he alone had hit the target. He immediately threw down his rifle, rushed into the field, flung the bloody fowl over one shoulder and triumphantly marched back to the blind with his first double header. Pat Brown just couldn't miss with Earl Warren.

"That vow of chastity really gets to me"

CHAPTER 4

During the summer of 1952, San Francisco papers overflowed with stories of how Richard M. Nixon was undermining Earl Warren's bid for the presidency. California's junior Senator had never forgiven the Governor for failing to back him during three previous Congressional and Senate campaigns. Warren, determined to maintain the bipartisan image that led to an unprecedented three terms as governor, had in fact refused to issue statements endorsing any of his party's nominees during the 1946 and 1950 campaigns. But if he ever did resume backing Republican candidates, Warren knew this unprincipled young Republican would not be among them. The California chief executive was disgusted by the savage tactics of Nixon and his hatchetman extraordinaire, Murray

Chotiner. Not since Lewis B. Mayer loosed MGM on Upton Sinclair's 1935 EPIC movement had there been more unprincipled tactics in California politics. Warren believed that Nixon's outrageous red-baiting of Democratic senatorial candidate Helen Gahagan Douglas in 1950 was beneath the dignity of either party. In addition, the Northern Californian was not about to enhance the power of a politician representing a rival region. The Governor knew his biggest threat was not the Democrats but the conservative power bloc building south of the Tehachapis.

After initially pledging his support to Warren in March 1952, Nixon was told that Eisenhower was considering him as a running mate, and quickly pole-vaulted over to the General's camp. Now anxious to stop the California Governor's bid, Nixon flew to Denver on the Fourth of July, where he joined the Warren train heading toward the Republican convention in Chicago. Minutes after Nixon climbed aboard, he and his allies began trying to persuade the Warren-pledged delegation to climb onto Ike's supposedly unbeatable bandwagon. The Governor's backers glared as Nixon hustled up and down the aisles, as if Ike had already promised him the vice-presidential nomination. Although the Senator laughed off rumors that it would be Ike and Dick in November, no one was surprised when Nixon slipped off the train at a suburban Chicago station to avoid a Warren rally staged for the press downtown.

This Nixon-led mutiny ended Warren's slim hope of upsetting Ike. Following the convention, Pat Brown's fourteen-year-old son eagerly followed charges that Nixon had profited from a secret slush fund. He was amazed at how the vice-presidential candidate managed to work his Oldsmobile and little dog, Checkers, into the televised denial.

But what really confounded Jerry was seeing Earl Warren stumping for Ike and Dick. Although he was humiliated by both men at the convention, here was the Governor, warning his party that Stevenson's election could stunt the progress of California, Oregon and Washington: "They tell our people that the development of the West will come to a halt; that there will be no more river development, no more hydroelectric energy, no more soil conservation or rural electrification. Out here Eisenhower stands for the development of our great river basins, the development of hydroelectric power, irrigation and all the other multiple purposes that water can be used for. Eisenhower believes that those things represent the unfinished business of America."

Pat Brown explained to his son that this sounded like the pitch of a man who was hoping for a Supreme Court appointment. Jerry, with the naivete of the very young, had difficulty believing a man of Warren's integrity would bargain so openly. But Pat didn't want to argue about it, and the boy finally dropped the subject. On the last day of September, 1953, Jerry opened the newspaper to read that Ike had named Earl

Warren the fifteenth Chief Justice of the United States Supreme Court.

At this particular time, the focus of the Brown family's attention was Jerry's education. The senior Brown was anxious for his son to enroll at Lowell High School. Both he and Bernice worried that another four years of Catholic education might persuade Jerry to enter the priesthood. And, indeed, on the eve of his first day in the ninth grade at Lowell High, the teenager announced his intention to continue his parochial education at Riordan High—a relatively new, cement-walled school named for an archbishop who had been run over by a train. Resigned to respect his son's desires for a parochial education, Pat was apprehensive about sending Jerry to an unproven school, where, according to one of Jerry's friends, uninspired teachers—called Brothers of Mary—warned the all-male student body about the dangers of public high schools, not the least of which are the "bloody Kotex shameless Protestant and Jewish girls were said to carelessly drop on dark stairways." No, Pat thought, Riordan was too much of a gamble. If Jerry insisted on transferring out of Lowell High, his parents' alma mater, then he would continue in the proven Jesuit school system, at St. Ignatius High. Jerry acquiesced.

Downplaying his relationship with the Attorney General, the new high school student distinguished himself in the oral arts. No one at St. Ignatius could match his verbal abilities. After winning the freshman elocution and sophomore oratorical contests, Jerry starred on the debate team. In the centuries-old tradition of the Society of Jesus, Brown learned how to argue any point. What astonished friends and teachers was his ability to humble others on issues he knew very little about. The technique was simple enough. He put opposing debaters, teachers, friends and relatives on the defensive with endless questions. Invariably his queries undercut the weakest part of the other person's argument. In just five minutes, he could unravel a theory that someone else had spent weeks developing. And frequently, victims of Brown's verbal acumen had to admit the precocious teenager was right.

Not long after being expelled for a day for ignoring a rector's command not to toss an empty lunch bag into the schoolyard, Jerry got back into the administration's good graces by becoming a yell leader. But his heart obviously wasn't in it. When the rest of the squad jumped up to cheer the St. Ignatius football team's grand entrances at Kezar Stadium, the politician's son barely moved a muscle. And more than once he was late for the kickoff.

Indeed, the teenager's inability to be on time for anything was apparent to all who knew him. Part of the morning routine for Jerry's school bus driver was honking the boy awake. Neighbors often saw the porch light go on as pajama-clad Pat opened the door and handed his half-dressed son a pair of pants to slip on inside the bus.

Despite his preoccupations, Jerry was popular with friends, who enjoyed cruising the city with him in his beat-up Plymouth — despite its weak brakes, which he supplemented with aggressive downshifting. On jaunts to coastal parks, Sausalito, and the Russian River, Jerry and his friend Peter Finnegan, a nephew of the St. Ignatius principal, began talking about the seminary as an outlet for their idealism. In this era before the birth of the Peace Corps, Vista, United Farm Workers, Southern Christian Leadership Council and the Free Speech Movement, the novitiate represented one of the few places an altruistic young Catholic could go to work toward the betterment of mankind.

Perpetually in the vanguard of church theology, the Jesuits had great intellectual appeal for Jerry, who was now a debating champion at St. Ignatius High. The fathers at the school suggested that no matter what shape his future took, Jerry would never regret continuing Jesuitical training. They knew firsthand what the Society intended when it set up its first San Francisco school in 1861: "Experience has proved that by this method are imparted the best literary education, the fullest knowledge of English and the most perfect training of the mind; and on the other hand, exemptions in this regard have been found to be a great source of idleness and indifference to study."

Jerry was also sensitive to the Ignatian ring of much of San Francisco's cultural scene in the mid-fifties. The Beat poets and writers who gathered at North Beach cafes flourished on an anti-materialistic philosophy challenging the economic thrust of the post-war era. They complained about the lack of moral and spiritual leadership among politicians. "I am waiting for Ike to act and I am waiting for the meek to be blessed and inherit the earth without taxes," Lawrence Ferlinghetti told coffee house audiences, while Gary Snyder (the son of an IWW organizer) helped popularize the search for wisdom through Zen meditation: "As Zen goes to *anything* direct — rocks or bushes or people — the Zen Master's presence is to help one keep attention undivided, to always look one step farther along, to simplify the mind: like a blade which sharpens to nothing." It was even possible to take off, like Jack Kerouac, and live along the byways in a marijuana dream.

But to middle-class idealists like Jerry, these cult figures appeared destined to suffer the fate of local predecessors like Frank Norris, Jack London and Ambrose Bierce. While their work enraged, enlightened and titillated the public, it was unlikely to result in significant political change. The dominant culture would merely embrace, merchandise and assimilate these fashionable heretics until the power of their ideas was spent. An effort to map out a bold new vision in the complacent fifties just didn't seem likely to succeed. Even Beat ideologues like Allen Ginsberg asked, "America, how can I write a holy litany in your silly mood?"

One way to sort out the contradictions and develop a workable strategy for the future was to retreat from society into the Sacred Heart novitiate at Los Gatos. Rereading the lives of the Jesuits, it seemed to Jerry there was no limit to what you might accomplish if you let go of your personal ambitions and committed your life to the greater glory of God, as his instrument.

With his increasing interest in theology, Jerry grew more absent-minded. One afternoon in April 1954 the aspiring young seminarian was so preoccupied that he forgot a girlfriend's invitation to stop by. By the time he arrived, his surprise birthday party was over.

After this memorable oversight, the Brown boy's friends joked that he was destined to be late to his own funeral. But Pat and Bernice were not amused. They were growing more and more concerned about Jerry's religious intensity. To try and divert his attention, Pat asked his millionaire high school fraternity brother, Norton Simon, to line up a summer job for Jerry. After school let out, Jerry and a friend took off for Coeur D'Alene, Idaho, where Simon had arranged jobs for them at the Ohio Match Company. As soon as they got across the Bay Bridge to Emeryville, Jerry's 1949 Dodge engine blew up. The boys finally made it to Idaho, but nothing Jerry saw there challenged his resolve to enter the novitiate that fall.

So, while the parents of other St. Ignatius students worried what their children were doing parked in their cars at Ocean Beach late into the night, Pat and Bernice continued to fret about their son's religious preoccupations. The Attorney General, who had recently incited the enmity of many devout Christians across California for banning Bible studies in the schools, found it difficult to reason with Jerry about the Jesuits. The lapsed Catholic who had renewed his vows next tried an indirect approach. He suggested that legal training would give Jerry more influence than any Jesuit could hope to have. Law, he told the boy, was the best route to political office where one could achieve goals the Society of Jesus espoused. But the younger Brown, just named "overachiever of the year" at St. Ignatius, wasn't interested.

Jerry had been around politics long enough to believe he never wanted to run for anything. The phony backslapping, endless platitudes and ingenuousness dismayed him. He believed little could be accomplished through politics as long as questions of right and wrong were subordinated to the individual ambitions of politicians. And in addition, elected leaders were eternally dissatisfied—as soon as they reached one office, they promptly turned their attention to trying for a higher one. From his own experience, Jerry knew all too well that the campaigning never stopped.

48

For this reason, he applauded Pat's decision to resist Democratic Party pressure to run against Warren's successor, Goodwin J. Knight, in 1954. As top dog in the newly formed progressive California Democratic Council (CDC), Brown, Sr. was seen as California's best liberal hope. A grassroots organization, the CDC was conceived by Pat and others in 1953 as a way of helping the faltering Democratic Party cope with cross-filing. Under the leadership of his old labor lawyer friend, Matthew Tobriner, the fledgling group set up a statewide network, drawing members from the moribund Democratic Clubs that sprang up to support Adlai Stevenson's 1952 presidential candidacy. The idea was to have the CDC endorse Democratic candidates before the primaries and thus block Republicans from winning both party nominations.

With Senator Joseph McCarthy running against the Red Peril in Washington, few California Democrats initially sought endorsement from this left-of-center organization. Most were afraid of being red-baited into oblivion, like Helen Gahagan Douglas, who had relied on Tobriner to chair the Northern California portion of her ill-fated 1950 senatorial campaign against Nixon. But a few brave faces, like Alan Cranston, did pop up out of the liberal underbrush. A devout Stevensonian from the Peninsula, who starred in track at Stanford, he worked as a foreign correspondent, and was at one time sued by Adolf Hitler for publishing an unauthorized translation of Der Fuehrer's work. Besides writing a book blasting American isolationism, and succeeding in the real estate business with help from his wealthy physician father, Cranston organized endlessly for the Democrats. When he and other kindred spirits came together for the first CDC convention, it was Attorney General Brown who delivered the keynote address.

CDC troops adored this Irish Catholic father figure who proved liberal Democrats could win statewide in California. And they listened carefully as he explained that progressives were not just bleeding hearts, but pragmatists who valued the dollar. They especially enjoyed his occasional malapropisms. One popped out when he suggested it was far cheaper to parole young offenders than put them in expensive state institutions like Ventura School for Girls. "Do you know," the Attorney General asked, "how much it costs to keep a woman in Ventura?"

So popular was Pat that his delegates were determined to draft him for the 1954 gubernatorial campaign. But Pat resisted: "My job as Attorney General is not yet complete. My first three years must not be sacrificed for personal advancement but must be utilized to meet the obligations of this office. Organized crime in California has been smashed. The network of gamblers and narcotics peddlers and prostitutes has been warned: 'Stay out of our state—there is no room for you here.'"

Like her son, Bernice cheered Pat's refusal to challenge Knight in the

1954 campaign. His re-election as Attorney General put off the grim prospect of moving to Sacramento. But Bernice continued to worry about Jerry's talk of making a lifetime commitment to the Jesuits and fervently hoped Pat could dissuade him. The family debate over Jerry's future continued for months, until finally Pat ended by refusing to sign the papers required for his admission to the novitiate. When he left Magellan Street in the fall of 1955 to attend Santa Clara University, his mother urged him not to feel defeated. If he still felt strongly about joining the Society after his freshman year, she and Pat would reconsider.

Just an hour's drive south of San Francisco, the Jesuit college reinforced this Catholic student's determination to become a seminarian. A member of the sanctuary society, Jerry helped officiate at religious ceremonies in his white cassock. And when he wasn't praying or studying in one of the mission-revival buildings, the seventeen-year-old student could be found arguing philosophical issues with classmates or dorm counselors Marc Poche and Frank Schober. These Santa Clara seniors sparred with Brown over his unwillingness to honor the school's 10 p.m. lights-out policy.

Jerry's fellow Santa Clara freshmen were impressed by his dedicated search for answers to insoluble religious questions. But few of them knew that he was the son of a prominent politician who was crusading to protect the public from both foreign and domestic enemies.

News media hailed the Attorney General's aggressive legal staff of 115 as it fought to realize vast state royalties from offshore oil drilling, convicted assemblymen for fraudulent resale of liquor licenses, recovered charitable trusts foolishly invested in race tracks and uncovered lumber overloading in Mendocino County. Pat also exposed mistreatment of state mental hospital patients, sued *Confidential* and *Whisper* magazines for publishing objectionable materials, prosecuted Yolo County policemen who staged lascivious stage shows, worked to keep California teenagers away from Tijuana vice and raided gambling parlors and bordellos from Pismo Beach to Eureka.

With the possible exception of J. Edgar Hoover, there wasn't a lawman in the country who could match Pat's record. During periodic visits to Santa Clara, the Attorney General cited these achievements as examples of the good lawyers could do in a democracy. But none of this swayed Jerry. On his eighteenth birthday, he arrived at Magellan Street to tell his parents that the Sacred Heart Novitiate would become his home in the fall. Bernice, who had never converted to Catholicism, did not try to hide her feelings. It was one thing for Jerry to harp at Ida about getting baptized, but how could a child who wasn't old enough to purchase a can of ale be allowed to abandon a promising future for a life of obscurity in sacerdotal robes?

Pat shared Bernice's concerns and was also troubled by the genetic implications of Jerry's choice. Although now a practicing Catholic, the Attorney General sounded like a liberal Protestant when it came to the subject of celibacy. "Those Jesuits are tough, hard-hitting guys," he explained. "They ought to perpetuate their kind. They're not like some of these orders who are a little effete. I don't mean queer or anything. But that vow of chastity really gets to me."

Yet Pat's concern about Jerry's withdrawal from the active gene pool was tempered by his common-sense expectation that the boy would ultimately leave the seminary, with its vows of poverty, chastity and obedience. "Son," he told the aspiring Jesuit, "you've got your father's genes. You'll never be able to live up to one of these vows."

"Which one, Dad?" asked Jerry.

"Obedience."

By mid-summer of 1956, Pat was busy preparing for the Democratic National Convention in Chicago. But before he left San Francisco, the Stevenson loyalist arranged a favor for his son and three of Jerry's old St. Ignatius classmates — Peter Finnegan, Frank Damrell and a husky young man who also happened to go by the name Jerry Brown. Pat called a business friend in New York and asked him to host the four young men on their last non-sectarian liberty. Within days, Magellan Street's "Little Jerry" Brown headed east with his friends. When they left, Pat suggested that Bernice join him in Illinois for the convention. But the boy's mother wanted to be home when Jerry returned from New York, so she could properly send him off to Los Gatos. Pat would have preferred to be home for that occasion, too, but Adlai Stevenson needed him. And although he didn't know it yet, a handsome young senator from Massachusetts was also about to solicit his aid.

In Chicago, the Attorney General was sought out by both John F. Kennedy and his younger brother, Robert. The junior Senator from Massachusetts was excited about his possibilities of getting on the vice-presidential ticket. Pat suggested he calm down and accept political reality. First, it was clear that Eisenhower would embarrass Stevenson at the polls in November. Kennedy had fine prospects in 1960, but if he ran this time, analysts would claim a voter backlash against Kennedy's Catholicism defeated the 1956 Democratic ticket.

The Senator thanked Brown for his advice, but went on to fight Estes Kefauver for the right to run with Adlai. When the chairman called for California's vote, Pat had no idea where his delegation stood. But instead of pausing to take an accurate head count, the San Franciscan simply eyeballed the California contingent and claimed his state cast 62 ballots for Kefauver and 30 for Kennedy. After the convention he confessed to friends that he "gave it to Kefauver because I wanted Kefauver to get the nomination over Kennedy. I didn't want Kennedy to be hurt. I felt he had a great future. Now it was really duplicitous on my part but I was sincere in wanting to save Kennedy for 1960."

By the time Pat returned to Magellan Street, Jerry had left for the novitiate at Los Gatos, giving his mother a set of plates. Despite Jerry's obvious sincerity, Pat remained convinced his son would not last long in his new environment. What will happen the first time he craves a Zimburger, fries and a chocolate shake? How will he bear those hot valley summers without swims in the Russian River? He simply could not envision his son where there was no golf, no movies, and no women.

Jerry Brown considered all of this as a friend drove him and Frank Damrell, Peter Finnegan and the other Jerry Brown down the Bayshore Freeway. As they passed through Millbrae, these new Ignatians watched the large planes lift over the bay toward destinations that would soon be out of bounds for them. In Palo Alto, Stanford's Hoover Tower reminded them they were giving up the obvious merits of co-education. Heading up Los Gatos' vineyard-covered slopes, everyone lit a last cigarette. There was time for one more drag as they approached the parking lot. Finally, they ground out their butts and walked through the gate to greet Sacred Heart's Master of Novices.

Like the forty other seminarians entering the novitiate with them, these three friends from San Francisco quickly fell into a daily routine that had varied only slightly since the sixteenth century. Soon after taking vows of poverty, chastity and obedience, the aspiring Jesuits began a thirty-day silent retreat. Guided by the Spiritual Exercises of St. Ignatius, they were taught how to apply zero-based thinking to matters of theology. Centuries before the rise of transcendental meditation and the human potential movement, the Society had developed this system to help seminarians transcend their pre-novitiate biases. A psychological masterpiece, the exercises helped "conquer oneself and regulate one's life and avoid coming to a determination through any inordinate affection."

The month-long process began by examining the purpose of man's existence. The retreatant was asked to visualize Satan on a throne in Babylon representing forces of evil. On the other side of the throne was the noble prince seeking support for his holy crusade. After pledging oneself to the Christian forces, meditation began on the life of Christ and the crucifixion.

This spiritual footwork was a prelude to the final stage of the exercise. Once the novice committed himself to the Savior, he came to the great fork in the spiritual road that distinguishes the Jesuits from other orders. It was not enough, taught St. Ignatius, merely to find God inside the monastery walls. The retreatant had to meditate on the idea that the spirit of God can be found everywhere. This doctrine, known as *contem-*

platio ad morem, enabled Jesuits to make their crucial break with older monastic orders. Four centuries later, the Society continued to teach novices how to pray and lead active lives. Contemplation and action went hand-in-hand for these modern-day papal soldiers.

Brown and his fellow novices rose at five each morning, meditated for an hour, listened to hour-long lectures on spirituality and then either worked in the garden, the kitchen, or outside, tending — and occasionally slaughtering — chickens. After another period of spiritual reading and then lunch, thirty minutes of theological conversation (often in Latin) with assigned companions was permitted. A similar period after dinner was the only other time during the day that speech was permitted. No one was allowed to speak at meals except for a reader who quoted from designated spiritual classics. At night they studied the lives of obscure Jesuits.

Totally cut off from print and electronic media, limited to weekly letters and monthly visits from family members, the novices broke their routine for only two reasons. Twice a week recreational activities were allowed at a nearby facility. And every September the young men of Los Gatos went on a thirty-day "Long Retreat." Ostensibly a spiritual odyssey for the seminarians, this excursion also enabled the California Province of the Society of Jesus to harvest grapes from its local vineyards. The fruit picked by this voluntary labor force was reserved for crushing into the novitiate's premium-priced dessert wines. While no threat to the large Christian Brothers operation in Napa Valley, the Los Gatos Jesuits did produce a Black Muscat favored by many California wine connoisseurs.

During monthly two-hour visits, Pat and Bernice searched for signs that their son was ready to doff his long black cassock and white collar. But as they strolled the floral gardens, Jerry made it clear that he was adjusting well to the vicissitudes of Jesuit life, including penitential practices. Bernice cringed when she heard him talk of "taking the discipline" by whipping himself with a cord and wrapping spiked chains about his limbs. And while it was true that the seminarian did limp with the links tightened about his ankle, Jerry found a way around self-flagellation, simulating the sound of whipping his buttocks by slapping the ropes on his bed.

When Pat and Bernice visited their son, Pat did most of the talking. Bernice walked along silently as father and son discussed theological matters. The Attorney General, now looking forward to running for the governorship, tried planting seeds of doubt in Jerry about the value of seminary life. In what seemed to be a role reversal, Pat was asking more questions than Jerry. The novice struggled for quick answers to Pat's skeptical inquiries about the rosary, sacraments, and confession. It would only be a matter of time, Pat hoped, before the seeds would germinate.

The Tower of Jello

CHAPTER 5

S turdily built of virgin redwood in 1877, the governor's mansion
served twelve heads of state prior to the Browns' arrival in 1959.
This fifteen-room, five-bath house had weathered handsomely. Even the
dynamite planted by assassins trying to blow up Governor William
Stephens in 1917 failed to damage anything beyond the kitchen and
pantry. Remodelled during World War II, when quality furnishings
were scarce, many of the rooms resembled Sears & Roebuck floor displays
from the forties. Even so, nothing on Sacramento's multiple listing
matched the gabled splendor of this ninety-year-old residence.

Pat was exhausted after his campaign. He had beaten William Knowland in the fall of 1958 and succeeded Goodwin Knight as Governor.

During the family's first weeks in the capital, Bernice was irritated by the noise of semis down-shifting outside the bedroom. Mechanics at the used foreign car lot across the street added to the noise by running engines all day long. For Pat, some of these domestic irritations were offset by the joys of being Governor, not the least of which were the toys of high office. Among them was his twin-engine state plane, Grizzly, in which he loved to survey his wide domain.

Pat's enthusiasm for his new job was evident in a letter he wrote to Jerry shortly after taking office:

It was certainly good seeing you at the inauguration. I suppose you noticed that you got a bigger hand than the new Governor. It just goes to show that people have a deep respect for anyone devoting himself to God. I was very proud of the entire family.

I have a topflight staff here at Sacramento and they are working awfully hard to bring my program into fruition. I can see some real thunderheads in the offing because we are really treading on some pretty sacred cows. I am trying to be very, very fair, but I sometimes find out that politics is not a matter of fairness but really doing something for your friends (which is human nature, I suppose).

We have a labor bill, a water bill and a budget that will really cause consternation. If all the forces join together I am afraid both Governor Brown and the state will be in trouble. There is one thing I am certain they won't say, however, and that is that I am indecisive or unable to make up my mind. People closest to me know that I really want to accomplish things and that I am not too much afraid of people I think are wrong. . . ."

Jerry put the Governor's letter down and thought about the challenges confronting his father and himself. In Sacramento, Pat was trying to put through a state water plan, a master plan for higher education, ban racial discrimination in businesses and unions, increase employment benefits, initiate a consumer protection office, establish an economic development agency, speed up freeway construction, increase taxes to make up past deficits, end cross-filing, and put an end to capital punishment. In Los Gatos, Jerry was trying to convince the Jesuit's California Province that he was old enough to read Teilhard de Chardin.

The seminarian had taken his vows shortly after celebrating his twentieth birthday. Promoted to the juniorate level on the fifteen-year path to ordination, he now lived at Sacred Heart's House of Classical Studies. His religious exercises were supplemented with coursework at the University of Santa Clara. By now, Brown was beginning to have serious doubts about the order's relevance. His reservations were shared by Peter Finnegan and Frank Damrell, who also wondered whether they could commit themselves to twelve more years of religious study.

All three were beginning to tire of the Society's pettiness, which appeared unrelated to serving God. Jerry was especially put off by a master who rebuked his charges for being too dependent on their morning coffee. After the Jesuit leader announced that, to encourage austerity, the beverage would no longer be served the politician's son asked: "Why not let coffee continue to be served so that the novices might be free to exercise their power to refuse to drink it?"

This caffeine skirmish was only the first of a series of minor struggles culminating in the battle to read the groundbreaking work of the late Pierre Teilhard de Chardin. Born and educated in France, the Jesuit paleontologist had been exiled to the Far East for expounding heretical views on evolution. In China, he distinguished himself in a variety of excavations that included the 1928 discovery of the Peking man. While excelling in the field, Teilhard also continued his redefinition of scientific and religious philosophy. Not since Galileo had a thinker ventured to offer such an all-inclusive view of the universe. His radical view of human evolution challenged the traditional notion that the creation was finished — that Jesus had come and gone leaving mankind in a static world:

> Christ is not a supernumerary added to the world as an extra, an embellishment, a king as we now crown kings, the owner of a great estate . . . he is the alpha and the omega, the beginning and the end, the foundation stone and the keystone, the fulfillment and the fulfiller. Jesus has never left but is present in his spirit in resurrectional triumph over sin, suffering, and death.

Man was seen not merely as God's lackey but a reflective center, an ego engaged in gathering up the whole universe in himself as center and moving out to personalize the whole world. Humans were able to control their environment and nature while working with God in the dynamic evolutionary sweep towards the Omega Point — the Supreme Conscious Personality in whom all others will achieve union and harmony.

Perhaps the most fascinating aspect of Teilhard's theory was its emphasis on synthesis. He saw men of opposing philosophies moving in different directions toward the same end. To speed progress toward unification and everlasting peace, he labored to reconcile humanism and grace, nature and the Cross, prudence and heroism, freedom and obedience, as well as other seemingly contradictory aspects of the dogma. In the paleontologist's eyes, the dialectic was merely part of an evolutionary process that would ultimatly converge at Omega. Horrified by this unorthodox view, Rome refused to let Teilhard publish his work. He died a semi-exile in New York's Central Park shortly after leaving Mass on Easter 1955 at St. Patrick's Cathedral.

The first of Teilhard's books, *Phenomenon of Man,* was published shortly before Jerry Brown entered the novitiate; it sold 70,000 copies in a week, and within a matter of months, publishers around the world were scrambling to get sequels on press. His thinking attracted considerable interest in San Francisco, which had long been a beachhead for radical ideology, like the Catholic pacifism brought south by inmates of a conscientious objectors' camp at Waldport, Oregon after World War II.

The California Province's refusal to let the juniors study Teilhard's visionary work added to Brown's skepticism of the Jesuit curriculum. Jerry discussed these concerns with his parents when they arrived for their monthly visits. "I sit here in poverty, but it isn't real poverty. I don't buy anything, I don't own anything, but I don't have to worry about it either. The mystical Three Degrees of Humility elude me, too. And chastity seems like just another form of detachment and separation. What is the point of being here?" Thrilled by his change of heart, Bernice wanted to pack up Jerry's cassocks and underwear and sweep him away before he changed his mind. But Pat, who had been trying all along to plant seeds of doubt in Jerry about being in the seminary, sensed it was not yet time to whisk him off. Instead he played devil's advocate. Striking a "Father Knows Best" pose that would have done Robert Young credit, he told his son, "I think you should stay until you're absolutely sure." So, with Pat's modest contribution and "Uncle Lou" Lurie's more generous subsidy to the Society, Jerry remained for the time being.

While his son struggled with whether or not to leave the novitiate, Governor Brown addressed the multiple challenges of his new administration. A forerunner of Lyndon Johnson's "Great Society," Brown's "Responsible Liberalism" initiated progressive reforms in housing, employment and social welfare that would be imitated nationally in the early sixties. He was determined that California would be the first state where "a young man or woman who has ability can go from kindergarten through graduate school without paying one cent in tuition." To this end, he developed a master plan that put new community college, state college and University of California branches in cities throughout the state. In addition, he pushed for funds to help school districts fight illiteracy and develop programs for the handicapped.

The new Brown administration took an activist approach to many pressing problems of the fast-growing state. Among others, Pat backed bills to equip cars with smog control devices, provide medical treatment for drug addicts, construct mass transit facilities, protect San Francisco Bay from excessive landfill and capture eighty percent of tidelands oil revenues for the state. At the same time, he moved ahead on his plan to undo the 160-acre limitation for federally irrigated water, which he had earlier supported as Attorney General in the 1902 Ivanhoe case.

Since the early 1930s, the Federal Bureau of Reclamation had been trying to put together a comprehensive water plan for California. The agency's Central Valley Project, an extensive network of dams and canals, already supplied water to agricultural interests. But large landholders, who had long taken advantage of paper shenanigans and federal non-enforcement to circumvent the 1902 law, were leery of any new projects. Even though the federal government was eager to impound north state water with a dam at Oroville and pump it over the Tehachapis to Southern California farms and communities, big landholders resisted the project. Likewise, when an opportunity arose to get more Colorado River water from Lake Mead, the big users magnanimously let the surplus go to Arizona. They didn't want any more Washington-financed water projects unless they won the Ivanhoe case. They feared that until the 160-acre limitation was thrown out, new Bureau of Reclamation construction would lead to applying the law. That would mean breaking up federally irrigated farms covering more than 160 acres, or losing the subsidized water.

After losing in the Supreme Court, agribusiness giants like Kern County Land, Standard Oil, DiGiorgio, Southern Pacific and Times-Mirror decided that another approach was needed. Accordingly, they got behind a state water project that would charge Californians $11 billion to build canals and pumping facilities, plus major dams at Oroville and San Luis. Governor Brown flew to Washington and told Congress it would no longer have to pay for the whole program. If the Bureau of Reclamation would simply enlarge existing canals and do groundwork for the San Luis Reservoir, his state would finance everything else. There was just one little favor the people of California wanted in return for assuming this burden. Since they were financing most of the new system, could Congress exempt project water from the 160-acre limitation?

Even though Washington refused to amend the 1902 law, Pat proceeded to ask the state legislature to put the water bond issue on the November 1960 ballot. He was a true believer in the economic value of public works projects, and saw numerous advantages to this idea. It would shift surplus water south, converting heretofore desert land to farms, and support urban development. The system would also mean the state could reduce reliance on disputed Colorado River sources shared with other states, such as Arizona. Finally, it would link up the two Californias. If people north and south could agree to share their natural assets, the entire state would benefit.

To make the program palatable to Northern California legislators opposed to subsidizing valley farmers and urban residents in the south, the Governor dropped the $11 billion price tag he quoted Congress the previous summer. Oportunistic accounting helped disguise most of the true costs and allowed him to claim the project could be completed for a bargain basement price of $1.75 billion. Best of all, Pat argued, water and power sales would ultimately make the venture self-liquidating.

When agricultural interests voiced concern about the acreage limitation, Pat promised that the federal code would not apply to farms receiving project water. The fact that this position violated the Supreme Court decision won by Brown as Attorney General two years earlier in the Ivanhoe case would make no difference. To get around this problem Governor Brown promised to make irrigation of any size farm kosher by establishing a two-tier rate structure that gave a break to the little guy:

> On land in excess of 160 acres, the price to be charged shall be the cost of delivering the water, including the market value of the power used to pump it to the land. For all others, the price shall be the cost of delivering the water, including only the actual cost of power to pump it. I believe these policies are fair and workable. They will give the small farmer a break in his battle to compete with the big mechanized farms yet they will not seek to force anyone to break up what he owns or pay more than is reasonable for delivering the water to his land.

But these compelling arguments didn't sway a key legislator from a rural Sierra county. After moral suasion failed to bring this swing voter around, Pat came up with a sweetener; he promised to expand the water plan by adding a small dam in the official's district. Thanks to this diplomatic stroke, the referendum bill sailed through the capitol and the Governor turned his attention to lobbying urban constituencies that would decide the issue that fall.

Southern Californians were told the water plan would eliminate the prospect of dry faucets and burned-out lawns. Skeptical Northern Californians were assured the program would end floods in their region. What conscientious citizen could oppose construction of the new Oroville dam that would prevent a repeat of the disastrous 1955 Feather River flood, which took thirty-six lives? The only problem with this argument was testimony given by Senator Thomas Kuchel in 1956 hearings on the same subject. He pointed out that "if the state had not indicated its interest in Oroville, we would have had a [federally financed] dam long before last year's flood at Oroville."

Thoughtful people within the Governor's own office challenged the wisdom of master builder Brown's monumental scheme. They worried that increasing water supplies to Southern California would bolster population in an area already beset by severe air pollution. But Pat countered that blocking new deliveries to this region wouldn't slow population growth. Immigrants from the rest of America would continue pouring into the Golden State even if they faced water rationing. And the Governor was convinced that failure to bring water to Southern California would only draw more newcomers into Northern California: "All these yokels from the southern states and from Iowa will come up to Northern California — to my country! The hell with it. Build the California Water Project and keep them down south."

This argument failed to persuade Brown's executive secretary, Fred Dutton, who worried that the $11 billion project would cost so much "that we'll drown all the school children and all the universities in the state."

"The hell with it," replied Pat, "we can have both. We're a rich state."

When further questions were raised about the environmental implications, Brown replied, "I'm an environmentalist but I'm also a builder; I love to see projects."

Soon critics around the state began denouncing this $11 billion water program that the administration continued to log at $1.75 billion. The Governor decided to respond via state wide television on the evening of January 20, 1960.

As Pat prepared for his broadcast in Los Angeles, Jerry was on the phone to his lapsed Jesuit friend Charles Fracchia, seeking a lift to Provincial headquarters in San Francisco. When Fracchia arrived, the junior piled his few belongings in the trunk, waved goodbye to his superiors and rode down the vineyard-covered hills of Sacred Heart toward foggy San Francisco. Certain it was time for him to leave the seminary, Jerry thought about a line he had just read in Boris Pasternak's new book, *Doctor Zhivago*: "Man is born to live, not to prepare to live."

The Governor's son repeated those words as he mounted the steps to Society headquarters and entered the somber Jesuit office. The black-robed master motioned the crewcut seminarian toward a chair. For a minute the room was silent, save for the ticking pendulum of a grandfather clock. Finally the official gestured toward a document on his uncluttered desk. "When I hand you this piece of paper," he told Brother Brown, "you are no longer a Jesuit. Are you sure this is what you want to do?" Jerry extended his hand to receive his separation papers and dashed out of the office as the clock gonged the hour.

Released from his vows of poverty, chastity and obedience, Brown rode back to Forest Hills with Fracchia. As their car swung down Magellan Street, Jerry felt relieved that his parents didn't put the old place on the market when they moved to the governor's mansion. Somehow the idea of strangers living in the family's Mediterranean homestead was unthinkable. The house was part of the Brown heritage, and Pat's son was delighted to know that his mother and father had sold it to his sister Cynthia and her husband, Attorney Joe Kelly.

Rushing up the familiar flight of stairs, along the second-story porch and in the front door, Jerry felt eighteen again. No longer did he have to meditate, wear his cassock, or abide by his vows. Unfortunately Pat, preoccupied with his Los Angeles TV pitch for the forthcoming water bond referendum, couldn't be part of the welcoming party. After changing into civvies, the ex-seminarian told his sister he planned to enroll at Berkeley. In Sacramento, Jerry's customarily reserved mother was so excited that she broke the story to the wire services.

> SACRAMENTO (AP)—Gov. Edmund G. Brown's only son, Gerald, is leaving a Catholic novitiate to take up psychiatry.
>
> Gerald wasn't available for comment but his mother, Mrs. Bernice Brown, confirmed that he is withdrawing from the Jesuit order's Sacred Heart Novitiate at Los Gatos.
>
> Mrs. Brown said Gerald wants to study medicine and psychiatry at the University of California instead of entering the priesthood.
>
> "He is particularly interested in people and feels he could make a real contribution there."
>
> Mrs. Brown, a Protestant, said she approves of her son's decision to leave the novitiate, just as she did his decision to enter 3½ years ago. "He's almost twenty-two and knows what he wants to do."

The chief executive was delighted by his son's decision to apply to UC's Berkeley campus. The University, which his parents hoped he would attend after St. Ignatius, was now administered by a labor mediator named Clark Kerr. Pat was impressed by the foresight of this educational statesman who expected enrollment to treble to 274,000 by the twenty-first century. And the Governor always felt reassured listening to Kerr scoff at suggestions that students organizing against capital punishment, nuclear testing, the House Un-American Activities Committee, compulsory ROTC, and other well-established ogres might disrupt the campus in Latin American fashion. At the Regents meetings, the university president assured Pat that despite their youthful idealism, the students were moving single-file toward the placement office. "The employers will love this generation," promised Kerr. "They aren't going to press many grievances. They are going to be easy to handle. There aren't going to be any riots."

This reassured Brown and his fellow Democratic appointees to the UC Regents, like old Lowell High School chum Norton Simon and millionaire oilman Edwin Pauley. And under the leadership of men like Kerr and Pauley, the University rushed forward to build new campuses at Santa Cruz, San Diego and Irvine.

While Clark Kerr moved ahead on his expansion plan for the University, which he characterized as "an imperative rather than a reasoned choice among elegant alternatives," Jerry Brown was trying to find a place for himself in the multiversity. He was now merely another aspiring transfer student putting his future in the hands of the institution Kerr described as a "mechanism" — a series of processes producing a series of results — a mechanism held together by administrative rules and powered by money."

Visiting the coffeehouses on Berkeley's Telegraph Avenue, the new civilian began to appreciate the transformation that had begun during his three-and-a-half years with the Jesuits. In 1956, rock and roll was the dominant cultural medium of his generation; the only serious intellectual movement in the Bay Area had been Beats reading their poetry to one another in North Beach coffeehouses. But now Kerouac, Ginsberg and Ferlinghetti were making the reading lists not only of the University, but in small high schools from San Diego to Michigan's Upper Peninsula. And rock and roll was turning out to be something less than the pulse of youth, as notable disc jockeys were indicted for accepting the bribes of record manufacturers anxious to hammer their songs into the new generation's subconscious.

Revelations that the airwaves weren't sacred came at a time when Jerry's old friends seemed to be getting tired of Elvis, Bobby Darin and Paul Anka. All over campus, students were now playing Pete Seeger versions of Woody Guthrie protest songs. At dinner they discussed the black student boycott of segregated Woolworth lunch counters that was spreading across the South. Talking with some of the more radical students, Jerry soon realized that issues like capital punishment, integration, and banning atmospheric nuclear tests were only part of a new commitment that transcended ideology. Unlike the thirties, there was no adherence to party doctrine. Berkeley radicals of the 1960s were starting from zero-based thinking, and seemed to have junked all the old rules.

This unsystematic approach made leaders like Clark Kerr optimistic. It was true, conceded the president, that campus "intellectuals are a particularly volatile element capable of extreme reactions to objective situations — more extreme than any group in society." But unlike himself, they had no master plan, no grand strategy; they were not *organized*. In fact, they seemed to shy away from any kind of long-range commitments. "They are," explained the UC president, "by nature irresponsible, in the sense that they have no continuing commitment to any single institution or philosophical outlook and they are not fully answerable for consequences. They are, as a result, never fully trusted by anybody, including themselves."

Kerr was convinced that these intellectual forces were doomed by the convergence of capitalism and communism. "The age of ideology fades" into a new era of undifferentiated "industrialism" with "bureaucratic managers and managerial bureaucrats" at the top. "Class warfare will be forgotten and in its place will be the bureaucratic contest. Memos will flow instead of blood. In this system, the successful manager will be "mostly a mediator. He wins few clear-cut victories; he must find satisfaction in being equally distasteful to each of his constituencies."

Although Kerr's futuristic view won him friends in the American Management Association, Pat wasn't buying. Somewhat naively, as it turned out, he continued to hold on to the notion that if he maintained a fair and reasonable middle position, he could please everyone, even on life-and-death issues. Nowhere was the Governor's determination to give both sides equal time better illustrated than in his handling of the Chessman case.

Since his conviction on seventeen counts of robbery, kidnapping and attempted rape in 1948, alleged Red Light Bandit Caryl Chessman had received seven court stays of execution. His fate caused the Governor, who had become an opponent of capital punishment during his Attorney General days, obvious agony. Pat's vacillation under pressure led San Quentin officials to joke that the thirty-eight-year-old prisoner walked in and out of the gas chamber so many times they had to re-pave death row.

Brown was plainly having difficulty stage-managing the fate of California's leading prisoner, who had complicated things by becoming a best-selling author behind bars and developing a sympathetic international following. Although Brown was sworn to uphold the law, he felt there was nothing to be gained by executing even a typical lifer — and Chessman was a sizeable cut above the average inmate of death row. Indeed, errors in the Chessman trial transcript and honest doubts about his guilt raised a moral issue that bothered many concerned men and women nationwide. Unfortunately for Chessman, however, Pat was also being pressured by law-and-order forces who were determined to end the prisoner's life on schedule in January 1960.

One of those most bothered by the moral issues involved in the Chessman case was a U.C. undergraduate named Jerry Brown. The student's concern caused him to get on the phone twelve hours before the scheduled execution and ask his father to grant a reprieve and request that the legislature pass a two-year moratorium on capital punishment. "You're not going to let Chessman die, are you?" the ex-seminarian asked his father.

"There isn't a chance in a thousand that the legislature would do it."

"If you were a doctor and had a chance to save a man's life — one chance in a thousand — wouldn't you do it?"

Pat finally agreed. He granted Chessman a 60-day reprieve and scheduled a special legislative session to take up a bill abolishing the death penalty.

As he put down the reciever, Jerry realized he had just demonstrated the kind of evolutionary potential Teilhard was talking about. In one long-distance conversation, he had accomplished more good than all the eloquent wires in Chessman's behalf from men like Albert Schweitzer, Pablo Casals and Aldous Huxley. Singlehandedly he had done what thousands of letter-writing intellectuals, anti-capital-punishment demonstrators and brief-laden defense attorneys couldn't. He had just saved a life with a collect call from a pay phone.

In the spring, the undergraduate moved into Berkeley's International House, on Piedmont Avenue. His father was still struggling to persuade the legislature to back his stand on capital punishment. But Pat's lobbying effort finally failed when the Senate Judiciary Committee defeated the death penalty moratorium bill eight to seven.

On the Mayday eve of Chessman's execution, Brown sat at his vast cork-covered desk reviewing the case once again with his clemency secretary Cecil Poole, finance director Hale Champion, ranking Assemblyman Jesse Unruh, and a delegation of concerned celebrities including Marlon Brando, Shirley MacLaine, Steve Allen, *Ugly American* co-author Eugene Burdick, and the convict's attorney. Their compassionate plea to spare the condemned man was brushed aside by Poole, who insisted the public would not tolerate another stay.

"Look, Governor," pleaded Brando, "we're planning to film the Caryl Chessman story. What you decide tonight will have a lot to do with how you'll be portrayed."

"Marlon," Brown replied, "you don't understand. Your movie couldn't be out for a year. The Los Angeles papers are crucifying me right now!"

The following morning, California's leading agnostic prisoner ate his final meal and received Protestant and Catholic chaplains still hoping for a last-minute conversion. Finally disappointed, the chaplains looked on as Chessman headed down death row. The bell-shaped gas chamber faced a row of bleachers, now occupied by reporters and VIP guests. After the straps were tightened at 10 a.m., the Governor got on the telephone in his office overlooking Capitol Park to pick up the play-by-play from prison officials. Brown sat quietly as word came that the cyanide pellets had been dropped in a bucket of sulfuric acid beneath the condemned man. Choking on the fumes, Chessman went into convulsions and then sagged forward. His eyes closed and fists unclenched. Six minutes later the warden announced that the trembling fingers had gone rigid. Brown looked up at clemency secretary Poole; the Red Light Bandit was dead.

Clinging to a copy of California's Constitution, Pat told waiting reporters that pardoning Chessman would have been "an impossible abuse of executive power. I don't know whether a governor can play God in these cases." Clark Kerr's prophecy about the collapse of ideology and the rise of a new industrial age was turning out to be somewhat off the mark. True, bureaucrats preferred to fight with memos, but it was clear there would continue to be moments like these, when blood would flow.

In Berkeley, Jerry Brown listened to students characterize his equivocating father as a "Tower of Jello" for executing a man on a conviction charge that didn't involve murder. Many of the same people who picketed to save the prisoner now planned to demonstrate against upcoming hearings of the House Un-American Activities Committee (HUAC) at San Francisco's City Hall. Chartered buses heading for this event met a few days later in front of Jerry's I-House residence. When the dissidents returned that evening, the Governor's son was horrified to learn that many peaceful protesters had been unceremoniously blasted down the steps of City Hall with fire hoses. The next morning Jerry went over to this domed building, where Pat had served as D.A., to check things out for himself. He sat quietly and listened to the men from Washington harass a handful of tired old Communists, most of whom had been under permanent FBI surveillance for years.

After leaving California, HUAC produced a film called "Operation Abolition," which contended that the entire San Francisco riot was communist-inspired and led. Shown in towns across the United States, this remarkable hatchet job held that peacefully picketing students who had been knocked down the steps by high-powered water jets were masterminding a frightening new brand of insurrection. California was characterized as a sanctuary for subversives who threatened everything good about American life from supermarkets to freeways.

After his initial look at confrontation politics, Jerry next turned to examining farm labor conditions with members of the campus Agricultural Organizing Committee and the Catholic Worker Movement. When the latter group's veteran leader, Dorothy Day, visited California, the Governor's son accompanied her and a dozen other students to valley fields near Stockton for a weekend of strawberry picking. On subsequent trips, Brown helped recruit a number of black teenagers from San Francisco's Hunter's Point to work on these farms. This effort was part of Youth for Service, a program designed to break up San Francisco's menacing street gangs. In charge was Percy Pinkney, who had recently given up leadership of the "baddest black gang in town" — the Aces. The local combat veteran had controlled a territory including the old Western Addition flats built by Jerry's grandparents. Brown was enthusiastic about the idea of helping urban delinquents by "borrowing" them from their troubled neighborhoods and exposing them to people and lifestyles different from their own. This project also fit right in with Pat's strategy of finding public service opportunities and jobs for young people. He frequently spoke with visitors about California's creative solutions to problems of the underclass.

By now, a stream of presidential hopefuls was passing through Sacramento to pay homage to the politician who would control the second largest delegation at the party's July convention in Los Angeles. Some guests followed up with thoughtful letters, like the one from Majority Leader Johnson's top aide, Bobby Baker.

> The Senator and I have discussed our meeting and we are unanimous in our appraisal that you certainly have all the characteristics necessary to be president of this great country. I might add, your wife would make a charming first lady.

Although Pat understood the underlying intention of such flattery, he was intrigued by the notion of becoming a convention king-maker and possibly ending up with the vice-presidential nomination. To maximize his own power, the Governor told leading candidates to stay out of the state's presidential primary. In exchange, he would see that the California delegation, while pledged to him as a favorite son, would include supporters of all the other aspirants. In July, the Governor flew south to manage state Democratic forces at the convention. Anxious to keep his family image intact for this command performance, he brought Bernice, Jerry and Kathy along.

The Browns especially enjoyed a party thrown for Senator John F. Kennedy by savings and loan leader, Bart Lytton. Nervous that outdoor acoustics might not be adequate for the occasion, the major Democratic contributor spent more than $15,000 lowering the entire garden of his Holmby Hills mansion. And to make sure guests didn't miss any of his comments to Kennedy, Lytton amplified them with a lavalier microphone.

For months, Governor Brown had been withholding his support from Senator Kennedy in the hope that Johnson or another non-Catholic might surge ahead and select him as running mate. This vacillation prompted the Massachusetts leader's staff to ridicule the Californian. But in the end, when it became clear that Catholic Kennedy was clearly in command, Brown swallowed his own hopes and endorsed him.

Unfortunately, the rest of the California delegation did not concur. Inside the Los Angeles Sports Arena, Pat faced a sudden revolt by Stevenson forces within the CDC. The state party chief, who had backed Adlai in 1952 and 1956, hopped around in front of the cameras and tried to bring the rebels into line. Although never a threat to Kennedy, die-hard Stevenson forces did finally force the California delegation into an open roll call, which many observers saw as an embarrassing defeat for Pat

Brown. After Kennedy's victory, the California governor somberly flew back to Sacramento. The only member of his family happy about the convention week was fifteen year old Kathy, who had managed to get a pass to see the filming of "Ozzie and Harriet" as well as a commissary lunch date with her TV heart throb, Ricky Nelson.

That fall, Pat fought to regain prestige he had lost during the convention with an endless campaign for the "Brown water bonds." Cruising the state eighteen hours a day, the Governor never passed up a chance to win another vote. Returning from a Napa Valley speech one afternoon, he motioned his chauffeur over to the shoulder. As soon as the car stopped, Pat dashed off into a vineyard to corner a farmer with his sales pitch. And after a long day's work at the Capitol, the chief executive could usually be found poolside in his bathing suit, talking water plan cost-benefit ratios to guests at the Mansion Inn.

Bernice, who was horrified by Pat's paddling about the swimming pool of this motel located across the street from their official residence, decided to take up a collection among her husband's friends to build a pool in the mansion's back yard. Pat himself, who seemed happy enough joking with motel guests, had no time to assist her and the project was abandoned.

Tired from the water bond campaign, Pat found himself plagued by brief memory lapses. The low point came one afternoon in Sacramento when he started to introduce his young traveling secretary whom he saw every day. "I'd like you to meet John . . ." said the Democratic leader, as he suddenly realized he couldn't remember the name of this aide who had been closer to him than his wife in recent months. As Brown sifted methodically through his mental Rolodex, the staff man stuck out a hand and said, "Hi, I'm John Vasconcellos."

In November 1960 while Kennedy was losing California's electoral votes to Richard Nixon, the electorate approved Pat's water plan. This was the crowning achievement of a two-year series of legislative triumphs. All his major programs, including the master plan for higher education, freeway construction program, substantial increases in the public school fund, tougher crime laws, reorganization of state departments and the ending of primary cross-filing had been enacted. The Governor had lost on just two major issues: the abolition of capital punishment and a $1.25 minimum wage for workers exempt from federal coverage.

Shortly after New Year's, the Browns flew back to snowy Washington where Earl Warren swore in President Kennedy. On inauguration eve, Bart Lytton's wife offered Kathy the services of a hairdresser brought along from Beverly Hills. After much discussion, the stylist backcombed the tenth grader's hair into a fashionable bouffant. Teased and sprayed to the consistency of cotton candy, Kathy's hair horrified her mother. Mrs. Lytton, coiffed like Madame Pompidou, tried to reassure Bernice that the puffy look put her daughter right in style with the new First Lady. But the Governor's wife remained in anguish all the way through Robert Frost's poetry and Kennedy's call for self-sacrifice.

Kathy, who grinned when family friends told her she could pass for twenty-four, thanks to the work of her new hairdresser, found it difficult to take her eyes off the new President. The school girl's dreams of Ricky Nelson evaporated as JFK smiled and said that national prestige lost to the Sputnik-shooting Russians would be regained by putting an American on the moon. Kathy nodded enthusiastically when JFK called for citizens to ask what they could do for their country, while Jerry kept wishing he would get on to the pressing Cuba issue. Months earlier the student had taken up this matter with Kennedy while riding with his father and the presidential candidate from the San Jose airport to an Oakland meeting. Jerry felt JFK was disappointingly evasive on recognition of Fidel Castro.

After the presidential inauguration, Jerry was continually frustrated in efforts to discuss this issue with his father. Pat argued simplistically that President Kennedy was correct in suggesting Castro might be turning Cuba into a base for Communist subversion in the Western hemisphere. The Havana leader's counter-claim that the CIA was trying to overthrow his government was dismissed as nonsense. Undergraduate Brown tried to make the Governor view the situation objectively.

"Have you considered the possibility that Kennedy and Castro might both be right?" he asked his father.

While the debate over Cuba continued in the Brown family, the Governor arranged for his son to visit state mental hospitals as part of his preparation for a career in psychiatry. But about this time, in the face of exacting science and math pre-requisites necessary for the field, Jerry realized his interests were more in the social sciences. After taking courses in the classics, the young Berkeley student found himself thinking about law school. Much had changed since his father first broached the idea as an alternative to the seminary. Brown, Sr., delighted at this turn, encouraged his son to visit a judge he had appointed to the District Court of Appeals, Matthew Tobriner. The old family friend advised Jerry not to be swayed by his father's desire to enroll him in Berkeley's inexpensive but prestigious Boalt Hall School of Law. The man who had brought Pat into the Democratic Party twenty-seven years earlier, suggested Jerry apply to his own alma mater, Yale University.

The idea appealed to Jerry, and soon Justice Tobriner was dictating a recommendation in his behalf. "Mr. Brown," he wrote the admissions committee in New Haven, "is not interested in the mechanics of law as such and I believe will develop into far more than the usual practicing lawyer. My conversation with him discloses that he is thoroughly versed in political theory, that he has a philosophical and searching turn of mind. May I add that he is likewise a modest and highly attractive person who has not been at all spoiled, as others might have been, by the high status of his father. In my opinion, he will develop into an outstanding student."

Jerry's acceptance notice came swiftly, but with it came a new problem. Even though Pat now earned more than $40,000 a year as Governor, he wasn't about to foot the bill for an expensive Ivy League education. After all, the alternative, Boalt Hall, charged no tuition and turned out men like Chief Justice Earl Warren. Pat, who had obtained his legal education through night courses and consistently championed high quality, low cost public education, saw no reason to send his son to Connecticut to learn how to practice law in California. Undaunted, Jerry returned to his old Sacred Heart benefactor, "Uncle Lou" Lurie. The millionaire real estate entrepreneur promptly agreed to set up a Yale fellowship in Jerry's name.

In the fall of 1961, the freshman law student flew to New Haven, while Pat rode north to trigger a historic dynamite blast at Oroville. As the dust settled over the damsite observation point, Governor Brown spoke theatrically of the many ways his new water project would "correct an accident of people and geography." The war between Northern and Southern California was being settled by re-engineering the state's hydrology. Soon the two regions would find common purpose along the five-hundred-mile-long, man-made river which he touted as responsible liberalism's great legacy to future generations.

"Thank God for the spectacle of students picketing"

CHAPTER 6

J erry Brown sat at attention amidst canary yellow legal pads, ice
water, and dour Kennedy aides in monogrammed shirts. At the
conference table, Arthur Schlesinger, Roswell Gilpatric, and Adam
Yarmolinsky were flanked by generals whose crowded lapels jingled every
time they reached for a panatella. These Washington men had come
together in a New York hotel room to advise the governors of a dozen
states on a matter of crucial national importance. All the state leaders,
including Pat Brown, were suitably escorted by their respective military
attaches. The impeccably organized host, Nelson Rockefeller, signaled a
liveried servant for a light by pressing a button beneath the table, and
then began by handing out a meticulous agenda on the subject at hand:

the urgent need for a comprehensive national fallout shelter program. The Yale law student, who had accompanied his father, listened to the Pentagon men lecture state leaders on their patriotic duty to build radiation refuges below ground. Absent these atomic age sanctuaries, they claimed, it was only a matter of time before the Russian air force dusted America's spacious skies with long-lived radionuclides.

Taking their cue from Rockefeller, the governors reviewed the central question of how to tactfully route people to the nearest bomb shelters. Radio, it was argued, could touch off the fearsome brand of panic generated by Orson Welles' War of the Worlds radio broadcast in 1938. The telephone system was vulnerable to sabotage, and electrical hook-ups were expensive. The group then discussed the possibility of financing an independent early warning system and whether Congress would pay for it. Or perhaps, as an alternative, it could be amortized with interstate bonds.

Listening closely, Jerry felt the fundamental issue of whether bomb shelters merited construction in the first place was being ignored. Finally, he leaned over and whispered in his father's ear: "Dad, you should see if an expensive bomb shelter program like this makes any sense in light of the vulnerability of American cities to atomic attack."

The California Governor raised the issue with Arthur Schlesinger, who brushed him aside like a kindergartener, "Pat, we've got to have them."

BUT WHY? Jerry wanted to cry. Why did we have to open the door to subterranean living? Wouldn't it be cheaper and safer for both nations to divest themselves of nuclear weapons? Why weren't these men working on strategies for peace instead of trying to appropriate taxpayers' funds for underground shelters? It was the kind of question Jerry would pose repeatedly during the sixties. And years later he would cite this meeting as an example of the central problem in government: "Conventional wisdom and group thinking conspire to prevent serious challenges to widely shared assumptions." Political energy always seems to focus on getting things accomplished. What was wrong with slowing things down or doing nothing at all until a clear plan of action emerged, Jerry would ask. Why did freeways have to be lengthened, rivers dammed and re-dammed, and universities turned into multiversities? And why couldn't government take a sabbatical and leave the people alone?

Jerry found himself thinking more about these questions as he flipped through the San Francisco newspapers his busy father sent to Yale in lieu of letters. The Sacramento stories all reinforced the obvious conclusion that most politicians had an inherent conflict of interest. The rift was not just between the competing demands of contributors who underwrote one's campaign at $1000 a plate dinners and the voters who subsisted on food stamps. Rather, the fragile nature of elected officials' careers made

71

rational thinking a luxury. To assure the longevity of his career, the politician had to maintain high visibility by coming out for issues strong, hard and often. Uncertainty, wavering or hedging were seen as signs of incompetence, as in the Chessman case. There was usually no time to develop a long-range humanist perspective like Adlai Stevenson's. Political points were gained by making snap judgments which created an illusion of decisiveness. What a politician had to say often mattered less than the fact that he operated in a crisis climate and cloaked his solutions in a patriotic banner.

Even Kennedy's Harvard intellectuals seemed to use this mindless approach when hawking absurdities like bomb shelters. And now, back in California, one of the all-time masters of style over substance, Richard Nixon, was getting ready to challenge Jerry's father. The Yale student had run into this ambitious Republican the previous year while attending the San Francisco Giants' season opener with his parents at Candlestick Park. Following a pre-game VIP lunch, the Browns and the Nixons shook hands and everyone walked out into the sunlit stadium. The former vice-president, who had lost the Golden State to Kennedy in 1960, was applauded vigorously. Native San Franciscan Pat, who had won a landslide victory in his last campaign, was annoyed by a deafening Bronx cheer.

When Nixon announced for the Republican gubernatorial nomination in the spring of 1962, Jerry was sure that the round of applause at Candlestick influenced his decision. Opinion polls giving the man from Whittier an early lead scared Pat. His first move was to go on an all-protein diet and cut out all drinks. For exercise Pat played golf seven days a week on suburban Sacramento links. Rising at 5 a.m., the Governor and Bernice were at the first tee by daybreak. There they sped through eighteen holes without benefit of caddy or cart. After losing thirty pounds in just forty days, Pat next recharged his spiritual batteries by heading down to the Jesuit's retreat house near Los Gatos. For three days the voluble politician remained in silent contemplation.

Brown got his first break with newspaper accounts of a secret $200,000 loan Howard Hughes had made to Nixon's pudgy brother, Donald. Although the former vice-president tried to sidestep the issue, it kept popping up everywhere he turned. Campaigning in San Francisco, he cracked open a crispy fortune cookie and found a strip asking "What about the Hughes loan?" The amusing story of this cookie, planted by Democratic prankster Dick Tuck, seemed of more interest to voters than the Republican candidate's recital of his achievements under Ike.

Like Knowland, Nixon claimed that after years in Washington his heart remained in California. Yet at the end of an eighteen-hour campaign day, the exhausted candidate unintentionally broke up audiences by declaring: "I'm running for the Governor of the United States."

A month into the campaign, Nixon sounded increasingly like George Orwell's vision of a politician who "has gone some distance toward turning himself into a machine. The appropriate noises are coming out of his larynx, but his brain is not involved as it would be if he were choosing his words for himself. If the speech he is making is one that he is accustomed to make over and over again, he may be almost unconscious of what he is saying, as one is when one utters the responses in church."

To help Nixon, campaign aide Murray Chotiner assigned someone to confiscate refuse from Brown headquarters, in the hope of finding useful information. The Republican also persuaded a friend at the phone company to release to them the numbers which would be used for a last-minute Democratic get-out-the-vote drive. Chotiner armed his troops with dimes and sent them running from one pay phone to the next. At each stop they called a different Brown number and dropped the phone. By the time they finished, receivers dangled off the hook in phone booths across the city. This destabilization program prevented scores of Brown volunteers from calling out to solicit support.

The Republican campaign manager, ad man H.R. "Bob" Haldeman, also exploited the Governor's longtime affiliation with the California Democratic Council. The Republicans put up $70,000 to form a phony "Committee for the Preservation of the Democratic Party in California." This group sent out 500,000 copies of a postcard poll to a carefully selected list of conservative Democrats who traditionally crossed over to the GOP. A cover letter charged that the entire Brown slate was controlled by CDC fanatics who wanted to seat Red China in the United Nations, ban atmospheric nuclear tests, abolish loyalty oaths and let Communists speak on college campuses. Right-wing Democrats were asked to complete a ballot on all these liberal dreams and contribute to the bogus Democratic fund.

Following up these phony postcard polls, Nixon barnstormed the state, charging that Pat supped with known Communists, refused to require university professors to sign a loyalty oath and failed to make local school boards root out Soviet subversion in the classroom. Simultaneously, supporters (working without Nixon's permission) circulated a doctored photograph of Brown supposedly bowing to Nikita Khruschev just before the Russian became the first world leader in history to be denied Disneyland hospitality. "Premier," read the caption, "we who admire you, we who respect you, welcome you to California."

Pat, not about to suffer this sort of attack quietly, went on the offensive. "I don't think anyone in my nineteen years of public service has accused me of being soft on the Communist threat," Pat convincingly told his many audiences. The Governor, who privately assured liberal friends that things would ease up after the election, told voters that the FBI had assured him they knew the identity of every California Communist from border to border. Under his administration, he maintained, there was no chance that subversives would ever orate at UC: "The President of the University and the fine Board of Regents composed of people like Mrs. Hearst and Mrs. Chandler can well take care of speakers on the campus." Moreover, "Our Regents, our Trustees and members of local boards of education are loyal and alert Americans. They are just as aware of the need for anti-Communist teaching as he [Nixon]."

The state, Pat added, was well-protected against enemy attack by "one of the nation's best civil defense organizations." As soon as the nuclear explosives started dropping, 30,000 emergency personnel equipped with 12,000 radio meters, and 105 radiological monitoring trailers would be out evacuating people from contaminated areas and sending them to fallout shelters stocked with more than three million bushels of wheat.

After cloaking himself in patriotism, the Governor wound up his Nixon assault by citing John Edgar Hoover's words of wisdom: "Reckless charges against individuals and false statements about the nature of Communism and the extent of its penetration into various areas of our life serve the cause of Communism by creating disunity among Americans."

The Republican candidate's assertions of subversion slacked off in late October, after Democratic state chairman Roger Kent uncovered the chicanery of Nixon's phony Democratic committee, won an injunction against further smear literature mailings, and turned the whole issue to Pat's benefit in the media. The day after the court issued its order, President Kennedy took to national television to announce that his U-2's had found Russian armed missile bases in Cuba capable of firing nuclear weapons 1,000 miles into American territory. To protect his country, the commander-in-chief ordered a naval blockade of the threatening island. Nixon, who had been trying to project a statesmanlike image, watched helplessly as Brown dropped campaigning, flew back to Washington, and huddled with Kennedy's staff.

Cheered by the knowledge that voters tended to rally around the ruling party in times of international crisis, Democratic leaders readied themselves for a last big push. Pat often put in eighteen-hour days mechanically spouting campaign cliches, and habitually ended in motel rooms which met the rigid standards prescribed by his re-election committee's advance manual: "When staying in hotels or motels, get a 'rate' for the party . . . $7 or $8 will cover most hotels."

Sound asleep as soon as he hit the pillow, the under-rested Governor often woke the next morning in such a haze that he had to scan his economy quarters for stationery pinpointing his whereabouts. One morning, particularly beat, he was horrified to find a half-dressed woman sharing his bed. Certain that Nixon's dirty tricksters had slipped a lady of the night in between the gubernatorial linen, he braced himself for the pop of news photographers' flashbulbs that would surely send Nixon to Sacramento. Then looking more closely, he recognized Bernice. "In the exhaustion and confusion," he recalled, "I had forgotten she had joined me the previous evening."

Pat's intensive campaigning culminated with a sweeping election day push across low-income Chicano and black precincts in South-Central and East Los Angeles. Here the Democrat had earned a good reputation by putting through fair housing and Fair Employment Practices legislation, while also working to eliminate de facto school segregation. To bolster the turnout, rotund assembly leader Jesse Unruh's janissaries handed out ten-dollar bills to 10,000 precinct workers, who spent the campaign's waning hours rounding up Brown supporters and ferrying them to the polls. The Governor's son, who had flown home from Yale, was out working minority precincts in San Francisco that final night. He campaigned hard in Hunter's Point with his Youth-for-Service friend, Percy Pinkney. Residents, who appreciatively remembered Jerry helping dismantle youth gangs several years before, were happy to see him back. One even gave Jerry a small cup as a gift. At poll closing time, when many voters were still in line waiting to cast their ballots, the Ivy Leaguer moved down the line cheerfully urging voters to hang in there until their turn came.

While her brother remained on duty in Hunter's Point, seventeen-year-old Kathleen, now attending Santa Catalina School in Monterey, was ushered into a sitting room where the nuns had set up a radio. She was allowed to remain past curfew with a classmate to catch the returns. When first tallies from Southern California precincts showed Nixon winning his home state, she called her father, weeping: "I don't care what happens, Dad, I'll always love you."

"What are you talking about," laughed Pat, who had just received late returns from San Francisco. "I've won."

The next morning, an ashen-faced, unshaven man elbowed press secretary Herb Klein off the Beverly Hilton's ballroom lectern to announce his political retirement. "Now that all the members of the press are so delighted that I have lost, I'd like to make a statement of my own. I believe Governor Brown has a heart, even though he believes I do not. I believe he is a good American, even though he believes I am not. I am proud of the fact that I defended my opponent's patriotism. You gentlemen didn't report it, but I am proud that I did that. I am proud also that I defended the fact that he was a man of good motive. I want that — for once, gentlemen — I would appreciate it if you would write what I say in that respect. I think it's very important that you write it in the lead, in the lead.

"Never in my sixteen years of campaigning have I complained to a publisher, to an editor, about the coverage of a reporter. I believe a reporter has got a right to write it as he feels it . . . I will say to a reporter sometimes that I think, well, look, I wish you would give my opponent the same going over that you gave me . . . I made a talk on television, a talk in which I made a flub . . . I made a flub in which I said I was running for Governor of the United States. *The Los Angeles Times* dutifully reported that. Mr. Brown, the last day, made a flub in which he said, 'I hope everybody wins. You vote the straight Democratic ticket, including Senator Kuchel' —a Republican. *The Los Angeles Times* did not report it.

"As I leave you, I want you to know — just think how much you're going to be missing. You won't have Nixon to kick around anymore because, gentlemen, this is my last press conference . . ."

Not since his dramatic response to the 1952 campaign's "Nixon Fund" had the Republican done a better job exploiting adverse circumstances. The loser's speech reaped a publicity bonanza that overshadowed national coverage of Brown's victory. Political analysts devoted more time to questions raised by the former vice-president than to analyzing Pat's success.

Even in victory there was some grumbling among the Democrats. Leaders of the California Democratic Council grimaced over Unruh's last-minute vote-buying binge in Los Angeles. "I don't like the picture of an armored truck driving up to Democratic headquarters with more than $100,000 in ten-dollar bills," complained the CDC's Paul Ziffren. "That's not the symbol of the party that many of us who worked for it for many years had in mind. If we condone the hiring of 10,000 workers in this election, what's to prevent the hiring of 100,000 in the next election?"

Back in Sacramento, Bernice began working with architects on blueprints for a spacious new governor's residence that would allow her second-term husband to enjoy the luxury of a stall shower. Determined to escape the noisy downtown location on Sixteenth Street, she explained: "It's impossible to have any kind of entertainment in the old mansion. There isn't any space where even a singer could stand." As the projected cost of the new state house rose from $475,000 to $875,000, Bernice rejected the suggestion that inclusion of live-in quarters was an extravagance. "At present everyone except the cook works by day. The Governor is servantless if he plans a party in the evening."

Bernice' campaign for someone to carry the canapes on the swing shift was of little interest to her son, who was now flirting with the civil rights movement at Yale. Like many of his law school friends, Jerry had become involved the previous fall after James Meredith's integration of the University of Mississippi touched off a riot. Jerry, his roommate Danny Greer, classmates like Frank Damrell (who had left Sacred Heart with Brown in 1960) and New Yorker Tony Kline listened to numerous civil rights talks. One was delivered by lawyer William Kuntsler, who was working on a suit against the Justice Department over failure to protect civil rights workers with federal marshals.

Anxious to find out what was really going on, Jerry accepted the suggestion of Bill Higgs, a Harvard-trained lawyer who was recruiting civil rights workers for the Northern Student Movement, to spend his spring vacation in Mississippi. But as he walked off the plane in Jackson, the Governor's son began to have second thoughts. His mind flashed to stories of voter registration organizers being harassed and jailed by redneck cops. At the big house Higgs had rented to lodge transient organizers, the Yale law student listened to a wide range of legitimate horror stories. A typical tale was the case of Emmett Till, a young black who had disappeared one day while working in the little town of Laurel and was now presumed dead.

Under these tense circumstances, Jerry decided it would be a good idea to remain in touch with home. "Someone like you could be in real danger in a situation like that, Jerry," Pat told him. "You really shouldn't be down there." The twenty-five-year-old assured his father that he was old enough to handle himself in Dixie. But after hanging up, he decided to follow Pat's suggestion to "make physical contact with state officials to enjoy the protection of establishment." Without bothering to call ahead for an appointment, he drove over to the state capitol, and barged into Governor Ross Barnett's office, holding out a palm: "Hi, my father is a friend of yours. I just wanted to come by to say hello."

When he finished chatting with Mississippi's leading segregationist, Jerry went out to visit local civil rights celebrities and shrines with Bill Higgs. One of their first visits was with the man Governor Barnett twice blocked from registering at the University of Mississippi — James Meredith. Next, the pair stopped at Jackson State College to hear about the recent murder of three black students by white vigilantes. Anxious to restore his visitor's fast disappearing peace of mind, Higgs headed north, through the peaceful magnolia-scented countryside. By the time they reached Greenwood, Jerry was thinking he might have been wiser to spend his spring break in Ft. Lauderdale.

In Greenwood, Brown was warmly received by the Rev. James Bevel and other organizers of a voter registration drive that was spreading across the South. But it was hard to keep his paranoia in check when all the civil rights workers kept one-upping each other with tales of their most recent death threats. These stories gained credence when a number of sympathetic blacks they visited were obviously squeamish about being seen with white organizers. Among them was a local doctor who flipped the blinds shut as soon as Brown and Higgs entered his office. "Whites and blacks have to be careful about being seen together," explained the trembling physician as he served Scotch and Pepsi on the rocks in Dixie cups.

At home in the executive mansion, Pat and Bernice began to wonder why Jerry hadn't called for several days. Both of them were sympathetic to the civil rights movement all their lives and neither had any use for bigotry or prejudice. Jewish voters had always contributed generously to Brown's campaign and if it hadn't been for the heavy black and Chicano turnout the previous fall, Richard Nixon might now reign in Sacramento. But there was a difference, they believed, between responsible liberal programs, such as the one Jerry supported to help delinquents at Hunter's Point, and radical agitators staging life-threatening confrontations on the south side of the Mason-Dixon line.

Adding to their anxiety was an unexpected call from Governor Barnett. "I think you ought to know," said the man from Jackson, "that Jerry is living with a very bad man. I think this Higgs is going to be indicted for fooling around with little boys. I just wanted to warn you because I think your son is in danger as long as he hangs around with him."

Normally, when he needed to find someone, Pat Brown could rely on local police agencies to locate them anywhere from the middle of Lake Tahoe to Santa Monica Bay. But this was different; he was not about to put the Mississippi State Police on Jerry's trail. There was nothing to do but wait by the phone. A few hours later, the Governor interrupted a conference to take a call from the only person who would be phoning him collect from the Deep South.

"It got really heavy," explained Pat's son from a New Orleans phone booth. "I was really nervous so I just decided to get out of there."

Jerry's friend Bill Higgs also fled Mississippi to avoid prosecution on morals charges involving a juvenile runaway who had been living at his Jackson house. After the civil rights organizer was tried and convicted in absentia, he told his Yale friend that the entire case was a fantasy trumped up by Mississippi officials anxious to dispose of him. This smear did not discourage Pat from thanking Barnett for taking time from his busy schedule to keep an eye on his boy: "Dear Ross," wrote the California Governor after Jerry was safely back in class at Yale. "Just a note to tell you that I very much appreciated your thoughtfulness in calling me about my son. Although you and I disagree vehemently on certain things, I am quite confident that we both are trying to carry on the traditions of our great country." And at year's end he furthered inter-state relations by airmailing the southern governor twenty-four one-pound packages of cellophane-wrapped walnuts.

By then Pat had turned his attention to another pressing domestic crisis. Winding up her convent studies, Kathy decided not to attend the modestly-priced University of California. Like her older brother, she ignored her parents' egalitarian arguments and insisted on private higher education. When the unrelenting Governor and his wife refused to sign her Stanford application, Kathy forged their names. Even after she was accepted, Pat and Bernice continued to refuse to underwrite this extravagance. Undaunted, she wrote a letter to "Uncle Lou" Lurie, who ponied up a $1,410 grant in the freshman's name.

Anxious to avoid further rebellion from his children, the Governor decided to plan their summer vacations. Jerry was discouraged from getting back into civil rights by being put to work in Paris as an assistant to the United States Ambassador to NATO. Kathy and her old Magellan Street girlfriend, Barbara DiGiorgio, were invited to accompany the Browns, press secretary Jack Burby and his wife on a six-week European tour. The party's first stop was Paris, where Jerry promptly invited everyone over for a look at his Left Bank garret.

The entourage followed Jerry across the Seine, down a narrow street, through a rusty iron gate, into a courtyard and up six flights of stairs. Winded by the time they reached the entryway, the group paused to catch their breath as Jerry fumbled with a key, opened the door to his one-bedroom quarters and flicked on a wall switch. As the lights came on, they could hear the sound of running water. Suddenly the noise stopped and a woman's soft voice from the bathroom rang out: "Jerry, is that you?" Without bothering to answer his girlfriend who, it turned out, had returned unannounced from a country weekend, the Governor's son quickly hustled everyone back down the six flights, through the courtyard, past the gate and down into the street. As the group neared the Seine, Bernice told her son: "I want you to come back and stay at our place."

Jerry refused, which was just as well since by the next day Bernice was ready to leave France. What persuaded her to cut short the family's Paris vacation was not the amorous adventures of her son, but the discovery that among her fellow hotel guests was a New York attorney retained by the Pepsi-Cola Company — none other than Richard Nixon. After avoiding him once in the lobby, she entered a Champs-Elysees restaurant and spotted those detestable Nixon eyes again. She decided then and there they would move on to Soest, Westphalia, the ancestral home of Pat's grandmother, Augusta Fiedler.

Arriving in Germany, Pat was touched by the turnout of German officials applauding the arrival of his handsome family. Raising his glass of schnapps to return their generous toast, he declared: "In the future I want to be known as the man from Soest." After motoring to Heidelberg, the party caught a flight to Berlin, where they climbed Potsdammer Platz observation platform for a look across the barbed wire into the binoculars of an East German guard. "Oh, I'm eyeball-to-eyeball with a Communist soldier," clowned the Governor as he waved to an unresponsive watchman. Thinking that his pretty teenage daughter might have better luck with the stone-faced sentry, he urged her to signal.

"Why should I wave?" asked Kathy.

"They're just innocent victims of circumstance," explained Pat as he raised his camera and tried to find the best angle. "What an immense failure the Wall is. How stupid can you get? Imagine if they put up a wall between Northern and Southern California."

Following a meeting with West Berlin Mayor Willy Brandt, the Browns crossed into the Communist sector, where they were followed by guards and newspeople. When Pat paused during his tour of Karl Marx Allee, an East German officer told him, "Governor Brown, I think you should know you are standing on the same spot as Mr. Nixon," during his recent visit. The Californian quickly stepped to one side.

Like the former vice-president, Pat was tempted to quarrel with his Communist hosts. But he had brought with him a serious impediment to any kind of serious debate.

"Daddy," Kathy yelled every time he started sounding contentious, "you are making a scene. Stop it."

In Rome, it was Kathy's usually patient mother who began making a scene. The source of her irritation was a delay on an appointment at the Vatican. After more than an hour went by, Bernice had had enough. "You can't keep the Governor of California waiting like this," she told her characteristically impatient husband. But Pat was prepared to wait all day. "After all," he told his wife, "it *is* the Pope."

Jerry was not to see his father again until November, at President Kennedy's funeral. Overwhelmed by endless electronic media babble about the back-to-back assassinations of the President and Lee Harvey Oswald, the Governor's son wished there were some way to throttle Walter Cronkite. But saturation coverage was not Pat's primary concern. At his Madison hotel room, the California Governor confessed nervousness over walking in John Kennedy's funeral procession. After his own experience in Mississippi, Jerry sympathized with his father and didn't smile when Pat asked for help getting into the bullet-proof vest.

In the spring of 1964, the twenty-six-year-old Brown continued to devote more time to bull sessions with his Yale friends than to his approaching final exams. Usually secretive about his identity, the Governor's son warned friends not to bring up California politics on double dates. Unlike many of his fellow law students, Jerry never tried to impress new acquaintances with his parentage. And wherever he went, Jerry's primary interests were philosophical. He loved to indulge in intellectual gamesmanship with classmate Don Burns, who had also come to Yale after quitting Jesuit seminary. One of their favorite sports was taunting Brown's roommate Danny Greer, who was Jewish, about his ignorance of theological matters.

Customarily, law school graduates spent their summer madly cramming for bar examinations. But Jerry Brown, who returned home to begin clerking for State Supreme Court Justice Matthew Tobriner, wasn't worried. Confident of his legal skills, he approached the big test like one more final. While his friends hung around to compare notes after turning in their papers, Jerry casually headed home to the lower half of a Berkeley brown shingle shared with old Yale classmate Tony Kline. As far as he was concerned, the bar was no sweat.

Instead of taking off for a post-exam vacation with exhausted friends, Jerry continued riding to his San Francisco job each morning in a car pool that included Kline, Frank Damrell and Don Burns. Tobriner valued the services of his defendant-conscious young aide who never knew when to quit. Indeed, Jerry frequently stayed up past midnight searching for legal authority that would help sell his point of view to the boss. Unlike fellow clerks, the Yale grad rebelled when Tobriner refused to go all the way with him on civil liberties issues. One disagreement was over the case of *People vs. Robinson,* where a lower court upheld conviction of a man after police found contraband in his car. Defense attorneys argued that the case should be thrown out because of illegal search and seizure. Jerry agreed, but his boss upheld the lower court ruling. It took Brown days to recover from this defeat.

In the fall, conversation in the Berkeley-San Francisco legal car pool focused on whether idealistic Berkeley students had the right to break a law forbidding political solicitation on campus. Working under the Free Speech Movement banner, twenty campus organizations ranging from Youth for Goldwater to the Independent Socialist Club set up card tables at an area near the main entrance, called the Bancroft Strip. This Hyde Park-type location had been used during the 1964 summer to gather support for various candidates at the Republican National Convention in San Francisco. But shortly before school resumed that fall, campus administrators decided to end all organizing on the strip by enforcing the flaunted law.

Riding across the Bay Bridge in the back seat of Tony Kline's Mercedes, Jerry argued against the Free Speech Movement. But when fellow lawyers like Paul Halvonik disagreed, he decided to check out the campus situation for himself. After work one day in early October, Jerry visited Sproul Plaza, where he found hundreds of students surrounding a police car. These demonstrators were effectively blocking the arrest of one of their leaders, Jack Weinberg, who became famous for warning that you should never trust anyone over thirty. The sight of the undergraduates chanting, obstructing justice, and taunting police reminded Brown of his Mississippi spring break. He had fled the civil rights battlefield to avoid getting caught in just this kind of showdown. But now it was apparent that civil disobedience techniques pioneered in the South were going to rattle his own neighborhood. And this, the Governor's son reported to his car pool friends, was scary: "I just don't see the point of breaking a law in support of some other grievance."

By late fall, the Berkeley campus found itself increasingly torn between the rigid and unimaginative administration of Chancellor Edward Strong and the increasingly militant students headed by Mario Savio, Jack Weinberg and others. Jerry continued to listen to the arguments of his pro-FSM friends, but remained unpersuaded. On December 2, the aspiring lawyer's worst fears were played out as eight hundred FSM supporters marched up the steps of Sproul Hall, Berkeley's administration building.

When news of this occupation reached Pat in Los Angeles, the Governor knew he had to move promptly. He was told by law enforcement officials on the scene that this supposedly spontaneous sit-in had been plotted weeks in advance. How else, it was contended, would the Jewish demonstrators have had time to assemble the Hanukah menorahs they were lighting on the chancellor's floor?

Particularly troubling to the Governor was the realization that he had no time to bob and weave. No legislature or court was going to help him this time. With children of the affluent revolting in front of the international eye of the television screen, he was going to have to take a firm stand. Pat deliberated with aides over conflicting recommendations from police and university administrators. The often heavy-handed Alameda County District Attorney's office urged the Governor to call in the police to break up the demonstration. But his friend, Clark Kerr, suggested instead that Pat go with him to Sproul Hall the following morning. Although the multiversity leader believed they might be able to talk the students into leaving voluntarily, Brown found the whole idea about as appealing as sitting ringside at Chessman's execution. He didn't like the idea of strapping on a bullet-proof vest to visit the alma mater of his wife, brother Frank, and son.

After promising the U.C. leader he would not send in the police, who were waiting nearby for word to move in, the chief executive received a call from his son. Jerry explained that a friend who knew Mario Savio felt something might be gained by putting the FSM leader in touch with the Governor. Pat agreed and seconds later he was listening to Savio comparing organizer's card tables on the Sather Gate strip to Vietnam. He insisted that U.C. regulations prohibiting students from soliciting for social and political causes on campus was an abridgement of their freedom. When the two men rang off, student organizers assembled nearby asked Jerry how the conversation had gone.

"I don't think they communicated very well," he responded.

By that time, his father was receiving the latest bulletin from Deputy Alameda County District Attorney Edwin Meese III. "They're busting up the place," Pat declared after receiving a totally false report that students had begun ransacking the office of U.C. president emeritus, Robert Gordon Sproul. "We have to go in."

Brown immediately called Kerr, who assured the Governor that the demonstration remained non-violent. Brown's aides suggested that Meese's charges be substantiated before moving in. But the degree to which students were breaking the law no longer mattered to the Governor. After months of what he considered to be U.C. administrative mismanagement, Pat decided to restore order. "We cannot compromise with revolution, whether at the University or any other place," explained the Governor. And at 3:30 a.m. he ordered the law officers to enter Sproul Hall. The police then kicked, clubbed, dragged, bumped and strong-armed students out of Sproul Hall and stuffed them into every available paddy wagon in Alameda County. Coverage of the mass arrests on a liberal Berkeley radio station was interspersed with selected excerpts from a commencement address Pat had delivered several years before at the University of Santa Clara:

Thank God for the spectacle of students picketing — even when they are picketing me at Sacramento and I think they are wrong — for students protesting and freedom-riding, for students going out into the fields with our migratory workers, and marching off to jail with our segregated Negroes. At last we're getting somewhere. The colleges have become boot camps for citizenship and citizen-leaders are marching out of them.

For a while it will be hard on us as administrators. Some students are going to be wrong, and some people will want to deny them the right to make mistakes. Administrators will have to wade through the angry letters and colleges will lose some donations. We governors will have to face indignant caravans and elected officials bent on dictating to state college faculties. But let us stand up for our students and be proud of them. If America is still on the way up, it will welcome this new, impatient, critical crop of young gadflies. It will be fearful only of the complacent and passive.

The morning after the Berkeley arrests, reporters inquired why he changed his mind about campus dissent. "There will be no anarchy," he replied, "and this is what has developed at the University of California." Asked if he felt police had used excessive force in clearing Sproul Hall, the Governor shrugged. "It could have been far worse. We could have used tear gas."

That same morning his son explained his father's military strategy to outraged car pool friends: "There wasn't any need for a sit-in. The whole thing was an unnecessary confrontation." Even after papers reported that President Sproul's office had never been entered by demonstrators, Jerry continued to support the mass arrests. It didn't matter that the raid had been based on a false premise or that students merely sought their first amendment rights. They had broken the law; therefore they should be punished. After all, the law was all that stood between organized society and chaos. Once individuals believed they could break society's rules with impunity, established order would collapse. That was why Jerry valued his opportunity to work with Justice Tobriner, where the kinds of issues raised by the Free Speech Movement could be resolved peacefully and rationally.

Unfortunately, one afternoon in late December, Jerry's clerkship was interrupted by a call from Sacramento. The Governor had just taken an advance peek at the names of Californians who passed the bar. The name of Tobriner's aide was not among them. When Jerry told his car pool what had happened, the driver, without taking his eyes off Bay Bridge traffic, deadpanned, "I didn't know they graded those things honestly." A few days later, following his father's instructions, the clerk threw some clothes in a suitcase and headed for the Governor's mansion. Upon arrival, wise Papa Pat cheered up his son with a totally uncharacteristic gift, keys to a new Chevrolet Nova. Jerry used the car for the next three months to commute to bar exam tutorials at McGeorge Law School in Sacramento.

The Turkey Has Landed

CHAPTER 7

I n the winter of 1965, the director of Sacramento's McGeorge Law
School took Jerry through a three-month bar review course. With his
help, Brown, Jr. passed the exam on the second try and was sworn in
with 211 other attorneys on June 15, at San Francisco's Veterans
Memorial Auditorium.

Unlike other parents, Pat and Bernice were celebrating more than the
beginning of their son's legal career, for after the ceremony, Jerry modestly told reporters he hoped to follow in his father's footsteps. "I have
some political ambitions when the time is right."

Matthew Tobriner tried to discourage his former law clerk from starting out in a corporate law firm, but like many young attorneys, Jerry

believed a business-oriented firm would be a sensible training ground. The judge, a labor attorney for thirty years before moving on to the bench, reminded Jerry of organized labor's key role in any successful Democratic campaign. Pat, Tobriner added, might never have become district attorney had it not been for key precinct work by old union clients."

Jerry listened politely as Tobriner advised him in his paneled chambers on McAllister Street, but he had already made up his mind. "I don't want to be in a firm that has a liberal or conservative label attached to it," he said. "If I get into politics, it might be detrimental."

"Well, there are a lot of good firms to choose from in San Francisco," replied the judge.

"No, I'm going to practice in Los Angeles. That's where the votes are. That's where the people are. If I want to get into politics, that's where I've got to go."

Anxious to preview the politically dominant Southern California metropolis, Jerry flew south in August 1965 to help troubleshoot the Watts riots for his father. The Governor, who was vacationing with Bernice in Greece when the forcible arrest of three black drunk driving suspects touched off civil disorder, caught the first jet west. At Kennedy Airport in New York, Pat called his office and within moments agreed to National Guard intervention. By the time he reached California, Watts resembled a war zone.

As Jerry's flight approached the Los Angeles International Airport, the battle area could be easily seen. As the "No Smoking" sign went on, the Jack Daniels-colored smog gave way to clouds of ash billowing up from the burning neighborhoods. Later, at the baggage area, Jerry was greeted by an old Yale classmate, who gave him a lift to a rundown section of Venice in his pickup truck.

A program entitled "The Eve of Destruction" just finished airing on the radio when the young men pulled up to an old church. There, local contacts had pulled together friends from Watts to confer privately with the Governor's son. Soon the basement walls resonated to the shouts of black leaders haranguing the young attorney for his father's decision to let guardsmen use South Central Los Angeles for "target practice."

Hours later, Jerry relayed these concerns to his father, who by then had arrived and was caucusing with aides at the Sheraton Town House. But the younger Brown's attention was quickly diverted when he was introduced to evangelist Billy Graham, who had just completed a helicopter tour of the riot area. Donning his Jesuitical thinking cap, Jerry fell into easy theological discourse with the internationally-respected Christian soldier. The Governor's aides glanced clockward, amazed that with Watts on the verge of becoming California's first urban forest fire, gubernatorial decision-making came to a standstill while Jerry played twenty religious questions. At last, Pat mercifully interrupted: "Jerry, please. Now is not the time."

After the last ambulance departed Watts on August 17, the box score for the six-day riot stood at 34 dead, 1,032 injured, 3,952 arrested. As crews began rebuilding more than $40 million worth of damaged property, Los Angeles Mayor Sam Yorty, blamed the insurrection on "outside agitators." He insisted that brutality complaints made against police chief William Parker were part of "a worldwide campaign by communists, communist dupes and sympathizers."

Yorty, who had broken into politics thirty years earlier on the left side of the state assembly, now apparently believed he could ride into the governor's office on the strength of a white backlash. Even though he became Mayor in 1961, thanks to heavy support from minority voters responding to his promise to dump "racist" police chief Parker, he was now anxious to back up the lawmen with new anti-riot legislation. He also allied himself with forces favoring an initiative repealing the state fair housing law, and pushed for anti-crime legislation.

Anxious to placate the right without losing crucial minority support, Pat also got behind three proposed anti-riot bills, while simultaneously opposing new legislative efforts to overturn fair housing. But this attempt to navigate a middle-road course failed to impress old CDC allies who sensed their main man was moving too far right. Determined to hold liberal support, Brown and State Controller, Alan Cranston (who lost a bid for the Democratic senatorial nomination to Pierre Salinger in 1964), compounded their difficulties by selecting Simon Casady, a mild-mannered El Cajon publisher with good liberal credentials to take over the organization in 1965.

Within months, the White House complained to Brown about the new CDC leader's crusade against LBJ's Vietnam policy. Canvassing California in his own plane, Casady used every available forum to preach against the war. The Governor and Controller caught up with the fifty-seven-year-old renegade at a fundraiser in San Francisco's Fairmont Hotel. This Nob Hill establishment, owned by Pat's multimillionaire friend Ben Swig, was the favored location for selling airline-type chicken dinners to Northern California Democrats at one-hundred dollars per plate. Following the banquet, the Governor took Casady aside and said: "I understand you're doing a great job, Si, but I think you ought to soft pedal that Vietnam business a little." Before the CDC chief had a chance to remind Brown that an anti-war platform had been endorsed at the organization's last convention, Cranston was at his side suggesting other issues to emphasize besides Southeast Asia. "It might be a good idea if you stuck to state issues, Si — like smog. Or saving the redwoods."

But unlike Cranston, Brown and Johnson, Si Casady didn't have to run for re-election. When American military involvement in Vietnam accelerated during the summer of 1965, Casady began denouncing the President as a "cowboy who shoots from the hip and not a very good cowboy at that." Soon Governor Brown was on the line from Sacramento. "Si, I've been back in Washington and the President is very disturbed about what you've been saying about Vietnam." Pat went on to suggest that Casady go to D.C. with a California group for a special Vietnam briefing. "If you come back and still have the same opinions, well, that's fine," said the Governor.

Casady, truly a man with a conscience, paid his way back to the District of Columbia. At the White House, foreign policy experts explained that the real reason Americans were in Vietnam was that Johnson didn't "want to see the white world which we've built up since the Reformation besieged by the rest of the world in the next ten or twenty years."

Furious over wasting money on an idiot's mission, Casady returned home and escalated his verbal assault on the war. His rhetoric peaked in Northern California's eggbasket, Petaluma, where critics complained that he devoted too much time to Vietnam at the expense of Brown's forthcoming re-election campaign. While agreeing with a questioner that Pat's re-election was important, Casady added, "Governors come and governors go . . . ."

This was too much for Pat. The next day Casady received another call from Sacramento.

"How are you, Si?"

"Fine; how are you?"

"Fine. Did you get my letter?"

"No. What letter?"

"I asked you to resign as president of CDC."

"Oh. What's the problem?"

"Si, I just don't think you should be saying the things you're saying about Vietnam, criticizing the President and criticizing me, while you're still president of the CDC. You have a right to your own opinion. But you occupy an official position within the party, just like I do. We can't always say the things we feel like saying. And Si?"

"Yes, Governor."

"I hope this won't interfere with our friendship."

When news of this demand broke, pickets from Berkeley's anti-war Vietnam Day Committee (VDC) piled into a car and drove to Magellan Street to demonstrate against Pat. Cynthia Kelly and her children looked down from the porch as the polite demonstrators waved placards reading "Upside Down with Brown" and "LBJ — Governor of California." Pat's old neighbors were leafleted with flyers denouncing the effort to sack Casady and urging Brown to call for immediate withdrawal of American troops from Vietnam. "We feel this is a dramatic way to protest the Governor's attempt to silence the peace movement," explained VDC leader Stephen Smale.

Casady, who, it turned out, was a tough man in a fight, resisted Brown's pressure to resign, prompting the Governor and Cranston to take their case before the CDC's 1966 convention in Bakersfield. "When you treat the President with contempt, me with contempt, the congressmen with contempt, you have forfeited the right to lead a Democratic organization," said the man who wanted to emulate Earl Warren and win a third term. In a bitter floor fight, the delegates agreed to oust Casady 1,001 to 859.

But this struggle was not without cost to the Governor, as it alienated many of his traditional liberal supporters. Coming as it did after the U.C. Berkeley arrests and the Watts riots, it seemed to show that the Governor was losing his political touch. Now worried about his chances for re-election, Brown knew he had to take action. When he did, he made another serious mistake.

Brown decided to undercut the primary campaign of his leading Republican opponent, San Francisco Mayor and dairy owner George Christopher. Determined to find something controversial in Christopher's past, Brown's researchers camped out in a microfilm room until they found a twenty-year-old story about the Republican's technical arrest for breaking state milk laws. By themselves the facts were hardly worth alluding to in campaign leaflets. But Pat knew a man who could transform yesterday's backpage news into headlines — his old acquaintance Drew Pearson. Once fed the story, the Washington columnist, who helped undermine Attorney General Howser in 1947, promptly recycled the obscure charges onto the front page. The San Francisco dairy owner professed his innocence, but voters put their trust in the muckraker. Christopher lost the primary, to the delight of Brown, who easily snuffed out Sam Yorty's aspirations. The campaign would be easy, Brown thought, now that he had beaten his principal opponent and assured the nomination of a man who never spent a day in political office — Ronald Reagan.

Like Pat, the actor-turned-candidate became a serious political contender only after changing party affiliation. During the forties, Reagan worked for liberal organizations like the Americans for Democratic Action and the United World Federalists (along with Alan Cranston). In 1950, he offered to endorse Helen Gahagan Douglas in her senatorial campaign against Richard Nixon. But the Democratic manager decided not to emboss Reagan's name on official stationery because of his left image.

Then in 1952, Reagan had a change of heart. Turned off by twenty years of Democratic monopoly and suddenly anxious to cut off the New Deal, Reagan voted for Dwight Eisenhower. Two years later he signed a $125,000 contract to host a weekly General Electric Corporation television series. As the firm's ambassador to the American people, he visited 125 GE plants and spoke to 250,000 employees. Gradually, his political views moved right and he adopted the anti-big government perspective that became his trademark. Reagan's plugs for rugged individualism drew rave reviews in the kilowatt kingdom. And key themes like opposition to "bureaucracy, planners, regulators, government red tape, the welfare state, and high taxes" not only played well to conservative audiences, but also brought a favorable response from the broad middle-class.

By the time G.E. cancelled its program in 1962, Reagan had changed his affiliation from Democrat to Republican. Now one of America's best-known TV hosts, the actor proved an effective fund raiser for his new party. In 1964, the year United States Borax Company picked him to host *Death Valley Days,* the one-time liberal became co-chairman of California Citizens for Barry Goldwater.

These were good credentials for a Southern California congressional race, but they seemed hardly sufficient to win the office that had eluded a former vice-president last time around. Pat looked upon his campaign against Reagan as mere formality along the way to his third term in office. At the age of sixty-one, he believed his record of positive achievement would sell without hype. During his eight years in Sacramento, he pushed through a comprehensive water plan that had tamed several of the wild rivers in the northern part of the state for the farmers in the southern regions; concrete was being poured for new U.C. campuses at San Diego, Irvine, and Santa Cruz; thousands of miles of freeway were constructed in response to California's love affair with the automobile; remote beaches and mountain peaks had been acquired for the state park system; social programs were initiated to assist the mentally ill, disabled and unemployed; and many laws had been passed banning discrimination against minorities in housing and employment.

Pat could now boast that California embraced "the greatest scientific and engineering community in the world" which "created and built machines to land on the moon, photograph Mars and circle the sun." He also modestly pointed out that during his terms, California had accumulated "more students in public higher education, more Nobel prize winners, more farm income, more public beaches and parks, more cars, more business investment, more of almost anything good you want to name than any other state in the Union."

Celebrating this millennium, he frequently reached back to a question Daniel Webster had once raised about the untamed West:

"What do we want with this vast, worthless area, this region of savages and wild beasts, of shifting sands and whirlpools of dust, of cactus and prairies dogs? To what use could we ever hope to put these great deserts or these great mountain ranges, impenetrable and covered to their base with eternal snow?"

"California," Brown replied, "is providing the answer to those questions and I believe will do so in the future with increasing emphasis."

Reagan, the retired Borax salesman, effectively undercut this optimism with a string of aphorisms, quips and one-liners that struck quick emotional pay dirt. Flying around the state in a converted DC-3 turkey freighter named "The Turkey," he skillfully promoted his laissez faire perspective. "Either the problems confronting us will be solved by those who believe in individual freedom — including the right of each person to spend as much of his own private wealth as possible — or by those who feel the government should have claim to more and more of the individual's earnings. What is needed now is an anti-revolution — a reformation of the reformers. Under the false title of liberalism, we have seen social engineers with calculation and the violence of centralized power confine, control, and direct the free rhythms of human life. They deny the validity of absolute moral values and reject the spiritual bases upon which that unique being — the individual person — is founded, and with that rejection, they destroy the philosophical foundation of our free society."

Whether in person or on TV, the Governor always made sure anyone in his audience beyond the fifth grade could understand him. Speech writers were careful not to include any language or reference beyond the grasp or experience of the average listener. Thus, Dostoevsky, Nietzsche, and even Shakespeare were out, while Americans like Lincoln, Jefferson, and the martyred Kennedy were often alluded to as paragons of sagacity. Phrases like "common purpose," "the unrelenting challenge," and "restless, driving, dynamic traditions" littered every speech. Middle-westerners such as Frost were in, while local talent like Ambrose Bierce never made it to the rough draft.

The campaign proved that Reagan understood the use of television better than Pat. The Governor's idea that TV didn't require much more than a blue shirt and matching tie proved naive now that he was up against a pro. While people still reacted well to Brown's personal appearances, Ronald Reagan's polished TV presentation played much better to audiences than Pat's old-fashioned homilies. McLuhan had obviously discovered something important. Applying his theory to Pat, it appeared the Governor hadn't lost his personableness, it just didn't transfer well to the small screen.

For example, when Pat was on the road preaching the gospel according to California, hosts sometimes introduced him as the kind of rube who wanders around in mismatched socks. One such gathering that year was at Washington's National Press Club, where reporters expected to have a few laughs at the Governor's expense. But when he finished his impassioned tribute to the Golden State, the audience was speechless. Finally a newsman in the rear broke the silence. "Governor," he asked, "how much is a one-way ticket to Calfornia?"

"Governor, how much is a one-way ticket to California?" Brown remembered that question as he watched media-Smoothie Reagan characterize mid-twentieth century California as the homeland of criminals, hoodlums, restless blacks, impatient students, lazy professors, vacillating administrators, cynical politicians and spendthrift governors. But even as he mocked Ronald Reagan as a "McLuhanesque cowboy in an electric-blue suit, ready to rid the state of modern bandits and troublemakers," the chief executive realized this Republican was toting live ammunition. The man who had begun his own career as a San Francisco D.A. in a campaign against gangsters, con artists, gamblers, abortionists, pornographers, and corrupt bureaucrats had to counter his opponent's call for a return to simpler and more orderly times. Governor Brown spoke out. "There are those who dream of retreat to a simpler, slower time. But that is not our way. California was built by pioneers of whom it was said: 'The cowards never started and the weak died by the way.' There can be no retreat — no drift to the past. Where one house stands, we must build another next door. It is because of our massive relentless growth that California has become the cutting edge of America."

The words made considerable sense, but in precincts where so many voters had pulled the Democratic lever during the Knowland and Nixon campaigns, they had little impact. Back-pedaling to conservative elements during the Berkeley crisis, supporting anti-riot legislation in the aftermath of the Watts riots, arm twisting with the CDC over Vietnam, and failure to aggressively push farm worker organizing legislation hurt Pat badly with many of his traditional supporters. Progressives who had promoted Brown as the great liberal hope in campaigns past decided to sit this one out.

By October, some of Pat's detractors, like *Ramparts* magazine, suggested he head for a phone booth and change in to a liberal Superman outfit: "Brown could recapture the elusive quality of vitality, turn tragedy to victory. Even now, after Chessman, after Delano, after Berkeley, after Watts, he could turn the wheel, inspire support, arouse enthusiasm. All he needs to do is to meet the issues, head on, chuck out the appeasers of racism, the apostles of caution, the vultures, and apply to the real issues of the state, one by one, the meaning behind the rhetoric of liberalism."

The former liberal believed expensive programmatic solutions only inflamed the greed of special interest groups. He claimed that the Governor's well-intentioned civil rights legislation had ended in mass murder at Watts and that an enormous cash investment in the state university system led to civil disobedience at Berkeley, where violence had given way to orgies that were "so vile I can't describe them to you."

While a case could be made that without Brown's reforms, the eventual cost in civil disorder would be far greater, few were interested in the judgment of history. Even casual students of current events could see that major elements of the California dream were taking a nightmarish turn. Heralded solutions to many everyday problems were obviously not working in this new era. For instance, Californians were finding it harder to enjoy their freeways now that they were trapped in bumper-to-bumper commuter traffic, and residents of some southern valleys were growing impatient with track meets cancelled due to smog alerts. And even those who disagreed with Reagan's rugged individualism had to admit it was becoming harder to raise a family while you also supported ever larger city, county, state and federal governments.

Pat, so confident when the campaign initially began, faced a precipitous decline at the polls. Suddenly, the man who sought to please both the right and the left seemed to have lost both, and wasn't at all sure what had gone wrong. Jerry, who was just then reading a book called *Understanding Media,* by a Canadian professor named Marshall McLuhan, thought he could explain his father's problem with reference to the author's theories.

McLuhan focused on two crucial ages. The first was the beginning of the fifteenth century, when Johann Gutenberg developed print. This led, in McLuhan's words, to "the separation of the senses, of functions, of operations of states emotional and political as well as of tasks." The second age began in the mid-twentieth century, when television again united man's auditory and tactile senses. No longer dependent merely on his vision, man could use all senses simultaneously. Television, in a sense, extended the central nervous system.

McLuhan went on to discuss the special properties of television and how it influenced style. In the realm of politics, for example, a TV spot is usually brief—a matter of minutes rather than paragraphs or pages. This made it imperative that a candidate not come forward with too much information in any one appearance or the viewing audience would experience stimulus overload. Also, because TV was a close-up medium, it was essential the candidate appear relaxed, spontaneous, and light. And, because TV cameras tended to exaggerate everything, it was important to be as low-key as possible. Jerry quickly understood why people were making such a fuss over McLuhan. Beyond the perplexing hyperbole was an essential fact of contemporary political life — *what* you said didn't matter as much as *how* you said it.

Television, Jerry realized, was spawning a new generation of political heroes like Ronald Reagan and threatening the careers of scores of old-style politicians like Pat Brown, in much the same way that the invention of the sound-track wrecked the careers of many great silent screen stars. Or, as Marshall McLuhan said, issues were becoming secondary to images.

At first it was difficult for Pat to admit he didn't have the right image for television. With the possible exception of Earl Warren, there had never been a California politician who exploited media more effectively than Brown himself. His first campaign success in 1942 was a textbook example of how to exploit the public's fear of political and criminal vice. He had repeatedly gone to Drew Pearson for crucial headlines in tight races. Newspaper morgues overflowed with photos of the racket-busting Attorney General patting himself on the back at press conferences. He had sold the water plan using TV ads frightening people with the specter of empty spigots during a drought. And in 1962, Pat had the pleasure of watching Richard Nixon bury himself before a television audience of millions.

Edmund G. Brown, Sr. thought he knew plenty about the electronic media. All you had to do was dress, talk and present yourself as a regular guy. Jovial and unpretentious, Pat could even turn his occasional bloopers to his advantage. People continued to chuckle over the time he referred to a disastrous series of Northern California floods as "the worst disaster in California since my election as Governor."

Pat took a different view. He believed the liberal troops that helped build his career had taken early retirement. A generation of liberal programs, beginning with the New Deal, had worked — assimilating many of the poor, oppressed minorities and struggling workers into the middle-class. No longer on welfare or unemployment, these one-time underdogs were now out pricing automatic garage door openers, and pool sweeps and flirting with the idea of voting for Ronald Reagan. He did not deny that "California and the nation are still blemished by pockets of poverty and groups of underdogs." But to try to save his campaign by an eleventh hour appeal to the left was, he believed, no answer to Reaganism.

In long campaign meetings, the staff agreed that positive documentation was needed for the media and the public showing what Brown had accomplished in office. With the help of Justice Matthew Tobriner, Stewart Udall, Erle Stanley Gardner, Wallace Stegner, and half a dozen others, he collaborated on a book describing what responsible liberalism had done for the people of California. Illustrated with landscape photographs by Ansel Adams, the volume was a 222-page advertisement for the Governor.

Scheduled for release at the height of the campaign, the handsome book, entitled *California: The Dynamic State,* bogged down in Brown administrative red tape. Preoccupied with personal appearances, the Governor procrastinated on approving the galleys. Instead he told television audiences: "Reagan's talent for the simple quip fits neatly into the needs of television news," and "if politicians offer little more than smiles, quips and simplistic advocacy, we might as well convert our city halls and capitol building into television studios and anticipate the tragic day when democracy will have withered away to leave a vacuum for demagogues to enter."

Desperate to stop Reagan, Pat — with Bernice's help — went into the sort of campaign overdrive that served him so well in past years. The state's first couple popped up on breakfast talk shows in Pasadena, noon-hour Fresno shopping center rallies, and nocturnal San Jose airport press conferences. The Governor's ads broke up Top 40 broadcasts, kept billboard crews busy on U.S. 101, and even slipped into the interval between the late show and the early morning meditation. Vaulting through the state's high and low lands, scrambling for last-minute votes, he was frequently tired and occasionally somnolent. In the past, fatigue made him absent-minded. His staff shuddered when they recalled the time the Governor decided to barnstorm Valley pear country at harvest season. After driving through many orchards where Chicanos were gathering ripe Bartlett pears, Brown had tipped his hat to the farm owner and asked, "What are you people growing up here?"

This time, with aides whispering vital details in his ear, Pat avoided similar mishaps in the campaign's debilitating final days. But the once iron grasp of the man who had shaken more hands than any California politician in either party went limp when the votes were counted. On election night, Ronald Reagan won by 993,000 votes. "To be frank," Pat admitted after it was over, "a majority of Californians were bored with me." The next morning booksellers throughout the state began returning unsold copies of *California: The Dynamic State* that had arrived only a week earlier. Even the modest $1.95 price and Ansel Adams' striking pictures of Yosemite's Half Dome couldn't tempt buyers. In all, 9,600 copies from the 10,000 volume run ended up at the Santa Barbara dump. The Turkey had landed in Sacramento and responsible liberalism was moving to Beverly Hills.

Pat with father, Edmund Brown.

Ida Schuckman Brown.

Photos courtesy of Governor and Mrs. Edmund G. Brown, Sr.

Bernice and Jerry Brown.

Bernice Brown's father, Captain Arthur Layne

Pat with younger brother Harold.

L to R, Dan Brophy and Pat "Trow" (nicknamed for his short rolled trousers) Brown.

98

Pat Brown in the Russian River, California.

Jerry, First Communion.

Jerry with older sisters

Jerry at his birthday party with neighborhood friends.

The Brown family.

Jerry Brown

Brown family dinner at the Governor's Mansion in Sacramento on inauguration night, January 1979. Seated, Ida Schuckman Brown with Charles Casey on her lap, Pat, Bernice, Kathleen with Kathleen Kelly. Standing, Jerry, Cynthia, Pat Casey, Joe Kelly and Barbara.

Jerry at Sacred Heart Novitiate, Los Gatos, California, 1958.

Governor Edmund Brown awards his son Jerry a Bachelor of Arts degree at commencement exercises, University of California, Berkeley, June 1961.

John F. Kennedy, Averell Harriman, Bernice and Pat Brown, Lady Bird and Lyndon Johnson.

Pat with Richard Nixon at a debate during the 1962 gubernatorial race.

Pat and Jerry.

L to R, Edmund G. Brown, Sr., Edmund G. Brown, Jr., Wally Lynn, Earl Warren, duck hunting at Lynn's ranch in Colusa.

Jerry at his inauguration ceremony for governor in 1975 with California Supreme Court Chief Justice Donald Wright and Leo McCarthy.

Jacques Cousteau with Jerry at Space Day.

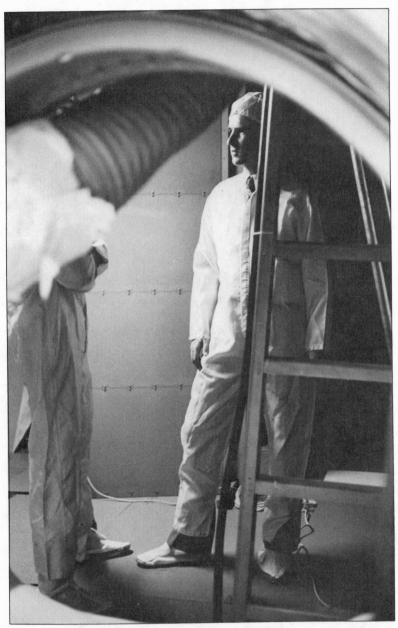

Jerry visiting NASA on a field trip to learn about the shuttle program.

Photo by Stewart Brand

PART 2

The New Spirit

"When you want to go left, you have to go right"

CHAPTER 8

R egardless of the weather, each day began in much the same way for Pat Brown. When the alarm clock went off, he unbuttoned and dropped his pajamas, dashed out to the patio and belly-flopped into his oval swimming pool, buck naked.

Following a ritual sprint, the new partner in Ball, Hunt, and Hart rolled onto his back and sniffed the arboreal splendor of Beverly Hills. Spurning offers to return to San Francisco, he had followed his son's lead south. Bay Area friends doubted the man from Forest Hills would be happy in Benedict Canyon, where tourists armed with maps of stars' homes patrolled the serpentine roads. But eight years in Sacramento had softened him to the virtues of a warm climate. And few things in Pat's new life gave him more delight than the chlorinated swimming hole in his backyard. "All my life," he confessed, "I've wanted a home with a pool."

The Browns politely attended the ceremony as the new Governor took the oath of office on January 2, 1967. Reagan insisted on being sworn in at midnight, when the constellations would be lined up in his favor. "For many years," Ronald Reagan told his late night audience, "you and I have been shushed like children and told there are no simple answers to the complex problems which are beyond our comprehension. Well, the truth is there are simple answers."

Following the ceremony, Pat handed Reagan the keys to the governor's mansion, which Reagan promptly declared a firetrap. He and Nancy retreated to a rented Tudor home nearby.

"I'm sorry you are leaving the mansion," Brown wrote the Reagans from Beverly Hills. "You would have found it comfortable once they had put in the new freeway along Thirtieth Street and the trucks no longer shifted gears on the street beneath the bedrooom.

"Also, I am sorry you are selling the Grizzly (Brown's plane). A chartered jet flies too high and too fast for you to get a good look at this great Golden State as you fly over. And that is one of the genuine satisfactions of being governor of this state — soaring over the cities and towns; the farms, the dams and canals; the colleges, the National Guard fighters on five-minute alert; the highways; all the things that make California the leader among equals in this Nation."

Reagan, whose first action as Governor was to dramatically "freeze" all state hiring, never answered Brown's letter. Instead, his executive secretary, Edwin Meese III, the young Alameda County Deputy D.A. and former tax collector instrumental in persuading Pat to authorize the December 1964 police raid at Berkeley, cleared all Democratic vestiges from the executive suite. Even Brown's imperial cork-covered desk, originally built by state prison inmates for Earl Warren, was sent down to storage. Pat would have loved to ship the California oak showpiece to his new office but that was ruled out by the General Services Administration. He had to settle for hundreds of jade, crystal, ivory, pewter and stainless steel mementos bestowed by appreciative dignitaries during his tenure.

Glancing at the spoils scattered about his Beverly Hills home, Pat felt like a Latin American leader in temporary exile. For reasons he could never fully articulate, the thirty-third governor believed his people would return him to office — perhaps as early as 1970. Bernice insisted his political career was complete, but Pat knew a man of his experience was always subject to a draft. While he lost badly, millions of Californians still proudly identified with the manifold accomplishments of the Brown era.

Pat and Bernice arrived in Beverly Hills less than a year after Jerry took a $640 a month job with Tuttle and Taylor, a corporate law firm in Century City. The senior Brown found the legal position for his son after Jerry returned from a five-month swing through Central and South America. That trip began with a visit to a family near Mexico City. After brushing up on his Spanish, Jerry then proceeded through Honduras, Guatemala, Costa Rica, Venezuela, Colombia and Peru. In Santiago, he worked briefly as a private investment consultant for the Chile-California program. Disappointed by this economic development project, he moved on to Uruguay and then Brazil, to look up an old Berkeley friend, Ann Mayno.

During the height of their romance at UC, the plant pathologist's parents had rushed up from Merced to meet the Governor and his wife. Pat and Bernice were somewhat put off by the visit, which seemed to them presumptuous and was, in any event, a false alarm. Ann decided not to marry. She received Jerry cordially in Brazil, but by the time he left for Acapulco, he knew there would be no reconciliation.

Returning to Los Angeles shortly before his twenty-eighth birthday, Jerry began following the case of condemned prisoner Aaron Mitchell, who killed a Sacramento policeman during a 1963 robbery attempt. Although Pat refused clemency to twenty men executed after Chessman, court decisions had left the San Quentin gas chamber dormant since 1963. Now death penalty critics were trying to make the prisoner's fate a partisan issue. At rallies all over California, Reagan was characterized as the GOP's new prince of capital punishment. Few of these demonstrators recalled it was Governor Brown who had denied Mitchell clemency a year earlier. On April 11, 1967, just hours after throwing the first ball at Anaheim stadium for the Angel's new season, Ronald Reagan rejected the condemned black man's last appeal for mercy.

When the execution began at 10:04 a.m. the following morning, Jerry Brown was at the San Quentin gate observing a vigil in the prisoner's behalf. The young lawyer, who had always opposed taking human life by court order, believed that asphyxiating a Chessman here and a Mitchell there only turned the serious issue of criminal justice into a cruel carnival act.

After Mitchell died, Jerry returned to Tuttle and Taylor. He had an informal arrangement with the firm which allowed him all the free time he needed even during normal business hours, as long as his work got done. Reflecting on his four years as an attorney, Brown later commented:"I enjoyed practicing law, but there were parts of it I didn't like. There's a certain abstract quality about it with respect to questions that I didn't find that interesting. I didn't find the problem-solving that interesting or that exciting or that challenging... [The practice of law] struck me as narrow and confining. The procedure certainly seems to take precedence over the substance. I can look back on cases now that went on for years and that really should have been just arbitrated instead of this very cumbersome procedure of discovery and correspondence back and forth and depositions and trials and appeals. If a solid arbitrator could have been presented with the competing arguments, a judgment could have been made in a matter of weeks instead of a matter of years. That's something that the entire legal system is going to have to confront, and I'm going to help 'em confront it."

By now, politics had become Jerry's main preoccupation. And unlike other ambitious Southern California political newcomers, Jerry did not have to run a mimeograph machine or walk precincts to move up the Democratic organizational ladder. Ex-Governor Brown was more than happy to arrange for the party's front door to be open when his son came calling. Shortly before Pat left office, he made a quick phone call to veteran Los Angeles County Supervisor, Ken Hahn. This gangling white man, who represented predominantly black precincts in and around Watts, listened to Pat candidly outline his dilemma. "Jerry wants to run and I can't appoint him to anything. Would you look around and see if you can appoint him to something." Hahn was amenable and saw to it that Jerry got a seat on the Los Angeles County Delinquency and Crime Commission. Jerry's old neighbors on Magellan Street in San Francisco, who recalled his childhood antics, were amused to learn he was breaking into politics on the wayward youth circuit.

Aware that the new appointee had marched in Berkeley anti-draft demonstrations, the other commissioners expected Brown to champion permissiveness. But from the first session, Jerry voiced strong opinions about the need for rigid enforcement of juvenile crime control laws. His experience with Percy Pinkney's Youth for Service in San Francisco had convinced Jerry that strict laws and harsh sanctions were the only answer to juvenile crime. Indeed, there was an Ignatian ring to the hard line he put forward, though by this time he had lost contact with the church. He argued that no one — whether adult or juvenile — was absolved of responsibility for misbehavior. And because Brown was so pessimistic about the likelihood of altering criminal patterns once they were ingrained, it was even more urgent that juveniles not be coddled.

While Jerry Brown was grappling with the problems of teenage tyranny, his father was working for Democratic Party leader, Lyndon Johnson, with the National Commission on Reform of the Federal Criminal Code. Brown, Sr., who as Governor allowed three dozen inmates to go to their court-ordered deaths at San Quentin, was now determined to abolish capital punishment. "No one has the right to play God with someone else's life," he argued at commission meetings in Washington. "Besides,

114

I don't think executions are an effective deterrent."

Pat's unqualified endorsement of the sanctity of human life surprised many. But he was quick to defend his record against those who recalled missed opportunities to save Chessman and his death row compadres. Going against popular sentiment at that time would have been political suicide for the Democrats, Brown explained. In fact, failure to gas the Red Light Bandit could have swept Dick Nixon into the governor's mansion enroute to the White House.

No one appreciated this point better than Jerry. He knew California Democrats had to temper progressive aims and come to terms with the strong law-and-order feeling in the state if they were to survive. That's why he valued Hahn's appointment. For here, at the outset of his political career, was an opportunity to establish that he was not just another liberal who blamed all criminal behavior on misguided toilet training. "Society, by setting forth clear penalties for certain kinds of conduct sets its public ratification on moral judgment that this is wrong behavior and that it is deserving of punishment irrespective of whether the punishment will deter, rehabilitate or any thing else. It is a way of society defining what is . . . seriously wrong.

"My philosophy is it is better to catch people at the beginning, give them a sentence that isn't, you know, necessarily of a Draconian period, but of a certain substantial time in prison; then let them out and then if he fails again, bring him back and keep him longer."

Friends kidded Jerry that he was starting to sound like Ronald Reagan, who had suggested a "bloodbath" might be the necessary solution to campus challenges posed by a new generation of Mario Savios and Jerry Rubins. But Brown insisted he had lost none of the old Sacred Heart compassion. "When you want to go left," he explained pragmatically, "you have to go right."

Unfortunately, going right on the Los Angeles delinquency commission appeared to have little practical effect. Jerry grew impatient listening to board certified scientists prate about "leakage," "communications ethos," and other psychobabble. It amazed him that soporific reports filled with recommendations on the latest methodology and sanctions for handling delinquents were mailed fourth-class to authorities and then dumped on the shelf, unread. Before long he complained publicly that advisory commissions had "less power than I'd realized."

By now, equally uninspired by Tuttle and Taylor assignments to mass produce memoranda, contracts, pleadings and legal boilerplate for corporate, collection and criminal cases, Jerry began to focus his political energy on matters of foreign policy. While reluctant to directly participate in demonstrations challenging America's military intervention in Southeast Asia, he was anxious to speak out at appropriate forums. In

October, he phoned Gerald Hill, the San Francisco attorney who replaced Si Casady as head of the CDC, and asked for a chance to address a divided CDC membership at a special Long Beach convention. Anti-war forces favoring complete withdrawal were excited when Jerry rose to address the meeting. They expected him to lend the famous Brown name to their cause. Instead, Jerry spent five minutes awkwardly endorsing an end to American bombing of North Vietnam and the beginning of truce talks.

This view, embraced by CDC moderates, prevailed over the more radical resolution to immediately send all American troops a ticket home. The losers did not accept defeat gracefully. They dismissed the winning platform as an easy out for Johnson, allowing him to continue committing ground forces as long as negotiations dragged on. To them, Jerry and other moderates were "hypocrites, hogging the middle of the road while strumming Phil Ochs' 'Love Me I'm a Liberal.'"

But Jerry Brown contended that moderation was necessary with regard to withdrawal of troops from Southeast Asia. At the very least, he believed moderation was necessary for him. Partially because he was seen as a responsible dissident, Brown was selected to serve as Southern California finance chairman for a CDC-backed peace slate which voted to endorse the presidential candidacy of Minnesota's Senator Eugene McCarthy. This grieved Pat. While he wanted a quick end to the war, the former Governor worried about Jerry breaking ranks with the national party—which was sure to back Johnson—and irreversibly branding himself a leftist.

During this controversy, Pat returned to Sacramento to attend a state luncheon at which his official portrait would be unveiled. Governor Ronald Reagan neither attended the luncheon nor scheduled any time to meet with Brown. Many politicians were disapproving of Reagan's tactlessness, but Pat let it pass.

In December, just four days after Pat was named to the regular state Democratic delegation pledged one-hundred percent for President Johnson, his son spoke at a Democratic peace slate fundraiser in Santa Monica. "Dad is wrong on Vietnam," Jerry asserted. "He thinks Johnson is right. If you disagree, he asks, 'What other course is there?' When people tell him, he doesn't listen."

In fact, Pat listened very carefully to the case made against the war by Jerry and others. He simply didn't believe in abandoning incumbent leadership because of a disagreement over foreign policy. No matter what your stance on the war, abandoning a Democratic president wasn't going to hasten the war's end. He was sure that if elected, hawks like Nixon or Goldwater would make Johnson look like a member of the War Resisters League. The important thing was to re-elect LBJ, who could win if dissidents like Jerry backed off. "I think it [the antiwar movement] is his

[Johnson's] only problem, other than not being a strong television personality," Pat insisted.

The war issue, which divided Democratic families all over America, sent the Browns moving in three political directions. While Pat sold one-hundred dollar plates for LBJ in Beverly Hills, Jerry looked for Gene McCarthy dollars among old school friends in Venice and Westwood. And in San Francisco, Jerry's brother-in-law, Joe Kelly (sister Cynthia's husband) was campaigning for Senator Robert Kennedy. In spite of their disagreements, Pat and Jerry remained friendly. To them the war issue was no more than an extension of the dinner table debates that began years ago on Magellan Street.

In March, Jerry headed for the annual CDC convention in Anaheim, where he served as co-chairman of the McCarthy peace slate. After listening to the Reverend Martin Luther King deliver the opening address, Brown, Jr. dissuaded fellow delegates from passing a resolution criticizing Bobby Kennedy's late entry into the presidential primaries. While the Massachusetts senator's candidacy clearly jeopardized McCarthy, Jerry discouraged gratuitous name-calling. "I think we should be cautious in criticizing Kennedy," he told Council leaders in the Disneyland Hotel suite of CDC leader, Gerald Hill. This low-key approach proved to be a good political move and enabled McCarthy forces to win ninety percent of the floor vote.

Prior to the convention, Pat threatened to quit the CDC if it sent an anti-LBJ delegation to the national convention. "One-hundred percent behind Johnson" and "confident that when he gets out and starts campaigning, the people will get behind him," the former Governor bemoaned the CDC's desertion in the President's hour of need. Despite Johnson's problems as commander-in-chief, Pat was convinced that his Great Society was the most progressive domestic program since the New Deal. Pat had a serious problem, though; if he quit the state's Democratic Council, he could be badly hurt if he decided to try a comeback against either Reagan or Senator George Murphy in 1970. What to do?

While trying to make up his mind, Pat continued stumping for Lyndon. At the end of March, reporters asked him about rumors that the President might not run for a second term. The former Governor dismissed such talk as the wishful thinking of Democratic rebels like Jerry. On the last day of the month, Pat again endorsed LBJ, this time in an Associated Press interview. Unfortunately, Pat's views, published in papers statewide, were undercut that evening when Johnson announced he would neither seek nor accept the Democratic nomination for a second term.

At McCarthy and Kennedy headquarters, the decision touched off celebrations. But four days later, elated campaign workers cancelled their precinct work to observe a period of mourning for Martin Luther King, who had been assassinated in Memphis. After the black leader's funeral, the rival peace candidates resumed the scramble for vital California votes. The sight of Bobby Kennedy campaigning for support from the poor on his parents' largesse was the subject of considerable kidding by the press corps. But back in Boston, Rose Kennedy saw nothing wrong with anteing up. "It's our money and we can spend it any way we want."

Jerry, now fully allied with the peace campaign, once again tried to convert Pat and his Beverly Hills friends to the McCarthy cause. But these old-time Democrats could not make the jump over to the Minnesotan's camp. On the other hand, those who knew both Jerry and McCarthy weren't surprised that the young Californian and the older Senator quickly became companions. Brown was officially adopted as part of McCarthy's braintrust as soon as his thorough grasp of the electoral process became evident. Traveling the state together, Brown and McCarthy mystified acquaintances by sometimes lapsing into Latin. While others worried about campaign minutiae, Jerry and Gene talked poetry and religious philosophy late into the night.

When Kennedy began moving ahead in the polls, some of McCarthy's advisors suggested he abandon his scholarly image and attack his opponent as a crass opportunist. But even during a statewide televised debate, the Democratic peace candidate refused to blast Kennedy. And even more damaging, McCarthy's dry, professorial delivery disappointed campaign workers.

After the debate, McCarthy and Brown arrived for dinner at the Fairmont, engrossed in a subtlety of Thomistic logic. Turning to his poet-in-residence, Robert Lowell, the Senator said, "I don't want to talk about politics tonight. Let's talk about Dante's Sixth Canto." Like an Oxford don at a reunion of his favorite students, McCarthy presided over a far-ranging colloquy on poetry, philosophy, psychology, writers and the human spirit.

Jerry characterized McCarthy as "a person whose thought I respect. His concepts that the process of government should be orderly, that institutions should be respected, that the cult of the individual politician or personality should be limited, avoided where possible . . ." were ideas Brown had considered himself. "Often it is very easy to get caught up in the emotion of the moment and personalize the chief executive's job. It's good to some extent to limit that, where possible . . ."

In the final weeks of the campaign, Jerry and Joe Kelly took turns lobbying Pat for his valuable endorsement. The ex-Governor's son was pleased by press reports indicating his father leaned toward McCarthy. His brother-in-law, Joe Kelly, cheered when Bobby's statewide campaign chairman, Jesse Unruh, said he had Pat's promise that he "would not work against Kennedy." The Senator had, after all, campaigned for

Brown in 1966. But neither man was genuinely surprised when, on primary day, Pat came out for Vice-President Hubert Humphrey. Old political friends, these two liberals had carried the progressive Democratic banner high during the silent fifties. Firm believers in the Union label, hot lunches for impoverished school children, and the National Association for the Advancement of Colored People (NAACP), their political lineage traced back to Franklin Delano Roosevelt.

On election night, Jerry Brown joined the McCarthy organization for a victory party at the Beverly Hilton. Early Northern California returns showed the Minnesotan in front. But by poll closing time, a CBS key precinct survey showed Kennedy winning. This projection, which came while McCarthy remained ahead in raw votes, quickly turned the celebration into a wake. The Minnesota Senator assured his troops this was only a sparring match T.K.O. enroute to a main event victory two months hence. But as he went around the room, bear-hugging loyalists and whispering "All the way to Chicago," political realists knew this poet from the plains had been knocked as cold as a Minneapolis winter.

Amidst the Hilton gloom that night, there was only one hopeful voice. In a corner, Jerry chatted thoughtfully with Harvard's Robert Lowell. "I'm not disillusioned," he said while McCarthy's glum staff members popped champagne corks off bottles optimistically purchased before the polls closed. "There's still potential for things to happen in government. I think we've all learned a lot about the nature of campaigning, the nature of politics."

As Lowell and Brown conversed, Kennedy's cheering workers at the Ambassador flashed before them on a nearby television screen. Long popular with presidents and potentates, the half-century old Ambassador Hotel had been a favorite of J. Edgar Hoover. Accompanied by bodyguards, he spent one month of each year at the Ambassador, in a bungalow next to his columnist friend, Walter Winchell. And the feared FBI chief wasn't the only conservative to favor the old hotel. Richard Nixon drafted his Checkers speech there sixteen years before. While not as plush as the Beverly Hilton, there was something romantic about the large, old-style building shaded by Hawaiian palms. Its Regency lobby, Grecian fountains, Mediterranean rooms, Coconut Grove, and vaulted ceilings made the eclectic Ambassador the perfect place to celebrate a California political triumph.

Now they could see Robert Kennedy brushing aside a tousled forelock and waving his arms in triumph. Next to him was his wife, Ethel, their children, and his mother, Rose. The Kennedys were laughing and crying at the same time, as were their friends and campaign workers. Remembering the media people waiting for him in an adjacent room, Kennedy excused himself and took a shortcut through the kitchen. Suddenly the dignified Ambassador Hotel was thrown into mass confusion and horror. By the time cameramen caught up with Kennedy, he was lying on the kitchen floor, mortally wounded. Minutes later he was enroute to Good Samaritan Hospital. The following afternoon, before the final votes were tabulated, he was given the last rites of the Roman Catholic Church. His western stepping stone led directly to Arlington Cemetery.

The assassination of Bobby Kennedy on his victory night gave new meaning to Lord Bryce's ninety-year-old warning about the "strange and dangerous" nature of California politics. For Jerry Brown and others in the McCarthy campaign, this murder was the nightmarish beginning of a downward spiral leading to the massacre at Chicago and the disastrous fall campaign.

In July, Jerry, along with other CDC leaders, flew to a Western States anti-war conference hoping to resuscitate the McCarthy campaign. The Minnesota Senator's delegation thought Edmund G. Brown, Jr.'s presence would help them lobby old-timers who remembered his father with affection. But after testing the political winds, Jerry decided not to lend his family name to what he was certain was a losing cause. Jerry remained loyal to McCarthy, but told CDC Chairman, Gerald Hill, "I want to be my own man."

In August, a few weeks after Richard Nixon was nominated by the GOP, Jerry Brown took a week's leave from his Tuttle and Taylor practice to attend the Democratic Convention in Chicago. Once there, both he and Pat worked hard to win the votes of uncommitted Kennedy delegates like Joe Kelly. But instead of coming out for either McCarthy or Humphrey, Jerry's brother-in-law and many other Kennedy delegates came out for a new hopeful from South Dakota — Senator George McGovern, who also had solid anti-war credentials, and a stronger record of support for traditional liberal issues than did McCarthy.

The emergence of yet another anti-war candidate was deeply disturbing to Pat. Who were Gene McCarthy and George McGovern to try to usurp the Party's leadership with a Johnny-come-lately gang of raga-muffins? The ex-Governor placed much of the blame for McCarthy's sudden ascendance on television, which tended to "focus on the ten sack-dressed, long-haired, screaming demonstrators or hecklers in an auditorium at the Johnson rallies, not on the thousand other individuals listening politely to the speaker." He believed the bedraggled-looking throngs of demonstrators were a sartorial time bomb and that the spectacle of "blacks with high, free-growing Afro hairstyles and young whites dressed in hippie-style clothes" parading for McCarthy was an instant voter turn-off that would return the country to the Republican Party, and probably Richard Nixon, in the fall. Conversely, Pat was convinced that the 1963 Washington civil rights march succeeded because "blacks and whites who demonstrated then were generally dressed in suits and ties and had orthodox haircuts."

The platform of the Democratic establishment as set forth by his father and Humphrey troubled Jerry almost as much as the sight of Chicago's finest lining the route to the International Amphitheatre. Not since the Watts riots had Jerry seen this much concentrated firepower. Convinced by now that McCarthy's cause was hopeless, he concentrated on a Vietnam peace resolution. After watching the status-quo-oriented majority quickly put this proposal to sleep, Jerry checked out of his hotel and headed for O'Hare Airport. He had been in the windy city only two days, but it was enough.

Back home in front of his TV, Jerry watched Chicago police shove screaming demonstrators through the Conrad Hilton's plate glass windows. And like millions of other Americans, he saw the bright hopes McCarthy had raised in New Hampshire collapse inside a convoy of paddy wagons.

Hubert Humphrey's campaign was badly tarnished by the bloodshed at the Convention. In addition, Democrats continued to bicker over Humphrey's lukewarm opposition to the war — all of this against a continuing backdrop of anti-war protests across the country. And while the many constituencies of the Democratic Party continued to square off against one another, Richard Nixon effectively mobilized the united support of Republicans and went on to win the election in November.

After he was sworn into office, America's first California-born president publicly thanked Pat Brown. At a White House dinner honoring Earl Warren, Richard Nixon cheerfully asked his former Democratic rival to take a bow. "I see my old friend Pat Brown is here tonight — Pat, I want to thank you for defeating me for Governor, because if I had defeated you, I would probably still be Governor, and I really think I can do more good as President of the United States."

Back in Los Angeles, local issues were becoming paramount to Jerry Brown, who had been hinting about his own campaign plans for nearly a year. When he dropped by the office of State Assemblyman David Roberti, campaign workers asked if Jerry planned to challenge the incumbent. "Oh, no," he said. "I'm running for Governor." No one knew if he was joking or not.

In early 1969, Jerry decided to run for the new Los Angeles Junior College Board. Local college trustees hardly enjoyed the prestige of legislators and constitutional officers, but it was a good place to start a political career. Opponents like Alex Aloia, an education professor at Loyola Marymount College, argued that aside from the lack of a famous name, they were better qualified than the inexperienced Brown. But Jerry remained confident that his talents were well-matched to the chal-

121

lenges of academic administration.

Given his political grounding, legal training and ecclesiastical bent, it was hardly surprising that Jerry Brown was more articulate, better informed, and able to field diverse questions with greater confidence than most of his opponents. Embellishing his campaign talks with Latin, Greek, religious, legal and philosophical insights, he sounded like the perfect Renaissance candidate. Thoroughly schooled in the antiquities, Jerry was nevertheless solidly planted in the twentieth century and promised to replace the district's "horse and buggy" accounting procedures with a "computerized system called PBBS." It was irrelevant that no one in the audience besides Brown knew what this acronym stood for. It sounded impressive and cost-effective.

His many strengths made Brown stand out amidst a field of 133 community college board candidates. An important ally in his campaign for media access was a cherubic journalist named Tom Quinn, who had been running for appointment to the Los Angeles Board of Education at the same time that Jerry was running for the community college board. Brown was curious how Quinn was able to get more coverage than himself.

When the two men met at a political gathering, Jerry was impressed with Quinn's knowledge of both printed and electronic media. Quinn's father, Joe, it turned out, owned the City News Service (CNS), which supplied most of the local news copy to the Los Angeles area, and the younger Quinn had grown up with the media in much the same way that Jerry had grown up with politics. With the aid of cub reporter Llew Werner, Quinn's team often scooped the wire services on local disasters, murders, and celebrity suicides.

Radio News West, as Quinn's agency was called, used an aggressive approach to hard news coverage which irritated competitors, particularly when they muddied adjacent reporters' tapes of live events by "accidently" scratching microphones. Once, when Werner showed up for a Nixon press conference in a disheveled cowboy outfit, the President refused to acknowledge his questions. At another session Quinn's lieutenant asked Spiro Agnew to elaborate on his suggestion that "all looters should be shot" and the Vice-President angrily walked out.

While livening up the local press corps, this team of media junkies also gained the grudging respect of their peers for some remarkable beats, like an exclusive interview with a hijacker who had commandeered a plane to London. As security police kept a nervous watch on the aircraft, Quinn's shoestring outfit phoned the Heathrow Airport tower and asked to be connected with the hijacker. They were put through and the hijacker supplied Radio News West with a fine interview that was promptly sold to the networks.

During Jerry's junior college board campaign, the Quinns were a dependable source of coverage. They gave good and frequent play to press releases, which were always welcomed by readers because of the well-known Brown name. If Jerry talked to a college audience and promised to expel ineffectual administrators and introduce "modern management techniques" to help the system prepare for doubling enrollments in the coming decade, the Quinns covered it, always adding the kicker — "Brown is the son of former State Governor Edmund G. "Pat" Brown and is one of 133 candidates for the seven trustee seats." This sort of billing made it easy for Jerry to place first in the April primary, take sixty-seven percent of the run-off vote, and even outpoll popular Democrats like Mayor Yorty, who had gained another term by defeating Tom Bradley.

With continued generous media coverage from the day he was sworn in, Jerry promptly went to work becoming a household name in Southern California. Confounding those who doubted that an obscure local board was the logical place to begin an up-tempo march to statewide office, Brown kicked off his term with a master politician's touch. He attacked the junior college's $23,000 budget for "press agents to toot our own horns." Radio, television and the press rushed to cover the new trustee's criticism of public relations expenditures. And when Jerry unsuccessfully tried to kill a $74,000 appropriation for administrative expenses, his picture made the *Los Angeles Times*. "The Board doesn't need separate offices," declared Brown, Jr. "It doesn't need bigger desks, doesn't need travel money or mileage money and certainly doesn't need two private secretaries who will each receive $900 a month plus fringe benefits." Appointing himself fiscal ombudsman, he swore to protest "every attempt to spend the taxpayers' money for any purpose not directly related to educating those students who want an education."

This cry for frugality was the first of Jerry's many successful moves to divorce himself from what he believed to be the greatest liability attached to his name — his father's reputation as a free spender. Jerry, one of the first Democratic politicians to recognize that you don't have to throw money at problems to be a liberal, genuinely believed that less was often more. Indeed, as he spoke on fiscal issues, he often sounded like a latter-day Calvin Coolidge.

During his two terms, Pat had challenged "the people of California to become involved with the big problems of their state, to care personally and deeply about them, and to pay the taxes to help solve them." Reagan had ousted Brown with a philosophy of cutting expenditures by reducing state government's role in health, education, welfare and other social services. Jerry was now suggesting government could expand the junior college system while simultaneously reducing property tax levies for

123

higher education. How did he propose to accomplish this? The answer was simple. Thanks to the fact that California's withholding tax was not being indexed, taxpayers were being pushed into higher tax brackets, yielding the state a $450 million "Reagan (income tax) surplus." Jerry wanted to use this surplus to finance junior college growth. And of course, the idea was well received by Los Angeles taxpayers, who had tired of the sort of problem-solving that always resulted in higher taxes.

Brown spoke in favor of campus civil rights and civil liberties during the new board's first meetings. But he dismayed old anti-war friends by helping draft a motion prohibiting out-of-district transfers for any student convicted of campus disruption during the previous three years. If passed, this would mean an undergraduate sentenced for sitting-in during an anti-war demonstration at a Northern California school couldn't enroll at a Los Angeles community college.

Yet on academic freedom issues, he took a broader view. Jerry repeatedly spoke against the dismissal of English instructor Deena Metzger for reading a poem called "Jehovah's Child" to her class. The Board was particularly offended by the passage which read, "In Christ's name kindness is sucking the cock of a turned cheek—Jesus style—Jehovah would have bitten it off." Although Brown conceded "the poem injects religion in a most unfavorable light," he believed she "should be given another chance to demonstrate her ability as a teacher."

As the Metzger dispute heated up, Brown argued that the disciplinary matter should be debated behind closed doors to keep "this from getting into the area of a witch hunt." But his bid for a secret session was defeated and on July 22, the Board had its first important policy confrontation.

Arriving in a suit which hung limply from his thin frame, Jerry nervously took his seat. During his superb campaign, he had promised to be an aggressive trustee because, "Recent events have made it crystal clear that the day of a passive board has long since passed. The Board must be . . . ultimately unafraid to make hard decisions and then stick to them, whatever the pressures."

But now that he was sworn in, his role seemed more difficult. While he sided with the Board's conservative bloc on halting transfers for campus law breakers, Jerry found himself on the liberal side when it came to the Metzger case and worried about emerging with a muddled identity that would satisfy neither constituency. He could, of course, abstain when the vote was called, but that was no solution either, since people might suggest he was as indecisive as his father. Clearly there was only one wise thing for Jerry to do in these difficult circumstances. Before either crucial question was moved, he packed up his briefcase and excused himself to attend to "urgent" Tuttle and Taylor business.

124

In Jerry's absence, the motion to fire Deena Metzger passed five-to-one. Nevertheless, Jerry continued to come forward at academic freedom rallies to speak out against her firing. At the same time, when he appeared before conservative groups dismayed by campus violence, he assured them, "Students who tend not to obey college rules should be suspended or expelled. Students who break the law should be arrested."

Carefully attuning his message to his audience, Jerry spent increasing time on self-promotion. He urged black newspaper editors to initiate a campaign to rename one of the college campuses for Martin Luther King, and commiserated with Chicanos about his unsuccessful efforts in getting school cafeterias to purchase only Union-picked lettuce. In talks before taxpayer groups, Jerry pledged to block construction of a new women's gym by accommodating the ladies in existing men's facilities.

Thanks to Tom Quinn and Llew Werner, Brown's activities got almost as much local airplay as Senator Cranston's. Motorists heading down the freeway heard reports of "how different he [Jerry] is from his father" on many stations. The Browns' contrasts in style and philosophy were a news hook that few reporters could resist. Typical was this account carried by City News Service that reached millions of Southern California readers and radio listeners:

> Edmund G. Brown, Jr. urges scrapping of the state's Master Plan for Higher Education — which his father helped write — and recommended a 'complete change' in California's approach to public schooling. Brown, a member of the L.A. Community College Board of Trustees, said priority should be given to converting the state's two-year junior colleges into regular four-year colleges. 'It makes sense to spend our limited funds where they do the most good,' Brown, son of former Governor Edmund G. (Pat) Brown, said.

Afterwards, district administrators politely replied that the new trustee had neither the experience nor credentials to justify his dramatic proposal. But Jerry came back with an interesting reply. "The times change; problems are different today than they were five years ago. Experience isn't especially relevant anymore." And that was why he was seriously thinking about proposing the elimination of doctoral degree requirements for college presidents. "What they learned to get that Ph.D.," Brown declared, "doesn't necessarily help them in confrontations [with students]."

Jerry was confident about his solutions to community college problems and had little patience for trustee meetings. Thus, while his outside talks and press releases assured him more coverage than the rest of the Board combined, he had the worst attendance record in the group.

Frequently the last to arrive, he repeatedly stepped out to make calls and was usually the first to leave. Typically, Brown returned to his law office to take calls from reporters who liked the clever ways he ridiculed Board decisions made in his absence.

And when he continually ended up on the losing side of Board issues, Jerry appeared in person to warn the Los Angeles Press Club that the ill-managed community college district was sinking fast. Rising confidently in the hot glow of TV lights on a late January 1970 morning, he introduced himself, along with fellow trustees Ken Washington and Fred Wyatt. "We often find ourselves voting together on the losing side of major issues," explained Jerry. "For the most part, we have confined our criticism of the Board majority to board meetings. The three of us have refrained from heated public discussions outside the board room to avoid unnecessary acrimony. Now, however, we feel compelled to speak out. I have just learned that at least one — and possibly all — of the schools in our junior college district may eventually lose their accreditation because of an irresponsible and possibly illegal fear campaign initiated by the Board's four-member majority.

"That majority seems intent on initiating a reign of fear on our junior college campuses. For reasons of their own, they have squandered district funds on petty personal projects; conducted the public's business in secret session; established a 'spy system' to frighten teachers; acted to inflame racial tension; undermined administrative authority; and even interfered in student body elections.

"This majority bloc appears to have a scheme to intimidate teachers and college presidents. Two of our presidents have already left and the Board majority has made it plain they want to fire three others who refuse to knuckle under to their irresponsible, and often expensive, demands.

"One of the most effective tools in this fear campaign is the consistent use of secret meetings to set district policy. These secret sessions may even violate the Brown Act because they are used to conduct the public's business behind closed doors.

"The machinations of the majority power-bloc have now become so dangerous to local education that the report of the College Accrediting Association may actually warn those four trustees to get back to the business of education or face possible loss of accreditation.

"If we lose accreditation, students attending our junior colleges will graduate with worthless degrees and will not be eligible for admission to any legitimate college or university. The students will suffer and the taxpayers' money will be thrown down the drain."

When reporters asked Brown if this media event was simply a warmup for a run at statewide office, the trustee replied: "Well, there are a lot of these charges, and everytime you say something, the other side says 'This

126

is politics.' I think we ought to deal with the facts, and what we do in our private lives I think is our business. I will tell you this. I'm a young man. I've gotten elected to this Board, and I don't feel that my election here as a trustee prevents my possibly seeking other offices. I very much am attracted to public life and I would be kidding you if I told you I was not seriously contemplating political office in this state. Yes, I am thinking of public office, I have always thought about it, and will continue to do so."

Members of the Board majority were outraged by some of Brown's tough charges at his first formal press conference. Afterwards, they reminded reporters the same trustee now denouncing "secret meetings," had fought for a closed session a few months earlier on the Metzger case. "Unfortunately," said trustee Robert Cline, "Mr. Brown has not been raised in the tradition of political truth and I think that some of the statements he has made should be considered in the light of that tradition."

When Edmund G. Brown, Jr. announced his candidacy for Secretary of State on March 2, 1970, he emphasized that he was not abandoning the college district. Higher office would give him the power to accomplish objectives he couldn't realize from a minority seat on a local school board. Los Angeles students weren't losing a trustee, they were gaining an ambassador to Sacramento. However, his commitment to civil and human rights did not mean he was willing to write a blank check for insurrectionists. As student demonstrations erupted on many California campuses, local police agencies discovered they were not equipped to handle the rebellious progeny of the middle-class. It was senseless, Brown argued, to pit community patrolmen against these often revolutionary tactics without providing them special training and improved weapons. Consequently he was asking the state for an "airborne campus strike force to curb student violence."

He wanted these troops to employ "hard-hitting, no-nonsense tactics to prevent what could be the most perilous year in the academic history of this country. Force members would have access to a fleet of jets equipped with the latest crowd-control devices, such as tranquilizer guns, wood pellet guns and water cannons."

"But, Mr. Brown," asked a South Gate Rotarian at one campaign talk, "what about the Presidential Commission's call for a cease fire among students, police and politicians?"

"That's a fine idea, and I'm sure the police and politicians would love to have a cease fire but I'm afraid the student radicals may not be agreeable. We could have had peace long ago if the bank-burners, brick-throwers and other militants had stopped their violent activities. Most students, most professors and virtually all taxpayers have always wanted

127

calm on our campuses but a few radicals and kooks have managed to keep our campuses aflame. College administrators, teachers and students are frightened about what this year may hold. We need tough measures to protect college campuses."

This stand hardly seemed in character for the young civil libertarian who had linked hands with civil rights, anti-war and farm workers' movements. Although he had just denounced his fellow trustees for intimidating the campus community with spies, Brown now endorsed police intervention in situations where students resorted to violence.

Friends like John Vasconcellos, once an aide to his father and now a state assemblyman representing San Jose, wrote asking Brown for an explanation of this new military policy that made Dr. S.I. Hayakawa, president of San Francisco State College, look like a pacifist. Reading over Jerry's remarks, Vasconcellos worried that his friend might be cutting loose from his political roots. Perhaps Brown planned to run as both liberal and conservative to avoid being slotted in one camp. Or perhaps he was afflicted by decisionitis — a chronic inability to commit either way for fear of tainting his record.

In early May, the Democratic candidate seemed to be sending a clear signal to his liberal friends when he moved to lower campus flags to half mast in memory of four Kent State University students slain by the Ohio National Guard. This gesture was rejected by the Board majority, who ridiculed him for trying to honor those "Midwestern hoodlums." As Richard Nixon's foreign legion invaded Cambodia later that week, the flag of every community college in the Los Angeles district continued to fly high. Brown, thoroughly disgusted by his fellow trustees' insensitivity, presumed campaigning for a state college militia that could promptly contain student demonstrations against this latest war escalation. Was this a contradiction? "Absolutely not," said the candidate, who claimed no inconsistency in his crusade for both academic freedom and a campus strike force.

Eugene J. McCarthy

Dear Friend:

What began in the cold of New Hampshire two years
ago continues today in individual campaigns across
the nation. One of the most significant, in my
view, is the race being run by Edmund G. Brown, Jr.,
a candidate for California Secretary of State.

Ed was there at the beginning. As a founder of
California's Democratic peace slate in October 1967,
he came forth when most people only privately voiced
their convictions. I believe Ed has the moral
courage to face problems long before most politicians
know they exist. He is the kind of person urgently
needed in public life.

Ed is one of the few outstanding young leaders who
has a realistic chance to be elected this year...
and I ask you to join me in doing everything possible to help him.

Campaigns are extremely costly. Ed is now making
the major media decisions for his race and within
the next few weeks must put up a substantial amount
of money for radio and television time. Without
your immediate financial support, it will be
impossible for him to wage a strong campaign.

He urgently needs your help. Please fill out and
return the enclosed contribution envelope today.

                    Sincerely yours,

                    Eugene McCarthy

"You almost cost me this election"

CHAPTER 9

With contributions generated by McCarthy's letter, Jerry bought broadcast time to make an important announcement — if elected he would work unceasingly to "take the price off public office." However, there hadn't been much of a price tag on the Secretary of State's Office that anyone was conscious of — at least not for the two generations that Frank Jordan and his recently deceased son, Frank Jordan, Jr., held it. With Frank, Sr. first elected in 1911, the Jordans made this office their personal fief for fifty-six years. Experts at routine paperwork and keeping a low profile, the Jordans achieved little beyond the ordinary. In fact, most people weren't sure what the function of the

Secretary of State's office was — except to provide permanent employment for the Jordans.

After her husband's death, Alberta Jordan, Frank, Jr.'s wife, announced she would run for the office to keep the family tradition alive. But Jerry Brown had other ideas. If the Jordans could spend several generations in Sacramento, why not the Browns? In announcing his candidacy, Jerry claimed it was time to put this "unknown, underrated, undeveloped job back to work for the people." When asked how this could be done, Edmund G. Brown, Jr. replied that the Secretary of State's office should function as a focus for campaign reform.

"Years ago," Brown explained, "candidates were able to finance campaigns with donations from friends and constituents. But today, in the age of television and expensive billboards, most candidates are forced to accept money from paid lobbyists and special interest groups. I believe this is inherently corrupting. This tragic situation must be changed. I believe it is essential for the taxpayers to know who's paying for the campaigns of our elected officials."

Determined to carry his message of accountable frugality to every town square in California, Jerry outspent his primary opponent, former state Senate President Pro Tem Hugh Burns, better than 24-to-1. This heavy-set Fresno legislator had served in Sacramento for more than three decades and was widely remembered for his ponderous leadership of the state's Un-American Activities Committee. As the state leader, Burns fought Pat Brown on many liberal issues, such as the elimination of primary cross-filing and the establishment of a fair housing law. He also helped the elder Brown move his water plan through the legislature. But by the time he faced Jerry in the spring of 1970, the valley Democrat had lost his spot as Senate leader in a showdown with the Reagan team. In addition, he had been touched by the breath of scandal. Early in 1969 Robert Fairbanks of the *Los Angeles Times* described how Burns shared a $500,000 profit on an insurance deal with a company that benefited from legislation he helped pass. Newspapers immediately called for a Legislative Ethics Committee investigation. But it was hard to initiate such an inquiry in the Senate, where the ethics group was chaired by Hugh M. Burns himself.

When he began his campaign against Jerry, the portly Senator found he couldn't rally more than a small number of the politicians and lobbyists who had supported him in past years. Indeed, the former President Pro Tem had difficulty even giving away campaign buttons and bumper stickers. Money, which had never been a problem for him in the previous campaigns, was trickling rather than cascading in. Jerry had an unfair advantage, Senator Burns complained, because his father could easily get cash from old appointees and others he had favored in years past. This

131

point was underscored by a form letter Pat sent prospective donors:

> Many times and in many ways you have helped me and other public officials. Now my son, Edmund G. Brown, Jr., is a candidate for Secretary of State. Ed has an excellent chance to be elected, but he urgently needs your financial assistance. I am asking everybody who receives this letter to contribute just $100. If you would like to give more, that will help make up for those who are unable to respond.

Much of the money for Jerry's campaign came from Brown loyalists who pledged $400,000 earlier that spring for a proposed Pat Brown gubernatorial campaign. When a private poll showed the former Governor a two-to-one favorite over either Jesse Unruh or Sam Yorty in the primary, fundraiser Eugene Wyman phoned Pat, urgently requesting he cut short his trip to Japan and rush home. The thought of another shot at Reagan excited Pat. Who was he to desert his party in its hour of need? But Bernice put a damper on his enthusiasm. "Jerry has just announced for Secretary of State," she told him by phone. "I don't think you ought to be doing anything to interfere in his career."

Much as he would have enjoyed beating Unruh and Yorty, not to mention the invigorating challenge of a Reagan rematch, the old campaigner knew his wife was right. Two Edmund G. Browns on the same ballot would be a mistake. While not yet a has-been, Pat was wise enough to realize that it was time for him to move aside and support his son. With some regret he said no to the Party and then, with genuine delight, watched as his son knocked Burns permanently out of the political ring with a million-vote primary victory. Clearly, Jerry Brown's style was catching on. Before long, loyal family friends, like hotelman Ben Swig, were rounding up their favorite "Checkbook Democrats" for creamed chicken fundraisers on behalf of Jerry.

After his inauguration, John F. Kennedy confessed the nadir of his 1960 fundraising campaign was watching Ben Swig make an unctuous pitch for money at a San Francisco Peninsula motel. In 1968, senatorial candidate Alan Cranston blushed when Swig locked the Fairmont dining room and refused to let anyone out to relieve themselves until they produced cash, check or IOU. Now it was Jerry's turn to move through this California political rite of passage as he collected money for his fall general election campaign. As soon as Swig bolted the doors, Brown confidently outlined his campus strike force plan for the captive audience. "Campus rules must be enforced in a tough and strict manner, and students who disobey regulations should be suspended or expelled — but not gunned down." This pragmatic humanitarianism was generously applauded by the Fairmont crowd, which bolstered Jerry's TV budget by $14,000.

132

Brown used his donations to produce impressive commercials claiming he was not for sale. Thanks to a $150,000 general campaign fund (compared to $60,000 raised by his Republican opponent, Los Angeles attorney James Flournoy), Jerry could even afford to announce the ultimate mid-campaign sacrifice. He was returning several thousand dollars worth of contributions received "with strings attached. The people who sent the money represent businesses that could benefit from actions of the Secretary of State." Jerry candidly added that not all members of his political braintrust were sanguine about returning the money. His own father suggested that "if I continue attacking lobbyists, I might not have any contributions from them." But the novice campaigner for statewide office, who was obviously learning fast, assured audiences he would prefer to take a campaign budget cut than fuel his populist effort with tainted money.

Zipping around the state, Jerry (aka Ed, Edmund and Pat, Jr.) excelled at the old California campaign trick of establishing multiple political identities. In black areas, Jerry was the "soul candidate." On the campus, he harked back to his early opposition to the Vietnam War, his co-chairmanship of the McCarthy campaign, and his fight to insure that only Union-picked lettuce would be served in community college cafeterias. Americans for Democratic Action were hopeful when Jerry promised to sue corrupt corporations, dishonest politicians and their multinational benefactors. Police audiences applauded when the candidate asked rhetorically "What is the role of the jails?" And then, after a dramatic pause, answered "To lock people up in."

While the Democrat's political personality fluctuated with the issues, the campaign did have a central theme — a photograph of Pat and Jerry Brown sitting down for a friendly talk. "Governor Brown's son earns full community support," "Black community supports Governor Brown's son," "Brown, Jr. pledges to carry on his father's tradition of working for equal rights for all programs to help the poor," were just several variations on a common theme which implied that the acorn hadn't fallen far from the sturdy oak tree.

Wherever he spoke, Jerry alluded to the advantages of growing up in the home of an elected official. "I've been around politicians all my life and want a chance to apply what I've learned." When voters questioned his credentials, he alluded to the delinquency and junior college board posts, his thorough classical education, and his law degree from Yale.

It wasn't surprising that, in California, liberal Democrats saw Jerry Brown as their party's greatest hope. According to the polls, he was the only challenger likely to stop the Reagan forces from sweeping all the California statewide constitutional offices — including Governor, Lieutenant Governor, Secretary of State, Attorney General, Treasurer, and

Controller. And it was genuinely refreshing to hear a lone voice crying out against the erosion of electoral honesty. "In politics," Brown complained, "we hear much about image and reality. Too often they bear little relationship to each other. But the image-making approach to politics is gaining momentum and popularity. It reflects a cynical, nihilistic attitude toward politics — without principle, essence or faith . . . I recall vividly the words of Adlai Stevenson, who said 'Let's talk sense to the American people, let's tell them the truth.' But that was before Vietnam, before Madison Avenue took over the running of campaigns, and before advertising executives were installed at the very center of our national government."

It was also, it must be said, before Jerry learned how expensive it was to put an egalitarian message across in a statewide campaign. With his early lead of fourteen percent over Flournoy in the polls gradually vanishing before the concerted attack of the Reagan team, he had to put himself in the public eye quickly. Instinctively, he headed up Benedict Canyon to the home of the one person he knew he could depend on.

"Pop," Jerry blurted out as Pat unlatched his front door, "I need more money for television."

With Pat's assistance, Jerry was able to finance additional TV spots, but in spite of money spent by both candidates for campaign coverage, the media paid little attention to the Secretary of State's race. And by election time that November, it was obvious that with Reagan riding high there was likely to be a Republican sweep. But on that day, Jerry Brown — like his father twenty years before him — was the only Democrat elected to fill state office, winning by 300,000 votes over James Flournoy.

On January 3, 1971 Jerry flew to Sacramento for his inauguration. Walking through Capitol Park with his old dorm advisor, Marc Poche, the new Secretary paused to enjoy the grounds. The more than four-hundred species of plants from all over the world made this forty-acre botanical garden a favorite spot of legislators, lobbyists, constituents and panhandlers. Camellias surrounding the statue of Franciscan missionary Junipero Serra were just beginning to bloom. Nearby were towering Deodar, Italian Stone Pines, Tulip trees, Southern Magnolias, Redwoods and Cypress, many of which had been thriving for nearly a generation when his grandmother, Ida, first passed through Sacramento in 1896. In the cactus garden were plants sent by school children at the request of Hiram Johnson in 1914. Next to the trout pond was a reproduction of the Liberty Bell cast in France, as well as the bell from the only battleship built on the Pacific Coast, the U.S.S. California.

At the Capitol entrance, Jerry walked past the symbol of his office — a ten-foot wide state seal cast in bronze by San Quentin inmates. The design, chosen by the state's founders, appealed to Jerry. It was a crowded montage including a grizzly bear, shafts of golden wheat, plump grapes, a pick-toting miner and Sierra peaks. The classicist in Brown was intrigued by the inclusion of the goddess Minerva springing full-grown from the brain of Jupiter. She had been worked in to symbolize the fact that California was admitted to the Union without going through the usual probationary period.

Later that day, the newly-elected Secretary of State headed up the Capitol steps to take the oath from Earl Warren before a homecoming audience including his parents, sisters and grandmother, Ida. Moving through the receiving line, he was at ease with everyone except Assemblyman John Vasconcellos. "I still have your letter," Jerry told the Assemblyman, who had inquired about Brown's campus police strike force proposal. "I haven't replied because I haven't thought of an answer yet."

Jerry had no desire to remain in the Capitol supervising state records, managing archives, chartering private corporations, commissioning notaries and recording trademarks. So, while keeping a ceremonial office with a small chandelier in Sacramento, he set up his main office in Los Angeles, at Century City. This fancy office complex was among the most expensive in the City. Arriving for work each day in a state Cadillac, Brown promptly began to assemble a braintrust that included the peripatetic news hound Tom Quinn, Llew Werner, who had worked with Quinn at Radio News West before joining Brown's campaign team, and a former Rand Corporation analyst named Richard Maullin, whom Jerry had met in Colombia in 1966, backed by a support staff plucked from local Catholic colleges.

Naturally, no upwardly mobile politician could hope to do his job without an intellectual utility man. John F. Kennedy had Arthur Schlesinger, Jr., Lyndon Johnson had Bill Moyers, Richard Nixon had H.R. Haldeman, and now Jerry Brown tapped Lorenzo Jacques Barzaghi. Officially, Barzaghi was employed as a $380-a-month file clerk, but calling him a paper shuffler was as misleading as referring to Ronald Reagan as a retired actor. Indeed, Barzaghi was quickly promoted and he became, and has remained, one of Brown's most trusted advisers. The slight Frenchman, who periodically shaved off his crew cut and sported a naked dome for a change of pace, often functioned as Jerry's "scout." Appearing without warning in staff meetings, he would prop himself against a door and listen to the proceedings as he stared up at the ceiling and puffed on a Camel. Often he remained motionless for an hour, never glancing at anyone or speaking a word. Then, suddenly — without explanation — this Tonto in state service disappeared as quietly as he had come. No one knew if he had slipped off to take a nap or report to his

135

Kemosabe.

Staff colleagues who were envious of Jacques' close relationship with Jerry kidded one another that Barzaghi seemed like a character out of a bad Malraux novel. But in candid moments, they were hard-pressed to explain what Brown's one-man braintrust actually did. Unlike Quinn, Maullin, Werner and other prominent aides, this combination clerk, chauffeur, fashion consultant, decorator and trusted friend had no discernible powers. Yet late at night, after everyone had gone home to their families and TV consoles, it was Jacques who lingered in the Secretary's offices.

Barzaghi's inscrutable manner was accentuated by fractured colloquialisms, but Jerry seemed to understand the Frenchman intuitively. Indeed, there were times when only a friendly look was sufficient to insure absolute understanding between them. Unlike everyone else Jerry knew in politics, Jacques rarely pressured him for an answer or a position. He wasn't preoccupied with reconciling past and present political behaviors and didn't believe that elected leaders needed either rear view mirrors or telescopes. "I only think in the present," he said. "The future doesn't belong to me. The past is already dead."

Like Jerry, who seldom made more than passing reference to his family history, Jacques preferred not to talk about his past. Born in Beausoleil, near the French Mediterranean Coast, the pensive immigrant was just three months younger than Jerry. But unlike Brown, Barzaghi's childhood was painful and lonely. Raised by his grandmother after his parents divorced, he was poor and frequently went hungry — often going to school without so much as a pretzel for lunch. Years later, following his father's example, Barzaghi joined the Merchant Marines and went to sea. After three trips around the world, he was drafted into DeGaulle's Algerian Army, where he saw action in the Sahara Campaign between 1958 and 1960.

Following his discharge, Barzaghi went to Paris to study acting, using the stage name, Lorenzo. In his first theater performance, he played the gypsy lover of a dying girl. Next, he portrayed a juvenile delinquent with a heart of gold in a message film. From these early experiences, Barzaghi learned that in the theater the real power rested with the director. Abandoning his acting ambitions, he soon went to work as an assistant director "and quickly learned that the director has to listen to the producer. That was when I got into production with Raoul Evy, who created Brigitte Bardot. He was the man who taught me that to make dollars, you have to compromise your beliefs and make stories about a decadent style of life. I got very disenchanted. Money wasn't important to me. For in the film world, I saw that the more dollars you make, the less you have."

Unlike his late father, who never realized a lifelong dream to live in America, Barzaghi's love affair with the New World didn't start until 1968. That was the year he and his wife, Tanya, the daughter of Eddie Constantine — an American-born entertainer who became a household word in Europe — crossed the Atlantic for a vacation. According to Barzaghi, "something" happened to him when a ruddy-faced drunk in the men's room at Kennedy Airport thrust a sack-clad whiskey bottle toward him to drink. Jacques' cinematic mind cut to the train rides of his youth, where as a hungry schoolboy he watched fellow passengers gorge themselves on meals from brown bags, avoiding the boy's stare. So, when Barzaghi put the whiskey bottle to his lips, he thought he was in paradise.

Jacques Barzaghi came back to earth with a thud a few days later as he toured Universal Studios. He was horrified at studio extravagance. "They spend so much on everything. According to Union rules, you have to have twenty-three different people to hold the nail and another to hammer it in. In France, people who work in film expect to do everything."

Hosts at the American Film Institute were interested in learning how Barzaghi assisted directors like Jean-Luc Godard to produce quality pictures for under $100,000. Soon the Institute invited Jacques to Utah to assist with a documentary about the American Indians' role in film. When Barzaghi arrived at the Navajo Reservation, the documentary's heavy-handed director was having difficulty getting the tribe to cooperate. Jacques quickly disappeared into the crowd. Before long, he re-emerged with several Indian leaders, all of them now in good spirits. Filming quickly resumed without incident. No one knew what Barzaghi had said to the Navahos, and typically, he didn't say. At the time the incident was a minor mystery, soon forgotten. It is worthy of note here only because it was this sort of sensitivity that was soon to make a deep impression on Jerry Brown.

When Jacques returned to Los Angeles, his wife Tanya filed for divorce and returned to France with their two daughters. He then started seeing Ann Campbell, an American who was close to the Barzaghis. In November 1970, the couple had a daughter. They married the following year, but separated soon after.

About this time, the U.S. Immigration Office informed Barzaghi that since he was no longer married, his days in the States were numbered. Although he didn't want to marry again just to get a green card, Jacques was desperate for a permanent visa. His friends, Linda and Rolando Klein, who worked with him at the American Film Institute, suggested that their friend Jerry Brown might be able to help. They followed up by having a dinner party and inviting the two men.

After an engrossing forty-five minute conversation about American

137

Indians, the cinema, and the state of the world generally with a pleasant-faced man wearing blue jeans, Barzaghi suddenly remembered the party was being held for him to cultivate an important official. Excusing himself, he sought out the Kleins and asked when the Secretary would arrive.

"Ah," said Linda, "but that's him over there, the man you were talking to in jeans."

"You're kidding," said Jacques.

"No, really. That's Jerry Brown."

Not only did the Secretary of State offer legal advice to help Barzaghi remain in America, he invited him to stop by his office. Soon Barzaghi was consulting for Friends of Edmund G. Brown, Jr., the campaign organization preparing for Jerry's run for the governorship in 1974. A position as a temporary clerical trainee in the Secretary of State's Office at $380 per month followed in 1972. By the end of the year, Jacques was promoted to permanent clerical assistant and given a forty-two dollar raise. He and his new wife, Connie (who Barzaghi met on a Roger Corman film set), frequently socialized with Jerry.

When people asked Jacques what he did for a living, the state worker liked to flash a copy of the new California Roster, a directory of state offices. Barzaghi and two other Brown aides had revamped this drab document, which now sported a free-flowing orange, green and blue collage on the cover. Some Sacramento traditionalists were horrified to see a psychedelic finger-painting replace the state seal, but the Secretary of State loved it.

Jerry was fond of Jacques and regarded him an astute judge of character. He frequently had Barzaghi conduct or sit in on job interviews and relied upon him to attract new talent and innovative ideas to the Capitol. With Jacques acting as Jerry's umbilical to the future, Brown began a series of wide-ranging discussions with scientists, ecologists, geologists, architects and others concerned about the shape of the coming decades. This was not difficult in a state which spawned a continuing procession of grassroots political movements, schools of Eastern philosophy, alternative medicines, gurus, celebrities, cults and technologies. As Barzaghi told Brown biographer Orville Schell: "Compared to all the other countries I have visited, there is nothing better than this place . . . If something starts, it starts in California. California moves all the time. But when you get a love of movement, there is also a possibility for new ideas . . . It's fabulous! Absolutely fabulous!. . . ."

Brown and Barzaghi began studying the new California constituencies, convinced they represented future electoral power. Long before most other mainstream politicians, they realized that a significant number of New Age interest groups already wielded considerable political influence. In a state where weak party structures had long confounded traditional politicians, it was arguable that many people identified more closely with concerns like solar power, spiritual awakening or healthy food than they did with Republicans and Democrats. Jerry Brown was particularly well-placed to understand this phenomenon. His father had become the most successful politician of his generation by campaigning industriously on both sides of the Party fence.

The necessity of embracing contradictory philosophies helped explain why Earl Warren (who Pat Brown would recall after Warren's death "didn't become a liberal until he got to Washington") supported concentration camps for Japanese-Americans during World War II; why no one worked harder to send Northern California water south than San Franciscan Pat Brown; why the CDC's leading Stevensonian, Alan Cranston, went to hawk for the Pentagon bomber budget in the Senate; why Ronald Reagan, whose political career had been spawned by fiscal angels from the oil industry and the highway lobby, eventually worked to establish a coastal protection commission and block a trans-Sierra freeway. All these winners learned quickly that a California politician who can be narrowly categorized — no matter what his or her philosophy — is already on the endangered species list. This was a lesson that Upton Sinclair, William Knowland, Jesse "Big Daddy" Unruh, George Murphy, John Tunney and S.I. Hayakawa, among others, failed to master.

Jerry Brown distinguished himself from his predecessors by not being defensive about his changes of heart or policy, which he referred to as "situation ethics." Jacques Barzaghi, who puzzled over Zen Koans like others pondered over chess moves, expressed his conviction that these juxtapositions were all part of the yin and yang of political life. People who complained that Jerry contradicted himself, simply didn't know their Chuang-tzu. "What is 'it,' is also 'other,' what is 'other' is also 'it.' " Teilhard de Chardin had also argued that only by knowing both sides can one unify antagonists. Thus, viewed with a proper spiritual perspective, Brown wasn't being a hypocrite when he jaywalked from one political ideology to another; he was simply pinning down his spiritual twin.

Here, then was the answer to Assemblyman Vasconcellos. It was possible to be a civil libertarian and still favor putting down student revolts with tranquilizer guns and water cannons. It was possible to be a humanist and at the same time a law-and-order man. Populist candidates could even outspend their more traditional opponents on television without feeling guilty. Indeed, in California, public officials had to serve several masters to survive. This meant periodically both befriending and offending nearly every constituency, or, in the words of that wily old survivor, Earl Warren, "Leadership, Not Politics."

Brown's vision of himself as an effective mediator is important in understanding his political persona. Darting back and forth between the power structure and its opponents of the moment, he felt his ability to unify opposites gave him an advantage over other officials who saw the world as an "us" against "them" proposition. Even before he was appointed or elected to public office, Jerry had some impact on the course of the Chessman case (and hence, many people have observed, an influence on his father's political career), put Mario Savio and Pat together on the same phone line, and talked peacefully with Watts leaders while troops under his father's command were fighting hand-to-hand in nearby black neighborhoods.

While this approach enjoyed some success in California, he had trouble applying it east of Reno. Glad-handing with Governor Ross Barnett one minute and chatting amiably with James Meredith the next alienated both and led to Jerry Brown's early departure from Mississippi in 1962. In New York, he couldn't get anyone to even question the assumptions behind the fallout shelter program. And in Mayor Daley's Chicago, he saw what happened when the New Spirit was greeted by an establishment with guns and police clubs and the will to use them. Like orange, lemon and avocado trees that flourish in the temperate western regions, Jerry, too, seemed to thrive best in the political climate of his warm native state.

From his new Century City vantage point on the old Fox lot, California's ranking Democrat became the Secretary of what seemed an endless procession of lawsuits, each backed by dozens of press releases. Sometimes it seemed that Brown filed the court actions as an excuse to lob media grenades at dishonest politicians, corrupt corporations, obsolete laws, special interest legislation and other enemies of the people. Indeed, so much litigation came out of Brown's office during the early days of his term that he was in court almost as often as Attorney General Evelle Younger. The Secretary was a master of his craft, adopting the bare knuckles, prosecutorial role that had done so much to advance his father's career. At the same time, he was smart enough to litigate selectively, avoiding inevitable no-win cases.

Early in his term, Jerry embarrassed the Attorney General by successfully challenging his ruling that college students were required to vote in their parents' district. Similarly, he used his seat on the state's reapportionment commission to question the legality of the Republican-controlled board. But perhaps his best-received move was requiring 134 candidates to file detailed fundraising reports. All of the politicians had complied with an Attorney General's campaign law requiring candidates to list contributors only by first initial and surname. The amount of the contribution did not have to be reported. In requiring more information,

Jerry noted he was challenging an Attorney General's opinion issued by Pat. "If you read my father's opinion allowing this," Jerry declared, "you will find it absurd."

Suddenly everyone from U.S. Senator George Murphy to his primary challenger, Norton Simon, was being threatened with six months to five years in jail for failure to make full and complete disclosure of their contributions. Jerry had clearly discovered some powerful imagery. Would elected state officials be put in prison if they disobeyed his new filing requirements? Absolutely, insisted the Secretary, who vowed to form a legal posse and round up political outlaws. He would not play favorites, he assured the public. Even Norton Simon, who had contributed generously to his father's many campaigns, was not going to get a break. "He was a schoolmate of my father's and my father appointed him to the Board of Regents of the University of California. I am obviously unhappy that his name appears on the list of candidates who did not file timely campaign contribution reports. However, it is clearly my duty to act against my friends when they violate the law, as well as against those people I do not know. To do otherwise would be a mockery of justice and a violation of my oath of office."

All this was a replay of the technique Jerry pioneered the year before with his community college board press conference on the imminent loss of accreditation. Just as no Los Angeles campus ever came close to being decertified, none of the 134 non-conforming candidates spent a day in jail (they all turned in the detailed reports required by the new Secretary of State). Jerry did try to initiate legal proceedings against a handful of late-filers, but this litigation collapsed when it turned out that one of the defendant's records had been lost by Brown's office.

Although no one was arrested, the publicity generated by the Secretary's stand attracted numerous reporters to the beachhouse he rented at Malibu. Against the sound of the Pacific surf lapping against the shore behind him, Jerry complained about "public office rapidly becoming a rich man's preserve. Each year it is more difficult for an honest man of moderate means to conduct an adequate campaign. Skyrocketing campaign costs have opened the door to influence-peddling by those who command sufficient resources to bankroll campaigns."

The Secretary wearily confessed to a reporter that he wasn't sure whether the public was ready for a politician like Jerry Brown. "It's still not clear what can be accomplished through politics. I have some reluctance about it — the whole game. I don't even know if I want to stay in state politics. I don't think you should stay in one field too long — you get rusty."

Even oceanfront living became boring to Jerry after a while. Tired of watching an ever-larger share of his $35,000 paycheck go to the tax man, he began searching for a house. One afternoon he phoned Bernice and asked her to meet him at Schwab's drugstore. Together they drove up into the Hollywood Hills for a look at what Jerry told her was his dream home. He was especially in love with the view, which on those rare, clear Los Angeles days reached all the way to Long Beach. "But," said his pragmatic mother as they walked around the property, "I think you should look at the erosion and all the underbrush. There's a real slide and fire danger. Also, the price is too high."

Jerry decided Bernice was right and didn't buy the property. Just the same, when he found a better place on Wonderland Drive in Laurel Canyon, he didn't invite his always sensible mother to inspect it. Instead, he asked her for a loan toward the down payment and the name of the banker who arranged the mortgage on their Benedict Canyon home. Bernice agreed to loan him the money and soon her banker was helping Jerry close escrow on his new three-bedroom home.

Just before Jerry moved into the new house, Pat and Bernice came over to have a look at their investment. Heading up the Canyon in the driving rain, they reached the gutted structure that was being remodeled under the supervision of Jacques Barzaghi. Stomping around in the mud, Pat moaned, "It's too small. We'll never get our money back."

"Remember what you said when I found the place on Magellan," replied Bernice.

"What's that?" asked Pat.

" 'I'll buy it if you want it, but it's the ugliest place I've ever seen.' "

Thanks to a sound remodeling job that extended the living room, Jerry's new home soon became his proudest asset, one that even his skeptical parents came to admire. On balmy afternoons, the Secretary sat out on his patio by the swimming pool sipping beer and philosophizing about the future of his state. But off in Sacramento, legislators were not impressed to hear the Secretary was carrying out his official duties in swim trunks. Already annoyed at Jerry Brown's portrayals of politicians as power-crazed sybarites, and infuriated by his insistence on detailed statements of campaign contributions, legislative leaders struck back by ridiculing his expensive office suite. "He likes it down in Century City next to his daddy," laughed Democratic San Francisco Assemblyman Willie Brown, Jr. Soon the legislator's colleagues voted to cut Jerry's budget, forcing him to move downtown to an ascetic state building and reduce his staff.

Even with a smaller staff, however, Jerry was hardly slowed. He was soon taking on corporate targets — including the oil companies — who he charged had secretly financed statewide ballot referendums to write laws favorable to themselves and thus avoid the legislative process. And if big oil wasn't a tough enough nut to crack, Jerry also decided to go after the President of the United States. A Tom Quinn—led team began investigating Frank DeMarco, the law partner of Nixon attorney Herbert Kalmbach. This group quickly discovered that President Nixon had backdated a deed relinquishing his vice-presidential papers for a half-million-dollar tax break. Here was national news, as was Jerry's subsequent successful move to revoke DeMarco's notary license. And when the President fired his Watergate Special Prosecutor Archibald Cox, Jerry Brown was the first California politician to call for Nixon's impeachment.

For a time, it seemed no issue was too obscure to escape the attention of this rambunctious new politician, who some felt cried "fire" for the sheer joy of racing to the scene, water hose in one hand and press release in the other. For instance, one afternoon the Secretary's office received a call from San Francisco Examiner reporter Lynn Ludlow. While working on a story about a fly-by-night dance parlor, Ludlow discovered the owner never posted a required bond with Brown's office. Following a hunch, the reporter learned that only a handful of more than 1,000 California dance schools complied with the bond regulation. Brown's office promised to quickly come up with comment for the story. But before Ludlow got his answer, papers all over California headlined Jerry's announced crackdown on parlors that failed to put up bonds. The Examiner was among the journals that gave the news big play. Ludlow's own story eventually wound up on page fifty-six. A year later the San Francisco reporter checked again and found that despite the announced cleanup, only a dozen schools had posted bonds.

Brown's failure to follow through on this and similar matters was less an indictment of his administrative skills than a reflection of his determination to remain on the front lines. Anxious to be the first politician to come forth on every major issue, he showed solidarity with Daniel Ellsberg and Anthony Russo by joining them at the Pentagon Papers trial, fought in the U.S. Supreme Court to win voting rights for ex-felons, sued backers of a "fraudulently qualified" initiative aimed at making California farms open shops, and helped a new People's Lobby draft a political reform initiative to limit state campaign advertising expenditures to about $900,000. Whether you liked Jerry Brown or not, you had to concede that he had quickly become the most dynamic Secretary of State in California history.

Yet no matter how many times Jerry led the evening news or argued before the Supreme Court, he saw himself as nothing more than the state's leading paper pusher. "The worst thing in the world," he complained to his friend Marc Poché over dinner in San Jose during the fall of 1973, "is to have a job where you can't do anything. All you do is draw public pay and drive around in a Cadillac. I want to be governor."

"I don't think you'd survive the primary," Marc told him. "You'll be characterized as being too young, aggressive, unseasoned and avaricious. Hang around four more years as Secretary of State and the voters will hand you the governorship."

"I don't want to wait around," replied Brown. "If the people don't want me to be governor, then there are a lot of other interesting things I can do. Life's too short. If you have an opportunity to do some good, you should seize it."

As Quinn, Werner, Barzaghi and other members of Brown's team fanned out for the 1974 Democratic primary, the candidate freely admitted it wasn't going to be easy converting his sixties idealism into a credible program for the seventies. After watching the New Frontier get shot down in Dallas, the Great Society take early retirement along the Pedernales, and personally stoking the Watergate bonfire, Jerry Brown was no blind optimist. "I've seen government all my life," he said repeatedly, "and I'm not bemused by it."

The answer to the nation's economic dilemma, Jerry modestly suggested, might be found in the provinces. "With the failures in Washington in the sixties and the start of general revenue-sharing, it's clear the states are going to have to take a positive role in planning. We have the sophistication here to do it, to develop our own transportation and housing and resource plans. The talent is here, in our universities and our industries, and if we get the leadership, California can be the leader of the country in these areas."

"Are there any models around?" asked Washington Post political columnist David Broder during a Los Angeles visit.

"I don't see any," replied Brown from his Laurel Canyon patio while an unidentified woman friend grilled dinner. "And that's one of the problems. But that's also what makes it exciting. We may create the new model here."

Eager to find a creative speech writer to help him carry his vision to the people of the state, Jerry approached another graduate of the McCarthy campaign — screenwriter and novelist Jeremy Larner. The talented young writer had profitably turned his experience in the peace movement into an imaginative script for Robert Redford. The resulting film, called "The Candidate," was particularly interesting to Jerry because it featured the son of a famed political leader campaigning successfully for an office of his own.

"You know that film was about me," Jerry told Larner, who tried in vain to convince him it was not.

"What about coming to work writing speeches for me?" the Secretary inquired.

Larner begged off, citing other interests and responsibilities.

144

After Larner turned him down, Jerry gave up his search for a speech writer and decided to rely on his own extemporaneous talents. Like many of Brown's major political decisions, this one was made quickly with positive results. Unlike his rivals, the Secretary did not read canned campaign rhetoric served up by political science majors with minors in English. In the spirit of McLuhan, he limited himself to pithy comments that left audiences hungry for more (and were eventually collected in a book entitled *Thoughts*). The details were supplied later in carefully written campaign pieces tagging him as the man "with the longest record of support for liberal causes among candidates now seeking the Democratic gubernatorial nomination." The mouth-watering leaflet itemized just a few highlights from Brown's decade of commitment to the left, the poor, blacks and radical students:

1960 — Opposed House Un-American Activities Committee investigations and publicly joined efforts to abolish HUAC.

1962 — Participated in civil rights activities in Jackson and Greenville, Mississippi.

1967 — Played key role in protest vigil outside of San Quentin prison the morning of California's last execution.

1967 — Helped form CDC's Peace Slate, which opposed President Johnson's Vietnam war policies.

1968 — Served as Southern California's vice-chairman and treasurer of Eugene McCarthy campaign.

1969 — Marched with Cesar Chavez during his farm workers organization campaign in the Coachella Valley.

1969 — Elected to Los Angeles Community College Board of Trustees where he became leader of the Board's liberal group.

1969 — Fought to allow SDS the right to hold meetings on campus.

1969 — Proposed boycott of non-union lettuce in college district's cafeterias.

1970 — Advocated naming junior college in south Los Angeles after Dr. Martin Luther King. Students at the school supported the move, but the school board's conservative bloc opposed it.

1970 — Supported students' call for a symbolic tribute honoring those slain at Kent State.

Thanks to deft campaign talk, superior organization, and his famous name, Brown easily won the Democratic nomination against a field that included Assembly Speaker Bob Moretti, and San Francisco Mayor Joe Alioto. After applauding the June passage of Proposition 9, which limited the statewide candidates' campaign expenditures to about $900,000 (the measure wasn't scheduled to take effect until the following year), Jerry set out to replenish his exhausted financial reserves. Even though he honestly supported limitations on political spending, he knew it would take plenty of money to get elected.

While Jerry solicited cash up and down the state's affluent urban corridors, he publicly complained politics had become a rich man's game. In fact, Brown told voters, the only way to take the price tag off political office was for both gubernatorial candidates to cancel all advertising. The idea of turning the McLuhan age on its head and returning to a stump-centered campaign was, of course, instantly rejected by Republican nominee Houston Flournoy. He knew Brown's name would put a lesser-known opponent at a disadvantage in an adless campaign. Nevertheless, after long negotiations the adversaries agreed to hold their media budgets to $900,000, the approximate limit stipulated by the state's new Political Reform Act. This was a significant sacrifice on Jerry's part, as he raised the entire $900,000 and could have easily collected more, while Flournoy was only able to raise $800,000.

Brown ran a soft sell campaign — an approach advised by his media expert — Jacques Barzaghi. Chosen to replace Brown's advertising agency, Jacques produced the candidate's TV commercials. To gain perspective, the Frenchman consulted the electoral mood polls run by Richard Maullin, the social scientist with experience at the Rand Corporation who had joined Jerry in 1971. Maullin determined the public wanted a non-controversial governor in 1974. He contended that the Watergate fury helped Brown's chances, but also argued that Jerry would have to be more restrained. According to Maullin, voters were looking for politicians who had not identified themselves with vexing issues like capital punishment, decriminalization of marijuana, or legalized abortion. This finding led to a simple strategy: avoid discussion of controversial issues, especially those where Jerry's views didn't coincide with the electorate's.

Campaign chief Quinn got just the dull campaign he wanted. Edmund Brown, Jr. called for sensible leadership, integrity, decency and other virtues no one could argue with. Ahead by twenty points in the summer polls, Jerry's victory seemed almost inevitable.

Of more immediate concern to the Brown family was the deteriorating health of the candidate's grandmother, Ida. Even though she had been ailing for several years, Ida Brown firmly resisted family pressure to abandon her beloved Sunset apartment at Seventeenth Avenue and Lincoln Way. Pat's brother Frank, who lived on nearby Sloat Boulevard, tried to at least drive her to the grocery store, but she insisted on making the five-block trip on foot. Only after several cancer operations slowed her gait did she finally agree to move in with Frank and his wife Jackie, in early 1974.

The Brown matriarch spent much of her time receiving a stream of family visitors, including Kathy, who arrived shortly after Jerry's June primary victory. "You've got to hang in there, Grandma," said the candidate's younger sister, who wanted Ida to see the inauguration of California's second Governor Brown. Although the nation had known a number of prominent political families, only one other, the Dockings of Kansas, had managed to put father and son in the top state office during the twentieth century. But Ida wasn't sure she would make it to Sacramento the following January. "I've lived a long time," she told Kathleen, "and there's only one thing I'm certain of. No one gets out of this life alive."

On July 5, Ida persuaded Frank and Jackie to take her to the Tudor Room at the Sheraton Palace for a plate of oysters and a scotch-on-the-rocks. The next morning, the ninety-six-year-old family matriarch awakened feeling ill. Her son advised her to rest. That afternoon she closed her eyes and died peacefully in her sleep.

The following morning, Frank, Pat, Harold and Connie discussed the funeral arrangements for their mother. Someone suggested burying Ida alongside her husband, Edmund, at Holy Cross Cemetery in suburban Colma, but it didn't seem right to lay these adversaries side by side near the San Andreas fault. "We were afraid putting them together would trigger another earthquake!" Frank explained to relatives as they rode three hours to lay Ida to rest in the family plot at Williams.

After his grandmother was buried, Jerry reflected on her long life. As a young boy he had spent nearly as much time with Ida as with his busy father. He realized that this individualist and free thinker, who remained relentlessly skeptical about both church and state until the day she died, helped him develop his own independent spirit. Jerry resolved to carry forward the memory of Ida Schuckman Brown. Confounding friends who claimed that "Jerry doesn't have a nostalgic bone in his body," the candidate brought his grandmother's story to millions of Californians. A campaign crew filmed Jerry talking about neighborhood crime with a group of elderly citizens. Shunning cue cards, he spoke from the heart about Ida's lifelong habit of taking a daily constitutional. But, said the candidate, in the last years of her life she sadly gave up these walks to avoid the muggers and purse-snatchers who were making the Sunset district nearly as dangerous as the Tenderloin.

It was a compelling ad echoing Pat's "Crack Down on Crime, Pick Brown This Time" campaign for District Attorney in 1943. And Jerry's pitch was a perfect lead-in to his crime-fighting program. The only problem with the commercial was that Ida Brown, her independent spirit intact to the last, never feared taking walks. Until the very end of her life, when illness forced her to move in with Frank, she regularly walked alone throughout the neighborhood. Even though Ida surely would have agreed something should be done to protect older citizens from mindless, urban crime, she hadn't let it slow her down.

Drawing attention to his late grandmother not only focused the public eye on his California roots, but also diffused Republican candidate Flournoy's blatant insinuations about Jerry's notorious bachelor status. Brown had never felt handicapped by being single and he didn't intend to apologize for it now. Casting back for a bipartisan example, Brown countered, "Lincoln didn't have a very satisfactory relationship with his wife, but he was a great president. In spite of Franklin and Eleanor Roosevelt's marital problems, Roosevelt was a great president."

Robert Pack, a Jerry Brown biographer, quotes Jerry as saying "I think the job's breakneck pace is incompatible with marriage. For two people to be together constantly takes a lot of consideration and attention. I don't have the time right now."

Pack also reported a rumor that certain strategists in Brown's 1974 campaign, bored and disgusted with repeated innuendos that Jerry might be gay, jested about producing a special television commercial. The joke was to have a beautiful Swedish blonde gaze into the camera and murmur, "I don't know a thing about American politics. All I know is, I'm voting for Jerry Brown because he's great in bed."

Flournoy soon realized that in California, which boasted as great a diversity of lifestyles as anywhere in the world, it was useless to belabor attacks on Jerry's sex life. He switched instead to needling Jerry about his privileged upbringing and limited experience "in the real world." How could a child of the ruling class possibly hope to lead a populist revolt, Flournoy asked.

Pat Brown countered that Jerry's youth was far from privileged. "We never really had any money," he told author Orville Schell. "And we never gave Jerry a goddamn thing."

Unlike his Peace and Freedom opponent who was out leafleting nude beaches in her birthday suit, Jerry avoided the wild gimmicks often associated with politics on North America's Pacific rim. To help minimize confrontations, he even refused to permit any other radio or TV station to pick up public television coverage of his second debate with Houston Flournoy. When the University of California's Irvine campus radio station asked him to waive a bipartisan pact banning pickup of the debate, Brown said no. He feared that by letting one station broadcast it, all would insist on the same right. Even Flournoy's willingness to make an exception just for U.C.I. didn't change Brown's mind. When he exlained his side of the story to a student audience, they responded with a Bronx cheer.

Jerry rarely experienced this sort of public humiliation, but he preferred the momentary antipathy of his student audience to over-exposure, which might tip his fifteen point lead in the polls. He was convinced it was wiser to down play the debates and stick to a low-key campaign emphasizing the tradition of "Roosevelt, Truman, Kennedy and Johnson until he got involved in the Vietnam War."

Notably missing from this list of guiding spiritual lights was a ranking local Democrat. "My father was governor," Jerry told audiences, "and I'm proud of the fact. But I'm running on my own record. I disagree with him on many things." What "The Spirit" (as friends now called him) promised voters was a chance " . . . to confront the confusion and hypocrisy of government. I've been around politics all my life and I think I'll have a fresh approach as governor. There are a lot of people who worked in my father's campaigns who won't support me. There's resistance from voters in the forty to fifty age group that I'm too young. But this generation — my generation — is one that is demanding change and imagination in government. That's why I think we're going to win. California will again have blue skies, an educational system second to none, and a prosperous economy."

By the campaign's final weeks, Jerry's lead had diminished. Where had he gone wrong? Had the election been in September, he might have won by a million votes. Now pollsters were predicting a photo finish. Were voters beginning to tire of the Brown wit and wisdom? Maybe Quinn, Barzaghi and Maullin had been wrong to advise Jerry, whose ideas were sometimes radical, occasionally brilliant, and periodically off-the-wall, to run a campaign with all the verve of a bowl of tapioca pudding. Maybe the voters had changed their minds and wanted a candidate with a strong political identity on the issues.

It was frustrating to Jerry that after months of continuous television exposure, polls showed that voters were having trouble separating his ideas from Houston Flournoy's. The Democrat found himself in the dilemma of all candidates who make their whistlestop tours on the prime-time caboose. While Brown tried to project a more liberal image, the electorate, watching him and Flournoy in thirty-second TV slots, seemed unable to distinguish between them. For example, when asked by pollsters, the voters did not know that Brown was against the death penalty, for the public employee's right to strike, and against laws punishing people for committing victimless crimes. Clearly Jerry had a marketing problem.

On election day, Brown opened the *Los Angeles Times* to read that his reassuring lead was now down to a scant four points. That night he won a narrow 179,000 vote victory. While hardly a mandate, this success was a remarkable come-back for a family humiliated by Ronald Reagan just eight years earlier.

At an election night celebration at the Beverly Hilton, Pat spoke long and enthusiastically about Jerry's success and the promise it held for the state. The old war horse, clearly enjoying the moment, went on and on. When he finally stopped, Jerry — tired and impatient — mumbled to him, "You almost cost me this election."

After he learned the remark was picked up by nearby mikes, the winner said he was only kidding. Some guests, who were acquainted with both father and son, didn't laugh.

In December Jerry's family traveled to Williams for the unveiling of his grandmother's tombstone. His father and uncles had wisely decided to postpone the carving until after the general election. Now it was time to raise the granite marker against a slate-colored sky. It read:

IDA SCHUCKMAN BROWN
Died July 6, 1974
Loving Mother of
Edmund G. Brown,
32nd Governor of the State of California,
Harold C. Brown,
Associate Justice, Circuit Court of Appeals,
Constance Carlson, Teacher
Frank M. Brown, Attorney
and
Grandmother of
Edmund G. Brown,
34th Governor of the State of California

"The administration is like a moving river and minutes have no relevance to where we'll be tomorrow"

CHAPTER 10

*I have abolished the whorehouses of France, Tangiers is the next to go.
My ambition is to be President despite the fact that I'm a Catholic.*

Allen Ginsberg
America

The moment he saw it, Jacques Barzaghi went for the brakes. But it was too late. The car's front end dropped into another chuckhole. As he was thrown up toward the ceiling, Jerry Brown looked over at his friend wondering if it was really such a good idea to go to Tassajara Hot Springs without an invitation.

All day long Brown and Barzaghi had been on the path toward the Monterey County Zen outpost owned by and for disciples of the San Francisco Zen Center. Friends of Barzaghi had visited Tassajara during the summer, when the retreat still accepted a few guests to defray expenses, but now the remote settlement east of Big Sur in the Santa Lucia mountains was closed to outsiders. Even California's new commander-in-chief couldn't get a reservation. Yet Jacques continued driving along the treacherous eighteen-mile Ventana Wilderness roadway, famous locally as a graveyard of clutches and axles. Unlike the new governor, Barzachi was not concerned about signs along the unimproved route proclaiming, "Don't Come," "Please Turn Back," and "Closed to the Public." As they lurched along at ten miles an hour, Jerry's empty stomach rumbled. Jacques urged his friend to be patient — he was convinced that the Zen retreat was the best possible place for Jerry to recharge after the election. The workaholic needed a place to cool out before taking over his new office.

Upon arrival, the uninvited guests were treated to vegetarian fare and provided sleeping accommodations in a nearby creekside cabin. Not since Sacred Heart had Jerry found any place more conducive to meditation. Nor was it surprising that a man attracted to the philosophic insights of Teilhard de Chardin would also be drawn to Zen Buddhism, with its emphasis on intuition and immediate feeling rather than reason and argument. For although Jerry Brown was adept at the almost aggressive use of reasoned argument, he also valued periods of silent contemplation. Despite his peripatetic lifestyle, he held strongly to the idea that one needed to occasionally come back to the source, the self.

Barzaghi was right. Jerry was immediately at home at Tassajara and comfortable with the Zen rituals, which were reminiscent of the Jesuit disciplines at the Sacred Heart novitiate. He also took immediately to Zen philosophy which taught that truth comes when words are discarded, that truth is outside of words. Zen coaxes the mind toward integration by carrying thought to its logical—and frequently absurd—extremes. It is a discipline in awareness which allows one to sense the interrelatedness of all things. The transformation of consciousness in Zen has been described as the correction of faulty perception, or the curing of a disease. Unlike the western emphasis on mastering more facts and greater skills, Zen focuses on the unlearning of wrong habits and opinions. It is an attempt to replace book knowledge with direct experience, and scholarliness with intuition. It is the awakening of the cognitive powers that will lead to realization of perfect enlightenment. According to Zen, the longer one can abstain from seeing things habitually, the more likely he or she can perceive their true nature. Habit kills intuition because it prevents the direct perception of experience. When dealing with problems, one must, according to Zen teachings, avoid becoming satisfied with intellectual solutions or losing oneself in facts, figures, proofs, or abstract truths, all of which prevent or obscure enlightenment. At Tassajara, Zen masters were able to work in harmony with the natural beauty of the California coastal mountains to provide an environment for disciples and friends to experience these teachings in an intense way—including meditation sessions, sparse vegetarian meals and simple sleeping arrangements.

The new Governor's visit to Tassajara made a deep impression. Though never given to extravagance, he still surprised friends when, after leaving the retreat and assuming his executive duties, he promptly began divesting his office of gubernatorial power symbols. He refused to authorize an official portrait of himself to replace the photograph of Ronald Reagan still on display in state buildings from Crescent City to San Ysidro. He rejected the Reagan's new $1.3 million redwood mansion—built at twice the cost of the dream home his mother had designed. Instead of this "Taj Mahal," he rented a $250 a month downtown apartment furnished inexpensively by the General Services Administration. He got his sheets and towels from Napa State Hospital, his furniture was recycled from other state-owned apartments and kitchen items were borrowed from the old governor's mansion. Jacques Barzaghi went shopping for a comfortable mattress and returned with one that rested on the floor without a frame.

"I try to live the way I've always lived," he explained to William F. Buckley, "which is in some sense impossible in the job I have. But a simpler view of life is coming upon us. I have no doubt about that. The accumulation of possessions and material indulgence is impossible over time because of the ecological limits imposed on this planet."

While his new team finished attending to domestic details, Jerry traveled the state attempting to articulate his unconventional and sometimes elusive approach to government. There was, the new governor believed, altogether too much documentation in government. Administrative codes, which filled thick volumes, made it impossible for agencies to be fair, effective and efficient. Instead of getting out in the field with their constituents, officials hid in their offices stroking one another with memoranda or talking to their dictation machines. Lunches were too frequently alcohol-laden affairs with self-interested lobbyists. It was time, the new Governor believed, for officials to abandon their elitist tools, get out from behind their gold nameplates and mingle with the huddled masses.

Just looking at Reagan's imperial furnishings annoyed Jerry during an executive suite tour following the inaugural. Tagging along was the Governor's father, who noted the Capitol Park view he used to enjoy was blocked by temporary buildings housing the legislature during Capitol reconstruction. Like museum visitors, they kept their hands off the Republican exhibit. But when he reached Reagan's desk, Pat, unable to resist, plopped down in the leather chair behind the desk, leaned back and swiveled. "God, this feels good after eight years," he told his son.

It was exciting to many observers that Jerry approached his task of governing with "lowered expectations" optimistically. He had not become a drop-out or a defeatist like so many others baptized in the protest movements of the sixties. And it was refreshing to see that along with his spirit of hope, Jerry was espousing simplicity in government.

Encouraged by the attention his refusal to sanction extravagance was generating, Jérry climbed into a 1974 Plymouth Satellite for the ride to a San Francisco City Hall reception. The car, destined to become the most famous production line vehicle in American automotive history, had been selected to replace Reagan's Cadillac limousine by Brown's new executive secretary, Gray Davis. The young attorney, who studied at Columbia Law School and won a bronze star for service in Vietnam, clearly knew how to communicate Jerry's style to the public.

Chosen because it had the best gas mileage and emitted the least pollutants of any vehicle in the state fleet, the Plymouth became an instantaneous expression of the governor's commitment to "taking the price off of public office." Tony Kline, who had come aboard as Brown's legal secretary, complained that the Chrysler product deprived the Governor of the dignity and seating comfort he deserved. But that was only because he failed to quickly grasp the obvious media value of this decision in an auto-crazed state. Even the functionally illiterate could see and appreciate that Jerry voluntarily elected to ride in a people's car without power windows.

Riding without a police escort was a relief for the Governor, who preferred to travel unencumbered. Another advantage to giving up the limousine was that it eliminated certain security risks. "I can remember a time when I was going to a [San Francisco] Giants [baseball] game in my father's [official] limousine driven by a highway patrolman. At one point as we drove through the crowd, people started pounding on the windows. It made me disinclined to have a limousine, let alone drive in one."

During the post-inauguration drive to San Francisco, Brown considered the fact that no real theme emerged from his nine-minute inaugural address, one of the shortest in California history. Always hesitant to give formal speeches, Jerry entertained the refreshing notion that the leading "vice in public affairs is the surplus of rhetoric and meaningless generalizations and abuse of the English language."

154

In San Francisco, Brown didn't impress anyone at first, treating his audience to cliches like "our first order of business is to regain the trust and confidence of the people." But then, in characteristic fashion, while taking questions from his audience, Jerry found a theme that would serve him well in many political crises ahead:

"Remember," he told local officials assembled before him, "government is not the work of one person. As a matter of fact, before I gave my speech today, I reread the last chapter of *War and Peace*. You take a look at it. It will indicate that the generals neither knew what they were doing nor did those that followed them. Thank you very much. Give me a hand. We've all got to work together."

While this notion—unlike some of Brown's other seminal tag lines—attracted little media attention, it should have, for it illuminated what, for lack of a better term, can be called the "New Spirit" pessimism of Jerry Brown. The Governor's reading of history from the Peloponnesian Wars to Vietnam convinced him that politicians were often just as ignorant as their constituents. Like Pulitzer prize-winning author David Halberstam, Brown believed statesmen who passed themselves off as the "best and the brightest" often turned out to be the worst and the most ignorant.

In the months that followed, several themes emerged. Perhaps the most pervasive was the new governor's outspoken criticism of traditional government. Much of this disillusionment apparently had its roots in his childhood experience as a politician's son. "I was attracted and repelled by what I saw of politics in my father's house. Attracted by the adventure, the opportunity. Repelled by the grasping, the artificiality, the obvious manipulation and role-playing, the repetition of emotion without feeling, particularly that — the repetition of emotion."

It genuinely frightened Brown that year after year politicians recycled the same stale cliches until their imaginations went completely to sleep. "I think people in government, from what I've seen, are the prisoners of a very small circle of people. They move from one banquet to another meeting, from one national chain hotel to another of the same nature. You may go to Europe, but you're still staying in the Sheraton Hotel. You talk to the same people, who are playing the same game. And the game is a recognition ritual, it's a reassurance ritual, it's a kind of here-we-are, the important people, let's exchange our important thoughts. What new thoughts come into that?" Brown asked.

Jerry Brown believed that California had changed since his father had been governor. It was becoming more and more apparent to him that spending lots of money to try to ameliorate social problems—the traditional response of liberal Democrats—was no longer working. He saw all sorts of institutions failing to solve the problems they were set up to deal with, in spite of inflated budgets. Huge allocations for health, education and welfare, for example, inevitably went to the bureaucrats and researchers, with the public receiving only a trickle. It was absurd, the Governor argued, to take more steps toward trying to improve the state's problems until it could be determined just what these problems were and what those steps should be.

At the outset, Jerry did some symbolic streamlining in the Capitol. First he did away with the tradition of the governor's office supplying briefcases to staffers at taxpayers' expense. From now on staff employees would have to tote paperwork on their own nickel. (Or, they could follow the example set by their new boss, who crammed concise lists into pockets stocked with Cheetos munched in lieu of lunch.) Then Brown cut back his own salary and the salaries of his staff by seven percent and authorized an across-the-board salary increase for state workers in an attempt to level income disparities. Then in his second week in office, the Governor announced his intention to return the more than 150 gifts received since his election.

Themes which began to emerge from Jerry's first political speeches sometimes sounded more like those of his predecessor than his father. Like Reagan, he called for less reliance on government, more responsibility for community problems to be taken by the "private sector," and rejected the assumption that you could correct all social evils simply by throwing money at them. But unlike Ronald Reagan, Brown demonstrated an interest in, and ability to communicate with, the state's most politically powerless groups — such as farm workers, blacks, back-to-the-landers, and women. From the beginning of his administration, he sought out Chicanos like Health and Welfare Services secretary Mario Obledo, blacks like Supreme Court Justice Wiley Manuel, and women like Adriana Gianturco, whom he appointed transportation secretary.

Like so many of his generation who came of political age in the sixties protesting against capital punishment, the draft, wars and presidents themselves, Jerry was frequently asked to suggest a reasonable alternative to the existing order. "People ask me 'What's your program?' What the hell does that mean? The program is to confront the confusion and hypocrisy of government. That's what's important . . . You don't have to *do* things. Maybe by avoiding doing things you accomplish quite a lot. Maybe if Kennedy had avoided the Bay of Pigs or Vietnam, that would have been quite an accomplishment . . . Inaction," Jerry believed, "may be the highest form of action" in many cases.

The Governor's promotion of "creative inaction," with its Zen Buddhist overtones, disappointed many old friends who expected the first governor with good liberal credentials from the sixties to eagerly pursue the kinds of programs that McCarthy and McGovern had espoused. In this sense, Jerry agreed with Werner Erhard, one of the more prominent figures in the human potential movement, who explained, "One creates from nothing. If you try to create from something, you're just changing something. So in order to create something, you first have to be able to create nothing."

This approach warned against the habitual thinking which blocked awareness of immediate reality. Zen, Erhardt, and many of the systems of thought subsumed under the human potential movement urged slowing things down so they could be experienced anew, without preconceptions. In addition, Jerry was interested in the teachings of many of these groups that each person is responsible for what happens in his or her life, and an individual creates his or her own reality. This was a very different philosophical starting point than that of traditional liberalism, which holds that society and its institutions are ultimately responsible for mankind's ills.

Although some of Jerry's aides, like Tom Quinn, Jacques Barzaghi and Llew Werner, were comfortable with his new age aphorisms, others had difficulty grappling with him. One who was initially baffled was Tony Kline, Jerry's legal secretary and former law school roommate. Fresh from Public Advocates, a liberal San Francisco-based public interest law group, Kline was anxious to continue the fight begun by the L.B.J.-sponsored legal services programs to help low-income people. He had recently blocked the construction of $3 billion worth of freeways designed to pave over miles of minority neighborhoods in cities like Oakland and Los Angeles. Kline also sued to equalize state aid to public school districts and filed an action against the Department of Corrections, alleging overcrowded and unsafe prison conditions. As a trial lawyer, one of Kline's biggest obstacles was the impossibly clogged American judicial system, where very little happens very slowly. Particularly frustrating was the incredible court log jam that slowed down adjudication, thus working to preserve the status quo. To try to ameliorate this, Kline strongly urged Jerry to immediately fill fifty-three accumulated court vacancies with humanitarian Democrats who would be more sympathetic to the plight of the poor. He was totally unprepared for the Governor's response.

"He started asking questions," Kline recalled. "He wanted to know why there were vacancies, where they were and how much the judges got paid. I said those questions are academic. You can start filling all these vacancies and get some judges who are socially conscious and from the minority community. But he insisted [on answers to his questions]."

When Kline studied the issue, he found out that "California has more judges and jails than any jurisdiction in the world. People in our state are the most litigious anywhere. Californians bring more civil disputes into court with greater frequency than anyone in the history of man." Finally, six months after asking Kline to get this information, Brown began filling the judicial vacancies. When he did, his appointments included many non-whites, women, young lawyers and people outside the traditional legal establishment.

An information freak, the Governor insisted on getting this sort of insight in many other areas. His need to know drove many staff members up the wall. One who had some difficulty was his health director, Jerry Lackner. A physician who had studied for a law degree at the University of Santa Clara with Marc Poché, Lackner had participated in most of the major protest movements of the past fifteen years. A dedicated organizer of UFW boycotts, he had eventually become the personal physician of Cesar Chavez. Unlike Brown, Lackner strongly believed that only government-sponsored health care delivery systems would ever truly meet the needs of the public. "If I had my way," confessed Lackner, "I'd devote the entire state budget to correcting our disaster in mental health, care for the poor and elderly." Jerry was too busy during the early days of his administration for Lackner to communicate these concerns.

Like Lackner, much of Jerry Brown's staff found him inaccessible. Agency secretaries soon complained that Jerry was two hours late to his own weekly cabinet meetings. Once, when he did finally join his staff during one of their sessions, Brown asked then-cabinet secretary David Fox why he was taking notes.

"Because that's what you do at meetings," replied the new man who had come up through the Los Angeles campaign organization.

"The administration is like a moving river," replied Jerry, "and minutes have no relevance to where we'll be tomorrow."

While he stopped taking notes, Fox continued issuing an agenda. But those who knew Brown best made no effort to get on the schedule. Jacques Barzaghi didn't even bother showing up for many of what he knew would be meaningless sessions. Executive Secretary Gray Davis, who put out the morning line on the Governor's state of mind, tried to improve things by prepping cabinet secretaries like Mario Obledo on issues that interested Jerry prior to his arrival. But Brown's ranking Chicano, who had come to Sacramento via the Mexican-American legal defense fund, smiled and shook his head when it was his turn.

"Don't you have that hospital thing you wanted to ask him about?" Davis inquired hopefully.

"No," replied Secretary Obledo perceptively. "He's not interested in that. I'll tell him about it when he's ready."

Often when Brown finally arrived at a meeting he would fall back on his familiar verbal agility, skirting the issues at hand and, instead, firing Socratic questions at the cabinet. When he tired of that, the Governor would sometimes play his people off against one another on any handy issue for no discernible reason. When this precipitated a free-ranging debate, he would happily participate as long as his attention was engaged. Often when he lost interest, he would simply wander off.

By the summer of 1975, formal cabinet meetings were a rare event. Instead, to pacify his secretaries who were complaining about their boss' inaccessibility, Jerry gave them direct "Jerry" phone lines. In theory this was great, but in practice Jerry's frustrated aides found the red phone was usually busy. The Governor's Agriculture and Services Secretary, Rose Bird, who had known Brown at Berkeley and served as Santa Clara County's public defender before enlisting with the state, was particularly upset by his unresponsiveness. In frustration, she retaliated by refusing to answer when Jerry finally returned her calls weeks later. "I had some controversial areas I needed to talk to him about," she explained, "and didn't appreciate his inaccessibility early on. I would get annoyed and start making a point of being less available to him just to let him know it's a two-way street."

At the same time, Jerry's health director, Jerome Lackner, who also doubled as his doctor, learned that the Governor was alternately not bothering to eat at all or feasting on greasy hamburgers and fries. A favorite trick of the Governor's during this period was to raid his secretaries' brown bags while explaining to the victims about the virtues of fasting. Lackner tried lecturing Jerry and when this didn't work, simply instructed the state dietician to have balanced meals brought in from a government cafeteria.

Wholesome food, including lots of fresh fruits and vegetables, replaced greasy Dennyburgers around the conference room table. There was also talk of getting the Governor to start breaking up his eighteen-hour day with exercise, but no one really pressed the issue, since in 1975 physical fitness was still high on the long list of mainstream virtues that didn't interest Jerry. He would not, for example, cut ribbons, kiss babies, christen freighters, use a speech writer, put on crazy hats, hand out souvenir pens at bill signings, or ride in motorcades. And he refused to let his picture be taken while he was eating. An important part of surviving on Jerry Brown's staff was to know better than to ask him to do any of these things.

Jetting around the state on commercial flights, Brown descended into California's urban centers articulating his vision of political reality. "No one is going to get everything they want, at least in the short term," Brown told one group of Democratic leaders, "but if you redefine what it is you want, we think you might be satisfied." The exposition of this thesis was then followed by Jerry's introduction to E.F. Schumacher, a British economist, and author of a popular economics book entitled *Small is Beautiful*. Increasingly Jerry turned to Schumacher when trying to explain not only that Californians would have to learn to get by with a less affluent lifestyle, but that they would be better off if they simplified their lives. According to Schumacher, "work and leisure are complementary parts of the same living process and cannot be separated without destroying the joy of work and the bliss of leisure." Buddhist economists urged a return to a smaller scale, where production was based upon physical and spiritual needs of the community, as well as the needs and limitations of the environment. It implied that human environments and institutions should be decentralized into manageable entities and that each person should have a recognized contribution to make. This message seemed to square well with Jerry's own religious training.

Holding out his robed arms at the University of Santa Clara's June commencement, he called on the graduates to employ the Society of Jesus' time-tested methods to spread not just their own faith, but the gospel of New Age politics. "You look back at the history of the Jesuits, they were born in the time when the assumptions on which European civilization had rested were being very much brought under question. That puts you, I think, right at the cutting edge and with that you have to pick up the burden, pick up the opportunity. When you look at the future you are going to see that a mere accumulation of possessions, the mere extension of what it's been before, denoted as wealth and prosperity, is going to change. People of this world are looking not only for freedom and the light of technology, but for the human spirit that will bring people together."

And how exactly did Brown propose to apply sixteenth-century religious philosophy to his contemporary realm? "A very famous Jesuit," explained the Governor, "saw the world as converging, the alpha and omega. I don't think anybody studies Greek anymore. I had to study it for a year in the seminary in order to get out. The only thing I can remember about Latin is I never learned a word of it. I often wondered whether anyone ever knew Latin, I think it was a well-kept secret. Everybody was faking for many years. But Father Teilhard de Chardin saw that there was an evolution of the mind as well as of the body. The evolution of the spirit was bringing the divergence of this planet together, not only the nuclear problems, the problem of food production, the problem of resources depletion, the problem of learning to live with people who are very different, the problem of one generation accepting the different lifestyle, of accepting one another. I think we can very well think of the philosophy that all diversity is being converged toward a

160

greater unit. That's the way I see things and it won't be done unless each one of us can do this for ourselves so that together we can do what none of us can do separately. When I say together, I don't just mean people in California, the blacks and the whites, the older people, the younger people, the east and the west and all the people who have to share with spaceship planet Earth . . . It depends on the nerve or the ability, and the willingness to approach the future which is never quite the same and in many ways carries on like we were in the past. The more things change, the more they stay the way they once were."

While Jerry's version of Teilhard suffered a bit in translation, he continued articulating this view at nearly every opportunity. Soon the Governor found it difficult to leave a dias without exalting "convergence" and "unity." For his new creed held that a political leader's first responsibility was to "articulate a common purpose and a common philosophy that we can all share."

Brown was convinced that government could never satisfy constituencies by simply funding more projects. After all, his father, the master builder, after giving the people of California the best freeway system in the world, a five-hundred-mile long aqueduct, dozens of state parks, seaside university campuses that made the cover of architectural magazines and dozens of other new programs and civic monuments, was voted out of office by a landslide.

Concluding that voters were never really satisfied by whatever government provided, Jerry decided that injecting a little religion into politics couldn't hurt. What Brown's church offered was neither pork barrel for the rich nor handouts for the poor, but an opportunity for people to redirect their lives away from materialism. Typical was a program enabling Californians to donate their time at mental hospitals. It was run by Brown's new director of volunteerism, Charles Baldwin. Always at Jerry's side when it came time to solicit donations of human capital, this quiet man, who had the only shaved head in the administration beside Barzaghi's, could barely contain his enthusiasm.

"Have you figured out what makes Jerry's talks so effective?" he asked as Brown was finishing a private talk with a group of New York businessmen. "He keeps it simple. Like Christ."

The analogy was not lost on Brown's disciples who had been lured to Sacramento by his humanitarian call—a call which often required considerable personal sacrifice. "When are you going to get your fat ass out of Hillsborough and do something for the people?" Brown asked businessman/donor Robert Batinovich when he hesitated over enlisting as chairman of the Public Utilities Commission. The fact that this thirty-seven-year-old millionaire had requested a few days to put his copy machine empire into trustworthy hands cut no mustard with Jerry.

161

When the Governor called, he obviously expected people to put down whatever they were doing and follow him. When pressed, Batinovich didn't disappoint and agreed to join overnight.

Before long, Sacramento began to resemble an intellectual Parris Island. No sacrifice of personal convenience, or even rest, was considered too much. One of Jerry's favorite techniques for working out compromises was the post-midnight bargaining session. He used this technique to great advantage to work out a compromise Agricultural Labor relations bill establishing election procedures for the farm workers. A nocturnal creature with a distinct advantage over conferees he called out of bed, Brown substituted his own quirky time schedule for the nine-to-five most everyone else preferred. Before long, early appointees like Dave Jensen, the first of seven press secretaries, Special Assistant for crises Carl Werthman and Business and Transportation Secretary Don Burns and others packed their bags and left. Most liked their jobs and most even liked and admired their boss. But working for a Jesuit/ Buddhist who thought sleep and food superfluous, could wear a person down in a hurry.

Those who remained in their seventy- to eighty-hour-a-week jobs were sometimes expected to put aside their personal views on a particular subject and labor for what the Governor decided to be the greater good. While Brown hired many of his staff members on the basis of their sixties activist credentials, he also insisted they look for ways to work constructively with old enemies. For example, certified liberals, progressives and conservationists like Tony Kline, Jerry Lackner, the Sierra Club's Claire Dedrick, and California Rural Legal Assistance founder Jim Lorenz occasionally found their names and talents touted in support of programs they didn't believe in. Speaking before a union group about the forthcoming $102 million Dumbarton Bridge planned to span lower San Francisco Bay, the Governor, who had made Dedrick Resources Secretary, said he wasn't worried about environmental opposition. "It's ready to go," he boasted. "There may be a few lawsuits. I may have to send in a few of my best environmental lawyers to fight lawsuits. One way or the other, we can swing that one, I think." Brown was right—the big building project moved right ahead.

But on the whole, the Governor opposed expansion of the freeway program his father had done so much to create. In November 1975, he made his case before six hundred San Diegans at a poor people's luncheon. "There's no free lunch in Sacramento," the Governor told proletarians who had filed in at five dollars per head. "And I guess not in San Diego either. You don't get something for nothing and I'm faced with the fact that the buck stops with me. In the golden years of this state, grandiose plans were made to build billions of dollars worth of freeways that transit gas tax (revenue) will no longer permit. That's just the way it is. In our society I think we've reached the pinnacle of ability to move from one place to another. Our transportation is the best on the planet. The problem is what do we find when we get there after we move from point A to point B? We find there are problems in education, health, employment and a lot of other areas more important than transportation."

In the back of the governor's makeshift mess hall a man rose to challenge this assumption. "Hundreds, perhaps thousands, of San Diegans are facing layoffs due to your policy of halting highway construction. Doesn't this bother your conscience?"

"All government bothers my conscience . . . We have to learn that there are limits and within those limits we have to work out the agenda of public service. Now that's the way I see it and I wouldn't call that necessarily conservative, not necessarily liberal. I just think that's the way it is. Now some have wondered what I have meant by lowering expectations. I must say that my expectations haven't been lowered. I've been putting in a twelve-hour day."

The verbal process of self-discovery was one of Jerry's strategies for creating order out of the bureaucratic labyrinth. "Don't write it down, say it," became the unofficial motto of his administration. The Governor's signature became a rare commodity. Letters, memos and reports of substance rarely went out over his name. It wasn't that Jerry was trying to be evasive with staff. He just wasn't the sort of person who would ever sit down and draft a position. Often he didn't know what he was thinking until after he said it. And even then he wasn't always sure what he meant.

Jerry believed the public's cynicism toward government related to a lack of accountability. "One great difference between the private and public sector is that when something goes wrong [in the public sector], the enterprise does not go bankrupt, it gets bigger. That's where the interesting difference is . . . If we're losing in Vietnam, the answer is not to get out, it's to put more troops in. If we have a particular school that has a problem, we throw more resources in. If things get worse, we add more resources. If a particular problem doesn't work, the answer is we haven't put enough money into it, we haven't tried it enough. So there's a strange correlation between funding and failure which turns on its head the normal reward system that the more you achieve the more you're rewarded."

Certainly there was some truth to Jerry's argument that the easiest way to change the way things had traditionally been done was to apply zero-based thinking. Like zero-based budgeting, where Brown insisted that bureaucrats ignore last year's ledger and justify each new financial request from scratch, Jerry himself insisted on searching for a fresh philosophical baseline. St. Ignatius, Sartre, Gandhi, Ivan Illich and Schumacher were among the thinkers that Brown often referred to at this stage, with Stewart Brand and Gerard O'Neill soon to be added. But although Jerry was famous for surrounding himself with the thoughts of these and other remarkable people, no one view prevailed. In a way mysterious to everyone, including himself, the Governor created his own synthesis in pursuit of what he called "yeasty change."

Unfortunately, some of his cabinet secretaries, like Rose Bird, were simply not zero-based thinkers. Methodically organized, she continued to resent the Governor's tendency to subvert agendas with mind-fogging digressions. "It's a technique of keeping everyone around you off base because people don't know what you are going to do. You have control over almost uncontrollable situations because everyone else is thrown off base. Things are not predictable. You are never sure what the Governor wants of you and it's hard to please that person. If you are not predictable then people aren't sure how to gain your favor, to know what you like or want.

"I think he surprised everyone at how astute he was. Before becoming governor, he had a tendency to be deceptively slight and quiet. But he absorbed very much. He was kind of like a medieval prince who watched the court for years. Initially, I was told to do everything through the governor. But I could never get an answer and finally came to the conclusion that he wanted you to make your own decisions. That was an effective tool because if you make decisions you are responsible. If you make a mistake the chief executive is not responsible. That is the genius of his system. If you do something wrong then it's your fault. Increasingly I found I couldn't work within that system as an organized person who is predictable."

Preble Stolz, a civil procedure and administrative law professor from UC Berkeley's Boalt Hall was an early casualty of the Governor's hide-and-seek administration. An aide with Pat's first legislative staff, he couldn't resist a chance to return to Sacramento to work for his son. "I loved working for Pat," he told friends who questioned why he would abandon the comforts of university life in temperate Berkeley to become Jerry's education advisor. "As a governor he had a genius for inspiring loyalty. He was a good government type who was interested in doing the right thing. Coming back fifteen years later gave me a real sense of deja vu. There are lots of similarities between the two men. Every so often Jerry laughs in a way that if you didn't see him, you'd swear it's Pat. And his half smile is his father's.

"I was warned it was going to be harder this time before I arrived. Rose Bird said, if you are looking for positive reinforcement, go work for someone else. His father used to read his memos. When I started with Jerry on the legislative staff, I made the mistake of thinking this was a way of communicating with him. Jerry communicates better orally."

Stolz, in an attempt to maintain his balance and sense of humor, devised an original way to reach the Governor. Although Jerry persisted in ignoring staff memos, he usually went through newspapers ahead of his staff, pinning down every mention of his administration, even finding isolated references at the bottom of back page stories. He responded to negative comments with a quick call to the subordinate he considered responsible. In addition, Jerry commonly scanned the wire service teletype in the pressroom. Stolz joked that if Jerry loved the press so much, why not con him into paying attention to his own staff by feeding their memos into the wire service teletypes.

When this suggestion got back to Jerry, it didn't amuse him. He was already worried that the print freaks on his staff would imprison him in their linear world. The real test of leadership, he believed, was to make decisions without reading supposedly requisite staff reports. Brown even hinted that Stolz and the rest of his staff would be wise to cut back their work-related reading and writing to make better use of the tactile senses. To help them along the way, he suggested the state "close down the xerox machine one day a week in honor of clear thinking."

Reducing the flow of information was also connected to another of Jerry's ideas. This had to do with jettisoning the cumbersome review process that traditionally followed the creation of a new program Jerry was totally against. "The idea of pilot projects which then result in additional data collection, which are then fed into comprehensive plans, which then allow a great deal of institutional communication between local, state and federal agencies and departments which then explore gaps in the data and the information and then provide technical assistance one to the other . . . I generally like things that have only one phase and are not comprehensive."

Preble Stolz and at least some of his colleagues applauded the Governor's determination to junk a losing bureaucratic system. The only problem, in their view, was that Jerry had not come up with something better. Living up to the Zen principle of non-action, the Governor often forced Stolz to guess what he wanted. This made it tough for the literal-minded education advisor to represent Brown's views on pending legislation. A case in point was a bill requiring state college trustees to hire professors on the basis of seniority rather than merit. Stolz told Jerry that this proposal, developed because of potential funding cuts, threatened the California State University board's academic freedom. The Governor seemed sympathetic and his aide came away from their discussion convinced his boss would veto the bill if passed. While this information comforted the bill's opponents, it did not stop its sponsors who put it through the legislature anyway. A short time later, Jerry signed the bill and it became Stolz's job to explain to the losing side that the measure became law over his personal objection.

Humiliations like these tended to destabilize life in the Governor's compound. Even chief-of-staff Gray Davis, who saw Jerry about twenty times a day, often sounded less than authoritative when staff members who couldn't communicate with Jerry tried to find out what was going on. The word around the Capitol was that Davis, who sat in his court-yard office late into the evening prophesizing the administration's future, had begun to sound like a cross between Jerry and psychic Jean Dixon. Others cracked that Brown was turning California into a whim-ocracy.

One early experimenter in Brown's first administration to strike a raw nerve with Brown was his Employment Development Director, Jim Lorenz. Like many of Jerry's first appointments, he used a prestigious [Harvard] law degree to try to help low-income people. A friend of Cesar Chavez and Ralph Nader, Lorenz saw government service as the logical extension of his pro-bono past with California Rural Legal Assistance. With Brown's apparent encouragement, he promptly drafted a plan to hire unemployed youths to work for nonprofit associations in their own community.

Unfortunately for Lorenz, a memo on this project, which was proposed to be funded with $155 million in state and federal funds, was leaked to the Knowland's *Oakland Tribune*. Here was an easy chance to needle the family that had sent the Senator from Formosa back to Alameda County. "Brown's Secret Worker State," a red-ink front-page banner headline screamed. The accompanying article accused the Governor of trying to use public funds to create 100,000 jobs as part of "a worker-controlled, virtual economic revolution in California." Brown promptly told inquiring reporters he'd never heard of Lorenz's strange idea. "I don't like plans. I don't deal in plans. That is just a bunch of paper." Then he fired Lorenz.

After leaving Sacramento, Lorenz wrote about his Capitol adventures. He portrayed his former boss as an opportunist with little trust or faith in the wisdom of mankind. "What did he think about when he meditated? Jerry was asked. 'I think about the shortness of life and the inevitability of death,' he supposedly replied. The quoted response sounded a litle false, a little melodramatic, but Jerry's conversation that late fall (of 1974) afternoon was much in the same vein. We were making a tour of his house. He was showing me the shotgun he kept by his bed. He looked up and flung his arm out in front of him. We had been talking about whether democracy was in its terminal stages.

" 'People will tear each other apart if given half a chance,' he exclaimed. 'Politics is a jungle, and it's getting worse. People want a dictator these days, a man on a white horse. They're looking for a man on a white horse to ride in and tell them what to do. A politician can do anything he wants so long as he manipulates the right symbols.' "

Jerry's unappealable decision to fire Lorenz frightened other members of his staff. "If he sees you in the media attributing a position to him," explained a subordinate in the wake of the employment director's sudden demise, "he'll call people and talk to them for two hours trying to reassure himself that this is really his position. If he disagrees with you, he'll call you in his office and chew you out for misrepresenting him: 'How do you get off saying that's my position? When you say that's my position, who's got the facts? Have you got the facts? It's things like this that make me wish I didn't have to rely on anyone. I wish I could do it all myself.' "

The Governor's despair reflected his deep distrust of agency secretaries, department directors and even governors who promised the undeliverable. "I want to cut government off at the pocketbook," he told his disciples. "The best way to run a freeway program is to say no freeways. People will never appreciate what you give them unless you make it a concession."

Concessions were only possible under special circumstances. "Who are you to give away any government service?" Jerry asked appointees who wanted to disperse small pieces of the state's surplus billions. "I'm governor and I give it away."

Brown's chronic evasiveness was becoming his professional trademark. And soon nearly every political scientist with a subscription to *Psychology Today* was trying to uncover the real Jerry Brown. Writing in *New West* magazine, psycho-historians from the Menninger clinic argued his unusual conduct was the result of a frantic, unending competition with his father. California historian Kevin Starr suggested that his entire administration was being run in accordance with St. Ignatius' Spiritual Exercises. Lorenz wrote that his former boss "used the nervous system of the media as a substitute for the corporeal presence he felt he lacked; wrapped himself in other people's identities in order to give himself meaning." And the Reverend Robert Ochs, a Jesuit who was also well-versed in Zen thought, analyzed Brown with the help of a system devised by famed Sufi instructor Oscar Ichazo. The Governor was typed as a fanatical "resent type" crusader with puritanical tendencies.

Nevertheless, by the end of 1975, there was hardly a person in America who had not heard of Brown's "New Spirit." Leaders in other states had begun imitating his frugality. In Massachusetts, Governor Michael Dukakis was riding the bus to work. Governor James Longley of Maine cut his $31,000 salary to $11,000. And in Georgia, a presidential candidate named Jimmy Carter was getting press for making his own bed. While he had not approached his father's impressive first year legislative record, there was no doubt Jerry had strummed a national nerve.

But his treatment in the local media continued to worry Jerry. His staff knew that something was brewing, but they didn't know what form it would take. In the early evening of March 12, 1975, the Governor did something which amazed even some members of his staff who thought they would never again be surprised by anything Jerry did—he invited four reporters into his office and announced his intention to enter the California presidential primary. "I'm raising ideas and expressing a certain philosophy I think deserves a hearing," explained Brown over freshly brewed coffee.

"Now, since you feel you have a philosophy that deserves a hearing," replied one of the reporters, "you must have decided what this philosophy is."

"Well, no," said the governor, "I think this is, I would still describe what I'm doing as something that develops and emerges."

"What would you be telling these people about yourself? What philosophy do you think needs telling about? What ideas?"

"Well, I think people are looking for new ideas, I think they're looking for a sense of hope, they're looking for a way to reconcile what are apparently contradictions in a society, which includes limited resources. We're at a point, we're saying the governor can't do anything, that's more a Republican approach.

"That doesn't seem to be working very well. Some of our traditional Democratic approaches are running into difficulty with our limited resources . . ."

"Do you see yourself in this potential role of articulating?"

"I think it would be a yeasty element in the primary process."

"Would you be trying to find a new path between the Democratic and Republican groups?"

"What I try to do is to avoid premature labeling. Certainly I think forming a wider coalition and bringing together different political groupings is essential if the society is to be governed. That means that what appear to be irreconcilable differences have to be brought together.

That is what leadership is doing. Somebody can bring together groups that normally were thought to be so divergent that that would be impossible in the past."

"You're not going to suggest that you're just indicating your intention to go ahead with a favorite son candidacy?"

"I wouldn't describe it as a favorite son, possibly a faithful son. I will continue to think very carefully. At least I'm going to be running in the California primary. I can do something."

"Do you believe in the next year you'll be eating more enchiladas, more ravioli?"

"Well, I'm going to go [eat some] tonight."

Jerry's late entry into the national primaries seemed both foolish and precipitous to many of his admirers. "It would be a mistake," wrote the nation's leading Jesuit magazine, *America,* "for him to move, after so little experience, into national politics. The misleading urgency of media age popularity needs restraining no less than bloated government budgets. For his part, Jerry Brown need not look to Gandhi or the Zen koans for wisdom in this respect. His first spiritual master says it well enough. 'Age quod agis,' Ignatius told his distracted young novices. 'Do what you are doing.' "

The Latin phrase was, in fact, a Brown favorite often included in his unprepared remarks. But the Society of Jesus failed to understand he could easily continue doing the same thing from the White House. It was all merely a matter of teaching the public the facts of contemporary political life. "I don't think the president runs the country, nor do I think the governor runs the state," Brown explained. "Government is part of an overall complex equation—social, economic, environmental. Within that limited framework a leader can set a tone, express a philosophy and describe a future that is either consistent with what is possible or not. That's what I'm going to try to do. The president has a tremendous responsibility as leader, as educator, as describer of the destiny that we have and can find."

Traveling cross-country to file in the out-of-state primaries that weren't either over or closed, Jerry found voters anxious to know what his zero-based thinking would do for them. Breaking with a forty-year-old Democratic tradition, he offered few tangible promises. Indeed, Brown's many gubernatorial accomplishments — ending the state oil depletion allowance, supporting coastline protection, bringing peace to strife-torn fields, funding urban parks, reducing penalties for possession of small quantities of marijuana, mandatory prison sentences for heroin users and armed robbers, banning bank redlining in low-income areas, forming a new agency to build and rehabilitate housing — were of little interest outside California. People in Oregon, Maryland, Rhode Island and other states, who couldn't care less that Jerry's appointments to high office were considered to be the best in generations of California government, were much more fascinated by the Governor's rhetoric. Urbanites did learn, however, it might become necessary to abandon their sinking cities in order to save them. For the Governor made it clear in New York that he opposed long-term federal aid for the city. Vietnam, he maintained, had established that money alone was insufficient to preserve a dying way of life. Perhaps it would be a useful experiment in cultural anthropology to simply cut off Washington's help and see what evolves. After all, explained the California leader, "There is an inherent ecological problem in trying to have so many people who are so different inhabiting the same turf. New York City may not have the survival power because of its centralization."

New York journalists characterized this as the sort of callous indifference that "could well have been spelled out by one of President Ford's speechwriters." But sensational headlines in the New York Post like: "JERRY BROWN: N.Y.C. MAY JUST HAVE TO GO" were oversimplifications. It wasn't that Brown, or many other Americans outside the big eastern and western cities, had anything against the Big Apple or for that matter Chicago, Detroit and other decaying metropolises. Jerry particularly enjoyed visiting New York and had many friends there. But he honestly believed that like citizens in every other part of America, New Yorkers were going to have to face up to the necessity of fiscal sacrifice. And when they inevitably did, Jerry wasn't sure that their way of life would survive.

Jerry wanted to emphasize that unlike most programmatic liberals who still dominated his party, he was not linked to potentially losing causes, like trying to rebuild east coast cities. As a politician of the future, he could move swiftly to the winning side. "Of all the candidates," he told a black political conference in Charlotte, North Carolina, "I represent an opportunity for fundamental change. I represent a generation that came of age in the civil rights movement and the anti-Vietnam war movement, and that can put behind use the malaise of the 1960s, Watergate, the CIA and the FBI violations. I am unencumbered by the baggage of the last ten years."

This was the Governor's instant answer to those who pointed out he was running on the thinnest substantive record of any major candidate. No declared or undeclared opponent — not Jimmy Carter, Hubert Humphrey, Frank Church, Morris Udall or Teddy Kennedy — enjoyed the independence that came with his lack of political baggage, Brown claimed. And Jerry even went so far as to argue that his mysterious ways would be useful in diplomatic matters, promising that if elected "Mao will have as much trouble figuring out our foreign policy as we have figuring out China's."

Lines like these went over well with voters, who appreciated the way Brown questioned the ability of governments to govern. Many also liked the idea that while liberal on human rights issues, he was sitting back, taking his time and using his influence to reduce the power and impact of government.

Entering a number of late primaries, the Governor did surprisingly well. In Maryland, Nevada and California he won outright. In New Jersey and Rhode Island, Jerry campaigned successfully for uncommitted slates backing his candidacy. In Oregon Brown extolled a bill he signed in California limiting the amount of water new toilets can hold. Jerry told students at the University of Oregon: "Instead of seven gallons of flush, you can only consume 3½ gallons of water . . . then we can leave more of your water in Oregon." This kind of talk went over well. Even though his name wasn't on the ballot 23% of the Democratic voters wrote in his name for President.

It was a stirring performance, one that more than achieved Brown's goal of demonstrating his appeal to the voters. Unfortunately for Jerry, however, those advisors who told him that he was starting too late were right. Although he had ridden out of the West to stun the political establishment, there was no way to really capitalize on this rousing last minute stampede to his banner. When the primary ended in June 1976, Jimmy Carter was far ahead in the delegate count, having collected many votes before Jerry ever announced his candidacy.

Never one to underestimate the value of symbolism, Jerry showed up for the New York primary in July and turned his back on the rooms reserved for him at the Hilton. Instead, he moved his team into the economical McAlpin, where every room was a double—you and your cockroach. In one meeting, a cockroach sat near the foot of Wisconsin Congressman Robert Kastenmeier for ten minutes. The mid-westerner watched nervously as the bug, which was out of Jerry's range of vision, moved toward his shoe. Finally, the lawmaker placed his empty styrofoam coffeecup over the surprise visitor, and made a hasty departure.

As the convention heated up, party elders asked Jerry to release all three hundred of his delegates to Jimmy Carter on the first ballot. Much to his annoyance his string of convention victories seemed to be viewed by Party pros as little more than an interesting footnote to the nomination of the former Georgia governor. But quitting made no sense to Jerry, even after he realized he was sure to lose. All his life people had been telling him to throttle back, that everything he wanted would come soon enough. He had never taken this sort of advice, choosing instead to plunge ahead defying the odds. Now, again, it was suggested that it was time for a polite retreat and that his efforts toward party unity would be appreciated by the delegates and remembered at future conventions. With much the same spirit that John Kennedy had exhibited when Pat advised him to be sensible and drop out of the vice-presidential race in 1956, Jerry said "No."

Unfortunately for the young California governor, there was no miracle in New York. Instead of the upset victory he had dreamed of, Jerry came home with nothing more than a suitcase full of feature stories probing the inner workings of his self-declared "uncandidacy." Speculations on his sex life seemed to be of particular interest to reporters just then. A highly placed *People Magazine* source wrote, "There is just nothing sensual about him. I can imagine him screwing a woman, but I can't imagine him making love." On the other hand, according to the Sunday supplement *Parade,* a woman who dated Brown found him to be "one of the brightest, most ironically witty men I've ever met. Also one of the most sexy."

Yet, as he unpacked in Sacramento, Jerry was not depressed. Although he was both understaffed and undercapitalized, he had won an impressive string of primary victories while demonstrating remarkable personal charisma and rapport with the youthful audiences that would form a solid base for future campaigns. Brown took particular pride in a lengthy cover story by Peter Chowka in *New Age Magazine* which pointed out he "has been touched by the revolution in consciousness of the last decade. He presently counts among his friends Ram Dass and the Buddhist poet Gary Snyder. Among his favorite writers are Hermann Hesse, Henry Miller, Doris Lessing and the Zen Catholic Thomas Merton. He is perhaps the highest elected official to participate regularly in Buddhist and Trappist retreats. He hints that meditation is a part of his regimen." Friends like Ram Dass praised Brown's "higher consciousness" that enabled him to "redesign the entire meaning and game of politics. . . .

"Adjectives like 'detached, enigmatic, mysterious, aloof,' though overused, still come to mind. Brown is in so many ways unlike any other political animal; rendering a precise description of him therefore in purely political terms, is truly difficult . . ."

The Great Seal of California

"We are going to look up, as we look down, as we look within"

CHAPTER II

Dennis Ghenke had just rounded the corner into the kitchen when he spotted the familiar red, hourglass-shaped spider crawling out of the trash compactor. Instinctively he whirled and swatted the glossy arachnid, lifted the corpse from the floor and flushed it down one of eight toilets in the $1.3 million residence.

Since agreeing to guard the governor's mansion Jerry Brown refused to move into, the General Services Administration's watchman had become something of an entymologist. Every day dozens of species died by his hand. And after taking the lives of more than a hundred black widows, he didn't fear the dread spider any more than an ordinary housefly.

Roaming the eleven-acre estate built in a walnut orchard, Ghenke tried to visualize what the mansion might look like if the Governor moved in. Certainly the peaceful feeling of the place would be changed by the sound of voices and surely they would install the missing hot tub and swimming pool. But Brown had refused to make the twenty-five minute drive to Carmichael to even look at the mansion, explaining, "It's a huge place with nine bedrooms and six bathrooms—I'd feel like Casper the Ghost wandering through it. Besides, I don't think it's appropriate for a governor to live like that when so many people are being asked to sacrifice."

In spite of the mansion being deserted, it often seemed as if other presences were around. "It's hard to explain, but sometimes I get the feeling someone is in the house watching me," said Ghenke. "No matter what I do, I just can't shake that notion."

The caretakers of the mansion were not the only people in Sacramento to sense an extraordinary presence. By the end of Jerry Brown's second year, the governor's office itself had become a meeting place for poets, visionaries, Zen priests, astronauts, Sufi dancers, and even some psychedelic heroes from the old Haight-Ashbury days. To traditionalists accustomed to a procession of politicians, accountants, lawyers and a scattering of buttoned-down celebrities, it was a nightmare.

At first, some of the Governor's less conventional visitors escaped notice amidst the rapid turnover of the demanding Brown administration. Indeed, it was hard to tell visitors from the always changing staff. Employment director Jim Lorenz, press secretaries Dave Jensen and Bill Stall, Legislative Secretary Marc Poche, Resources Secretary Claire Dedrick, Agriculture and Services Secretary Rose Bird, Business and Transportation Secretary Don Burns, and Legislative Aide Preble Stolz were just a few of Brown's early appointees who opted out, were asked to leave, or were transferred to positions in the courts or on commissions. Many others who had come to Sacramento at some personal sacrifice to lend their talents and energies to the new administration, were surprised to find that they couldn't survive Jerry Brown's boot camp.

Musical chairs at the cabinet level meant names on the Governor's hot line phone console were always out-of-date. For a while, a light-hearted proposal circulated that secretarial name plates on agency buildings around town be replaced with chalkboards. As people came and went, it was apparent the distance Jerry kept between himself and many of his aides had certain advantages. For instance, after fired Employment Development Director Jim Lorenz announced he was going to write a critical book on the administration, chief-of-staff Gray Davis was able to point out, "he only saw the Governor three times during his career up here."

Part of the reason Brown didn't see his top aides on a regular basis was his unusual schedule. Unlike his father, Jerry didn't divide his day in fifteen-minute blocks. He preferred to deal with pressing issues on an ad hoc basis. And while the matter at hand — whether it be farm workers' union problems, a water resource project, or a proposal for a waterless toilet — received his undivided attention, unrelated matters, even if important, remained on the back burner.

Understandably, Jerry's insistence on doing his own research on issues that interested him slowed decision-making. While those around him often fretted because important issues went undecided while the Governor plunged into some new enthusiasm, Jerry himself was unperturbed, commenting: "Man has never been consuming so much as we're consuming now. We're consuming information. That's one way of looking at it. We're consuming products: food, cars, people, relationships, space, time. It seems to me the acceleration of consumption is such that we've never had to face what we are today and unless you slow that down, people just get dizzy."

When Jerry said he wanted "to slow things down so I understand them better," he was also talking about the way many of his aides made decisions as if they were on an assembly line. He felt that if his questions changed the way people thought, decisions might be delayed but would be the better for it. "If you ask something in a way that really seeks out the meaning of the situation or the assumptions on which a statement was made, that requires a pause and requires a reflection . . . the traditional satyagraha. Isn't that what Gandhi talked about—'expose the truth in the situation and then people, by recognizing it, are moved by it?' . . . People who stand for an idea that has energy connected with it, that's power . . ."

But Jerry's passion for questioning everyone and everything went deeper than his desire for informed decisions. Jerry was simply a very curious man. This was another reason why he surrounded himself with people who were examining the mind-boggling problems of post-industrial society from odd, interesting and hopefully enlightening angles. Buckminster Fuller, Gary Snyder, Gregory Bateson, Herman Kahn, Rusty Schweickart, Sim Van der Ryn and Thomas Szasz were merely the first wave of intellectuals and New Age pioneers sought out by Brown. Like Teddy Roosevelt, who found the presidency to be a "Bully Pulpit," Jerry was exhilarated by the notion that whomever he invited to the Capitol was almost always sure to come. For example, when he wanted to deepen his understanding of Buddhist economics, he arranged a visit with *Small is Beautiful* author E.F. Schumacher. When he wanted to discuss Zen Buddhist attitudes toward capital punishment, he spent an evening with Baker-roshi at the San Francisco Zen

Center. Because Jerry's interests were wide-ranging, so too were his guests. At one time or another he invited experts to enlighten him on waterless privies, alchemy, solar cow washers, new games, jojoba oil and collapsible bicycles. Unlike other politicians, Brown looked beyond corporate skyscrapers and university labs for ideas. If this meant raiding ashrams, fiberglass domes, monasteries, back-to-the-land communes and New Age think tanks, well, why not?

When it came time to plan the January 1976 Governor's Prayer Breakfast, Jacques Barzaghi came up with a unique idea. Instead of the usual inter-denominational choirs and non-sectarian sermons, why not invite Marin County's Sufi Choir to sing and dance for the 1,400 government workers and business guests? Surprisingly, the ceremony worked, and many people who previously thought Sufi meant either a small dog or raw fish at a Japanese restaurant, were delighted. Like other Barzaghi productions, this one succeeded in sending a friendly signal to devotees of religions gaining favor with the younger generation, as well as enlightening many members of Sacramento's political ghetto.

One problem with the diverse ideas which moved through the Governor's office was that they were speeding through so fast the Governor had difficulty fully assimilating them. Although he was a quick study, there were times when his seemingly erudite references masked only partial digestion of ideas. He was criticized for this in publications ranging from *Rolling Stone* to the *New York Review of Books*. In the rock journal, a Maryland student asked the Governor his reaction to the last two chapters of *Small is Beautiful* (where Schumacher called for a gradual conversion to a system of decentralized socialism, with the workers and communities controlling the factories).

"Well," said Brown, "I'm not sure I know what you're referring to. Those last chapters are kind of vague."

"They were the only specific chapters in the book," argued *Rolling Stone*'s reporter Joe Klein.

"Well, to tell you the truth," admitted Brown, "I only skimmed them."

And when the *New York Review*'s Gary Wills, who had devoted a chapter of his book, *Bare Ruined Choirs,* to Teilhard, tried to discuss the Jesuit philosopher, Brown begged off. "Oh, I don't feel I really understand him."

The fact that Jerry remained uncertain about the teachings of Schumacher and Teilhard said more about his attention span than it did about his intelligence. The Governor was interested in their ideas, to be sure, but they were only some of the many competing belief systems vying for his time. Given the demands of office, it was impossible for him to master all the subjects that interested him. That was why his insights at times seemed a mile wide and only a few inches deep. Brown appreciated this problem and tried to be honest about it. That was why he spent so much of his time doing fact-finding and bringing up ideas for discussion. Without professing to know the answers himself, he hoped to at least begin asking the right questions.

An important part of Jerry's approach involved a technique he learned from his father—the surprise visit. Suspicious of "red carpet tours," Pat Brown dropped in, unannounced, at several mental health facilities in 1959. Like many states, California's mental hospitals had become holding institutions for thousands of patients. Soon after he took office, Pat arranged for two undercover agents to become orderlies at Ventura's Camarillo State Hospital. The cuckoo's nest-like atmosphere they described in their report read like a horror story. Almost every charge that had been levied against the managers of these facilities—from staff brutality to feces-strewn corridors—proved true. Appalled, Pat brought in a new health director who established modern programs and replaced the menial aides known as "bughousers," with a better-trained cadre of paramedics called psychiatric technicians. Not surprisingly, many patients written off as hospital lifers began showing significant improvement and were eventually released.

Committed to monitoring the progress of the new programs, Pat continued making impromptu visits to the facilities. "Frequently I literally slipped into a mental hospital by the back door, alone or perhaps with only one aide," he explained. "I did not arrive with an entourage of staff assistants, experts and television cameras. On these visits, I did not want a ballyhooed publicity circus."

Many of Pat's improvements were early targets of Ronald Reagan's fiscal austerity program. The Republican announced his intention to cut the mental health budget by $17.7 million, fire 3,700 employees, shut down 14 outpatient psychiatric clinics, close a 400-bed alcohol treatment center, eliminate 80 state hospital wards and dismiss the state's psychiatric technicians. Although adverse public reaction persuaded Reagan to soften his position, he succeeded in shutting down the clinics and reducing the mental hospital payroll by 2,000 during his first term.

Cuts like these led to overcrowding, seriously undermining the effectiveness of many surviving Pat Brown programs. By the time Jerry took office, frightening stories about the hospitals again appeared regularly in his daily news summary. When Jerry did not take timely action on these reports, friends like Supreme Court Justice Tobriner began to worry that perhaps he lacked his father's compassion for this forgotten minority. Tobriner pointed out to Jerry that many of these Californians, who were doubled up in dirty wards, inadequately fed, and poorly supervised, knew far too much about the meaning of lowered expectations. Arguably, Jerry might be doing the middle-class a favor when he urged them to stop calling out to Sacramento or Washington to solve all their problems and start developing their own community resources, but what about the plight of these disturbed people whose inner reserves were depleted? "Jerry, you've got to empathize more with the people," Tobriner urged.

The Governor found this suggestion somewhat disturbing. Maybe he was isolating himself like a college professor drifting away from teaching to the laboratory. Perhaps he had been spending too much time with intellectuals to keep in close touch with the human condition. "I feel as governor I should experience what other people experience," announced Brown as he began a series of impromptu visits to the state hospitals, just as his father had done nearly twenty years earlier. Pacing the wards with a media accompaniment, he held the hands of bedridden patients and announced this was the ideal place to begin "a new era of welcoming citizens to share in the work of civilized society." The Governor suggested Californians might find more meaning in their lives by volunteering at their neighborhood mental hospital. If they would just donate a few hours a day, mental health costs would drop and so would state taxes. More important, the people who took the time to help would probably learn a great deal about themselves.

Jerry's interest in the problems of the mentally ill reflected some of the thinking of a man who was the bete noire of orthodox psychiatry, Dr. Thomas Szasz. The controversial physician told Jerry that as long as government continued subsidizing medical care, the demand for it would be limitless. In part, that was because it was difficult to define who actually needed treatment. According to Szasz, working toward a solution of what was called mental illness meant recasting the "whole nonsense about mental illness into ordinary language . . . into problems of housing, of economics, of family relations . . . I believe that if the psychiatrization of our society could be reversed, if psychiatric power could be reduced or abolished, then people would be forced to assume more responsibility for their lives. There would be much less deviance than we now have."

Clearly, the radical change of attitude toward mental illness that Szasz advocated was unlikely, and in any case, more profound than anything Jerry could accomplish. But community volunteers would at least provide some sorely-needed assistance and at the same time help keep costs down. The response to Jerry's petition for volunteers was disappointing. Many of those showing up were Hare Krishnas and Scientologists, who made hospital employees nervous. But both groups were finally welcomed when their leaders promised not to proselytize and the

179

Krishna people even agreed to leave their saffron robes at home.

Unable to institute Szasz's extreme ideas and to generate interest in his volunteer program, the Governor began mapping out a more conventional $70 million plan to upgrade state hospitals. While details of this program were being put together, one of the Governor's earlier triumphs—the Agricultural Labor Relations Board—threatened to unravel and he was forced to shift much of his attention to the crisis in the fields.

Since his Secretary of State days, Brown had been a close friend of Cesar Chavez's United Farm Workers Union. In 1972 he helped discredit and defeat an agribusiness initiative to make the fields an open shop by pointing out that many of the signatures turned in to qualify this ballot measure were obtained illegally. Three years later, after Jerry was elected Governor, the farm workers were one of the first beneficiaries of the new administration. During marathon bargaining sessions, Brown persuaded the growers to compromise on their longstanding opposition to union representation. After more than a decade of lettuce boycotts, 100-mile marches, and other protests, the Governor coaxed these bitter antagonists into signing a peace pact in Sacramento. This historic measure, which received the legislature's blessing in the form of the Agricultural Labor Relations Act, established a commission to supervise representation elections (ALRB). For the first time, Mexican-American field workers were brought under the umbrella of meaningful government protection.

One of the first discoveries of the new ALRB commissioners, however, was that the $6.8 million budgeted wasn't nearly enough to carry out their mandate to supervise all necessary elections. And when requests for a supplemental $3.8 million appropriation were turned down by the legislature at the behest of agribusiness interests, the ALRB was out of business. By February 1976 representation elections stopped. In response, the farm workers promptly began gathering signatures for an initiative that would force the legislature to appropriate the additional $3.8 million. Brown plunged into this dispute, supporting the union's demand for more funding. And while the initiative itself was defeated in November 1976, the Governor helped the ALRB get more state funding to resume monitoring elections.

Knowing any successful political leader had to stay in the public's eye, Jerry looked for another cause to champion. John Kennedy, for example, had identified himself with the plight of coal miners in West Virginia during his presidential campaign and had used that identification as a metaphor to illustrate his deep concern for the down-trodden. Was there something comparable Jerry could do in California? One possibility was to simply walk across the street and commiserate with the habitues of California's wine country—the downtown shopping mall. No, Jerry's advisors concluded, the imagery wasn't quite right. Americans didn't love the unemployed if they clutched bottles of Ripple. Brown finally found the cause he needed in San Francisco, with the help of his friend Percy Pinkney from Hunter's Point who he had met while working there as a college student volunteer. It was the eleven-story Yerba Buena Annex on Turk Street in the Fillmore section of the city, just a few blocks from where Pat had grown up. The project, known by its 211 resident families as the Pink Palace, was the kind of place where children saw more rats than dogs and cats and lived amidst constant murders, rapes, armed robberies, muggings, and drug-pushing.

After work one Friday night in early January, Brown changed from his grey pinstripes into a lumberjack shirt and slacks, flew down to San Francisco and hopped into Pinkney's unmarked panel truck which was waiting for him at the airport. The former leader of the Aces headed up the Bayshore Freeway to the area dominated by shabby apartment houses and storefronts shuttered with iron gates. Pinkney drove the Governor around the projects until he had seen his fill of hookers and pimps. Then the two men headed up to the $84-a-month, four room apartment of Virginia Herrera, who was recently featured in a *San Francisco Chronicle* story on the troubled highrise. "I have come to see for myself the conditions which exist and what is going on," explained the Governor to Mrs. Herrera.

On his tour of the building, Jerry met tenants who had lost the entire contents of their apartments, even their beds, to vandals, and was told that some occupants were afraid to go to sleep at night out of fear for their children and belongings. The Governor was told that project dealers moved more drugs in a day than did many pharmacists.

"Hey, Governor, can you get me a job?" one junkie asked Brown as they rode an elevator together.

"I'm trying to do something about the employment picture in this state. We're going to get the Employment Development Department working on it," Jerry replied.

Back in Mrs. Herrera's apartment, Jerry munched barbecued chicken and listened to a neighboring mother complain about the difficulty of motivating children to strive for something decent. "They see the pimps and the pushers doing good every day. So what's the use of trying? It makes no difference anyway."

Brown was sympathetic. "It used to be that there were two parts of town and that if you worked hard, you could move to the other side of town," he later told a reporter. "But in a lot of cases, it's not working."

Later, the Governor prepared to unroll a sleeping bag Percy had brought along. But Mrs. Herrera insisted on sending two daughters downstairs to stay with a neighbor so Jerry could use their room. Percy slept on the floor. As it turned out, it didn't make much difference where they bedded down, as neither man could sleep because of the noise outside.

In the morning, Jerry and Percy breakfasted on eggs and biscuits and then looked on as welfare mothers clustered in the downstairs lobby to grab their checks from the postman before thieves had a chance to snatch the payments from the mailboxes.

"This is Governor Brown," said Pinkney, trying to break the ice with tenants.

"Who you kidding?" asked one of the women, breaking into a laugh.

Only when the tenants saw reporters approaching the project were they persuaded that Mrs. Herrera's overnight guest was no imposter. The press got some fine pictures of Jerry standing amidst heaps of uncollected garbage next to a wall defaced with graffiti. Then Jerry posed with Mrs. Herrera, denouncing the society which had created this sort of horror chamber. "People are afraid to go out of their homes," he said. "People are living in fear. The garbage is all over. The electricity doesn't work. The mailboxes are ripped off. The dope-sellers and hypes are all around. This is the flip side of progress. It's a crazy scene. It's very far from the American dream."

From the projects, the Governor and Percy drove to a nearby church on Geary Boulevard to attend a memorial service for Martin Luther King, Jr. Mayor George Moscone was also there, but Brown spent most of his time rehashing his experience at the Pink Palace with city police chief Charles Gain. Outside the church, the Governor announced to city officials he would allocate funds to beef up Pink Palace security.

Some of the media were not impressed, however, and several editorial writers later suggested Jerry could never solve complex social problems with the Buddhist economics he'd been preaching for the past two years. "The poor cannot lower their expectations much further," editorialized the *San Jose Mercury*. "Jerry Brown needs to go back to Sacramento and consider how he can help the economy expand so that jobs will be created to spring them from the poverty trap."

Jerry realized that he faced a peculiarly twentieth century philosophical dilemma. How could he reconcile Schumacher's version of small, human-scale industries with the state's need for rapid industrial expansion? This problem was dramatized when several large firms announced their interest in establishing large plants that didn't meet the state's environmental standards. Brown's administration had recently taken a lot of heat for not supporting construction of a new Dow Chemical plant on the Sacramento River Delta, because of the high probability of serious air pollution. Now there was even more pressure to junk environmental safeguards to make room for plants that would employ thousands of Californians.

When none of his career civil servants could come up with a feasible way to integrate job-producing, heavy industry and the New Age, Jerry sought out new part-time employee, Stewart Brand. This retired Merry Prankster, who earned his place in counter-culture folklore by serving LSD to guests at San Francisco's 1966 Trips Festival, went on to publish the Whole Earth Catalogue. Then, he amazed even those comfortable with the bizarre and unusual by having a party and giving away a large portion of the profits to anyone who put out a hand.

In the 1970's, Brand founded and edited the *Co-Evolution Quarterly*, a New Age cross between *Popular Mechanics* and *Scientific American*, with just enough R. Crumb comics and articles by intellectual heroes like Gregory Bateson to keep readers on their toes. Just as every intellectual of the late 1920's had a copy of H.L. Mencken's *American Mercury* on the coffee table and no liberal knight in John Kennedy's Camelot could ride into battle without a copy of the *New Republic*, the *Co-Evolution Quarterly* was the Bible of the New Age intellectuals surrounding Jerry Brown.

By 1977, Brand had become one of the most important new faces in the Brown administration even though he only spent one day a week in Sacramento. And it fell to him to reveal how Jerry could promote rapid economic expansion without trashing the environment. Brand proposed making California the scientific capital of the world and suggested the best way to accomplish this was to reach for the stars. The state, he contended, should become the launching pad both for space colonization and the clean, hi-tech industries it would generate.

Jerry was fascinated with Brand's ideas; but how did you get a space program going, the Governor wondered. Again, Jerry was talking to the right person. Brand had been a space enthusiast for years and even had a relationship of sorts with NASA dating back to the mid-sixties, when he wandered around Berkeley, Harvard, MIT and Columbia in a white jumpsuit and top hat wearing a signboard asking: "Why haven't we seen a picture of the whole earth yet?" Thanks to this well-publicized campaign and the efforts of others, NASA did release black and white satellite pictures of the earth in 1967, followed by color prints in 1968. In the process, Brand learned his way around the space program and later placed a picture of the earthshot from space on the cover of his vastly popular catalogue. To him, the photograph was "the mandala for the ecological religion gradually taking shape that would unite people of many different faiths."

One of the young NASA people most impressed by Brand's self-styled campaign was Astronaut Rusty Schweickart, who circled the moon on Apollo 9 in 1969. Now parked at a Payload Department desk job, the astronaut was discouraged by Congress' refusal to give NASA the increase necessary to speed up outer space development. He had written a lively article in the *Co-Evolution Quarterly* about the potential of orbiting colonies advocated by Princeton physicist Gerard O'Neill. When Brand got Schweickart together with Brown and suggested that Jerry might want to follow up his recent "Whale Day" event with a Space Day, Schweickart had a brainstorm. Why not time it in conjunction with the first free flight of the Space Shuttle Enterprise in August? It would be the biggest boost for NASA since the Kennedy era.

Brown liked the idea. He could revive Kennedy's dwindling space program and, by linking it to the ecology movement, turn a six-minute flight into one of the most important journeys since Columbus weighed anchor on the Santa Maria. Here was the next giant step for mankind in Teilhard's "dynamic evolutionary sweep upwards and onwards." As presiding Governor, he could become America's pioneer whole earth statesman, and the first write-in candidate for President of the Universe.

NASA was ecstatic about the Governor of California's willingness to invest in the space program. To build the case for Space Day, NASA put together a morning-long symposium at its Ames Laboratory in Sunnyvale. Experts gathered in an effort to show the Governor how satellite technology could be applied to the state's resource problems in areas like soil conservation, hydrology and forest practices. Among authorities assembled for this July 1977 program was Professor Donna Haskins of Humboldt State University. Well-versed in space satellite reconnaissance of Northern California forest resources, Haskins brought topographic maps demonstrating soil erosion in the Eel River, clear-cutting of the forests, and even the spread of the north coast marijuana farms many experts thought were now California's largest cash crop. She believed that detailed satellite photos of Northern California would be helpful in resource planning and management.

After Haskins explained her NASA research for five minutes in the over-crowded Moffett Field research office, Governor Brown began to fire questions at her and she suddenly found herself on the defensive.

"Now what do you do with this information? What's the practical payoff?" Brown demanded. "What are you trying to get? What happens at the end of the line?"

"Information like this is control information," explained Haskins clutching her laminated government dog tag.

"Are you trying to find out how many trees there are? How many fish there are? What is it? What's the practical payoff?"

"The status of hardwood in the region."

"I thought lumber companies already know that."

"They have never taken these surveys."

"I think," interjected Rusty Schweickart, "that the Governor wants to know how you apply this information."

But before Haskins could respond, Brown cut her off: "I'm still trying to find out what you get."

"We're trying to find out what the problems are," replied Haskins.

"One of the big controversies is the extent of erosion caused by cutting redwoods. Some say that the cutting causes siltation that leads to flooding in the creek and jeopardizes precious trees by undermining their root structure. But the lumber companies say all that is caused by cutting done 20 years ago."

"We are looking at that."

"How do you do that?"

"Look," she screamed at the Governor, "I'm not a geologist. I'm a scientist. I hire people."

Brown kept on firing questions with the consistency of a pitching machine as Schweickart cupped a hand to his mouth and whispered to a neighboring NASA official: "It's hard to get him to understand. He doesn't see the payoff. He thinks the agencies have all this information when they really don't."

That afternoon, NASA's Gerard O'Neill talked with the Governor about some of the possible payoffs of space colonization. Listening to the physicist's admittedly grandiose vision, Jerry was fascinated by the possibility, however remote, that man would have a second chance to create a sensible society in a wholesome new environment. Of course, there were political risks—people accustomed to his sermons about an era of limits were sure to have difficulty adjusting to billions spent for space colonization. And environmentalists of the back-to-Walden Pond school might well cringe both at the price tag and also because so many other fruits of technology—such as automobiles, pesticides, and nuclear power—had created vast new problems in the name of solving old ones. But Jerry believed any vision as large as mankind moving into space was sure to arouse opposition.

In the Governor's mind, the exploration of space was assigned a position fundamentally different from other government programs. In an age when even liberals acknowledged that public funds had not solved social ills, something revolutionary was needed. True, Roosevelt and his followers, like Pat Brown, had helped millions of Americans with programs like social security and Medicare, and even Jerry's own California Conservation Corps had been successful. Still, the government remained unable to guarantee everyone a decent standard of living, good education, quality health care and other basic necessities of life. Now, in the mid-seventies, even people who believed government had to maintain a safety net of social programs to protect the poor, old and infirm were beginning to admit the country lacked the political and financial resources to make FDR's dream of a comfortable life for all a reality.

One constructive new approach, Jerry believed, was to tap some of the imaginative resources in California's higher education system to create new technologies. But in addition to looking for ways to implement these bright ideas on earth, O'Neill and others now convinced the Governor it was wise to also pay attention to the high frontier, where revolutionary change was possible. On paper, what O'Neill proposed made sense. Just as it was easier to walk in a gravity-free world, it was easier to build new structures where environmental impact statements weren't required. And as long as cheap energy could be beamed back to earth, financing construction of space colonies would be no problem.

Jerry Brown was hooked. He hired Rusty Schweickart and committed himself to going ahead with Space Day. California's first astronaut moved into a windowless office in the research section of the Capitol and soon plans for Space Day were in full swing. Celebrities like Carl Sagan and Jacques Cousteau enthusiastically agreed to attend, as Brown's aides started joking about pinning on Junior Bird Man wings. Not to be outdone, Jacques Barzaghi went to work on a whole earth mural that would dominate the Space Day podium, while press secretary Elisabeth Coleman began stuffing hundreds of blue kits with posters of the Viking mission, LANDSAT photomosaics of the 48 contiguous states, and Enterprise paintings suitable for framing. Receptionists cleared the walls of the Governor's lobby to accommodate an exhibit of Mars photographs, and propped up an astronaut mannequin in a chair. Many visitors touched the lifelike dummy to assure themselves it was not one of Rusty Schweickart's friends.

In the weeks before Space Day, the Govenor was in an excited mental orbit that left little time for the terrestrial problems of California. Policy decisions languished as Brown rushed off with Brand and Schweickart to tour NASA facilities. Staff meetings were cancelled as the Governor donned a bunny suit to climb aboard the Enterprise for a guided tour with astronaut Deke Slayton. And those who did get to see Jerry were hard put to explain to him how their earth-bound programs could be of help in space.

Finally, in early August 1977, the big day arrived. Among the space groupies who showed up was ex-Harvard professor Timothy Leary. Although not invited to the dias, he managed to give nearly as many interviews as Jerry Brown. Skipping over inquiries about new revelations that the LSD he slipped his early 1960's Harvard students was financed by covert CIA grants, Leary endorsed O'Neill's nirvana. This man who had gained fame behind the slogan "turn on, tune in, drop out" moved about in baggy white slacks embracing technocrats whose main concern was going straight up. For more than a year, old friends had ridiculed Leary's impassioned ravings about the evolutionary necessity of starting fresh in outer space. But now, with O'Neill and Brown, he found both the prophet and architect necessary for the practical advancement of his view that man must embrace the cosmos. "Intelligent people can't help but favor this. It's a great imperative. We're getting squeezed out the same way intellectuals were pushed out of Europe in the eighteenth and nineteenth centuries. All the good people moved here from the old world and then gradually the east coast filled up and people began to realize that California was a better place to be. Now there is nowhere left for smart Americans to go but out into high orbit. I love that phrase (high orbit) all the NASA people use. We were talking about high orbit long before the space program."

Bubbling with enthusiasm, the psychedelic prince almost jogged over to congratulate the man responsible for this quantum leap in political thinking. The slim, forty-year-old Governor with a retreating hairline and an artful touch of grey at the temples looked around to make sure no photographers were watching before smiling and shaking hands with Leary. Only Jerry's flushed right cheek betrayed his outward calm. (Even his doctor, Jerome Lackner, couldn't explain why one side of the Governor's face went crimson in moments of stress.)

To confirm the significance of the event Brown equated with "the gold rush and the creation of the airplane industry," he gave both the opening and closing remarks. After thanking Stewart Brand for "showing me that ecology and technology find a unity in space," he explained: "We are going into space as a species. It is only a question of when and who and what kind of leadership will take us there. You have to keep on going, you have to keep on pushing because that is the human impulse. And instead of fighting it or ignoring it, you have to develop it and respect it and encourage it and celebrate it.

"As I try to sum up all this," said Brown, "I don't know whether I have all the words to do it. But as I was sitting there listening to the last speaker, mulling over in my mind what I might say, I remembered reading an article in a British publication that said something about America being on the decline, being where England was a few decades ago. I, for one, don't really believe that. Through the sixties we've seen a lot of problems, some not too many miles from here. Just about twelve years ago to the day, the Watts riots were in progress and this was a battle station. Since that time we've had the Vietnam War and Watergate and a number of things. But throughout all that turmoil we've still pushed forward so that tomorrow morning we can take a look at the space shuttle and all experience the excitement that brings to our state, to our country and to the whole planet.

"As we sit in this audience, people not too many blocks from here, many of them from very modest backgrounds, low income, even poverty backgrounds, are looking to a future. Through two-way communications, using satellite and instructional television we can take the work in the Mediterranean, at Harvard, at Berkeley, right into the ghettos and the low-income high schools and let the young people of this state sense what is possible. We can inspire them and summon up the talent that they have.

"We don't know if all these ideas that have been spun out about the future will work—some of them may be failures—but there's no doubt that we're going to look up, as we look down, as we look within.

"This is a rather limited piece of material that we all inhabit. It is a world of limits—limits psychologically, spiritually, politically, ecologically—but through respecting and reverencing the limits, endless possibilities emerge. As I look out into space and as I look at the possibilities that an expanding universe and an expanding exploration of that universe make possible, I sense in my own mind not only immediate benefits in a practical economic sense but in a far more profound way for the people of this earth. The earth map is drenched in the blood of a thousand, a million conflicts over recorded history. We're divided among arbitrary geographical lines, separated into ethnic categories, and divided along various linguistic groups. But when we look at the earth and the human species from a few hundred miles up, we can't help but sense the oneness of the human race and of this species that has been part of the universe for such a limited period of time.

"I also think of the closing frontier, the closing of the west and what that does to the psychology of people. As long as there is a safety valve of unexplored frontiers, the creative, the aggressive, the exploitative urges of human beings can be channeled into long-term possibilities and benefits. But as those frontiers close down and people begin to turn in upon themselves—that jeopardizes the democratic fabric. The mind of man will develop and will expand technologies. Some of them are destructive. Some of them kill millions of people. And some of them open up untold new horizons. That is where space is.

"It's not a waste of money, it's not a depleting asset, it's an expanding asset and through the creation of new wealth we make possible the redistribution of more wealth to those who don't have it. When we look at the underdeveloped countries, we want a planet that they can inherit and we want a quality of life that they can have. And they're not going to get it unless we make the investments to stretch and challenge all the thinking that the human mind is capable of.

"When the day of manufacturing in space occurs and extraterrestrial material is added into the economic equation, then the old economic rules no longer apply. That's a moment and a time that many of us are going to witness . . . It's all there just waiting for you and the rest of the people who stand behind you throughout this world waiting to get into the oceans — to understand ourselves and create the quality of life that our evolutionary potential really justifies."

Jerry finished to a standing ovation. "We've got to go all the way in all directions," cried Jacques Cousteau from his seat beside the Governor.

Just then, guests sitting near the exit heard the chanting voices outside. Investigation revealed they were from a delegation representing five-hundred bus drivers recently laid-off by the L.A. Rapid Transit District. "Jobs on Earth, Not in Space," cried the unemployed pickets police kept cordoned away from Space Day participants climbing into an Apollo 14 command module. Helmeted officers pushed the frustrated bus drivers back when the Governor crossed the street to join a catered buffet dinner in progress in the main museum building. Spotting a woman waving a "Brown hire an earthling" placard, the Governor halted.

"What's this all about?" he asked.

"Governor," said the demonstrator, "how can you talk about spending all this money on going into space when the city doesn't even have enough funds to maintain bus service at the present inadequate levels. We need jobs."

"Well, unemployment is coming down from ten percent to seven percent."

"That doesn't help us much."

"I don't have all the answers. If I could figure out the answers, I would. But I'm working on it."

"Don't forget us, Governor. People don't need rockets, they need buses."

"I don't know about buses. What do you think about buses?"

Before any of the demonstrators could come back with an answer, the Governor was in pursuit of the cocktail hot dogs, tacos and spicy meatballs, which he found on tables scattered amidst the technological exhibits.

Most of the guests that evening were only mildly interested in museum displays of old technologic triumphs like the Harbor Freeway and Hoover Dam. The only exhibit most people queued up for was Jerry Brown. Just about everyone wanted a close look at the man who was linking western civilization's future with the space shuttle. While President Carter had allowed inflation to reduce NASA's launching power, Jerry Brown promised to reawaken John Kennedy's grand vision of man leaving his home planet, and at the same time, advocated an intellectual synthesis of space exploration and environmentalism. Some staff members, like state architect Sim Van Der Ryn and energy advisor Wilson

Clark, argued that Brown's promoting the space program diverted much-needed attention and money for more immediate concerns at home. Denying he was a traitor for advocating leaving the mother planet, Brown felt there wasn't a moment to lose: "Move fast when you know you're right."

Sipping Napa Valley chablis after supper, the Governor witnessed the beginning of his conceptual merger. Jacques Cousteau, in a black jumpsuit, articulated the many ways satellite surveillance could help save the oceans. Then NASA administrator Robert Frosch told Brown his agency would be delighted to match a $100,000 state grant for whale spotting with heat sensitive monitors. "We could get a pilot thing going. Whales blow out a lot of hot water and create a great deal of activity when they make love."

"What did you think of Space Day?" Gray Davis asked Carl Sagan later that evening on the drive up to the NASA complex at Edwards Air Force Base in the Mojave Desert.

"Oh, I think your Governor's terrific. I really think he's got a lot of integrity. When I sent him my new book, *Dragons of Eden,* Brown wrote me a thank-you note saying he was going to send it to the state library."

"You wouldn't believe the trouble not accepting gifts has caused us."

"Sure, but at least he's honest. He did a great job today. Most politicians think two, or at most six, years ahead. Corporate executives think of the next shareholders meeting. But Brown is different. He's a real visionary who has a chance of moving the space program along. Now, if we could just fire the NASA public relations department."

The next morning wide patches of cirrus clouds rolled across the sky threatening the visibility on this special day. But by the time Brown's party had finished short-cutting through cactus flats, the clouds had moved on to Barstow. At the VIP viewing stand, concessionaires were busy dispensing hot coffee and rolls. Jerry and his guests moved beneath the brown awnings toward color-TV monitors which were trained on the shuttle vehicle piggybacked atop its 747 mother ship. Perhaps Los Angeles Times cartoonist Paul Conrad had summed up this odd technological couple best with a drawing of the pair captioned: "Not tonight, honey, I'm tired."

The guests were excited. The Boeing pilot, they knew, would climb to 24,000 feet before firing the explosive bolts and releasing the Enterprise which was designed to operate on seven-to-thirty-day missions at an altitude of 100 to 600 miles. No longer would expensive ground rocket launches be required to put these unmanned vehicles into orbit. The shuttle, that was designed to eventually take off like an airplane, would handle space-bound payloads like Federal Express. The project's obvious revenue-generating potential delighted assembled dignitaries

190

such as Senator Barry Goldwater, his son, Congressman Barry Goldwater, Jr., and astronaut Harrison Schmidt, who had come back from
space to win a U.S. Senate seat in New Mexico. For the first time,
manned orbiting vehicles would be able to launch, repair and retrieve
satellites.

Many of the two hundred reporters present admitted they were having difficulty reconciling this $100 billion project with their vision of
Jerry Brown. "Governor," ABC's Jules Bergmann asked fifty-one minutes before the launch, "only a short time ago you were advocating less
is more. Now you want to spend all this money in space. How do you
explain this?"

"In space limits are endless. In space there's a chance to sense the
oneness of the human species. Today the NASA budget is only slightly
larger than our state surplus. Given a choice I think most people will
want to invest in space. As shuttles leave here every week, they will
make possible new wealth for solving problems back home. Every state
department is now evaluating application of satellite technology. This
shot today is like closing the last gap in the transcontinental railroad. I
would find it fascinating to fly on the shuttle."

"What do you say to critics who say we can put a man on the moon
but can't solve the problems of our cities?"

"We can be mining the moon in fifteen years."

Following the interview, Brown returned to the viewing stand where
Carl Sagan watched the 747 move toward the flight line on an overhead
screen. "Do you really want to watch this on TV?" asked Brown with
one hand on his binoculars.

"TV makes it real," replied the Cornell guest without taking his eyes
off the screen.

The governor took a folding chair and joined Sagan to watch the
mated ships take off. Nearby someone was passing around copies of a
reader's letter to the editor of a San Francisco newspaper:

"Governor Brown's space program is the most intelligent thing any
politician has done for a long time. Many politicians these days find it
too easy to jump on the bandwagon of overzealous environmentalists.
The industrialized nations are stranded in a technological wasteland.
The way out is not to abandon technology but improve it. We need
more visionaries like Jerry Brown if the planet is to survive today's
paranoid death culture. Von Braun has given us the rocket and gone; it
is up to us now whether it brings us life or death."

Finally it was NASA's turn to make good on Brown's hyperspace
rhetoric. Senator Barry Goldwater, easy to spot in his pink silk shirt,
watched the 747 level off at 24,000 feet, then told a NASA leader
alongside, "This thing better work if you want any more money."

191

"Don't worry, it will," replied his host as explosive bolts detonated on computer signal, sending the now unmated shuttle into a six-mile-long landing pattern which ended in the dusty lake bed. Many Trekkies parked in the viewing area were disappointed, complaining the brief show lacked the fiery color and high decibel roar of Cape Kennedy space shots. But after trailing the descending Enterprise with his binoculars, Jerry Brown was plainly delighted that space colonization could be accomplished with a launch technology civilized enough for neighborhood airports.

By now Rusty Schweickart was jumping up and down. "When I saw the sun rise today, it was the dawn of a new era." The Governor kept time to the astronaut's beat: "When I saw it come down out of the sun, I couldn't help but be struck by limitless possibilities." Even Barry Goldwater was impressed. "Not bad, not bad," said the senator looking over toward Brown. "Now where the hell was he when the California delegation put on its big push for aerospace and defense appropriations last year? He's finally wising up and getting serious about politics. He's finally realized all this environmental emphasis and anti-growth doesn't fly with a guy who has to put a roof over his head and feed a family."

On schedule, the gubernatorial party returned to their Plymouth Satellites for the ride to a waiting Army helicopter. Led by a general who didn't know where he was going, they drove around in circles looking for the aircraft that would take them across the San Bernardino Mountains to visit a solar home project. Jerry hardly noticed they were lost. He was preoccupied with the idea that through NASA he had found a new constituency far larger than his home state. Whether he would be able to turn space lovers into Brown voters was another problem.

And there were still many questions to be answered before Jerry himself would feel completely comfortable with the exploration of space. Would the shuttle be a true mass transit system into space or merely a limousine for a self-selected elite? Were O'Neill's colonies a "self-sufficient paradise" or merely a way for the affluent educated to abandon seemingly hopeless causes, such as the eradication of poverty and hunger on earth. Would the solar power collected by these pioneers be beamed earthward as civilian heat or military death rays? Would the depopulated earth become a Garden of Eden or a nursing home for those who didn't qualify to live in the twilight zone? After all, Jerry was the first to admit that technology's answers to the wretched excesses of the industrial age didn't come with a money-back guarantee. And he didn't need a neurologist to know that looking up, as you looked down, as you looked within could give you a headache.

The Pizza Diplomat

CHAPTER 12

Sad-eyed mothers, feral-faced men, children with twisted shapes, as if reflected in fun-house mirrors, and mushroom-shaped clouds hovering over polluted oceans seemed unlikely subjects for an art exhibit in the Governor's executive offices. Yet these were the paintings that appeared along the corridor where Jerry Brown and his top aides worked after the Martian landscapes exhibited in honor of "Space Day" came down in the fall of 1977. Jacques Barzaghi spent two years assembling the show, chosen from the best work of inmates of the California Department of Corrections. The hit of the show was a picture of a flaming nude redhead, later moved to a private corridor after Barzaghi decided the Governor couldn't have her hanging in the lobby where tourists in polyester suits strolled with their small children. The fantasy goddess from Folsom Prison was finally hung outside Tony Kline's office, increasing traffic to the legal affairs department.

Although no one noticed it the day the exhibit was hung, one portrait painted by a Vacaville inmate/artist bore a striking resemblance to a prominent state leader. If you overlooked the thick neck, weak jaw and Malibu tan, the subject was clearly Edmund G. Brown, Jr. Word spread quickly that the Governor had finally allowed his likeness to hang on the wall of the Capitol. But by the time curious legislators scurried to Brown's office for a peek, the entire exhibit had been crated and returned to the Department of Corrections.

It is true Jerry did not like photographs of himself. After two-and-one-half years in office, he still frustrated school children who successfully collected pictures of the governors of the other forty-nine states by refusing to send his. But this was not the reason the prison art exhibit came down. It was simply that Jerry had conflicting views on the therapeutic value of painting and similar activities to rehabilitate prisoners. The Governor was, in fact, extremely skeptical that any amount of therapy could change people and did not want to be seen as endorsing it.

"I think human nature has some basic fundamental weaknesses that are always going to be there no matter what we do, no matter what psychological studies ever develop or produce or conclude," said Brown. "There is a lot of good that we can do but there is a lot of evil that we are capable of, and that's just the way the world is. I didn't make it that way. I don't find much use or comfort for these great analytical studies of why crime is caused and how we can mold people's minds by various forms of treatment and manipulation and government intervention. I think they have very modest potential. I think we have to tell people that when they are arrested, or they are found guilty, that we may not have the method of changing their minds or winning over their minds and hearts, but we do have a method to at least take them out of circulation."

Jerry Brown had always supported strict law enforcement even if it meant that more men and women went to jail during his administration than under any of his predecessors. He was having trouble selling his compromise $19 billion plan to finish off the California Water Project started by his father seventeen years earlier. His spirited advocacy of conservation, solar energy and other human-scale energy technologies at the expense of nuclear power damaged his relationship with big business. And his August 1977 veto of capital punishment legislation had been over-ridden by the legislature. But he could take solace from the fact that his anti-crime program sailed through both houses without a snag. By the middle of Jerry's third year in office, laws were on the books stipulating those who used a gun in a holdup automatically went to prison, requiring mandatory sentences for parolees who committed violent crimes, making it a felony to threaten others "in order to achieve social or political goals." (Not every new law made penalties harsher, however. California was one of the first states to virtually decriminalize the possession of small amounts of marijuana.)

In addition to tougher criminal laws, Jerry turned the state cookie jar upside down and found $90 million worth of crumbs for new prison construction. But first he took a long, careful look at how money was currently being allocated in existing prisons. Brown believed the state's reserves could no longer subsidize teaching inmates how to carve serpentine and read Chaucer in the vague hope that one day they might join the Kiwanis or become part of cafe society. As a psychology major in college, Brown once toured state mental hospitals to learn how to correct deviant behavior. Now he accepted the inevitability of increased crime and the necessity for larger jails. Law enforcement was not an economic or social issue, but mostly a housing problem, Jerry Brown believed. The cost effective way to protect the public was to "rehabilitate jails, not people... When my father ran for district attorney in 1942," Jerry liked to point out, "he had a little sign with his picture on the front side, and on the back it said 'Crack down on crime, pick Brown this time.' Ever since then, the crime rate has soared. Since 1942 it must have gone up at least 2,000 percent. Through Republican and Democratic administrations the fact remained that for many people in this society, crime in fact pays... you might think that is somewhat pessimistic — I think it is realistic."

When Jerry put through tough anti-crime legislation, he knew he risked angering civil rights allies who saw these bills as a thinly-veiled attempt to round up minorities. Accordingly, Brown linked his crime proposals to needed anti-discrimination legislation supported by the black and Chicano communities.

In September 1977, Brown flew to the Los Angeles International Airport Hyatt House to perform what some aides viewed as a tightrope act without a net. Flanked by all of Southern California's ranking black politicians, Brown put his name to an anti-redlining bill that forced banks to authorize loans in high risk minority communities.

For his second act, Jerry called forward district attorneys from the city and county of Los Angeles, Santa Ana police chief Ray Johnson and Republican Senator George Deukmejian, who planned to run for Attorney General the following year. In rapid succession he signed nine bills to lengthen jail sentences for repeat offenders, limit pornography, quash terrorism, stop attacks on the blind, elderly and disabled, while also granting $1.5 million to supplement local prosecutors' efforts.

"This is quite a significant block of crime legislation signed here today," Brown said. "I don't think it's liberal or conservative, left or right, Republican or Democratic. I think it's an attempt of everyone, regardless of their affiliation, to solve societal problems. Each year I've signed very tough crime measures. My administration has seen more appropriate legislation signed on criminal justice than any administration in the last ten years."

After the ceremony a reporter asked the Governor how he planned to pay for the increased court load generated by his new laws. "We'll get those trials so we won't need as many judges in Los Angeles," said Brown, turning to face another reporter.

"How does this relate to your opposition to the death penalty?"

"There is no dichotomy. It's part of a continual effort to make this a safer place."

But what about the fact that tough law and order bills would hit hardest in minority areas where unemployment caused the state's worst crime problems? Wouldn't this hurt the Governor's support with blacks and Chicanos who had opposed Reagan's attempts to enact similar measures?

"He can get away with it," replied Los Angeles County Supervisor Hahn, the man who had appointed Jerry to the Delinquency Commission back in 1967, "because he has a liberal image. Minorities will support him."

"You bet," replied Senator Holden, a Hahn protege who had begun his political career in the supervisor's office. "Reagan would probably not have introduced bills this tough. It would have been embarrassing to him. But they can't embarrass us. This goes to show that the Democrats are the real crime fighters."

While the two men continued talking, reporters had begun to fire questions at the Governor about a topic more important to many than crime — taxes. In recent years there had been several unsuccessful legislative attempts to limit property taxes which, in some areas, were rising at a rate of twenty-five to fifty percent a year and threatening the ability of some Californians to live in their own homes.

"There are political considerations at work," said Brown to a blue minicam. "When liberals get something, conservatives want something and vice versa. I'm worried about the middle-class property owner. Some want limits on local government spending and some want more police, more jails, more gas chambers, more roads, childcare for children, better schools, nursing homes for parents. I'm going to veto most of the legislation increasing spending because I want to see if people really want it. . . ."

Then, in answer to a question about the 1984 Olympic games, Jerry added, "I paid my own way to the Olympic committee meeting in Denver. I want a Spartan Olympics in Los Angeles. An 'era of limits'

Olympics. I don't say they have to sleep in church basements, but I don't want Olympics in the spirit of Rome in its declining era. I want a return to the spirit of Sparta . . ."

But though the 1984 Olympics were important to many, Jerry was more concerned with a problem he'd neglected during his first years in office — how to attract new industry to California. Dow Chemical's recent decision to cancel a Delta plant because of California's tough Brown-sponsored environmental restrictions suggested to many that the Governor was no friend of big business. Indeed, executives surveyed by a private survey research organization ranked California forty-ninth among the states in receptivity to corporate interests. And labor union interests and others were concerned that the Governor had shown little concern about trying to reduce the state's perennial unemployment problem.

One way to try to negate the perception that he was anti-big business was through the media. Since news flowed west, Brown decided he would pay a visit to the power elite in New York. In late October 1977 he bought tickets to Manhattan for himself, his new Business and Transportation Secretary Richard Silberman, Executive Secretary Gray Davis, Press Secretary Elisabeth Coleman and Public Utilities Commission Chairman Robert Batinovich.

Since joining Brown's bobbing ark earlier in the year, forty-eight-year-old multimillionaire Richard Silberman had become Jerry's constant traveling companion. Some of the Governor's staff, remembering his earlier obsession with lowered expectations, jibed that in his effort to communicate with the business community, he had elevated Silberman to California's de facto "prime minister." As well as heading the group running Southern California's First National Bank, being a major investor in San Diego's Bazaar del Mundo shopping complex, and chairman of the San Diego Development Corporation, Silberman had also worked in aerospace and operated electronics companies. This diverse background, plus his fundraising experience with Alan Cranston's organization and Brown's 1976 presidential campaign, made him an ideal economic tutor for the Governor. Separated from his wife, Silberman had no conflicting family obligations and was free to accompany the Governor on his erratic flights.

A man who respected a well-turned phrase, Silberman originated the "California Means Business" slogan displayed on buttons (made in New Jersey) distributed by the administration. But this was just one of the techniques of basic business boosterism that Silberman suggested to Jerry on a business recruitment trip to Japan. The visit was designed to counter Brown's anti-industry reputation resulting from the Dow Chemical pullout, by attempting to entice certain Japanese plants to relocate in California. In Tokyo, the Governor congratulated Honda officials for their fuel-efficient subcompacts with good smog controls that humiliated the Big Three's behemoths. While Honda's economics were hardly Buddhist, this achievement, Jerry said, made the Asian firm welcome to further industrialize California. The Governor argued that construction of a California plant would increase sales of Hondas on the west coast. And in a state where over half the new cars sold were imported, it seemed reasonable, the Governor hinted, to insist that manufacturers build vehicles locally. Jerry proved to be no master of industrial diplomacy, however, and Honda settled in Marysville, Ohio, whose buttons proclaimed "Profit is Not a Dirty Word." This decision, it should be noted, was apparently made because of lower costs and Ohio's geographic proximity to many of the nation's leading markets.

Undiscouraged, Silberman turned to his first love — food-franchising — and helped Jerry win a new multinational friend, the world's second-ranked cola maker, Pepsico. In early September, lobbyist Ethan Wagner asked Tony Kline for administrative support of a bill exempting the firm from California's "tied-house law." This statute prohibited alcoholic beverage manufacturers from owning retail liquor licenses. Because Pepsico was also the holder of several French vineyards, this meant it was technically unable to complete acquisition of Pizza Hut, where beer was sold on tap. Brown's lawyer felt he could get a quick yes on the exemption required. "The Governor is preoccupied with a million things. It's the hectic last two weeks of the legislative session. It [the merger] would bring extra capital into the state by building 250 new Pizza Huts in five years."

But none of these considerations addressed the social policy issues that mattered most to Brown. Taking time from a schedule already jammed with other legislative matters, the Governor asked Kline what Pepsico intended to do for the people of the state in return for the right to sell beer over the pizza counter? Kline said, "I made the Pepsico case and in the process of debating it, Jerry went beyond the company's argument. I argued more jobs would be provided by putting Pizza Huts in high unemployment areas. He wanted to know what guarantees we could get."

Kline communicated Jerry's concerns to Ethan Wagner, who reassured him that his client, Pepsico, would guarantee new pizza parlors for minority businessmen operating in economically depressed areas. When Brown received word that the company was willing to cooperate with his franchise restrictions, he decided to help redraft the exemption bill for Pepsico with Kline and Silberman. After stipulating that the firm must also embark on an affirmative action plan, the men examined several other possibilities. Jerry's proposal to make the new pizza franchises solar-powered was rejected because of cost considerations. But Brown was able to work in a clause that the franchises must serve "wholesome and nutritious" food.

Pepsico, now retaining Jerry's former seminary classmate Frank Damrell as legal counsel, dispatched executive Walter Rosensteil from New York to review the changes. After agreeing in principle, the visiting executive found himself face-to-face with the Governor. "I'm glad you perceived your self-interest," said Brown, alluding to the $400 million merger hinging on this settlement. "Frankly, I'm less interested in helping large multinationals open new fast food chains in California than I am in providing help to those who need it." After a forty-five minute talk on corporate ethics and responsibility, Rosensteil said he was troubled by Brown's stipulation that every pizza be "wholesome and nutritious."

"I ate it," Jerry said, having sampled the dish at Oakland's Eastmont Mall following a fundraiser. "Don't you think it's wholesome?"

Pepsico's vice-president agreed his food was wholesome, but he objected to inclusion of vague language in a bill empowering the state to take away liquor licenses in the event of non-compliance. Pepsico trusted Brown's people, but who knew what his successor's appointees would consider "wholesome and nutritious"? "We don't want the Alcoholic Beverage Control Commission deciding to change everything in 1983," explained Rosensteil. Accordingly the clause "wholesome and nutritious" was struck. The final bill, clearly stipulating minority ownership and affirmative action goals, passed both houses. Brown signed it shortly before leaving for New York.

Silberman believed this diplomacy showed Jerry's "uncanny ability to sort out what is significant and what is insignificant. I'd like to see his influence in the state, nation and the world expanded. I see him providing some of the world's needs." Glancing toward his boss as the Newark-bound jet prepared to take off, he suggested these Pizza Huts were part of Brown's emerging political universe. "It's the genius of the capitalist system in this country that you can make a profit in combination with progressive goals. Private business is healthier and profit potential higher because of affirmative action. There's tremendous underutilization of minorities and women. They may rejuvenate the success ethic. For as you bring groups into business that have been excluded they become part of the process. You get access to ideas for new markets. They make business more efficient. I say to people in industry today that white males are culturally deprived because they haven't had an opportunity to work with more women and minorities.

"It's one thing to get a report saying this is what women and men think. It's another thing to hear it from women or minorities with equal votes across the room. At Jack in the Box we had a large group of restaurants sold back to minorities. The only restaurants in Watts not burned down (in the 1965 riots) were ours. The owners and managers were black. There was a *Los Angeles Times* picture of the rioters and cops eating together at a Jack in the Box during all the trouble. I still have it."

Flying over Las Vegas, and then Monument Valley, passengers were beginning to line up in the galley for a deli brunch. But at the moment, bagels, cream cheese and lox were of less interest to Jerry Brown than Robert Batinovich, and he moved to sit next to him. This man, whose innovative policies as head of the state's Public Utilities Commission made him one of Brown's most controversial appointees, was a personal friend of Jerry's. Batinovich pushed regulations rewarding utilities for encouraging energy conservation. He was also well along in the effort to force the utilities to refund huge amounts of money collected from ratepayers for tax liabilities the utilities escaped thanks to loopholes. In addition, the PUC set a national example by emphasizing solar, geo-thermal, wind, co-generation and other alternatives to traditional gener-ation methods. And a new rate structure rewarded conservation while the state's utilities were being prodded to come up with plans to subsidize home insulation programs. Like Jim Lorenz, Rose Bird, Tony Kline, Mario Obledo, Claire Dedrick, Jerome Lackner and Caltrans director Adriana Gianturco, Batinovich had become a liberal lightning rod for Jerry.

Like Silberman and others in the administration, Bat, as he was called, received calls from Pat Brown on behalf of law clients like SOHIO, a firm anxious to build a Long Beach terminal for Alaskan crude that could be shipped east through a pipeline. Jerry believed these corporations made a mistake hiring the former governor to try to influence his son. "It's no asset to know anyone in government," he told Bat. "It's a liability. I never talk to my father [about his clients]. If my father calls you, don't return his calls."

Stories like these inevitably promoted Oedipal imagery and specula-tions about Jerry's relationship with Pat. Strains were apparent from time to time, especially one day when Jerry made Pat cool his heels for hours in Jacques Barzaghi's waiting room. And like most parents, Pat sometimes complained Jerry didn't consult him often enough. "He com-plained about me not calling him," Jerry said, "and he's been in Japan for three weeks." Nevertheless, observers felt that as Jerry established himself on his own terms, the two men became closer. As the years passed, the younger Brown, who once spoke out against his father's policies, began referring to Pat as "the best Governor California ever had."

Jerry talked through most of the flight, asking Batinovich all sorts of questions about energy — including how much power it took to run a Sony TV and a VW Rabbit. At lunch time he opted not to eat, remarking, not completely coherently, "Most of us are doing things we don't really need. We just keep doing them. For instance, I don't really believe in scholastic aptitude tests."

When the party reached New York, Jerry saved money by paying ten dollars a night to use a friend's apartment, the little-lamented McAlpin Hotel having closed. The following morning the Governor kicked off his laissez-faire visit with the president of the New York stock exchange. Later, at a luncheon hosted by Lazard Freres' partner, Felix Rohatyn, at the City Mid-Day Club, Brown told investment bankers that California liked big business. As his prime rib got cold, the Governor explained how Buddhist economics could work for billion dollar companies. "There are limits. There may be limits to any state. There may be limits to New York City. You have to learn to live with it and maintain prosperity and I think that's possible."

In a sense, Jerry was advocating playing both ends of the economic spectrum against the middle-class. Under his grand design, the poor would continue to be subsidized, while corporations could look forward to new state tax breaks, like the abolition of California's inventory tax. (Brown was convinced this was necessary to lure industry to the Golden State.) Unfortunately, the middle-class, exempt from welfare and corporate tax privileges, would be squeezed, suffering a continued loss in government services and giving up larger and larger chunks of their paychecks as inflation pushed them into higher income-tax brackets. There was absolutely no way to avoid this, the Governor believed, in a world where problems like the population explosion, reduced supply of cheap natural resources, and pollution conspired to reduce the quality of life worldwide. Space colonization offered hope for the future, but in the short run, people would have to get by with less. This, the Governor argued, need not be as devastating as some imagined, since consumption of more and more material goods would never lead to happiness.

There were obviously many Californians who had no use for Brown's Buddhist economics, especially when he appeared to applaud the prospect of lowered expectations. But even those skeptical of Jerry agreed with him about one thing — the middle-class dream of owning a ranch house, a Buick and membership in the country club was in trouble. Many found it impossible to qualify to buy a house — even with two incomes. The $30,000 starter house of a few years ago now cost $80,000 to $150,000 in many areas. Indeed, the state's high cost of living was making it harder for families to avoid deficit spending. Psychologists said economic pressure was replacing sex as the leading domestic problem in a state where fifty percent of the marriages ended within five years and

Charles Sherman's *How to Do Your Own Divorce in California* was the best selling regional book, year after year.

But the economic squeeze on the middle-class aside, New Yorkers told Brown his support for the environmental and consumer movements threatened their ability to make a profit. It wasn't true, insisted Silberman, who argued that the costs for these beneficial programs could be passed along to the consumer. "We in California are willing to pay a higher price for a way of life," he told listeners.

Selling this idea was part of Brown's emerging economic strategy. The state, he believed, had proven "a very ineffective and inefficient way of providing what a family should do." And this failure of government to deal with middle-class pressures created an opportunity for the private sector to offer technological as well as spiritual answers. One way to do this was through advanced electronics. Indeed, as a staff member joked, the microprocessor could take on many of the roles traditionally played by Sacramento, not to mention its potential as a mother/father surrogate.

The idea of computerized *in loco parentis* seemed fantastic at first, but the more Jerry thought about it, the more sense it made. There was no doubt in his mind that the vanishing American family life was about to make a comeback. A good example was the education industry. Students could attend college at their living room TV screen, thus saving on room and board. Once free of the obligation to provide additional schools, the state could facilitate this transition into the McLuhan age by investing in such things as the $5.8 million Syncom IV communications satellite, which would transmit educational programming to the home.

Before almost any other major politician, Jerry Brown understood that the electronic revolution going on in places like Silicon Valley was more than just a way to rake in capital and employ a lot of people. Computers providing individuals with fast, efficient access to good information were likely to become the network that reunited families and communities. In much the same way that the deaf communicated with one another on teletypes, home computers would link the individual to society at large in unique ways. Some systems would minimize dependence on at least some traditional government services, such as public libraries. As funding cutbacks reduced the level of police and fire protection, computerized security systems plugged into private alarm services would help fill the gap. And if the state couldn't provide enough staffing for day care services, at least there would be plenty of low-cost video games to educate and entertain the kids. "The profit motive," explained the Governor, "builds on a basic aspect of human nature. You know you can call it profit or greed or self-assertion or self-seeking. That is part of our make-up and a system that takes advantage of that is certainly in tune with human nature."

At a more practical level, Jerry argued that California schools should tighten their math and science requirements so that graduates would be ready to participate in the electronic industries. Tax incentives and government loan funds were also made available to stimulate formation of high tech companies which, Brown was one of the first to claim, were the key to the reindustrialization of America.

It was one thing to favor the new, clean high technology industries — within a few years after Jerry discovered them, almost every politician did — but where did large corporations in more traditional industries fit into Jerry's New Age structure, his New York audiences wanted to know. Right in the middle, he claimed. For although he continued to lead the fight against controversial polluting industries — especially nuclear plants — Jerry was now convinced that big business itself wasn't the problem. As his friend Linda Ronstadt put it, "You can say what you want about big multinationals running the country, but the fact remains that we need them, we need their services, we need jobs from them, and they are in a better position to decide what's going to be good for the economic climate of the country and for the rest of the world."

Watching Brown leave the private mid-day club with one of several Montecruz Dunhill cigars tucked into the breast pocket of his pinstripe suit, his gratified audience talked warmly of their guest of honor. The governor of California, one corporation president remarked to a reporter, "hardly sounded like a western Luddite."

"I learned a lot," Jerry explained on his way uptown. "I used to talk about the virtues of bigness with a beginner's mind. Now I'm beginning to see the advantages of experience."

At a private meeting with a number of executives in the Barclay Hotel, Brown referred to the Pizza Hut deal to illustrate his commitment to minorities. "You have a profit line you look at and I have a quality of life line that I have to look at," explained Brown.

"The Governor is willing to use his office for special interest legislation in California," Silberman added.

"That's right," said George Weissman, Vice-Chairman of Phillip Morris. His firm, a major stockholder in the Irvine Corporation, had recently found Jerry tough but helpful. In the fifties, Pat worked with Irvine ranch's majority heiress, Joan Irvine Burt, to defeat conservationists trying to block a new town of 100,000. After she won, Pat selected the new community for a University of California campus to spur development. By 1976, the original population projection had quadrupled to 400,000 and the Orange County Fair Housing Council sued to compel inclusion of several thousand units for low-income service employees.

Irvine Corporation responded with legislation banning all lawsuits attempting to rezone improvement districts selling bonds prior to 1972.

After this bill (which neatly grandfathered in Irvine) passed the legislature, Brown's legal staff suggested to opponents who urged him to veto it that they might lose everything if they didn't compromise on a minimum of 725 low-income housing units. While this represented less than one percent of the community, it was the best Irvine Corporation would do. Afraid the Governor might sign the bill and kill their suit, the Fair Housing Council reluctantly accepted what they considered to be a disappointing solution.

Encouraged by his initial New York appearances, Jerry charged through back-to-back meetings the following day with the editorial boards of *Time, Newsweek,* and the *New York Times.* Here in the den of eastern mass mediadom, the Governor spoke without notes or preparation. What he said was usually as much of a surprise to his staff as it was to his audiences. And at the very least, this off-the-cuff approach made Jerry something of a novelty in the all-too-familiar world of canned political rhetoric. Often, however, it was difficult for an audience to understand what the Governor meant or said without a translation. "I think all this forecasting isn't all that essential," he told *Times* editors. "It's more for appearance's sake. What's important? What you know, what you don't know and what's possible are political realities that are very hard to manipulate. Often your most important task is to preside with confidence over things you can't control."

"What I'm really interested in are things that bring people together. At the space shuttle shot we had Birch Society Congressman John Rousselot, Senator Barry Goldwater, Tim Leary, Jacques Cousteau, Gerard O'Neill and Rusty Schweickart all out there together. That's a very diverse group of people. If they all feel happy launching things into space then why not let them? I remember after the shuttle shot these people with pyramid domes on their heads came up to me and said, 'Governor, I'm glad to see you're centered.' "

"How does your support for the 1984 Los Angeles Olympics square with lowered expectations?" asked one of the editors.

"We have the Los Angeles River that we can put some water in for rowing. We won't build a roof on the stadium. We'll sell Olympic umbrellas. That is "small is beautiful." We always have church basements for big overflows. I think the main problem is going to be smog. We have to turn down electricity so there's less smog and the athletes can run without getting emphysema."

After the meeting, Gray Davis left to make a phone call while Jerry sat quietly staring at the only object gracing the conference room walls — a painting of Henry Luce near the end of his reign. "Gee," said the governor, "this is depressing just going around talking like this. I think the world is out of control."

An hour later the gubernatorial party joined *Newsweek*'s editorial board for lamb chops at the Century Club. This time Jerry cut his Steve Martin routine short. "No one wants to be constrained. We have civil rights. But we don't have civil duties." Although he didn't have a thesis to offer, the guest of honor did attempt to blend a few opposites in his political Osterizer.

"From the Junior League to the Black Panthers, from the farm workers and Hari Krishna to the phone company, folks want to be part of the structure. The Black Panthers have gotten parents to give two hours a day to help kids in school. The Mormons have programs to take care of their own. But a lot of people don't want to get involved and you have a fragmented society. The government has to pick up the pieces . . . I say, 'When was the last time you went to a nursing home or mental hospital?' Last year I was preaching doom and gloom. This year I think things are looking up."

"When you were pessimistic did you say the same thing?" asked a senior editor having trouble following Brown's muddy stream of consciousness.

"I was just seeing a different reality," said Jerry. "I wasn't pessimistic. I'm no expert. I know less than most of you people. I know what I read in *Newsweek* and *Time*."

What the governor saw in these publications was not a source of joy. "The foundation of news media is to provide more fillers to stimulate people to overconsumption. There is so much good news in the commercials that they have to run negative filler to depress people to stimulate them to overconsumption. Bad news makes you so damn neurotic that it stimulates people to overconsumption. Part of my platform will be retribalization — to have TV coverage of the meeting of the editors of *Newsweek*, *Time* and the *New York Times*."

At the *New York Times* office Jerry told Tom Wicker about a *Los Angeles Times* piece on his first year headlined "Brown Changes Nothing."

"Maybe I haven't . . . Some executives from San Francisco's Emporium came to me seeking tax money to clean up the drunks on Market Street. I said, 'Why not leave them on the street as examples of casualties of capitalism . . .'"

"What about this space thing, governor?"

"One of the reasons I like the space program is that you can take all the military industrial complex types and let them build their erector sets in outer space. People want limits but they also want dreams."

"It's kind of like Rosenthal, the guy who invented the brasserie," explained Silberman. "Suddenly more and more people wanted it and it created new wealth."

That evening after Jerry delivered an uninspired speech at the Waldorf, Gray Davis told him to get some sleep. "You've had a tough day. Tomorrow we've got to see all those bankers and editors."

"I know," replied Brown, as the two men climbed into an unmarked police sedan. "They're going to want to know what I think about the balance of payments and I'll say I don't know."

Not ready to call it a night, Jerry gave the driver an address on the affluent upper East side. A few minutes later their plainclothes driver pulled up to the 79th Street home of Lally Weymouth, a writer and sister of the *Washington Post* publisher. Inside they found a ruddy Norman Mailer apologizing to his hostess for throwing a drink in Gore Vidal's face and then punching him in the mouth. Moving over toward the carpet soaked by Mailer's cocktail, Brown scanned the other guests. Jacqueline Onassis was there and so were Barbara Walters, Gay Talese and CBS's Bill Paley. Towering over the crowd was John Kenneth Galbraith. Indeed, there were so many celebrities no one seemed to even notice Jerry Brown. Finally a young woman who had been staring at him approached. "Excuse me, I understand you're a governor. Just exactly what are you governor of?"

"Oh, just some little province out in the west," the Governor answered.

On the way back to his friend's apartment, Jerry asked the young sedan driver: "Do you take people around like this all day?"

"Oh, no. This is only part-time work for me. I'm studying psychotherapy."

"Hmmm," Brown said while the car cruised through perfectly sequenced green turn signals, "I'm not so sure the psyche is amenable to therapy."

On the Road

CHAPTER 13

How did we organize anything? How did Francis Xavier organize anything? How did Francis De Sales, St. Francis of Assisi, Ignatius Loyola? Where are all those people? It seems to me the streets are just waiting for a new St. Francis to appear.

Raindrops splattered against the Satellite's windshield as it emerged from the Bay Bridge's lower deck and crossed the four-lane prairie into Oakland. Unlike San Francisco, where residents complained about high-rise proliferation, or San Jose, where silicon chips profits threatened to put two Datsun 280Zs in every garage, the Bay Area's third largest city was distinguished by a low-rise skyline and a surplus of used Detroit iron. Many of the landmark buildings from Jack London's day which helped make this a pleasant, if somewhat sleepy, city had been torn down as part of one or another ill-fated "revitalization project." Now the Tribune Tower, built by the Knowlands in 1923, provided an aging salmon-colored apostrophe to miles of federally-sponsored parking lots local residents referred to as "urban removal." Indeed, once potential investors were told they could park here around the clock for less than the cost of twenty minutes in San Francisco, they didn't want to hear more.

By the mid-1970's, new business was unwilling to settle in the community where Pat Brown learned bipartisan strategy from Earl Warren and Jerry Brown had marched in 1966 to "Stop the Draft." Now, in November 1977, the Governor was returning to attempt to administer cardio-pulmonary resuscitation to the city which boasted California's largest minority population. Before World War II, 93.5 percent of Oakland was white. This balance began to tip after Pearl Harbor, when blacks arrived by the trainload to work in the Kaiser shipyards. Now over half the community was black, and commercial flight had reduced what was left of the City Center to a sad assortment of empty, decaying office space difficult to rent at any price.

The city's new containerized shipping facilities had stolen big business from San Francisco, whose once thriving wharves had been taken over by tourist dives selling baked potatoes for $1.50; portside land was attracting new business; residential areas had some of the region's best housing bargains; and hills were dominated by redwood parks. But downtown Oakland, with its high unemployment rate and unskilled minority population, was sinking so fast that many predicted that in ten years there would be little left except air bubbles.

With more than 61,000 city residents (about 18.7 percent) living below the poverty level, Oakland qualified for nearly every urban welfare program ever funded by Federal government. A good chunk of this money was invested in a project called Oakland City Center, which was designed to revitalize the downtown area. Complete with a cement waterfall and an $80-a-night Hyatt Hotel crowned by a rotating restaurant, this fifteen square block project had long been a dream of local politicians, planners, developers and investors. To free up space for the one-million square foot shopping center, which developers hoped would be anchored by Bullock's, Liberty House and J.C. Penney, blocks of small businesses, offices and homes were cleared. In addition to the stores, a convention center and five new office buildings, one as high as seventy-eight stories, were planned.

"Thunder across the bay" was the way Oakland's redevelopment director John B. Williams described this new commercial adventure. Even local business leaders were amazed by the scope of what they began referring to as "John Williams' medicine show." But City Center's founding father insisted that his dream was only a small part of the coming economic renaissance. In addition to its strategic location, Oakland had another advantage, Williams claimed. By the 1990's, California would be America's first third-world state, with minority residents making up more than half the population. It seemed logical to Williams that the first major city in the state dominated by nonwhites should be the laboratory for a new brand of multi-ethnic urban capitalism.

For a while, the City Center concept seemed feasible—the federal, state and local governments would spend $100 million, as 356 families were relocated and commercial stores were razed. After the wrecking companies finished demolishing stores and offices, the land would be sold at bargain prices to City Center development interests that included minority investors.

By the time of the Governor's 1977 visit, much had changed. The residents and merchants living in the area earmarked for urban renewal programs had moved and the land had been cleared. Then, just about on schedule for such things, the project began to falter. Only two office buildings and an underground garage had been completed. A third office structure and several other high-rises were in the works, along with the Hyatt Regency. But the shopping center that was to be the heart of this project, as well as the convention center, were dead. And the developer's solemn promise to cut a group of minority investors in on profits from the new Clorox Building was also broken, contributing to the feeling of displeasure mounting in the minority community. Except for the increased incidence of drug deals consummated on the street, there was less retail trade in Oakland's downtown area than on the day City Center was proposed.

"Every day is Ground Hog day," cracked community activist Paul Cobb. The leader of a group called Oakland Citizens Committee for Urban Renewal, Cobb was particularly dismayed that Grubb and Ellis, the developer, failed to make good on its pledge to turn the handful of new City Center buildings into a minority employment base. "They wouldn't even let us sweep the floors and take out the garbage in the Clorox Building. And that's one thing we Oakland blacks know how to do. We have a lot of janitorial companies."

For Jerry Brown, the continuing drama of disintegration in downtown Oakland was a microcosm of what was occurring all across urban America. Urban renewal failed in Oakland just as it failed as a national policy. But what next? What could California do to turn this situation around in its own cities? Stung by press criticism that ventures like his Pink Palace visit only camouflaged government inaction in deteriorating metropolitan areas, the Governor came up with a comprehensive plan for rebuilding this city of 355,000. This was something of a reversal for the politician who prided himself on keeping a low profile. As far back as his days on the Los Angeles County Delinquency and Crime Commission, Brown had been justifiably suspicious of carefully annotated studies and master plans. Still, if he could help orchestrate a policy that turned things around in downtown Oakland, he would have done something that eluded most leaders of urban America, something that would be of vital interest to citizens east of the Sierra.

The previous year, Brown got his feet wet in Oakland politics by involving himself in a proposal to complete Oakland's Grove-Shafter freeway. Thanks to Tony Kline's Public Advocates, construction of a 1.3 mile strip through a low-income downtown Oakland area was enjoined in the early seventies. Federal courts granted injunctive relief because the state failed to provide satisfactory relocation housing for residents in the $30 million project's path. But even after the low-income home owners resettled, the project remained stalled, because it was difficult to justify the expenditure from a transportation standpoint. Who needed a freeway, it was argued by many, when six surface lanes with timed signals already allowed traffic to zip swiftly through this bombed-out looking section and connect with the Nimitz freeway? Making the already uncongested road part of the interstate highway network would at best reduce driving time by one or two minutes.

However, Oakland development interests anxious to breathe life into the City Center project came up with an imaginative argument for completion of the road. They claimed major department stores wouldn't commit themselves to the new development unless the final stretch of freeway was finished. Merchandisers, it was contended, thought that suburbanites would ignore a department store complex in a poor black area unless they could drive their cars from the freeway off-ramp directly into a guarded parking garage. In addition, the limited access road would physically isolate the black neighborhood from the proposed project so that shoppers wouldn't have to see much of the low-income community.

Interestingly, these avowedly racist arguments for the new road didn't seem to bother Black Panther leader, Elaine Brown, who saw increased building development downtown as a major source of minority jobs. Her organization soon joined white business interests anxious to complete the marginal freeway. Even Tony Kline's former clients in the anti-highway suit now begged Governor Brown for eight limited access lanes.

"I was an advocate for people with clear interests," recalled the Governor's legal secretary. "Here you are surrounded by competing interest groups and trying to resolve conflicting interests. You are forced to look at interests you weren't concerned about at the time you won the suit. Unemployment is high and labor wants job-producing enterprises."

No one, Jerry Brown included, seriously challenged the racist assumptions underlying the case for what was essentially a $30 million off-ramp. Even Gray Davis casually admitted that developers wanted the freeway finished so "white customers could get into the parking lot without seeing any black faces." But their case was well-received by the Governor's office in 1976 because minority community leaders with political ambitions of their own were behind the project. The freeway extension, they argued, would make it possible to complete City Center which would produce both construction and eventually retailing jobs for the minority community.

Jerry was delighted by this alliance of interest groups who usually opposed one another. Here was an opportunity to promote interracial harmony only eight years after Panther leader Huey P. Newton intimidated then-Governor Ronald Reagan by marching his well-armed, paramilitary cadre into the Capitol rotunda. With Tony Kline now escorting Newton's successor, Elaine Brown, around Jerry's office, the Governor sensed an opportunity for an urban triumph.

Elaine Brown, who lost a 1976 bid for the Mayor's office in Oakland, believed economic progress was in the best interests of black and white Oakland. Jerry now hoped to persuade venture capitalists to come together with the revolutionary black socialists to lure suburban residents back to the Oakland ghetto. This, he believed, would create both work for the hard-core unemployed and profits for department store owners. If it was successful, it would clearly demonstrate that with a creative approach, the battle line that divided much of urban America need not be fixed forever.

While Jerry Brown certainly didn't believe that government intervention would transform Oakland's East Fourteenth Street into a replica of Beverly Hills' Rodeo Drive, he was convinced some sort of a plan had to be put forward before it was too late. "In another five years," Brown said, "we will need the Army, not in the Panama Canal, but in the cities of our nation to defend ourselves against the people who have lost hope, who have no jobs, who are living in the burned-out, miserable buildings that once were the pride of the country."

Hopefully, Oakland was not going to suffer this fate. Jerry had already announced a number of programs to spark an economic renaissance here. Besides the $30 million Grove-Shafter freeway completion, he was talking about a $21 to $35 million state building, a solar demonstration project that would provide jobs for twenty to thirty Oakland technicians, plus $1.25 million for parks and $250,000 to beef up law enforcement.

When Jerry arrived at City Hall in November 1977, Oakland's mayor

Lionel Wilson was there to call Jerry's arrival "Truly a historic official moment in the state of California. I don't ever remember a governor of this state ever being in these council chambers. I've lived here since I was a little kid and I don't think your father was ever here."

A novel part of Brown's new urban strategy was the California National Guard headed by his former University of Santa Clara counselor, Frank Schober. General Schober wanted to create an urban training program by imitating the California Conservation Corps model that put young people to work in rural areas. California Army Reserve units would no longer be composed of weekend soldiers called up to douse fires and rescue flood victims. Now they would become a permanent urban peace-keeping force composed of low-income and jobless young people.

"It has always struck me," said Brown to reporters filling the gallery, "that so many institutions are underutilized. I think it would be a good idea to set up an Oakland Guard to teach unemployed youth skills and then, six months later, obtain a job from employers. The Guard has a $137 million budget, training programs and the discipline and inspiration to help people find their way in life. My perception is as we pile on new programs we neglect old programs. We have light bulbs, chairs and pieces of paper. The infrastructure is here. What has been lacking is the social glue."

Thanks to $315,000 in federal CETA funds, Jerry announced that Oakland Guard members could now complete their training at military camps and find employment with no expenditure of state funds. Not only would these 200 to 500 men and women soldiers help remedy Schober's recruitment problem, they would also be available for instant call-up to fight violence in their hometown. And if the program worked in Oakland, other potentially unstable minority neighborhoods from Hunter's Point to East Los Angeles would eventually have their own state Guard units.

Brown believed that the Guard offered a chance to make a meaningful dent in the city's unemployment statistics where they needed it the most — minority youth. "The thing that troubles me about most of these liberal plans to make things better is that they are so disconnected from the subjects of their sympathy. It's not just a question of creating more jobs, it's a question of who get jobs."

General Schober's first Oakland recruit was eighteen-year-old Dale Reed. Dressed in a bright yellow shirt and orange polyester slacks, the new guardsman grinned obligingly for the TV cameras.

"Are we starting a new unit or a basketball team here?" Mayor Wilson joked to Schober, as reporters moved toward the six-foot, four-inch inductee. Even Governor Brown stood back to let the press have fun with the young man fate had plucked from the unemployment line.

"Mr. Reed," asked a woman in a peasant dress from a San Francisco TV station, "What would you do if you were called up by the Guard to put down trouble in your neighborhood?"

"I'd go."

"Would you shoot at your friends?"

"I'd feel bad about facing them, but I wouldn't have any choice. That's my job now."

Schober's imagination was also applauded a few minutes later by editors of the *Oakland Tribune* in their twentieth floor conference room. They believed the Guard was an important step in rebuilding their city. The once-powerful paper that provided the political and financial resources for Bill Knowland to make it into the Senate was no longer owned by his heirs. After losing to Pat Brown in 1958, Bill had literally run the *Tribune* into the ground with an editorial policy so ill-tempered that it opposed almost everything that happened after 1928 — political or otherwise. Knowland had pressured the University of California to adopt the ban on political organizing that led to the Free Speech Movement. And he answered CORE demonstrators protesting racist employment practices at Jack London Square restaurants by personally charging through their picket lines to dine alone at the Sea Wolf.

In 1972, Knowland divorced his wife, married a Las Vegas showgirl and promptly ran up debts totalling almost $1 million, using his *Tribune* stock as collateral. Marital problems persuaded his second wife to move back to Las Vegas where Knowland visited on weekends. Then the kidnapping of *Atlanta Constitution* editor Reg Murphy and the Patty Hearst case made the publisher a nervous wreck, fearing that he, too, would be abducted. Bill Knowland became a sad caricature of himself, never without a walkie-talkie connection to security guards even though by early 1974 he didn't have enough money to pay an imminently due bank note. Brooding over the prospect of relinquishing his *Tribune* stock, he drove to his summer home an hour north of San Francisco. There, on February 22, 1974, the Senator from Formosa walked down the swollen Russian River and shot himself in the head.

In 1976, after Bill's son Joe and nephew Jay failed to turn the badly ailing paper around, it was purchased by Combined Communications. This company — based in the mid-west — quickly learned how difficult it was to run a newspaper in a distressed city. Jerry responded to the problems sketched out for him by an all-white cast of Trib leaders in their chartreuse penthouse.

"I had three morning paper routes," Brown said. "I remember riding down through the eucalyptus in the foggy mornings."

"We can't find carriers willing to work rough territories in the morning," said the new publisher with his hand clenched around a glass of orange juice.

"That's a paradox," said Brown. "The unemployed can't get jobs which creates crime which makes it hard to find carriers. That's reinforcing synergism, the negative connection. Things get worse and worse. The inner city is a meat grinder that regurgitates anyone with any skill. Maybe Oakland is the place to test the concepts that I talk about. When I signed the Pizza Hut bill, some people looked at it as a joke. I think it's interesting. The Alcoholic Beverage Control Commission made it a condition of the license that minority jobs in these restaurants not be dead-end jobs. So now when you see a kid drinking Pepsi, instead of that multinational capital going to New York or Britain or Taiwan or Russia, it comes back to Oakland. That's my concept. I don't know whether it will work. It may just be a lot of rhetoric but I want to take all these great schemes we talk about in Sacramento and on interview shows and try to match it to your needs.

"Flight from schools is another problem. Very few people in my administration have kids in downtown Sacramento schools. They all move one district out. So if great liberals don't want to be in schools, what can you expect? Success in life is defined as getting out of Oakland."

"He's right," laughed an editorial writer, "there is no here, here. That's our problem."

"You have to create the illusion of success that will be transformed into the reality of success," said the Governor. "You need a police chief who says things are safe and they will be safe."

"We haven't conveyed that to people in Oakland," agreed an editor. "We have an obligation to try to change that image. Let's start an ad campaign that says, 'All the benefits of San Francisco with half the problems.'"

"Say 'In Oakland you have half as much chance of being mugged as in San Francisco,'" suggested Brown, who added, "Anyway, I am trying to use the symbols and institutions and money and send it into Oakland... The military isn't too popular after Vietnam. But we've got $137 million for the Guard and ought to put some of it in the cities. If we can't revitalize the cities here, then we can just write off urban America..."

Although the new publishers of the *Oakland Tribune* were impressed by Jerry Brown, they were even more impressed by the dismal status of their own bottom line and sold out to the Gannett chain. This sort of turnover was part of the problem the Governor ran into in trying to implement his urban strategy. Groups he counted on weren't always dependable. For example, Black Panther chairman Elaine Brown, so helpful in the job-producing Grove-Shafter freeway completion in 1976, later resigned and went incommunicado. Party members speculated she had left quietly to make way for Huey P. Newton's return from Cuban exile. If so, it was a wise choice, because like Caligula, the young emperor of the Panthers was surrounded by bloodshed from the moment he returned to Alameda County in 1977. Understandably, Jerry suddenly stopped mentioning the Panthers in his calls for togetherness.

Another problem Jerry faced was his relationship with local officials, such as Mayor Wilson, as well as with county supervisors and urban renewal groups — all of whom were slow to invite Jerry back. During his Oakland kickoff, the Governor promised to make himself available for five to ten hours every two or three months. However, the city's leaders preferred to muddle along with their economic blight instead of risking their personal authority and prestige by involving the Governor. If the state wanted to hand Oakland a pile of money, they would take it fast enough, but no one seemed too interested in giving up his or her own power to Jerry Brown.

The fate of Brown's urban strategy was most affected by Mayor Wilson's ambition to turn Oakland into a strong mayor-type government like San Francisco. This meant adjusting his salary from $15,000 to the $65,000 to $75,000 range. As a full-time administrator, he would take over most of the city manager's duties and acquire the power to hire and fire department heads.

Anticipating this change, Wilson decided it was no longer prudent to let a variety of state and federal agencies administer community projects. Instead he decided to centralize control of all money coming in from Sacramento and Washington by funneling it through a new superagency called the Office of Economic Development and Employment (OEDE). This agency would be headed by Wilson loyalist Juan Lopez, who had experience with a savings and loan business in the minority community. With the clout of OEDE sending funds into the community, Wilson's historically ceremonial office would begin to acquire real economic power. In effect, the Mayor, working through Lopez, could control how federal and state grants were spent. Unfortunately, before the OEDE began coordinating the city's outside government funding for business, housing, employment and social welfare projects, it was discovered that $34,000 was missing from government agencies already under Lopez's supervision. At a trial, the OEDE coordinator pleaded guilty to taking the money through a payroll scam, and was sentenced to the California Department of Corrections at Vacaville.

Wilson eventually found a new OEDE director and his hand-picked Charter Review Board recommended a city-wide referendum on his strong-mayor proposal. In the meantime, most of Brown's programs were either ignored or put on the back burner. For example, when it came time to purchase land for the multi-million dollar state office building proposed by the Governor, problems developed. First, a preferred site was sold to a private company. Then, budget limitations prevented construction of the state building on a second site. Eventually, as Oakland officials dilly-dallied past June 1978, Proposition 13—motivated economics killed the whole idea.

In the end, the only one of Brown's Oakland programs to get off the ground was the Oakland Guard. General Schober did manage to recruit 500 trainees, some of whom became full-fledged Guard members. Unfortunately, however, the program never became a model, like the successful California Conservation Corps which put recruits to work clearing streams, building solar projects and doing reforestation. Apparently, training young minorities to defend the Wells Fargo Bank or Capwell's Department Store against tomorrow's rioters didn't capture their imaginations the way CCC's projects did.

Through much of 1977, the Governor travelled the state trying to put new programs together. But periodically he took a break and retreated to the Tassajara Zen community to rest and think. One fall day he rose at 5 a.m. to catch a truck ride out of the remote mountain resort into Monterey. Brown now resumed a nonstop series of meetings and appearances that brought him to Sacramento's Arbor restaurant.

Although he arrived after the 10 p.m. closing time, tired employees agreed to put together a bean salad for the Governor's dinner. Then, without explanation, he cancelled the order and shifted a few lettuce leaves and beans off a plate ordered by another member of his party. Striking up a conversation with three waitresses, he asked about their salaries — how much didn't they report on their taxes, why didn't they organize a union, wouldn't they enjoy trading off jobs with the cooks from time to time?

When the Arbor people decided to lock up, the Governor, still full of energy, took his entourage across the street to a bar. Tossing a handful of singles on the table for a round of drinks, he talked business with Gray Davis for a little while. Gradually he turned his attention to some of the Arbor waitresses who had joined Jerry's party. By 1 a.m., some of his guests were ready to go home and Davis was close to nodding off. Many were no longer listening when Jerry reached into his breast pocket and pulled out a list of programs begun since he was governor. "People say I don't do anything, that I'm all style and no substance. Now here are seventeen positive, constructive things my administration's accomplished. There's the solar tax credit, anti-redlining bill to protect minority home buyers, and the Serrano Act that equalizes tax revenue for school districts. I established a housing finance agency, created a California Conservation Corps, established a rural health services program, appointed more women and minorities to the judiciary than any other California governor, put through a bill requiring that public members constitute a majority of boards and commissions in most fields . . ."

When Brown finished, the two remaining waitresses politely excused themselves. Disappointed that they didn't let him accompany them to the door, the Governor trailed behind. Outside he watched the women disappear into a dark parking lot.

"Do you think it's safe for them to walk alone?" he asked Gray Davis. "Maybe we should go with them."

"They're okay, Jerry," replied the chief-of-staff.

"Why did they want to leave?"

"They all have very involved lives. Come on, let's call it a day."

Wherever he went in the fall of 1977, Brown was sensitive to accusations that too many of his actions had been calculated to gain him political advantage and didn't really benefit the people. Thus in November, when Los Angeles papers wrote that Metropolitan State Hospital was in crisis because of inadequate staffing, poor record keeping, maintenance and sanitation, Jerry made immediate plans to visit the Norwalk wards.

A year earlier he had authorized $1.5 million to hire 122 emergency psychiatric hospital employees. Now he learned that due to bureaucratic confusion, only one of these spots had been filled. In marathon sessions with hospital administrators, the Governor, Health Director Jerry Lackner, and Jacques Barzaghi tried once again to help rescue Metropolitan. They mapped out a program for hiring more employees, correcting the administration's bookkeeping problems, and providing supplemental funds. Brown pledged a new $70 million fund for upgrading the state's psychiatric facilities which would make 1978 California's "year of mental health." After going thirty hours with only a short break for sleep, the tired group broke to let Brown address TV reporters.

Channel 2's minicam reporter Linda Douglas got to the Governor first in the corridor. Brown indicated, "We want to have adequate care for Metro so that when someone leaves, we'll be able to continue helping him . . ."

Later in the evening, Brown stopped to catch the second installment of a three-part KCBS series on his political career. He saw an unflattering piece capped by anchorwoman Connie Chung's statement that, "Everything he is doing is calculated toward the presidency. He has deep, cold ambitions."

"The media creates reality," observed Barzaghi as Chung proceeded to make fun of Brown's Latin aphorisms and ingeniously showed him taking firm positions on both sides of several major issues.

After being subjected to a media slaughter in the state's biggest city, Brown retired to his favorite restaurant, El Adobe, on Hollywood's Melrose Avenue. None of the fans who lined up outside the studio across the street for a "Laverne and Shirley" taping noticed Jerry as he arrived with Barzaghi, a psychiatrist who was advising him on the mental hospital crisis, and Channel 2's Linda Douglas.

The governor asked for a pitcher of margaritas, burritos, and an order of guacamole while Jacques consulted the doctor about chest pains that had begun bothering him during a lengthy meeting the night before. "Here," said the physician as he scribbled down a note on a pad. "When you get back to Sacramento, ask your doctor to give you this test. It will tell whether or not you've had a heart attack."

"You mean I may have already had one?" cried Jacques nervously reaching for a cigarette.

"Happens all the time," said the doctor.

Oblivious to the conversation going on beside him, the visibly exhausted Brown began asking Linda Douglas questions about Connie Chung. "She had to get in that question about whether or not I'm a homosexual. What about her? Does she have a boyfriend?"

"I think she's got one in New York," said Linda.

"No one here?"

"I don't think so. All she does is work."

"Let's ask her when was the last time she got laid."

"Right," said the psychiatrist, "and enjoyed it."

"That would be great," replied the Governor. "When was the last time you got laid and enjoyed it?"

A few minutes later the restaurant's co-owner Frank Casado came over and presented a bill to his good friend who promptly objected: "Thirty-one dollars for a couple of burritos, guacamole and some margaritas."

"It includes dinners ordered by your security men."

"Hey," said the Governor, who refused a salary increase above $49,000. "I'm not paying for those freeloaders. Let them pay for their own meals [from the state travel allowance]. They are state employees. We don't pay for them."

Saving money was still a priority for the Governor two weeks later when he stood at the Laker Airlines counter in Queens, New York. "I don't understand," he told the agent. "The flight is $135 plus $2 for breakfast. That only comes to $137."

"You're forgetting the tax, Governor."

"How much is that?"

"$3."

"Hey, Dick," he yelled over his shoulder to Silberman, "is that 6% sales tax?"

When sixty-six-year-old *Small is Beautiful* author E.F. Schumacher died of a heart attack on September 4 in the midst of a Swiss lecture tour, Brown had eulogized him as "one of the few men able to articulate the importance of the spiritual over the material." Now, on this budget flight across the Atlantic, Brown was preparing remarks for the Buddhist economist's requiem mass. There wasn't time for the governor to reread the whole book before he reached London. Instead he sat up underlining key phrases and making notes like a student cramming for a final exam.

On the page before him, Brown slowly drew a dark circle around the economist's assertion that "All the indications are that the present structure of large-scale industrial enterprise, in spite of heavy taxation and an endless proliferation of legislation, is not conducive to the public welfare."

"I don't think you can take this too literally," the Governor said while economic advisor Richard Silberman sliced wedges of Gouda cheese brought along from Sacramento. All the way across the Atlantic, Silberman, who did not trust airline food, catered an eclectic but tasty meal out of his carry-on bag. Appointing himself the Governor's inflight nutritionist, he laid out a fine spread of cheeses, oranges, bananas, apples, and premium California chablis served in paper cups. "The airlines simply don't understand food," explained the man from Jack in the Box. "They're trying to compete with restaurants. That's impossible when you have to reheat. They should stick with reconstituted items like stew and chili that improve with age."

While Silberman served up trail mix for dessert, Brown talked about Schumacher's ideology: "Corporate America has a stake in revitalization. These people intend to be around for a long time and you have to be responsive. Just as you take capital out, you have to put it back."

As the plane approached Ireland, Brown found more places where he disagreed with Schumacher. "Look here," said the Governor, "on page 269 he says it's dangerous to mix business and politics. Then he says nationalized enterprises should have a statutory obligation to serve the public interest in all respects. That's confusing.

"Now on 294 he doesn't seem to think more resources, wealth, education and research will automatically improve things. He wants 'the development of a lifestyle which accords to material things their proper, legitimate place which is secondary and not primary.' I'm not ready to come down on those questions yet. Do you think the whole world is going to go to Mendocino and get into composting?"

The sun was beginning to rise when Brown put down the paperback and with a sigh pulled a grey blanket over his head. He felt comfortable with the phrase "small is beautiful," but had problems because the ideology relied primarily on nineteenth-century economic philosophy and experiences of third-world countries. It was well and good to write utopian prose, but Schumacher didn't tell him how many Hondas they had in Lesotho. What did they know about the Jojoba bean in Senegal?

219

How many satellites had been launched in Bangladesh? Perhaps these nations could survive in a cooperative, agrarian society with help from intermediate technologists, and maybe some of their people would want to remain as an earth caretaker force after space migration began. Nonetheless, you couldn't take Schumacher too literally. The Governor had supported back-to-the-land types who constructed safe non-code homes in the state's northwestern and mountain counties; he had done more to encourage alternative energy technologies than any other political leader in the world; he was probably the least lavish governor in America; but Brown was beginning to understand the limits of how far he could push the idea of voluntary simplicity on those still hooked by America's materialist dream. Especially in minority communities, Jerry was beginning to realize what Pat had always known — when you've come up the hard way, the dream of a house in the suburbs, two cars, a box seat at the baseball game and occasional dinners of surf and turf is a small piece of heaven, and definitely worth going after.

When the plane landed at Gatwick Airport, Brown shook hands with the DC-10's leather-jacketed owner, Sir Freddie Laker. Then he ran into an embarrassing situation in the baggage area. Schumacher's widow, Verena, who in kindness had come to meet Jerry's flight, suggested that he join her for the ride into town on a train. This was fine with Jerry, but unfortunately, Dick Silberman had asked Lazard Freres' friend from Paris, David Karr, to meet the plane. The investment banker had come with a Jaguar-made Daimler limo and backup sedan. He suggested the two vehicles would insure an on-time arrival for the Governor's first appointment — a meeting with twenty international bankers at Hambros Bank. This made sense, and after greeting Mrs. Schumacher, Brown and his party split up into the two Daimlers.

This initial conflict of whether to take a few minutes longer and ride the energy-efficient train or speed off in a symbol of conspicuous consumption was to dog the entire trip. Jerry repeatedly found himself caught between two poles. The purpose of his trip was to try to get international capitalists with economic power to create jobs in California at the same time that Jerry met with Schumacher's followers and spoke at his memorial service. These two groups, of course, were ideological enemies for good reason. Jerry apparently thought he could find a way to synthesize "less is more" and "California means business." He was wrong.

Arriving in London, the Daimlers pulled alongside the New Hyde Park Hotel, a luxurious member of the world-wide Trust Forte chain. After the men went inside for coffee Brown's chauffeur asked Karr's driver, "Which one is the governor?" The man poked a finger in the direction of the guest wearing a tired blazer and faded tie. "Ah," said the chauffeur, "I was wondering who the scruffy one was."

An hour later Jerry, Silberman and Karr arrived in the Hambros Bank board room to try to persuade twenty officers of leading European, Asian and American banks to invest billions of dollars in California. Twenty guests, all in dark suits, listened carefully while the sleep-deprived governor characterized the wonders of California's $180 billion-a-year economy. "Our market is growing at ten to eleven percent annually," boasted the Governor. "We've created a million new jobs in the past couple years. We have tremendous oceans, mountains, cultures and an intellectual climate that makes our state the kind of place where foreign investors have traditionally found a very good return on their investment."

Then Jerry went on to deal with rumors he understood were worrying the bankers. Did he champion a new ecological religion subordinating profits to environmental considerations? "It's simply not true," explained Brown. "What we are trying to do is show that human and corporate values are not incompatible. I'd prefer not to have any new nuclear power plants lining the coast. But at the same time, we just broke ground for a new Miller's brewery that will provide five hundred jobs. So now, instead of having dangerous plutonium-laden generators lining our beaches, we'll have more people on the sand drinking beer. Everybody wins."

While this off-the-wall humor intrigued the bankers, it did not distract them from their concern about what Brown intended to do with the California unitary taxation system they despised. Under the unitary tax, the state assessed foreign companies doing business in California on the basis of their world-wide earnings. Controller Kenneth Cory believed his system protected the state against financial manipulation by overseas companies. Without it, the argument went, firms could sell their plants' raw materials at an inflated price and show a paper loss. This way they avoided paying their fair tax in California while booking profits in foreign nations where taxes were lower. Big business replied that elimination of the unitary tax would help California by bringing in more multinational enterprises. Increased profits realized by this tax break would be reinvested into new factories and jobs. The bottom line was, if they weren't accommodated, the firms intended to shift their dollars out of state.

Martin Huff, head of the California Franchise Tax Board, claimed that abandoning unitary taxation could cost the state $125 million. For that reason, Brown wrote the Senate Foreign Relations Committee early in 1977 complaining that the Anglo-American treaty would "take over $100 million from the state of California and give it to certain multinational corporations. This is not only bad government, but also infringes on state's rights."

Then, during his Japanese trip in 1977, Jerry ran headlong into an economic fact of life he hadn't anticipated. The Japanese told him he would not attract industry to California as long as the unitary tax existed. On his return to the States Jerry researched the tax issue with his advisors and concluded that Huff had given him "flaky data." Brown now contended that the state would lose $25 million or less by abolishing the tax — a loss that would be more than offset by new companies locating in the state. So, he could in all honesty now tell his London hosts he was "in favor of abolishing the unitary tax. I'm also trying to abolish the inventory tax," Jerry added. The businessmen glanced approvingly at each other and the Governor as the meeting convened.

The following morning, Brown and Silberman met for breakfast with Verena Schumacher and leaders of the late economist's intermediate technology development group. The British ate kippers, porridge and cold toast as Jerry and his aides asked questions about people's willingness to embrace voluntary simplicity as Schumacher conceived it. "After all," said the Governor, "it's fine to talk about replacing giant corporations with small scale producers more responsive to human needs. But are people ready to adopt an increasingly frugal lifestyle?"

"Fritz believed England may become the first country in the world to do that voluntarily," said Mrs. Schumacher. "Our group wants people to face up to the reality of Britain's economic decline and adopt a simpler way of life. We're greatly encouraged by the fact that our young people seem to be showing less interest in creature comforts than their parents."

"In other words," Brown suggested, "people here are ready to accept the Gandhian notion of enough for everyone's need but not for everyone's greed. Frugality and simplicity are catching on."

Silberman smiled in agreement while pointing at his digital watch. The Californians were late for a meeting with the chairman of British Petroleum. After politely excusing themselves, they rode over to King's Row where the oil company representatives waited in a beige townhouse sandwiched between Arab embassies. BP held a majority interest in Standard Oil of Ohio which was trying to build a $500 million Long Beach terminal for Alaskan crude. The plan was to ship the petroleum via pipeline to the midwest. At a private meeting, Brown said he was all for the project as long as the oil firm would help improve California air quality standards. The governor invited a BP officer to fly to Sacramento at the week's end for meetings to move this super project ahead. (The two men would meet again in California. But the anti-pollution laws adopted earlier in Jerry's administration and the state's unwillingness to modify permit procedures ultimately helped persuade BP Standard to drop the project.)

By now it was time to head over to the Schumacher memorial. In an unintentional but hilarious plug for appropriate technology, Karr's fat cat limo broke down, forcing the governor to taxi to the pre-requiem mass press conference. He was fifteen minutes late. "Mr. Brown," shouted one of several dozen reporters gathered in the Westminster Cathedral annex as he spotted the Governor leaving the cab, "why are you here?"

"I came at the request of the Schumacher family," he explained. "The man we honor here today opened our eyes at a time when the value of bigness was overstated. He taught us the worth of smaller things and focused our attention on an economics where people are at the center. His unique moral perspective is applicable in both developing and indus- trialized nations. For instance, we in California have opened the first office of appropriate technology anywhere."

"Governor," inquired another journalist, "did you take your chances on Laker standby like everyone else?"

"Absolutely," said Brown, without botherng to go into the meticu- lous advance arrangements his staff had made with the airline.

"You weren't given any special treatment?"

"I stood in line with cash in my pocket like everyone else," replied the leader as Silberman tried hard to suppress a grin. Laker had, he knew, provided transportation to the terminal, permitted them to waive the three-hour, pre-flight check-in deadline and in their own promotional self-interest, alerted national media to the visit. There was no way Sky- train would have bumped Jerry Brown.

"Sir," said a television reporter, "whenever we read about you, we see the word 'eccentric.' "

"I haven't read that. It must just be in the press over here."

"A lot of people wonder about your frugality."

"I think the closer leaders can be to the lifestyle of the people the better off we all are. I prefer to the extent that I can to simplify all the rituals, wining and dining that have become part of politics. I don't do much entertaining. If people want to see me, I serve them a cup of coffee. On special occasions maybe I'll throw in some cold cuts and cheese. You see, as pressure on our resources grows, I think there is going to be an expansion of voluntary simplicity. If you are at the bottom, voluntary simplicity appears necessary. If you are at the top, it looks frugal. But it's all part of reconciling class conflicts."

When he mounted the altar of Westminster Cathedral a few minutes later, Brown was amazed to find himself facing a crowd of 1,200 over- flowing the pews. Schumacher devotees had come from all over the British Commonwealth, France, Germany, Scandinavia, Africa, India, and North and South America to recite the liturgy of the eucharist in this chilly sanctuary. And as the Yehudi Menuhin Orchestra broke into Bach's Air from Suite III in D, Dick Silberman and David Karr stepped out for Big Macs at a McDonald's across the street. By the time they returned, Yehudi Menuhin had finished most of Bach's violin concerto in A minor.

From their vantage point in the transept, Brown's two friends watched the Governor move to the pulpit beneath England's largest rood, a thirty-foot high cross bearing symbols of the four evangelists on its front terminals and our Lady of Sorrows on the back. "I first met E.F. Schumacher at a Buddhist monastery in San Francisco that was symbolic of the paradox and contradiction that often flows through his ideas but also the potentiality and synthesis of bringing people and things together. What struck me both about his ideas and himself is really the utter simplicity that is contained and which he has expressed.

"So often in politics and government, words lose their meaning and they lose their meaning because people have stopped listening because the information being conveyed just doesn't strike a resonant chord. And on that first visit I saw people listening to Fritz and communicating with him about his fundamental ideas. It is a paradox that in a state as big and prosperous as California that the notion of small and intermediate technology would capture the enthusiasm that it has and young people of all walks of life are responding to the book. Listening to his lecture I felt the same thing myself.

"After that first visit, he came to California again and spoke in Sacramento to government officials. The room was crowded. Sitting in the glow of what he had to say, there was a warm, very excited, very enthusiastic feeling, and in an age of skepticism and cynicism, wherever there is a good idea that moves people in a positive and constructive way, people are going to rush to that idea. They are going to celebrate it and share it with as many people as possible. Certainly Fritz Schumacher had that idea. The idea of appropriate technology is asking the question of what service and what mechanism and what technology is appropriate for what particular problem and also asking the question of what are the means and what are the ends that people use when you challenge some fundamental beliefs of modern society. You have to do so out of the context in which you live, the context that finds its essence in Buddhism, Catholicism, Christianity, Judaism, Islam. All the great religions of the world come down to the same thing and that is the central idea that he expressed in his last book, *The Guide for the Perplexed*. . . . And that idea is basically one of culture, of sharing, of individual reality, social diversity and decentralization. The very important idea, the very difficult idea is to communicate. That's why his ideas are so important and powerful.

"And that's the reason I came over here. I wanted to confirm the contribution he has made and will continue to make. It's not a program. He didn't do it with a six-point plan or some kind of economic scheme

224

that is going to revolutionize the world but rather out of the simplicity of his own conversation, of his own way, the idea of example . . .

"In his book, he called attention to the idea that when we speak of GNP, into that goes auto accidents, cancer, as well as production. He emphasized the focus should be on the quality of life and the sharing of the good things that we create and produce. He quoted the word of Gandhi. The world right now has enough for the people's need but not enough for their greed.

"That was the essence of his message. He attempted to synthesize the contradictions between Buddhism and Catholicism, between the developed world and the undeveloped world. All those things come together in the simple way he expressed himself. And I hope I can just emulate some of those thoughts and apply them in practical, day-to-day activities that my own government has. And that's why I would say that this government and this world needs not just another political program, but another person, another hundred persons, like Fritz Schumacher."

Jerry Brown returned to his seat as the congregation began to sing the final hymn, "Jerusalem." When the service ended, he shook hands with the Archbishop of Westminster and then ducked out a side door for the four-block ride to the New Westminster Hotel. Waiting in a rear conference room was yet another group of international businessmen brought together by Sir Jeffrey Hart, the head of global recording company, EMI. Here, just minutes after resting his case for appropriate technology, Brown told these executives and bankers he was confident the U.S. Senate would soon pass the treaty banning unitary taxation.

Reading about the Governor's reassurances to the industrialists, Schumacher's people were offended. Brown's actions were in clear contradiction to his professed admiration of Schumacher, who believed that "all the educational, medical and research institutions in any society, whether rich or poor, bestow incalculable benefits upon private enterprise — benefits for which private enterprise does not pay directly as a matter of course, but only indirectly by way of taxes, which are resisted, resented, campaigned against and often skillfully avoided. Private enterprise claims that its profits are being earned by its own efforts, and that a substantial part of them is then taxed away by public authorities. This is not a correct reflection of the truth, generally speaking. The truth is that a large part of the costs of private enterprise has been borne by the public authorities — because they pay for the infrastructure — and that the profits of private enterprise therefore greatly overstate its achievement."

Schumacher further believed the present taxation system failed because it encouraged corporations to avoid paying their fair share through loopholes written by friendly legislators. He proposed decentralized socialism or co-operative ownership. This way companies would no longer pay direct taxes. Instead, half of each corporation's shares would be put in the hands of public board members living in the enterprise's home town. While this "public hand" enjoyed no managerial rights, it would control distribution of an "equity share" amounting to half the firm's profits. This way local residents could give half the net to their community. Since workers sat on this board, they would naturally see some of these profits maintained the infrastructure necessary for the corporation's continued prosperity. And at the same time, they would protect their neighborhood's interests far more effectively than a national government hundreds of miles away.

Schumacher's people did not understand that while Brown had a great deal of respect for Schumacher, he accepted his ideas more as sign posts pointing vaguely in the direction of a better society, rather than as a detailed road map of how to get there. If some detours were necessary through the board rooms of the internationl conglomerates to keep the economy going in the meantime, he as governor of America's largest state was ready.

Without ever really trying to explain how he could link the simplicity of Schumacher with multinational corporate politics or the space coloni- zation ideas of Gerard O'Neill, Jerry hopped in a cab to Heathrow. After fifty-one hours in Great Britain, the Governor took off for California, coach class, on a non-stop TWA 747. The $486 ticket cost more than Laker, but Jerry was expected to keynote a Los Angeles banquet that evening with a group of labor leaders and didn't have time to return through New York via Skytrain. While Brown settled into his seat for the ten-hour flight, Silberman began pacing the aisle, passing out Famous Amos chocolate chip cookies from a grocery sack.

An hour later Brown and Silberman dozed as the plane followed the great circle route over Scotland and Greenland. But by the time the jet reached Canada's Baffin Island, the Governor was reading an article in Stewart Brand's *Co-Evolution Quarterly* about Thomas Merton's simple cabin in the Kentucky Hills. "Think of it," Merton wrote one rainy night, "all that speech pouring down, selling nothing, judging no- body . . . What a thing it is to sit absolutely alone, in the forest, at night, cherished by this wonderful, unintelligible, perfectly innocent speech, the most comforting speech in the world, the talk that rain makes by itself all over the ridges . . . Nobody started it, nobody is going to stop it. It will talk as long as it wants, this rain. As long as it talks, I am going to listen."

Later, after a nap, Brown reflected happily on the Schumacher me- morial. "I've got a lot of people out there."

"Out where?" someone asked.

"Those people in Westminster Cathedral—from Zambia, Canada,

Germany, England — it's all interconnected — all part of it. You know that woman who was interviewing me just now at the airport? She knows Stewart Brand. She's been to the Zen Center. They're everywhere."

Schumacher may not have had all the answers, but Jerry genuinely felt he was right on when he wrote: "Modern man's attempt to live without religion has proven a failure." Faith and morals, Jerry was convinced, were every bit as important to the present generation of leaders as they were to Francis Xavier, Francis de Sales, St. Francis and Ignatius Loyola. Picking up a copy of Schumacher's requiem mass, he read from Matthew (25: 31–46):

" . . . Come, O blessed of my Father, inherit the kingdom prepared for you from the foundation of the world for I was hungry and you gave me food, I was thirsty and you gave me drink, I was a stranger and you welcomed me, I was naked and you clothed me, I was sick and you visited me, I was in prison and you came to me."

"If people would take this seriously," said Brown, unintentionally echoing his grandmother Ida and father Pat, "what a force this would be. If every Catholic spent a few hours a week in human service, it would be good."

But how to put this message across when the corporate elite was only interested in seeing that this year's bottom line was bigger and blacker than any in the past, and his job almost demanded that he woo corporations with power to make a dent in California's unemployment statistics? It was one thing for Jerry to celebrate the intelligence and far-reaching sensitivity of many of his friends and advisors, but quite another to translate these visions into work-a-day reality. It was easier for Jerry to look ahead. "I'm more future-oriented," he would explain. "I've got to think about the future. Our system is fairly disruptable . . . Technical innovation is important in a competitive world like ours. We are but one speck, we have to push forward, open up frontiers, new paths. Where do people go when they can't fit in? Space opens up possibilities."

"Besides," Brown added a few minutes later as the 747's flaps dropped, "why not explore the universe?" It's interesting. Where does it end? If it ends, what's on the other side? And if it doesn't end, how can it go on forever?"

"I don't have to answer people who say California is a bunch of crazy people"

CHAPTER 14

olitical adversaries since 1971, both Jerry Brown and Attorney
General Evelle Younger began warming up for their main event
bout in early 1978. As the June primary approached, each assured his
respective party he was the gubernatorial candidate who could best woo
middle-of-the-road voters and make off with the election in November.
And each could back up his claim — Jerry by pointing to his proven
ability to pull support across party lines, and Younger by referring to his
twenty-year string of victories in public life. In much the same way Pat
Brown started his career as the token Democrat in Earl Warren's cabinet,
Younger was the only successful GOP candidate for state wide constitutional office in 1974. And as Attorney General, he had compiled a record

of support for environmental- and consumer-oriented causes that earned him the respect of many moderate Californians.

Brown and Younger first clashed when Jerry, newly elected as Secretary of State, began his crusade to be California's first electoral process ombudsman. One issue involved the new right of eighteen-year-olds to vote. The Attorney General, reflecting a GOP concern that liberal eighteen to twenty-one-year-olds could take over some college towns, ruled young voters legally resided with their parents. This meant that they had to vote at home, thereby diluting benefits Democrats expected from the lowered voting age.

In 1971, Jerry Brown filed suit arguing that Younger's ruling violated the voting rights of college students. His opinion was vindicated when the state Supreme Court held that young voters could register where they attended school.

Again in 1972 the two men clashed — this time over the efforts of the Attorney General and Governor Reagan to crush the United Farm Workers through Proposition 22. This measure would have required an open shop for agribusiness, meaning farm workers could opt out of a union selected by a majority of the job force. Unions hated the open shop because it meant workers could enjoy the benefits of representation without having to pay dues. Jerry's discovery that there were unlawfully-obtained signatures on petitions qualifying Proposition 22 generated enough adverse publicity to help defeat the measure in November. This saved the closed shop, a crucial victory in the farm workers' long struggle to represent California's field hands.

This bitter personal defeat was one of the reasons the Attorney General was anxious for a chance to take Jerry on in a statewide campaign. But Younger also believed the Governor was ripe for the picking, that he was out of synch with the electorate on a number of issues, including capital punishment. As part of his strategy to reclaim the governorship for the GOP, Younger promised speedy execution of everyone on death row. Although Jerry had a fairly good record on law-and-order issues, Younger believed that he was too soft when it came to executions and that Californians would register their disapproval at the polls.

Like Muhammed Ali before a big fight, the Republican enjoyed himself in the primaries. While campaigning against his chief opponent, Los Angeles Police Chief Ed Davis, the Attorney General told the people of California what he was going to do to Jerry Brown. When he was through, Younger boasted, the Democrat would be the youngest has-been in California politics.

Brown, facing an easy primary campaign against obscure college professors, retirees, and under-employed artists, emphasized his record of frugality. This included $2 billion worth of appropriation vetoes, sponsoring a historic $1 billion state income tax cut and being the first governor in twenty years to serve without a single general tax increase. He pointed out the latest state budget was $10.6 million less than the previous year, the first time in seventeen years that spending decreased.

Not to be out law-and-ordered, Brown also talked about a fifty-eight percent increase in the number of convicted felons sent to state prison between 1975 and 1978. Once his credentials as both a tough and frugal governor were in order, Jerry reminded labor of his support for stronger safety laws and equal employment guidelines, as well as a new ban on forced retirement of older workers. Environmentalists were told about achievements of prominent appointees like the Nature Conservancy's Huey Johnson, who initiated pioneering programs in urban ecology, and the Sierra Club's Claire Dedrick, who with public interest lawyer John Bryson brought sound environmental and energy conservation policies to the Public Utilities Commission.

No governor, Jerry added, ever appointed more women and minorities to judicial positions, and his Department of Consumer Affairs had succeeded at cleaning up some long-standing business abuses. The Governor frequently added that under his leadership, the state was becoming a national leader in energy production from solar, geothermal, wind, and co-generation. Finally, Jerry argued that during his first three years new jobs in California — many of them in technologically advanced fields — increased seventy-three percent faster than the national average.

Jerry joked about Democratic primary opponent Lowell Darling, who was conducting a light-hearted Pat Paulsen campaign out of his pink 1956 Plymouth. Armed with twelve-foot long needles, this conceptual artist claimed urban acupuncture could solve sewage problems. He pledged to prevent earthquakes by sewing up the San Andreas fault, abolish all taxes, segregate all the state's billboards in one tiny cluster, scrap the space shuttle, wipe out parking tickets, divide the state into smoking and non-smoking regions, give everyone Wednesdays off and reduce Orwellian paranoia by banning the year 1984. In addition, Darling promised to use the state highway budget to hire people to be themselves. For every $500 million frozen in road construction, he said, 16,666 people could be employed at $30,000. "And," the artist added in speeches around the state, "if elected, I would hire Jerry Brown to do the same job he is doing now."

Although that tag line never failed to get a big laugh wherever the thirty-five-year-old Hollywood candidate spoke, many Democrats weren't sure they could handle more of Jerry. The sharpest attacks came from the left. In a ten-page broadside, the Americans for Democratic Action warned: "Within the next few months, California and the rest of the nation will be inundated with the accomplishments of Governor Jerry

Brown. Millions of dollars will be spent to publicize the man who wants to be re-elected governor of California in 1978 and go on to capture the presidency in 1980. Politically, the Governor is a combination of Don Juan and Machiavelli. He's glib, charming and extraordinarily skillful in the handling of the truth, a masterful politician in his use of patronage, public relations and the understanding of power. His commitment to progressive government has weakened as his presidential ambitions have grown. California lags behind many other states in dealing with issues of concern to liberals. Much of Brown's support among liberals, labor, minorities and environmentalists has been maintained by patronage and rhetoric rather than accomplishments. Buzz words and public relations do not solve state or national problems."

Evelle Younger made no secret of his opinion that Jerry Brown was the worst governor in California history. The Governor's opposition to nuclear power, his appointment of liberal judges like Rose Bird, failure to build new freeways, and his "no growth" philosophy were all portrayed as elitist, unrepresentative, and ignorant. "It's not good enough to say lower your expectations," argued Younger. "California wasn't settled by people who came over the mountains to lower their expectations."

Specifically, the Attorney General advocated firing Air Resources Board chairman Tom Quinn, whose air pollution enforcement policies, he contended, upset California industry. Younger argued that Quinn's smog control policies were responsible for "housing and apartment short-ages, the upward spiral of housing costs and an overtaxing of existing sewage facilities." But as the campaign heated up, both Brown and Younger found themselves upstaged by a loud, often profane old charac-ter by the name of Howard Jarvis.

Since the Boston Tea Party, Americans have periodically tried to get back at unpopular government policies by refusing to pay for them. Most of the time, anti-tax crusaders have been beaten or compromised by the establishment. And the larger the amounts of money at stake, the more likely the crusaders are to be beaten. Howard Jarvis, with sidekick Paul Gann, proved to be an exception.

Virtually every politician, newspaper, tax reform group, union, civic association and major business in Califronia initially opposed the tax-cutting drive of this stocky businessman who represented small land-lords. But in the tradition of other great single-issue movements, Jarvis went to the people with his crusade to lower property taxes by fifty-seven percent and limit future increases to just two percent of market value per year. This proposal, presented to the voters as Proposition 13, was cleverly drawn to take advantage of a phenomenon Carey McWilliams, author of *California, The Great Exception,* had identified a generation earlier.

"Californians have become so used to the idea of experimentation — they have had to experiment so often — that they are psychologically prepared to try anything. Experience has taught them that almost 'anything' might work in California; you never know."

In principle, the traditional system of levies on real property appeared to be an equitable way to tax real wealth. But several factors had combined to turn this method into an unfair burden on home owners in the 1970's. Economy moves at the state level systematically increased local government's share of "partnership programs" funded jointly by municipalities and Sacramento. By mandating new or improved programs without financing them, Brown and the legislature forced counties and cities to pick up the tab. In addition, state administrative agencies were also busy drafting regulations in areas like mental health that required counties to initiate expensive services. To make matters worse, local contributions to many partnership programs were calculated on the basis of formulas sensitive to inflation, such as the assessed valuation of real property, while the state's share was fixed.

The combined impact of these new factors strained local governments. For instance, in Alameda County, the homeland of the Governor's urban strategy, property taxpayers had to make up $4.8 million on underfunding of partnership programs, $2 million in Medi-Cal reimbursement, $2.2 million on county overmatch and pay $1.7 million for state-mandated programs in 1977. Thirty percent of the total tax levy was going to support the state and its required programs. To meet all state costs, many county commissioners were forced to decrease support of local programs, leaving less money for municipalities to meet their minimum daily requirements. Funds siphoned off in this manner contributed to California's growing state surplus.

All of these problems were compounded by the rapid inflation of real estate values. Suddenly, houses that cost $40,000 a few years before were re-assessed at $80,000 or even $100,000. For some Californians on fixed incomes, this reassessment was tantamount to the confiscation of their homes.

Against this background, California had a large budget surplus. These reserve funds were a matter of great pride to the Governor. Everywhere Brown traveled he cited them as an example of his fiscal integrity. However, he didn't credit the man who made a good part of this accumulated bounty possible — Ronald Reagan. Because of income tax indexing initiated during the latter's administration, inflation automatically moved taxpayers up into even higher tax brackets. This meant every time a wage earner received a cost of living increase, even if it was only enough to keep up with inflation, the state took a bigger share. However, this hidden tax increase, buried as it was by withholding, was one few people initially understood as clearly as their $1,000 or $2,000 property tax jump.

In 1977, Assembly Minority Leader Paul Priolo of Malibu proposed a legislative package that included indexing income taxes and limiting state and local government spending increases to the rate of inflation. Brown didn't support income tax relief because he felt the state couldn't afford to lose that much revenue without unreasonable service cuts. Instead, he wrestled with the legislature on property tax relief. That year, the legislature considered three property tax reform bills, S.B. 154, S.B. 12, and S.B. 1.

S.B. 154 was designed to provide direct property tax assistance to renters, senior citizens and the poor, and increase the maximum state income tax bracket from eleven to twenty percent. S.B. 12 endorsed a split roll that allowed businesses to be assessed higher property tax rates than home owners. It also provided limited property tax assistance for senior citizens and ways for counties to limit their share of welfare and medical program costs.

According to the California Tax Reform Association's legislative advocate Dean Tipps, "Of these three, Senate Bill 154 was the most progressive. It was supported by organized labor, senior citizens, community groups, consumer advocates, tax reformers and political groups. But it was opposed by Jerry Brown. Instead, he supported S.B. 12 — the only one of the three bills that failed to close a single tax loophole and provided the least relief to home owners, renters and senior citizens. Along with Jerry, the real estate and business lobbies supported S.B. 12."

Despite Brown's efforts, S.B. 12 was soundly defeated in 1977. "It's like a shotgun wedding and the bridegroom isn't quite ready to go to the altar," the Governor explained after losing. "The senators should go home and meditate."

Early in 1978, when it became clear that due to good economic conditions and continued inflation, the state surplus was steadily growing larger, Jerry switched his support to a compromise plan which did afford home owners a considerable tax saving. This measure, S.B. 1, called for rebating a portion of the taxes paid on the first $67,000 value of a home to a maximum of $700. It also called for reducing home owners' taxes by about one-third without changing the rate for commercial property.

Endorsed by the legislature, S.B. 1 went on the June ballot as Proposition 8 with the Governor and many leading politicians believing that it would ensure the defeat of Proposition 13. Jerry remarked: "I think Proposition 13 will be defeated and I will do anything I can to see that happens. The Jarvis amendment is a tax trap."

Before audiences, the Governor noted nearly every important California politician opposed Jarvis-Gann. Even several of his potential opponents in the Republican primary were against the measure, with Evelle Younger refusing to campaign for it, explaining, "There are many problems with Proposition 13."

Brown was also encouraged by the fact that major contributors from both parties and big business backed a multi-million dollar campaign against Jarvis-Gann. The same Ethan Wagner who had helped forge the Pizza Hut pact a few months earlier now commanded the anti-Proposition 13 media drive with his colleague, Chuck Winner. The team enjoyed the best record of any political consulting firm in the state. They believed the best strategy to beat the initiative was to alarm the electorate so thoroughly that voters would be afraid to support it. Using figures worked up at UCLA's graduate school of management, the Winner/Wagner team claimed: "Should Californians vote yes on Proposition 13, there would be a job loss of 451,300 positions in the combined public and private sectors, the state unemployment rate would rise (from 6 percent to 10.1 percent), and total income for California would drop by $4.8 billion. In contrast, if Proposition 8 passes, there would be an eventual job gain of 48,000, a reduction in state unemployment from 6.0 percent to 5.6 percent, and an increase of over $2 billion in income for Californians."

Moving swiftly into big dollar combat, the state's political and economic leadership, including many big banks and corporations, financed a campaign reminiscent of the depression battle against Upton Sinclair's EPIC movement. Jarvis was villified as a dirty-mouthed old man selfishly trying to sink everything that made California work. At one time or another it was claimed that emergency services, schools, police, public health, transit and libraries would all be crippled by his wild scheme. By voting for Jarvis-Gann, Californians would be voluntarily signing up for a new Dark Age.

Like his son, Pat Brown took an apocalyptic view of Proposition 13. He believed the initiative threatened the great legislative monuments erected during his two terms. The Beverly Hills attorney was sure that passage of the initiative would hamstring local communities, forcing the state to bail them out. As a result, Sacramento would be forced to cut all sorts of humanitarian programs.

In addition the university system, state parks, mental hospitals, and urban strategy might all be reduced to subsistence level. And Jerry certainly wouldn't have funds necesary to complete the water plan. "If I were a Communist," cried Pat, "and wanted to destroy this country, I would support the Jarvis Amendment."

It was true that if you unclenched the tax crusader's often-raised right fist and stuck a shoe in it, he bore a vague resemblance to Khrushchev at the United Nations. Philosophically, however, he had more in common with Sinclair Lewis' George Babbitt than Marx, Engels or Lenin. Like Babbitt — Zenith, Ohio's hottest realtor — Howard Jarvis, backed by fellow crusader Paul Gann, saw the home owner as the fulcrum balancing western civilization. Governor Brown frequently pointed out that: "In California you don't mess with a man's car or his guns." Now Jarvis argued it was time to add a man's "castle" to that list.

In the early spring of 1978, most of the state's leaders still thought Proposition 13 would lose. After all, other radical tax reforms — like the ones proposed by Upton Sinclair, Francis Townsend (with his Old Age Revolving Pension movement), and the Allen brothers' ("Ham 'n Eggs for California") social security supplement scheme — all lost at the polls on election day. This last proposal, which would have entitled everyone over the age of fifty to a $30 check each Thursday, was initially extremely popular when proposed in 1938. Its promoters, Willis and Lawrence Allen, who had previously promoted "Grey Gone" hair tonic, had considerable experience in the selling of illusions. It even looked like they had a good shot at putting "Ham 'n Eggs" over until reporters discovered they were profiting off the grassroots campaign. After media exposes derailed key support in the campaign's final week, the measure was beaten by 255,000 votes.

But unlike the leaders of these earlier movements, Jarvis didn't characterize himself as a humanitarian and wasn't the least bit interested in balancing historic economic inequities. Quite the contrary, he was a middle-class rebel who wanted to "show the politicians who's boss" and get low-income Americans off the backs of home owners.

In the ill-fated 1966 Pat Brown campaign book, *California: The Dynamic State,* UC city planning professor William L.C. Wheaton isolated the political strain Jarvis hoped he could harness to start an epidemic. "Higher levels of government are regarded by some Californians with a curious and incomprehensible disdain. Sacramento is treated with a hostility reserved in the east for Moscow. In California, Washington is as alien to many as Peking. Thus, Californians treat their government in which they play so active a part as an object of distrust. Too many Californians will literally bite the hand that feeds them — the various institutions that make possible the California way of life, its increasing urbanization and its continuing prosperity and growth."

Wheaton and Pat Brown argued that this was a self-defeating attitude. To achieve the optimum society, "The mistrust, the little faith, the fear and the penury with which Californians have viewed their governments

235

must give way to confidence in the democratic process and the government institutions which have allowed the state to prosper. That, in turn, must be followed by that boldness of invention and willingness to invest money, effort and faith which characterized those who built the state and its institutions."

Jerry Brown, Evelle Younger and most other "responsible" politicians were initially lulled into a sense of false security by the fact that Jarvis had made several unsuccessful attempts to roll back property taxes over the years. But this time angry home owners lined up to sign his petitions. Because Sacramento failed to find an agreeable formula to remedy soaring assessments, the retired manufacturer began to find voters intrigued by his easy answers. In the words of Lord Bryce, Californians impatient "with the slow approach of the millenium" were always hot "to try instant, even if perilous, remedies for present evils."

Jerry argued that the issue wasn't as simple as Jarvis suggested. The electorate, he claimed, had to distinguish between the desirability of an "era of limits," and the perils of Proposition 13-produced fiscal anarchy. Slashing property taxes without restricting the state's municipal finance system was an invitation to California's greatest disaster since the 1906 earthquake.

In Brown's view, much of the state surplus was needed to implement the California Supreme Court *Serrano* decision that required equalization of local school district taxation and expenditure, and provide funds for new mental health programs, the $5.8 million space communications satellite project, and to cover any losses caused by the elimination of business inventory taxation and unitary taxation. In addition, many recent victories, such as low- and moderate-income housing programs, solar demonstration projects, reforestation and energy conservation would be jeopardized if Proposition 13 succeeded.

Until the last month of the campaign, many observers felt that although Proposition 13 did well in the polls, it would ultimately be rejected by the voters. However, in the final primary weeks Brown's hopes for a Proposition 8 victory were dashed by the Los Angeles County Tax Assessor when he mailed greatly increased property tax bills to thousands of home owners. This was like pinching an angry Doberman and the pro-Proposition 13 campaign received a terrific boost. Property owners were mad as hell and support for Jarvis' tax-cutting scheme was the best way to insure that the legislature and Governor got the message.

With the polls showing Proposition 13 was a sure winner in late May, Jerry stopped campaigning against the initiative he had characterized as "consumer fraud, expensive, unworkable and crazy, the biggest can of worms the state has ever seen." Wisely, it turned out, he retreated to Sacramento to prepare for Proposition 13's inevitable victory.

On primary election night, victor Evelle Younger had a reason to smile. He not only won the Republican nomination, but showed significant improvement when matched in trial heats against Brown. Four months earlier, the polls showed the Governor leading Younger by twenty percentage points. Now, after Jerry spent almost $1 million on his easy primary campaign, the Republican had closed the gap. Best of all, Younger felt he could easily portray himself as the more fiscally responsible candidate and cash in on Proposition 13. Although he opposed Jarvis-Gann too, the Attorney General had been less strident on the subject than Jerry. Younger was convinced the incumbent governor was going to be the real casualty of this initiative. The Republican felt so confident that he and his wife Mildred boarded a plane to Hawaii for a week's rest and recuperation prior to beginning his general election campaign.

When he returned tanned and rested, Younger was, for all practical purposes, out of the running. In one of the most remarkable California political comebacks since Nixon's "Checkers" speech, Brown used Younger's absence to reincarnate himself as a born-again supporter of the Proposition he had campaigned against. The Governor, adopting a nonstop schedule reminiscent of his father's race-horse campaigns, reminded voters of his refusal to accept the mansion, limousine, private jet and other perks of high office and commended his administration for not squandering the state's budget surplus. Then, while claiming, with considerable justification, that his call for lowered expectations helped spawn the Jarvis movement, Jerry promptly began cancelling state programs. Every time he killed a program, he made a big press conference splash. Predictably, liberals howled. And just as predictably the anti-tax crusaders cheered. As this performance was repeated again and again over the next days and weeks, it gradually began to dawn on the fiscal conservatives that they were also cheering Jerry Brown.

Time Magazine called the performance a verbal "pirouette that would have dazzled Diaghilev." Doonesbury got a laugh with strips about the "Jarvis-Brown" amendment. Even Evelle Younger tried to joke, "I just heard Jerry Brown on TV and I swear he sounded just like Howard Jarvis."

State employees unintentionally helped Jerry formulate his new image by booing him on the Capitol lawn for vetoing their 2.5 percent pay raise. And as the campaign progressed, thousands of laid-off county employees, led by a wheelchair regiment of disabled Californians, gathered outside the Governor's office. The chief executive denied them an audience. Even Jerry's sister Kathleen helped her brother look like

Scrooge. Leading a delegation of educators to the Capitol, Kathy, who had been elected to the Los Angeles County School Board, chided her brother for suggesting teachers wasted public funds. To prove her point, Kathleen asked for school board representatives to indicate if they had cut out summer sessions. "Show my brother what we're doing to cut the frills out of public education," Rice said, as Board representatives raised their hands. Then turning to Brown, she asked, "What about the long term? We can open school if we get some [state aid], but we have to look down the road.'"

Jerry enjoyed the best of two worlds. He proposed state bail-outs for school districts, police and fire departments and other agencies providing essential services by dipping into the $7.3 billion surplus, and at the same time, he got headlines for his symbolic cuts. Best of all, from a politician's point of view, the surplus allowed some flexibility in deciding which constituencies to rescue. Unintentionally Jarvis and Gann had created a new kind of patronage power. Through his Department of Finance, Jerry Brown could define how much was available and who would receive aid. Proposition 13 required a whole new budget bill by the July 1 deadline and the Governor was the only one with the staff to determine where the surplus should go. The legislature was not in a good position to haggle.

Under terms of Brown's bail-out bill, implementation of Serrano's equalized school district funding was delayed a year. Instead, the schools received $2.2 billion in emergency relief, while counties, cities and special districts picked up another $1.85 million. In addition, the state promised to assume locally funded Medi-Cal and welfare costs, while also making $900,000 available for emergency loans.

Doling out the surplus was easy compared to slicing the new budget from $17.4 billion to $14.7 billion. Working around the clock, the finance department tore apart the old budget, in the process erasing a blackboard full of Jerry's pet projects. The Governor's heralded "year of mental health" died in July 1978 with only $2 million of the funds for new programs, new staff and salary increases surviving. A $500 million package for alternate energy development, energy conservation and refor-estation was cut to $10 million. Plans to start the state's new housing agency with $300 million worth of low- and moderate-income units were cancelled. The Department of Corrections learned it would have to drop $90 million worth of new penitentiaries and canine narcotics detection teams from its shopping list. Even the Governor's beloved $5.8 million space communications satellite program was cancelled.

These budget slashings created a bull market for Golden State horror stories. Most of them were illustrated with predictable pictures of closed parks, drained swimming pools, locked libraries and unswept streets.

Many stories were exaggerated. Although some state employees were laid off, the blind failed to obtain increases in their welfare payments, Medi-Cal's abortion payments were cut back, and a few mental patients were temporarily housed in jail cells because state hospitals had no vacancies, the state of California did not cease to function.

Jerry Brown himself was not discouraged. "I don't think California needs to be defensive. We are the number one state. Proposition 13 is passing around the country, we are setting a tone. I talked with a delegation from Yugoslavia and even in Yugoslavia they're talking about Proposition 13, so I am proud of this state, proud of what the people are doing and I don't have to answer marginal critics or people who come out and say California is a bunch of crazy people."

Center stage in the state's big budget cut drama, Brown kept himself on the front page while Younger's political prospects sank steadily toward the obituary section. The ever-flexible Governor, remembering his father's loss to Reagan in 1966, calmly engineered one of the state's great flip-flops. And once set on his new course, he was able to dominate events.

In addition to his success in presenting himself to the electorate as a tightwad, Jerry had another big advantage. He was able to call on many people he and Jacques Barzaghi befriended during his first term — minorities, ecologists, women's rights organizations, senior citizens groups, farm workers, mass transit enthusiasts, veterans and New Age visionaries of many stripes. These special interest groups felt the young Governor was open to their proposals in a way no other major politician was likely to be. Even Brown's opposition to the death penalty was offset by the law-and-order record of an incumbent who put more law-breakers in jail than any predecessor. Most of the major GOP issues — such as reduced state spending, economic development, support for local police agencies and anti-drug peddling legislation — were either captured or nullified by Jerry's ability to spread himself across the political landscape.

By the end of July 1978, the Governor was so far ahead in the polls that he began to drift away from substantive issues like taxation to glittering generalities about the eighties. In Los Angeles, he even convened his own mini-United Nations at the Convention Center to salute California's diverse cultural heritage, and incidentally aid his re-election campaign. Like his 1975 Poor People's Lunch in San Diego, this affair was designed to attract ordinary citizens who couldn't afford to sup for $100 a plate at the Century Plaza. Encouraged by door prizes that included two dinners at the El Adobe restaurant, plus gift certificates from clothier friend Jerry Magnin and Raintree Cleaners, more than 2,000 donors payed $25 a plate for jellied roast beef. Operating with the glee of a Heinz man asked to show off his 57 varieties, campaign manager

Gray Davis proudly surveyed Jerry's eclectic constituency. Turks, Greeks, Jews and Arabs — they were all there — all seemingly delighted to be part of Jerry's coalition. The Koreans were stationed at table 246, devotees of the late Chiang Kai Shek were seated at 242, the paraplegics at 12, and halfway back in the auditorium, the shaved heads of a Hari Krishna delegation in pumpkin-colored robes bobbed to the movements of the Ballet Folklorico.

"Perhaps you remember when the Governor said he wanted priests, nuns and the Hari Krishna to volunteer for work at the mental hospital," whispered Brown donor Jayadhisa Daja. "That was the first time a political person has ever paid any attention to us. We did it for a year-and-a-half and then found it difficult to keep twenty or thirty people going. But we're still interested in Brown because he likes things that interest us, such as Indian culture, meditation and higher consciousness. Whatever a great man does, all the world follows."

Soon Motown's Bloodstones appeared on the stage to the obvious delight of those at the Sikh Dharma table. While their turbans and white gowns produced a few double takes, they seemed no less comfortable than a nearby group of Sumo wrestlers. Executive coordinator Krishna Kaur Khalsa remarked: "We appreciate the fact that he has the courage to live the life he wants and is not pushed by the pressures of the job. It doesn't matter what pressures you have, you should stand up to them. I like the way he switched around on Proposition 13. It's a wise man who realizes when he has made an unwise choice. He doesn't need to stand behind his ego. He's not attached to anything. He can flow with things and go the way he wants to go. I hope that through him, more people will have the courage to live a righteous life in government."

This view was shared by Dan Maziaz, co-founder of the New Age Caucus group. He too, believed that the cure for the disease of our time was essentially metaphysical. "Ten years ago or so, only the most perceptive prophet could have foreseen New Age thought leaving the incense filled, esoteric chambers of its origin to expand dramatically all over the American scene. Ten years ago a New Age political movement would have drawn amused chuckles from established politicians. Today, however, such a movement would draw the politicians' anxious attention and respect, for these people know only too well that Americans are more disappointed and disgusted with politics and government than ever before. More and more citizens shun the regular parties and register as independents, if they bother to register at all. There is an expectant feeling in the air. New Age people are sensing that the time is super-ripe for a fresh, original, nonpartisan New Age political movement.

"The numbers of people who would support a New Age political movement are growing daily. If properly organized and publicized, such a movement would immediately have a large and powerful base of support. In California alone, there are 4,000 to 5,000 New Age locations (meditation, yoga and growth centers, rural communes, health food stores and restaurants, coops, holistic health centers and so forth). New Age people directly associated with these locations number between 300,000 and 500,000, while millions of Californians use these facilities. If organized together to promote New Age ideals in the political and social sectors, these locations and people could be vitally instrumental in influencing government and society in California. We could be — very quickly — a positive and most formidable political force. Nor is our strength confined only to California. Recent studies show increasing support all over America for 'simple living and high thinking,' the basic lifestyle of the new age.

"Jerry Brown is leaning in the New Age direction. In his heart he's into decentralization and deinstitutionalization of society rather than having big institutions that aren't serving those interests. That's why Proposition 13 was so important. It gave him a chance to come out against institutions and scale down some institutions. You see the energy crisis, environmental pollution, inflation, social alienation, and spiritual starvation all are forcing Americans to reconsider their priorities and direction in life. The flow of history is aggravating the problems that make New Age solutions no longer utopian fantasies but urgent necessities."

Struggling to recoup his losses and revitalize his campaign, Evelle Younger claimed Jerry's lack of compassion made him a poor leader. "I do think I like more people than the Governor does. I've never seen any great demonstration of warmth on his part. He lacks the Irish charm of his father," the Republican candidate said. Unfortunately for the Attorney General, few people were listening.

In the meantime, Jerry's fervent support of Proposition 13 demonstrated how difficult it was to reconcile retrenchment with growth. As people all over California clamored for the state to bail out their favorite program, Jerry dished out bits and pieces of the surplus. At the same time, finance director Richard Silberman claimed Brown-sponsored cutbacks had a "generally minimal" effect on state government. While this contained an element of truth in the short run, the Proposition 13 meat ax would certainly create vast problems when the surplus was spent.

Thanks to Jarvis, property owners won a needed tax break. But his poorly-designed solution to the problem also let landlords and corporations off the hook to the tune of $2.8 billion dollars in tax revenue every year. If there were any low-income citizens, tenants, or mentally ill Californians who benefitted from Proposition 13 tax breaks, they were certainly hard to find.

And even worse, for a state that prided itself on its tradition of grass roots democracy, Proposition 13 greatly increased Sacramento's control over municipal affairs and services. The Capitol, not the municipality, now held new purse strings. A system of exorbitant property assessments was replaced with one effectively preventing most cities from financing needed municipal services through new tax revenues. And voting new tax levies now required a two-thirds majority. This local option to pay for better services was further restricted by a Jarvis provision limiting real property assessment increases to two percent per year unless home owner- ship changed. All this added up to the fact that city officials would have to decide which firehouses, police stations, and schools to close during the coming year.

Jerry could be fairly faulted not for changing his stand on Proposition 13, but for how he did it. The proposition, while responding to a real need, was loaded with fiscal time bombs sure to detonate in the years ahead. Brown's uncritical cheerleading for the new law was helping his campaign, but many thoughtful observers expressed dismay. Some felt he could beat Younger while also educating voters on the need for future Proposition 13 modification. One possibility was a split-tax roll plan that would increase levies on corporations while leaving them at a low level for home owners.

The Governor called on his family less in the 1978 campaign than he had in other years because of favorable polls. Just the same, they all supported his decision to concentrate on the larger urban areas himself by working smaller cities like Eureka, Pismo Beach, Sonora, Santa Cruz, Santa Rosa, and Santa Maria.

Occasionally family members came together for special events, like a women's luncheon for Brown at San Francisco's Sheraton Palace in mid- October. Leading off the testimonials was thirty-two-year-old Kathleen, who upstaged her more modest brother with a purple suit, leather boots and a Bella Abzug hat: "We have managed to place representatives of the Brown family philosophy in key areas of the state. Barbara is in charge of the Sacramento area, Cynthia has San Francisco, and I suppose I'm in charge of the L.A. area, although I don't know that he thinks I'm doing a good job representing his philosphy. But we are also in a position to give him advice on plumbing, grocery bills and other things that my brother doesn't know much about."

Following her to the dias was Bernice who had ornamented her grey suit with a pearl necklace. "I'm proud of both my governors. People say he's different from his father. Well, he has different genes in him. They are of different generations and serve different constituencies. Pat was governor in the turbulent 60's. We were in a period of great growth then. Half a million people were moving to California every year. So I'm proud of both my governors. I think each in his own way has contributed quite a lot."

Flying about the state in a Cessna, so he could get into small airports, Pat spotted many of his freeways, dams, reservoirs, university campuses and ocean front parks. At seventy-three, the former Governor toured with all the energy of that first run for the San Francisco D.A.'s office back in 1928. He whisked through twelve- and fourteen-hour days that exhausted Mark Adams, the thirty-year-old aide who accompanied him.

On a warm Saturday near the end of the campaign, he arrived at the Salinas Airport. Kathy O'Boyle, a local Democratic organizer, met him and ushered him into the back of her wide-body Checker sedan for a ride past great packing houses to the Italian Villa. Walking into the gloomy restaurant, the elder Brown, now having trouble with his eyesight, grumbled, "There are two things I object to — dark rooms and women in boots. Now, where is the banquet hall where I'm supposed to talk?"

"Back there," said a waitress without a hint of recognition.

Pat moved slowly through the dining room where families munched cheese burgers and chicken-fried steak. Finally, just as he was about to turn the corner to meet his audience, a rancher in jeans and work boots pushed back his chair, and rising with a smile stuck out his hand. "Hi, Governor," the rancher said.

"Hi, how ya' doing," Pat greeted the man.

"You see," Pat then said turning to O'Boyle, "there's still someone who recognizes me."

Just then, Bev Hudson of KSBW-TV/Salinas bustled in with a camera on her shoulder and asked Pat if he would mind stepping outside. "I understand you're campaigning for your son," she said while focusing in with the rig that included a mike mounted on the left side of the film magazine. "People want to know why he changed on Proposition 13. If you can answer that in thirty seconds, I'd appreciate it."

"That's a lot to say in thirty seconds," said Pat.

"Well, that's all the time we have," replied the young reporter. "Better than having to edit it down. Now could you say a few words so I can get a level."

"This is Pat Brown, campaigning for his son, the Governor."

"Fine, let's go."

"Well, my son, Governor Brown, as you know, opposed Proposition 13. But after the people voted for it overwhelmingly, he did everything he could to make it work. . . ."

When the interview finished, Pat walked into the banquet room to find a group including a local supervisor, a carpenters' and joiners' union business agent, a Spanish translator, a rancher, a college professor and four Democratic party volunteers waiting to hear his remarks. Aide Mark

243

Adams complained about the sparse turnout but Pat spoke to them with the same enthusiasm he displayed before a full Ambassador ballroom.

"When I was studying law," he said, after ordering a Crab Louie, "I was dating a teacher named Bernice Layne who went to school at Berkeley. Every night after class I'd get forty nickels and keep plunking them in the phone to talk to her. I remember one weekend four of us went to the Russian River and they said if you mention Bernice Layne's name once more, we'll throw you in the river. I didn't mention a word about her the whole time. Only after the trip was over and we were about fifteen miles down the road to San Francisco did I blurt out, 'It was a great trip but I sure did miss Bernice.' They turned around, drove back to the river and threw me in.

"You know, my grandfather crossed the plains in 1852 and arrived in Colusa County. He patented 350 acres and his oldest son developed 2,670 acres which was left to me and my brother. We lease it out and hope one of my grandchildren will be interested in farming and take it over.

"You know, I'd like to see Jerry get married. I don't know how that would work with Linda Ronstadt with her working as much as she does. I think he'll get married."

Rambling on about quality of life, nuclear power and the tax revolt, Pat suggested it "was much easier for me to invest in roads, beaches and parks. People want to cut down. I invested millions in education at Santa Barbara and some professors took me on there yesterday because Jerry hasn't given them enough money. But overall he has an enviable record."

Pat was particularly proud of Jerry's willingness to take principled stands in defense of unpopular issues. "Consider capital punishment. People want it overwhelmingly. I was for capital punishment as district attorney and, I can't remember for sure, as attorney general, too. Then I changed as governor. I've never convinced anyone. I had no say on Caryl Chessman. If I had my way, I'd have commuted him from capital punishment to life. After I gassed thirty-three of those poor bastards and was out of office, the Supreme Court decided they should not have been killed. Of course, it was ex post facto. So I stopped talking about capital punishment at parties."

"I still think you did the right thing on Chessman," said a volunteer across the table.

"How is it campaigning for your son?" asked Jim Hunter, a rancher who had worked for Pat during his gubernatorial campaigns and been a Jerry Brown delegate at the '76 Democratic National Convention.

"It's not so bad. I had a great time. I went back to Harvard Law School — me a night law school student going back to Harvard — and they told me I appointed the best state supreme court in the country."

244

After lunch, the former Governor took a cigar from his grey suit pocket and lit up. "The Irish are the best politicians in the world because they are lovers. You've got to love human beings to be a good politician. The Irish are great politicians. Mayor Daley was a great mayor.

"I think 13 is going to cause a lot of problems. It drives me crazy to see women in Bel Air raise their maids 10¢ an hour to clean houses, that will save $25,000 (on property taxes) thanks to Jarvis. People are selfish. You know, if they quote me on the speech I made in San Luis Obispo, Jerry will be mad. I told them savings and loans profits are obscene."

"Why did Nixon lose?" asked Nick Mascovich of Carpenters' and Joiners' Local 925.

"Well, people in California can see through a phony politician," suggested rancher Jim Hunter.

Pat tapped his cigar on an ashtray rim: "Well, they apparently saw through me, too, if your theory is right."

"Well, I don't think you're right," said Hunter. "I don't think they are politically illiterate. But in the long run, in our country, good people don't survive."

"Maybe I'm fatheaded," said Pat, "but I think people regarded me as a strong candidate. I see Younger came out for the New Mellones dam [on the Stanislaus River]. He's got a real TV blitz going, but I think Jerry has blunted them. He's been a tightwad. He's been a conservative Democrat. If I had been governor, I would have signed an increase for widows and orphans (welfare payments)."

"Jerry doesn't have your compassion," said Democratic organizer, Kathy O'Boyle. "This is our problem in attracting support."

After paying the bill, O'Boyle drove Pat and Mark Adams across the Salinas Valley to KMST-TV in Monterey. Inside he was interviewed by a young woman wearing jeans and a blue sweater.

"Mr. Brown," she asked, "if you were governor now, would you handle things the same way he has?"

"I don't think I would have gone as far out on Proposition 13 as he has done, but looking back I think he's done a good job."

"Then you don't think it's a phony stand he's taken?"

"No, he's made it work. He could have subverted it. I think he's done a great job. You know, today it's tough balancing the environment and economy. The fact that he is doing so well is a compliment to his talent. I think I would complete the freeways with 2 or 3¢ gas tax but he said no new taxes and lived up to it."

"What about the presidency?"

"I don't think he should even think about it. He has to be re-elected governor and the presidency is something he should put aside."

After finishing, Pat grabbed the newswoman's hands, "I'll watch this at 6 o'clock."

Heading past Cannery Row for a fundraiser at a Carmel friend's home, Pat reminisced about the super highway beneath them. "We had a big fight over the freeway here. It was a can of worms. One of the nuns called me from Santa Catalina where Kathy went to school and said, 'Governor, you're not going to condemn me. We didn't.'

"That Linda Ronstadt," he rambled on, "she must have a lot of boyfriends. That would be difficult for a singer doing all those concerts being married to a politician stuck in all those Sacramento meetings. It would be very difficult."

The Jerry Brown
Ten Percent

CHAPTER 15

"P eople have asked me why do I change my mind," Jerry Brown
recounted. "Well, when I find something doesn't work, then I try
something else. The worst thing is to get stuck in a position and just
blindly keep banging your head against the wall. I've made mistakes."

Answering skeptics who felt his first term lacked programmatic
clarity, Jerry began his second with a specific proposal — a call for a
constitutional amendment to balance the federal budget. The Governor
advocated a constitutional convention be called by the votes of two-thirds
of the state legislature to deal with his proposal.

One of the first mainstream politicians to support what many liberals
thought to be a dangerously kooky idea, Brown's proposal generated a

considerable chorus of support among fiscal conservatives and taxpayer groups. But after the media send-up and the dramatic speeches were done, Jerry again found he was far ahead of his time and wasn't able to drum up nearly enough support in the state legislatures to get the convention called.

The failure of Brown's balanced budget proposal to fly was symptomatic of a larger problem. After defeating Younger, Jerry seemed to have lost his knack for spotting and backing winning issues. In a sense, he was like a great basketball player who had suddenly lost his shooting eye — his teammates kept tossing him the ball and he kept launching twenty-footers, but not many made the basket. Of course, even sure-shooters have off days, and a few are wise enough to toss someone else the ball and wait for their timing to return. Adopting the slogan "Protect the Earth, Serve the People, Explore the Universe," he announced that he would again run for the presidency.

Challenging Jimmy Carter seemed like a terrible idea to most of Jerry Brown's supporters. Although his public approval rating, buoyed by the 1978 victory, was holding up fairly well in California, Brown had no national organization and little support east of the Sierra. The danger, many thought, was that by running for president without doing his homework, he risked both embarrassing himself nationally as well as being criticized at home for not tending to state business. There were some advisors who even dared to suggest that if he failed badly, people would compare him to Harold Stassen — the boy wonder governor of Minnesota and perennial presidential candidate.

Jerry didn't listen to his advisors, preferring instead to believe he could regain the magic that had almost won him the nomination last time around; but his advisors proved correct. The same candidate who came from nowhere to beat the Carter slate in half a dozen states in 1976 was now finding it difficult to generate any significant national support. It didn't matter whether he borrowed a cup of ideological parsimony from conservative economist Milton Friedman or appropriated a pint of John Kenneth Galbraith's faith in central planning — no one listened. Brown, it seemed, was becoming the forgotten Californian.

Familiarity seemed to breed contempt when it came to Jerry's national image. The more the Democratic political establishment saw of Jerry, the less they liked him. *Chicago Sun Times* columnist Mike Royko nicknamed him "Governor Moonbeam." In Doonesbury, cartoonist Gary Trudeau played with rumors that Brown tried to close a race track at the bidding of a reputed gangster. The series, banned by many newspapers fearful of libeling labor lawyer Sidney Korshak, featured Jerry's imag-

248

inary symbolist, Duane Delacourt (formerly with the Carter staff) doping out press conference strategy with Gray Davis. "I thought I'd say that Brown is intrigued by the Mafia only as a source of ideas. I'll point out that organized crime is one of the few labor intensive industries to be both self-regulatory and cost efficient."

Another critic who wasn't laughing was Shirley Wechsler, executive director of the Americans for Democratic Action Southern California Chapter. She accused Brown of pushing "destructive programs catering to baser mob instincts because he can't provide decent solutions to the state's problems. Brown's only real commitments are to his own aggrandizement and his quest for the presidency. He will do or say anything — even risk the destruction of the Bill of Rights — in his pursuit of power. Brown's obvious pandering to what he considers the mood of the moment makes him a national peril. He's not a liberal, he's not a moderate and he's not a conservative. Typhoid Jerry is a virus in the body politic."

Screenwriter and novelist Jeremy Larner, who once turned down a job with Brown, agreed. "It would be unfair to suggest that Brown's attacks on the bureaucracy are without merit or conviction, or that they have not led to some imaginative, effective appointments. A few of Brown's token showcase programs, such as the Conservation Corps, are based on good ideas. The trouble is — and this is why the ADA is finally right about him — most of these actions are insignificant when compared with the impact of his fiscal conservatism. No matter how you slice it, fiscal conservatism in the larger areas of human need leads to greater inequity, unemployment and social meanness. By social meanness I refer to the old American attitude that the more fortunate have to punish the less fortunate if they are to hang on to what they've got . . ."

Jerry's long-time friend John Vasconcellos, the state assemblyman now representing the legislature's "open feeling" wing, put the problem slightly differently. "He doesn't have humanitarian vision as a basis for redesigning society. I'd like to think there is something growing as far as affirmation of innocence. He believes in original sin and has a negative view of human nature . . . Jerry speaks the cynicism that is endemic in our time."

Indeed, Jerry's popularity was at such low ebb that some opponents of the call for a constitutional convention to balance the budget actually saw Jerry's support for the measure as aiding them. Massachusetts Lieutenant Governor Thomas P. O'Neill even went so far as to say: "Since Governor Brown infused himself into this issue [the balanced budget convention], he's caused the National Taxpayers Union to defend him ninety percent of the time and the issue ten percent of the time. He has taken their eyes off the ball and those politics are working in our best interest."

By the spring of 1979 some out-of-state politicians were telling Jerry to stay home when he announced his intention to come calling. Others tried to use his poor image to advance their own ends. For instance, when he arrived to address the New Hampshire state legislature on the merits of budget-balancing, Brown discovered he'd been set up. The speaking schedule, arranged by the Republican majority leader of the granite state's House of Representatives, put Brown ahead of Democratic Governor Hugh Gallen. This constituted a political embarrassment to the New Hampshire leader, who suggested "We would be conducting the affairs of state a lot more quietly if Governor Brown weren't here."

Jerry, doing his best not to look the fool, declared: "I am not going to be a party to a snub of the governor of New Hampshire." He then cancelled his appearance and attempted to avert some of the negative publicity by taking off to Africa with Linda Ronstadt. There he embarked on a tour of wildlife sanctuaries, villages and desert research centers. In Monrovia, Liberia, the couple toured with aide Jacques Barzaghi. Together they celebrated the Governor's forty-first birthday at the mansion of Liberia's president, William Tolbert. Jerry looked on with pride as Linda bravely volunteered to let a snake charmer wrap one of his reptiles around her wrists.

Normally, media interest in the couple's several-year-old romance was confined to the gossip columns. However, Kenya, the second stop on their tour, changed that. In early 1979 the streets of Nairobi were filled with scores of reporters unable to get across the Ugandan border to cover the overthrow of Idi Amin. While waiting to get clearance, they cast about for news scraps that would justify their expense accounts and forestall their being yanked back to Chicago, Rotterdam, or Manchester. Against this background, Jerry and Linda's arrival in town was a miracle, even to the most agnostic foreign correspondents. The politician and the rock star exploring the African bush were heralded as big news.

Jerry and Linda played a lot better on the home front than Idi Amin ever did. The result of the first filings was a flood of calls and cables from editors and producers back in the States crying for more copy. Almost immediately the Ronstadt/Brown romance became the sensation of the season. Linda, even though she often got top billing, was so annoyed by all the "illicit romance on the dark continent" stories that she threatened to fly home. Jerry, afraid that this would make him look more foolish than he already did, talked her out of it.

Of course, the media hoopla was ludicrous. Linda and Jerry often wined and dined together and neither was in the least secretive about their relationship. And until now, media coverage of their romance was for the most part friendly and low-key. Now, suddenly, they were "news," and at least some reporters delighted in trying to make Jerry seem ridiculous, or at least lacking in common sense. Page one articles, network coverage, a *People Magazine* story and the cover of *Newsweek* were among the media fallout. Although Linda was intelligent and shared many of the Governor's interests (she was a daily reader of the *Wall Street Journal* and *New York Times,* and persuasively argued with Jerry to oppose new nuclear power plants), she was usually portrayed as little more than a singing sex kitten.

Some political pundits claimed that Jerry had capriciously hurt his career by openly traveling with Linda, but Jerry didn't give a damn. He refused to believe the public still demanded unmarried public figures to hide or deny their romantic involvements. And even if the establishment press disapproved, the country was full of voters who would be delighted to spend a week in Africa with someone as lovely as Linda Ronstadt.

Many reporters speculated about the couple's possible marriage plans. One story suggested they planned to wed on the slopes of Mt. Kilimanjaro. This caused Linda to snap: "I only came here for a vacation and the rumors about us getting married are ridiculous." Jerry, who often argued that family life was incompatible with his erratic lifestyle, simply shrugged and refused to discuss the issue.

The confirmed bachelor had become adept at ducking questions about his personal life. He often cited California's fifty percent divorce rate as a reason not to rush into matrimony. While conventional political wisdom held that a family was as much of an asset as a full house at a $1,000 a plate fundraiser, Jerry was unimpressed. At times he even seemed to enjoy the vast rumor mill fueled by his bachelorhood.

For a while a story circulated that a Berkeley woman startled in the middle of the night was convinced she had nabbed a burglar, only to find the Governor tiptoeing toward her roommate's bedroom. On another occasion, a top aide recounted an incident that occurred in Jackson, California. This small gold country town just an hour out of Sacramento was once a favorite among elected officials. Indeed, when he was running for governor in 1958, Pat called it the "legislatures' bedroom. They'd drive up to Jackson whenever they wanted a little extra-curricular activity." When Pat became governor, he promptly "closed the whorehouses which had been running from time immemorial."

Now a favorite Mother Lode stop for tourists wanting the flavor of the old digs and a good meal, Jackson featured a restored hotel where Jerry and several aides sometimes enjoyed dinner. In the course of one particular evening, the Governor struck up a friendship with an attractive young woman. Eventually the two wandered off and disappeared upstairs. Jerry's aides, joking he still had some catching up do to from the seminary, also went upstairs to bed. Later that night, guests in the hotel were awakened by the slamming of doors and the loud voice of a woman. Jerry's companion, it turned out, was furious because during the night California's 34th chief executive gulped down the glass of water which sat on the night table and with it several hundred dollars worth of contact lenses.

When asked if this story was true, Brown laughed, paused a minute, and then denied it. But whether or not "the great contact lens caper," as it is known to some insiders, ever actually occurred, it is undeniable that when Pat years ago expressed skepticism that Jerry would keep his Jesuit vows—of celibacy, or obedience—he was right!

The publicity accompanying Jerry Brown's African safari with Ronstadt demonstrated that although the public wasn't terribly interested in Jerry's second run for the White House, they were fascinated by his personal life. Unfortunately for reporters charged with getting interesting copy, Jerry's life wasn't very glamorous. Indeed, despite a number of friendly, but often casual, romances, he probably had less of a private life than most politicians. People wanted to know what he did for fun. The truth was quite ordinary. Early in the morning Jerry jogged, having decided in 1978 that exercise and the New Age were not incompatible. Occasionally he went to a movie, standing in line for tickets like everyone else. Periodically Jerry and Linda saw a country and western show at the Palomino Club in Burbank. But Brown spent most of his spare time reading. There was no television at the Governor's apartment and he seldom watched in his office.

Jerry's fascination with the written word was no publicity hype. When you visited his suite, you were struck with the hundreds of books and magazines which sat in small piles throughout his rooms. In addition to nearly fifty pages of newspaper and magazine clippings compiled each day by his research office, the Governor seemed to inhale books. At one point he was simultaneously reading Thomas Szasz's *The Myth of Psychiatry*, Ivan Illich's *Deschooling Society*, Gregory Bateson's *The Politics of Ecology*, and E.F. Schumacher's *A Guide for the Perplexed*. *The New Yorker*, *Nation*, *Economist*, *World Press Review*, *Business Week*, *New York Times Book Review*, *Village Voice*, *National Review* and *Level 5* (the space lobby's magazine) were just some of the dozens of magazines that customarily littered the long table where Ronald Reagan's bottle of jelly beans once sat. It was a standing joke among the staff that half a dozen people could be kept waiting for appointments while Brown finished rereading *Criminal Justice, Criminal Violence* by Charles Silberman or *Energy Futures* by the Harvard Energy Project.

Brown's heavy reading was increasingly obvious in his talks as he had a sort of fly paper mind. Whether it was data on the state of the microprocessing industry, unemployment, acid rain or Medi-Cal cost overruns, once a particular fact touched Jerry's brain, it usually stuck. Nevertheless, while Brown's public talks impressed some reporters, students and intellectuals, they were not enough to overcome the "California flake" image or form the basis for a national political campaign. Even if Jerry had been widely popular in 1980, he might have had difficulty financing and organizing a national campaign. As it was, he found himself in the position of a small public television station with superior programming, but a two-bit transmitter, trying to compete with the networks.

By May 1979 it was clear that Brown's major political assets — energy, inquisitiveness and a droll sense of humor — were not going to reverse his declining fortunes. In fact, polls conducted that month showed him slipping even further toward political oblivion. When the public was asked about the impact of the Africa trip, twenty-six percent of those polled said they felt less supportive of Jerry's presidential campaign, while twelve percent believed it helped him. The balance thought it didn't make any difference. By comparison, fifteen percent thought less of Linda after she made the trip while ten percent liked her more.

One of the places that bad publicity hurt Brown most, of course, was the pocket book. When the Governor tried to solicit money for his second presidential campaign, it was obvious that Democrats who hadn't already forgotten him were trying to. Anxious to demonstrate his national appeal, Brown tried to set up campaign organizations in states like Texas. In Dallas he explained how his space program would help the local economy. Reminding crowds he was America's only governor with an astronaut on his staff, he reassured them: "If I get a chance, I will have a lot more astronauts working for me."

Didn't funding a new space program jeopardize potential tax cuts? Perhaps it did, admitted Brown; then he added, "What are they [tax-payers] going to do with that $50 [from Carter's projected tax cut] . . . People think they can consume their way to greatness."

Like most of his trips, this one to Texas generated lots of publicity, but failed to pump life into his campaign. In the fall of 1979 things were so bad, unless Linda Rondstadt was at his side Brown couldn't entice reporters to travel with him. The fact that Jerry's campaign was doing badly was the main reason for his lack of media attention, of course. But traveling a vintage D.C. that would have been at home on the Casablanca movie set, while other candidates traveled in jets didn't help him recruit many reporters.

It was disappointing to Brown that the imagery which was so refreshing to the public in 1976 didn't seem to work for him any more. Not only was no one interested in the old Plymouth, now pushing 150,000 miles (or seem to care that he kept a small menagerie of ceramic turtles and *Rules of the Society of Jesus* on his desk), no one seemed to listen when the California Governor discussed substantive issues like balancing the budget, or creating a credit-rationing system to stimulate small businesses while choking off giant loans for wasteful corporate takeovers and other nonproductive purposes.

In January 1980, Brown hoped to boost his chances in a Des Moines, Iowa debate against Carter and Teddy Kennedy. Then, at the last moment, the President cancelled because of the Iran hostage crisis. A candidate without a podium, Jerry flew from one prairie town to the next, often addressing crowds small enough to fit into a church basement. When his pitch to one Dubuque town hall audience failed to light a political bonfire, the Governor pleaded: "Well, if you don't feel you can vote for me . . . at least don't vote for those other two (Carter and Kennedy)."

Ignored in the midwest, Jerry flew on to New Hampshire to campaign for the February primary. By the time he arrived, reporters had already put him on the endangered political species list. Why was he pursuing a hopeless cause, they asked him. Brown replied that he had an important message for America. "We are doing what every empire does prior to its collapse. You cannot be addicted to mounting levels of public and private debt and not expect to overdose at some point. Every other country has done that. Germany, Brazil, Argentina, Chile, Uruguay, Roman Empire. You should look at it. We are in that stage . . . This path is not right. It is not sustainable. And it will lead to collapse. Or to war. Or both. And I believe that. That is why I am running."

While the media followed Carter, Kennedy, Reagan and Anderson, Jerry traveled about advocating a prescription for change. Surprisingly, even though he had little or no advance work, small but interested crowds began to show up and listen respectfully. They questioned Brown on his views on alternative energy and his support for new technologies and seemed impressed by his familiarity with the issues. It was an odd paradox. While the political mainstream was writing him off as if he were a has-been, a handful of supporters treated him almost like a guru. His opposition to nuclear power plant construction, for example, cemented his old bond with environmentalists. And when he talked about curbing conspicuous consumption, the accomplishments of the California Conservation Corps, small-scale hydroelectric ventures and doing something for the hungry third world, the relatively few who listened applauded a fresh point of view. His audiences of serious men and women—many dressed in plaid flannel shirts and work boots— grew. And much to the surprise of an occasional reporter who showed up for one of Brown's talks, his audience applauded his conviction that personal sacrifice was a necessary part of achieving a better America.

The Browns, of course, had always talked about the importance of hard work and personal sacrifice. Pat frequently told voters the only way they could improve their schools, roads, beaches, courts, parks and water supplies was to pay for them. Jerry came from another direction and argued that the steady depletion of natural resources necessitated a revival of the Puritan ethic. "Maybe everyone is going to have to start working again on Saturday," he suggested in a call for increased self-reliance that was, at the very least, refreshingly different than "more for everyone" messages of the other candidates.

But in New Hampshire, despite his small band of supporters, the majority of the state was clearly not buying Jerry's Puritan message. At "candidates' nights" in various school gymnasiums, Brown was often humiliated by union and teacher groups bussed in by Kennedy and Carter's well-paid advance people with instructions to cheer raucously for their man. Outspent and underorganized, Jerry didn't have to look at the polls to know that he was almost out of the race. As his campaign funds dwindled, he considered firing his small staff, and then announced he would hitchhike and beg for table scraps if necessary. "I am broke and in trouble," he admitted, "and that's why I am just like America."

Even the eleventh hour arrival of Linda Ronstadt ("I don't do political songs—only the politics of the heart") couldn't help California's "faithful" son, who captured only ten percent of the vote, running a poor third to Kennedy and Carter. "How did McCarthy do it?" queried the defeated Governor as his volunteers broke camp and took the Greyound Bus to Maine.

While Jerry's chances appeared to have sunk below hopeless, observant Maine Democrats were perplexed by some of his turnouts. Wherever he went now, no matter how bad his organization, how non-existent his publicity, or how erratic his schedule, groups of intelligent-looking, hard-working men and women awaited. In the small coastal town of Belfast, for example, a local leader looked out at an unfamiliar audience of bearded men and women in puffy down jackets and whispered to Jacques Barzaghi: "Who are these people? I've never seen any of them before."

As the campaign staggered on these same audiences were always there. They seemed different in spirit and appearance than the crowds greeting Carter and Kennedy, and described themselves as urban drop-outs, windmill entrepreneurs, passive solar home builders, organic farmers, wellness experts and anti-nuclear power organizers. And instead of passively listening to Brown, they actively engaged him in dialogue, sometimes challenging and at other times agreeing. Jerry seemed to draw energy from the verbal give and take.

The group, christened the "Jerry Brown ten percent" by campaign aide Fred Branfman, provided the psychic rewards that kept the candidate going. Exaggerating its importance, however, caused Jerry to make another poor decision. Believing that in a more progressive state he might atract enough supporters to win, Jerry ignored the advice of realists and took his bedraggled campaign on to Wisconsin. Casting himself in the LaFollette populist tradition, he traveled the state for several weeks, capping his campaign with a half-hour live television broadcast from the steps of the Madison state capitol. Produced by Francis Ford Coppola and his brother August, the $35,000 show required both a complicated state-of-the-art $500,000 Swiss projection system and three garden variety American flags. The idea was to create a media event so entertaining that the people of Wisconsin would start listening to Jerry's political views.

On the big night, searchlights illuminated the Capitol as the *Godfather* director hovered above in his chartered helicopter and a live audience clustered around steel barrels of burning oak. Meanwhile, rock promoter Bill Graham, who had catapulted groups like the Grateful Dead and Jefferson Starship (nee Airplane) into super stardom, tried to warm up the crowd with jibes like "Coke is bad for your sex life."

But Jerry's miracle in Wisconsin was not to be. Once again his luck and timing, so infallible four years before, failed him miserably. The first catastrophe could and should have been foreseen. Jerry's "special" pre-empted Peter Cottontail — a popular Easter show. Jerry just didn't make it with tens of thousands of disappointed Wisconsin kids who had been looking forward to the pesky rabbit. But the pre-emption faux pas turned out to be the least of his problems. The much balleyhooed chromakey system, which superimposed Brown's image against scenes of urban and country life across Wisconsin as he spoke, screwed up. First, viewers saw the Governor's head elongate and split in half. Soon a gaggle of electronic worms began walking across Brown's two faces. With a platoon of invertebrates now dancing on his cheek, Jerry wound up his talk with a thumbnail biography. Explaining his decision to enter the seminary, he told the crowd: "I wanted to find out what was inside me. I wanted to find God. I really didn't want politics." Then, after remarking that it was the Jesuit ideal which persuaded him to go into public service, the Governor invited the crowd to join him in a patriotic gesture. "I pledge allegiance to the flag of the United States of America . . ." he began, as a wayward space capsule tumbled across Coppola's screen.

By this time calls [unfavorable by a margin of six-to-one] were flooding in to Brown headquarters in Milwaukee. Many viewers were furious that such a poor performance by the California governor had been permitted to pre-empt the ever-competent rabbit.

On April Fool's Day the Governor received only eight percent of the

Wisconsin votes and gave up. "The lesson I take from the 1980 campaign is that voters feel I am not ready to be President." A Wisconsin newspaper reporter who had savaged Brown throughout the campaign shed tears as Brown added: "I feel strangely good. I am setting out to build a new future. My message is true, truer than has yet been felt."

While Ted Kennedy vainly struggled to catch up with Carter, Brown now put his energies into unifying the party. At the August Democratic Convention in New York, he warned about the danger posed by a Republican well-known to his family. "Do not be fooled by those false prophets who would tell you little difference separates our party from theirs — our nominee from Ronald Reagan. Do not forget that Ronald Reagan was nominated by and is ultimately accountable to the party of Nixon and Ford, the party of Hoover and Calvin Coolidge, the party of Warren Harding and William McKinley. That is not our party. That is not you. Ronald Reagan quotes the words of Roosevelt, but forgets these of Abraham Lincoln: 'The dogmas of the quiet past are inadequate to the stormy present. The occasion is piled high with difficulty and we must rise and act anew. We must disenthrall ourselves and then we shall save our country.'

"Even if the American people give Ronald Reagan his Kemp-Roth tax cuts, his nuclear bombs, his breeder reactors, and his superiority over Russian imperialism, I shall say it will be as verbal cellophane and an empty symbol when marshalled against the outraged emity of the emerging one billion hungry people. Without hope, their last refuge will be revolution, anarchy and terrorism. We cannot sustain a way of life that uses one-third of the world's basic resources for but a few percent of its people. In a world made small by jets and satellite communication, our oceans and our missiles will not protect us if we separate ourselves from the wider longing of humanity. Liberty for us? Certainly. It is our most precious possession. But also justice for all, wherever on this earth. That is the advance that can become the dream of tomorrow. Let us save our dying cities. Let us lift up the least among us."

Partially pre-empted on one network by a Pepsi commercial, Brown's remarks won slim coverage. Yet after the convention, there was some evidence that the Jerry Brown ten percent had won a few new recruits. "I don't think many people noticed, but somebody finally made a highly intelligent speech to the Democratic Convention," wrote columnist Mike Royko. "It dealt with issues that haven't been talked about. And it passed almost unnoticed, which is what usually happens to thoughtful observation made at a political convention. The speech was made by Jerry Brown, governor of California who is sometimes referred to as Governor Moonbeam. I have to admit that I gave him that unhappy label. I'm sorry I did it, because the more I see of Brown, the more I am convinced that he has been the only Democrat in this year's politics who understands what the country will be up against in the future. That's been Brown's problem as a national candidate. He won't talk about creating millions of make-work jobs, spending billions of dollars, following economic policies that will lead to even higher inflation, and getting involved in a mad arms race that will probably blow us all up. He won't pander to organized labor, tell a well-fed and materialistic America that it is deprived or try to convince voters that only the federal government is capable of solving our problems . . . People just don't talk that way at political conventions: Make do with less? Quality? Quantity? Less greed and selfishness? That's the way most of us have to live, but it isn't the kind of political rhetoric that brings standing ovations. Which Brown didn't get. I hope Brown is still around in 1984. I think the moonbeam has landed with his feet on the ground."

On to Uranus

CHAPTER 16

By early 1981, with former President Carter keeping a low profile in Georgia and Reaganomics standing tall on the Potomac, several political commentators began rehabilitating Jerry Brown's national image. Like Mike Royko, who once saw Jerry as the Mad Hatter of politics and was now almost a Brown booster, writers of both the left and right began applauding a number of Brown's stands. Descriptions like "thought provoking" and "ahead of his times" appeared more and more often about the same man whom most analysts had consigned to oblivion the year before. Perhaps what was most interesting about Jerry's resurgence was it came from both ends of the political spectrum. Thus, conservatives like syndicated columnists George Will and Evans and

Novak, as well as left liberals such as the *Village Voice*'s James Ridgeway and Alexander Cockburn, all agreed the California governor was talking sense.

"There is no politician who had more to do with framing the political issues of the 1980 election," wrote Ridgeway and Cockburn, "but who himself was so totally obliterated in the process as Jerry Brown." And George Will suggested: "By expressing too many trendy ideas in trendy idioms, Brown armed critics who consider him fluffy-headed. But today he is not trendy; he is leaning against the wind — a gale really — of disparagement of government. His ideas have serious pedigrees and represent a logical extension of twentieth century democratic policy, which is more than many prominent Democrats can claim."

Like a rowboat salesman in a flood, Brown suddenly looked wonderful to Democratic liberals frightened by the deluge of Reaganomics. A few years back many of these progressives argued that Jerry's anti-spending ethic and his support for tough law-and-order legislation made him a closet conservative. But with men like Haig and Watt voicing policies dangerously close to "nuking the whales," the governor of California no longer had to convince anyone he was a liberal.

Brown's support for environmental causes, his wholesale appointment of women and minorities to influential positions and call for the nation to redirect its vast pension fund investment toward more socially responsible objectives stood in healthy contrast to current Washington philosophy. In addition, Jerry was finally getting credit for pioneering the political argument that America should be directed away from failing smokestack industries toward new high technology fields. A survey by *Common Cause* rated California's energy policies "excellent" thanks to fuel-conserving codes, solar development and incentives for evolving alternate power sources.

Brown further strengthened his liberal base when he reassumed his initial position on the unitary taxation of multinationals. Originally Jerry endorsed the system, which assessed international firms doing business in California on a percentage of their profits from worldwide operations. Later he reversed this position in an effort to entice big business to California. Then, in 1981, when it was clear that President Reagan's plan to abolish the unitary tax would cost California five-hundred million to one billion dollars per year, he again changed his mind. Considering the substantial tax breaks already enjoyed by big business as a result of Proposition 13, as well as the state's fiscal crunch, Jerry once again defended the unitary tax.

Even some of the concepts which had targeted him as "flaky," "out of touch," and "weird" in years past were now beginning to make sense to many Californians. Few as yet seriously argued the desirability of the government putting $100 billion into space colonies — that price tag seemed out of the question in an era of limits. But some of the relatively modest projects Jerry directly supported — such as a California space satellite for communication and resource evaluation, scientific ventures associated with NASA's space shuttle and bullet trains to link up the Los Angeles-San Diego corridor — were now taken seriously. So was Brown's insistence that schools focus more attention on mathematics and the sciences so that young people could survive in the computer age. Also, his demand for additional government and private sector contributions to computer, robotic, and genetic industries made him look farseeing, as politicians around the world suddenly discovered there was more gold in Silicon Valley than there ever had been in the Sierras.

Convinced his record of achievement as Governor gave him a secure base with liberal young people and minorities, Jerry now demonstrated the flip side of his political personality. When chief-of-staff Gray Davis resigned in late 1981 to campaign for the state assembly seat from Beverly Hills, Jerry replaced him with an iconoclastic, loud-mouthed Republican named B.T. Collins. This disabled Green Beret, who earned his Purple Heart in Vietnam, promptly announced: "The first thing I'm going to do [as chief-of-staff] is get that guy to wash his hair. It's disgusting — all that . . . grease. Not even dandruff could get through."

B.T., as he was known to almost everyone, earned his political spurs by running Jerry's California Conservation Corps. He did it so efficiently, more than two dozen states and several foreign countries sent representatives to learn how the C.C.C. recruited unemployed youths off the streets and convinced them to work hard for lousy pay. B.T. was successful in part because he realized that a social worker can get a lot done in America if he presents his ideas in the rhetoric of the right.

In the 1981 legislative session, and then again in the spring of 1982, Brown's top aide lobbied for belt-tightening to avoid new taxes. At the same time, Collins argued Brown's case for more prison construction funds. "Since 1975," explained the top deputy, "California has enacted more anti-crime legislation than any other state. As a result, our state's prison population is going to increase from 30,000 to 45,000. If we don't build some good prisons, these people will be out on the street. We don't have room for them in the Governor's office."

Among the anti-crime bills Brown took credit for during his governorship was a determinate sentencing measure that led to mandatory [stricter] sentencing for using a gun while committing a crime, assaults on the elderly, sale of heroin or PCP, rape, or child molesting. This kind of legislation, as well as the tougher attitude of many state trial judges, nudged the occupancy rate of most state prisons well over one hundred percent. Overflow inmates were doubled up in one-person cells, or

261

housed in temporary quarters like mobile homes. To alleviate overcrowding, the Governor urged constituents to support a June ballot measure that would appropriate $495 million for new prison construction.

This tough stand on crime was part of the platform Jerry was fashioning for his next political campaign — a run for the U.S. Senate. Like Ronald Reagan, Brown decided to honor California's precedent of restricting governors to eight years in office (only Earl Warren managed to buck the tradition). But unlike Reagan, who went back to his ranch until it was time for another run at the presidency, Brown preferred to bide his time in the Capitol. To accomplish this, he'd have to challenge Republican U.S. Senator, S.I. Hayakawa. This official, who opposed the Panama Canal treaty saying, "We stole it fair and square," and was widely reputed to snore through Senate hearings, looked like an easy target. During his one term, the aging semanticist and former president of San Francisco State College repeatedly shot himself in the foot by changing his mind on issues. He once even astonished colleagues by voting against his own bill to extend economic sanctions against Zimbabwe, Rhodesia. On another occasion, he sponsored legislation for new federal earthquake research and then tried to delete the $100 million necessary to fund the study. He also hurt his re-election chances by opposing reparations for his fellow Japanese interned during World War II, holding firm to his conviction that the government was right to imprison Japanese even though they were guilty of no disloyal acts. Finally, in the midst of the energy crisis, Hayakawa antagonized another large constituency by arguing that "the poor don't need gas because they're not working."

Heartened by polls showing him ahead of the Republican Senator, Brown began looking confidently toward Washington. But the same survey research that encouraged Jerry also encouraged herds of Republicans seeking a chance to lay the Brown dynasty to rest in November. Prominent among the Republican senatorial primary front runners were San Diego's Mayor Pete Wilson, Representative Barry Goldwater, Jr., and the first Congressman to call for Nixon's resignation from the White House, Representative Pete McCloskey. Also filing were the President's daughter by Jane Wyman, Maureen Reagan, as well as conservative Republicans Robert Dornan and John Schmitz.

By early in 1982 Hayakawa's tendency to contradict himself persuaded some reporters and voters that he was confused and unreliable. Polls underscored this point by showing Hayakawa was the only one of the four leading Republican candidates who couldn't beat Brown. While the Senator claimed he could easily win re-election, his financial backers were less sanguine. During the 1976 campaign, Hayakawa received financial assistance from Reagan friends like Justin Dart and Holmes Tuttle.

These men, used to funding winners, apparently also believed Hayakawa couldn't beat Jerry in 1982 and switched their support to Barry Goldwater, Jr. Unable to raise big money, Hayakawa reluctantly dropped out of the race.

In the meantime, Pete Wilson, who had run a poor fourth against Evelle Younger in the 1978 Republican GOP primary, vied with McCloskey for support from the more moderate wing of the party. Although McCloskey was not popular with many conservatives, several polls showed that he would run the strongest race against Jerry Brown.

The Governor spent much of the winter and spring of 1982 raising money for the fall general election campaign. Speaking to business audiences, he frequently alluded to how well B.T. Collins was minding the store back in Sacramento. He reminded the business community that he abolished capital gains tax on corporations with less than five-hundred employees, was holding the line on the state budget, and not raising taxes despite anguished cries for help from cities and counties now feeling the full brunt of Proposition 13 cuts. Meanwhile, the contributions of Brown aides like Resources Secretary Huey Johnson, Transportation Secretary Adriana Gianturco and Consumer Affairs Director Richard Spohn were visible evidence of Jerry's commitment to causes like environmentalism, mass transit and consumer fairness. In the 1981 legislative session, the Governor supported an expansion of small claims court, diversion of state money to help Amtrak run more California trains, as well as bills protecting wilderness from logging and other development. At the same time, Energy Commission Chairman Rusty Schweickart continued pushing for more co-generation — the recycling of waste heat from industry to produce cheap electricity.

It was not so much that these programs were individually spectacular, or even that taken together they established California as a leader in adopting innovative new programs, that suddenly made Jerry Brown's administration seem fresh and exciting. It was more what Ronald Reagan failed to do that made Jerry look good. Those who believed some government planning was necessary to solve the nation's problems, were horrified by "laissez-faire" Washington. As a result they increasingly found themselves focusing on what was happening in Sacramento. Liberals who once feared Jerry was becoming too conservative, now counted it as a plus that Sacramento planners remained interested in protecting the wilderness, encouraging alternatives to the automobile, helping the poor and advocating the immediate end to the dumping of hazardous waste materials. In short, Reagan's stampede to stripmine Washington of large deposits of the New Deal, New Frontier, and Great Society programs gave new meaning to Carey McWilliams' phrase, "California, the great exception."

As Jerry addressed senatorial fundraisers, observers noticed a fundamental change in his campaign style. The fractured monologues of years past were now reasonably well-organized speeches with a beginning, middle and end, thanks to the polish of speech writer Fred Branfman. While Jerry continued to write his own first drafts, Branfman transformed these often sketchy themes into precise, understandable English. His efforts to communicate better earned Jerry new respect from a variety of groups. These ranged from checkbook Democrats who loved and supported Pat and never quite warmed to his son to recent U.S. immigrants ready to identify with any political leader sympathetic to their concerns.

A fundraiser at the Ambassador Hotel's Coconut Grove in February 1982 was typical. Pat usually made a few remarks first. "I'm probably the oldest person in this room," he began. "My grandparents on my father's side come from Ireland and my mother's side from Germany. I was district attorney in San Francisco for seven years, attorney general for eight years and governor for eight years. I've never been in a meeting with people from so many different countries. I couldn't help but think how great it is when we can live together with this diversity of citizenship and backgrounds. Life is rougher and tougher today than when I was a kid. Sometimes I get depressed. I was governor for eight years. Jerry has been governor for seven years, one month and twelve days. The world is tougher today than when I was Governor. It's hard trying to get enough money and keeping us cool. We think Jerry has been a great governor and will be an even greater senator."

A moment later, Jerry followed his father to the podium. After calling Pat California's greatest governor, he began to speak in a relaxed, informal manner. "One of my grandfathers was a policeman and the other was a gambler. Everyone was always afraid one would arrest the other. That's the basis of my split personality. My mom's a Protestant and my dad's a Catholic, but I've been able to synthesize these differences. Some people haven't been able to conceptualize my political philosophy. Maybe someday someone will give it a name.

"Here in California the Democrats have struck gold in areas conventional politicians have ignored. The neighborhoods keep changing here. There are no flip flops in a dead culture, just a flop. We've gone from Pat Brown, to Ronald Reagan, to me. Now if that isn't a flip flop I don't know what is. I'm not trying to flip flop, I'm trying to reflect the diverse constituency.

"As I was writing my state of the state speech, I thought of all the trouble my own great grandfather encountered coming out here in 1852 from Saint Louis in a covered wagon. The trip took six months and he left a diary of all the suffering and difficulties. His family was Irish and they came because there weren't enough potatoes. The ones on my great grandmother's side came from Germany. They were draft dodgers. What inspires me is reflecting on that struggle to reach California. Imagine no doctors, no Medi-Cal, no Blue Cross, no lawyers, no judges, no reporters and no politicians. They were just a bunch of people looking for a new life. They didn't really know what they were going to get.

"The problems we are facing today are insignificant compared to what they faced. As we look around the world we see a lot of problems. We see a financial system that's overextended, poverty and starvation. We now have the wherewithal to eliminate ignorance and starvation instead of fighting over a declining economy. Our best days are ahead of us."

Brown then talked about renewing America's commitment to education, particularly in science and mathematics. "Each person is going to have to do more, and learn more. We don't cut back in the schools, research and training or at the National Institute of Health because that is what will allow us to expand into the third world and make things work. As they have more purchasing power they buy more from us and strengthen the U.S.

"Our model for the 80's is not Hoover, Harding or Coolidge. Today the only people following that fellow Milton Friedman's economics are Chile and England and we know that is a disaster. If we play by the rules of Adam Smith and everyone else plays by the rules of strategic economic planning, we're going to be in trouble. We're going to have to have life-long learning in an era when *Newsweek* predicts forty million jobs are going to be automated. We are going to have to work harder. We have to cooperate, if we don't want to go down the dark dismal path that leads to nuclear silence."

During his 1982 primary campaign Jerry acted as if his real opponent wasn't any of the Democrats challenging him in June, or even the Republican senatorial nominee, but the Reagan White House. And the Governor wasn't wrong.

"Jerry Brown is our number one target as far as I'm concerned," said White House director of political affairs, Ed Rollins. "His [Jerry's] philosophy is 180 degrees from where we are. It's important that we not have a senator from the President's home state sitting here nit-picking the President on everything he does and playing it back to his home base."

In addition to the Reagan administration's determination to stop Brown, there were three substantive issues that threatened to damage Jerry's campaign. At the head of the list was the fly. In the spring of 1981, the Governor learned something of the limits of the new biological technologies when overnight the pesky Mediterranean fruit fly emerged as a deadly threat to California's largest industry — agriculture. As an environmentalist, Brown was reluctant to commence aerial spraying of the pest, which had been discovered chewing its way through Santa Clara Valley. Most environmentalists favored sticking to ground spraying techniques used to eliminate the flies first discovered there in 1980. What no one knew in the spring of 1981 was that some of the millions of supposedly sterile Peruvian medflies officials brought in to breed with ground-spraying survivors were both fertile and pregnant. This monumental error, attributed to the U.S. Department of Agriculture and a Peruvian laboratory, elevated the problem to crisis proportions.

Brown personally consulted entomologists, pharmacologists and physicians. As always when a big decision was to be made, he did much of his own research. Experts convinced Jerry there were unacceptable health risks associated with the aerial application of malathion. Citing these opinions and the views of his own committee of technical experts, the Governor announced a continued ban on aerial spraying on July 9, 1981. This infuriated agribusiness interests who claimed they already received a verbal promise from the State Food and Agriculture Department to begin spraying from the air with malathion if and when the medfly got out of control. The farmers immediately appealed to President Reagan for protection. Overnight the U.S. Secretary of Agriculture threatened to quarantine all unfumigated California fruit and vegetables from affected areas unless aerial spraying commenced. Brown now had no choice, and on July 14, he authorized sending up the helicopters.

The Governor told disappointed environmentalists that Reagan held a gun to his head. Unless the helicopters started dusting immediately, all fruit in affected areas would have to be fumigated. Malathion, he claimed, was less toxic than the proposed fumigants. B.T. Collins, who had been hit repeatedly with malathion during his Vietnam hitch, tried to reassure California Conservation Corps crews stripping fruit off trees in the Santa Clara Valley. At the command center in Agnew State Hospital, he insisted exposure to the pesticide wouldn't endanger their health. As proof he poured himself a glass of malathion and chugged it in front of his troops. "It's not that I care about you," Collins told them in his best tough-Marine manner, "I just don't want any lawsuits."

The medfly operation, which cost over $1 billion, soon gave rise to a new cottage industry — medfly souvenir traps complete with flies that looked like Governor Brown. Even loyal staff members who felt Jerry was unfairly blamed for the medfly outbreak admitted the crisis was poorly managed. Probably the Brown administration's big mistake was in making contradictory promises to different constituencies. Pledging to residents of the medfly area that he would protect their health by not spraying from the air, at the same time that farmers were told he would unleash helicopters if necessary, raised expectations on both sides. When

266

he finally reversed his anti-spraying stance, inhabitants of the Santa Clara Valley claimed they had been double-crossed. At the same time angry farmers claimed the crisis would have been avoided in the first place if he had only listened to their recommendation to start spraying months earlier. Meanwhile, Californians who had no strong feelings either way didn't enjoy sweltering in freeway lines at medfly checkpoints and being forced to destroy gardens.

Brown was correct when he argued Reagan held a gun to his head on the aerial spraying matter, but the fact that the USDA sent in pregnant medflies was not an acceptable excuse for why the problem got out of hand. Many observers pointed out that it was the job of the governor and his staff to set up monitoring procedures to prevent accidents like the spread of fertile flies from happening in the first place. And many Californians believed that Brown and his staff should have moved faster and more efficiently once the crisis was recognized. For all his homework, it was obvious Jerry Brown had been badly hurt by the fly. If the pest appeared in sufficient numbers in the spring and summer of 1982, it might even be fatal to the Governor's fall campaign.

At the same time the medfly was threatening California farmers, the taxing limitations of Proposition 13 were threatening the survival of many traditional governmental functions. For example, in Oakland, Brown's one-time showcase city, twenty-four of the community's thirty-five branch libraries closed by 1981. No longer was there a state surplus to bail out these and other casualties of the post-Proposition 13 era. The legislature, concerned about how this problem was hurting California education, passed a two-year $18 million library relief bill in late 1980. Brown vetoed it, announcing that the state didn't have the money. On the same day, however, he signed a bill to reduce racetrack taxes by $18 million. Apparently the state's race course owners were better organized than its library users. Many criticized Jerry's decision on these two bills, pointing out that it was a good example of how his failure to adopt and follow coherent priorities sometimes resulted in hasty, bad decision-making.

A year after the $18 million veto, the California Library Association estimated ten percent of the state's branches were forced to shut down due to insufficient funds. Hours were cut back nineteen percent and book purchases fell twelve percent. Obviously this made it harder for young people to master the skills necessary to become part of the technological vanguard foreseen by Governor Brown. With their local branch library closed after school, the only technology some of these children were likely to master was how to turn the channels on their TV sets. As Oakland writer William Allan put it: "In my community, the Glenview library is a center that authors use, artists come there, children and seniors are always there; it's a place of lifelong learning, and now unemployment helps fill seats. You walk past these days, the shades are drawn, children peer in the windows, go to the doors, knock seeking entrance. They don't believe what's happening and think if they go there every day, that the doors will be opened and they can go back in to their enjoyment. They watch the seniors, their friends, stroll by and ask them, 'Mister, is it going to open soon? What's up? I need some books.' "

But the libraries were just one problem area. Californians, long proud of their first-rate public services, began to feel the cutbacks in a number of significant ways. Personnel cuts meant reduced staffing for many local police agencies at the same time that people were demanding more protection from criminals. Fire services were also being reduced at both the community and state level. Even California's proudest asset — its outstanding highway system — began to develop enough potholes to rival New York. Especially hard hit were school districts, some of which were even having difficulty supplying books to students. Non-essential repair services were also being neglected in a number of state and local programs. This deferred maintenance meant that in the long run residents were going to have to pay higher prices to repair roadways, sewers, parks and public buildings. Staffing cuts were also a problem in many municipalities, eviscerating planning, zoning and public works departments in particular and thus making it difficult for cities to intelligently plan for their own survival.

To generate more money for programs cut by Proposition 13, the 1982 legislature began studying new revenue-producing tax schemes. One was a split roll property taxation idea that could raise corporate property tax assessments, while leaving Proposition 13 in place for home owners. Another idea was increasing the tax on oil taken from California wells. Brown was noncommittal on both ideas. Instead he preferred to address his first priority — a balanced budget — by cutting expenditures. This task, difficult in any year, was complicated by the recession, which worked to reduce state revenues.

One way to achieve savings, of course, was to eliminate state jobs, one by one. To reduce the payroll, agencies were told they could only be credited for required budget cuts by reducing their payrolls. A kind of fiscal neutron bomb, this approach, mandated by the legislature, hurt people while leaving programs intact. In effect, many agency heads could keep programs as long as they got rid of enough employees. Eventually Brown's proposed state budget was cut by $1.3 billion to $26.5 billion. Among the recommended changes were eliminating increases in Medi-Cal provider rates, reductions in some funding rates for growing school districts, a freeze on new state capitol outlays, reduced travel budgets, and a $250 million decrease in local government funding.

Cutting back was a painful process, but the Governor, who continued to push for a constitutional convention to balance the federal budget, believed it was important. State spending was another area where Brown looked prescient. Derided by many liberals when he first proposed a balanced budget amendment in 1978, the concept gradually gained support when Reagan's tax cuts for the wealthy, combined with big defense budgets, created a federal deficit of frightening proportions. By May 1982, with the support of only three more states needed to call a constitutional convention, even Congress appeared anxious to grapple with some kind of budget balancing scheme.

As always, however, Jerry's parsimony was selective. He continued to spend when he felt the public needed or wanted something badly enough. And one thing the almost fourteen million Californians who lived south of the Tehachapi Mountains always thought they needed was water. Thus, Brown continued to support a peripheral canal that would ultimately cost $19 billion and add at least $645 a year to each Southern California customer's annual water bill by the year 2000. This giant project, an extension of the water plan designed by Pat Brown, also required vast amounts of expensive energy to pump the Sacramento River south to the state's arid areas.

The peripheral canal plan had been around for many years. Traditionally, Northern Californians, especially those living near the Sacramento River Delta and San Francisco Bay, opposed it fearing that substantially reduced river flow would produce a number of environmental changes. One danger was that reduced flow of fresh water would bring the salt barrier (the point where tidal Pacific salt water meets clear Sierra runoff) upstream. This could disrupt and possibly ruin parts of the Delta ecology. Opposition also came from outdoors enthusiasts and others who felt that if the great canal was built, several wild Northern California rivers would surely be dammed to provide water necessary to fill up the ditch in dry years. Southern California agricultural and development interests argued that without the water, their desert civilization would dry up and blow away.

Jerry tried to placate both sides by drafting and supporting compromise legislation tying wilderness protection for north coast rivers and strict standards for Delta water quality to construction of the canal. This was his way of reassuring environmentalists that the last free-running streams of the north would not also be captured by the thirsty south. During 1977 it looked as if Jerry's attempt at a compromise might work, when both the traditionally anti-canal Sierra Club and a number of Southern California land corporations agreed to cooperate. But even before Jerry's canal bill passed the 1980 legislature, his coalition fell apart. First the Sierra Club rank-and-file forced conservative leadership to disavow support; then some big land owners in the southern regions reneged. These business interests concluded they would be better off killing the compromise and later trying to pass a canal bill free of environmental trade-offs.

This great water fight would be decided in a canal referendum on the June 1982 ballot. Much to Jerry's chagrin, the anti-land forces were led by members of the fragile coalition he put together in 1977 to support the canal. Thus the Sierra Club joined other environmental organizations to form an unlikely alliance with agricultural interests, like the J.G. Boswell Company who rejected north coast river safeguards entirely.

Brown's old allies breaking ranks and campaigning against his canal compromise demonstrated just how easy it was for a politician to make enemies in California. Even though the majority of Californians supported Jerry's position on the canal in an April 1982 poll conducted by the Field organization, the Governor's early spring public approval rating showed that forty-one percent of the electorate thought he was doing a poor or very poor job. (Seven years earlier, that figure had stood at just sixteen percent.) And while Jerry did manage to pick up a few points on the three leading Republican contenders in an April Field poll, he still remained from ten to seventeen percent behind Goldwater, Wilson and McCloskey.

At Jerry Brown waffle breakfasts, candidates like Pete McCloskey helped themselves to "malathion syrup" as they laughed about Jerry's problems. At one Republican gathering, complete with souvenir medfly traps, McCloskey played on Jerry's inability to balance the state's competing interests. "I'd like to run against him in November," said the congressman from San Mateo County, "but the important thing is that whomever we pick, we've all got. to get behind him to beat Jerry Brown." Standing at the serving table with an apron tied around his waist, Gary Shansby, head of the Shaklee Corporation and the San Francisco Chamber of Commerce, agreed. "Brown must be stopped. He's young and he's dangerous."

The GOP was heartened by Field polls now showing that over twenty-two percent of the electorate was turned off by Jerry's frequent policy flip-flops. Of course, changing your mind was nothing new in California politics. It took a former Democrat like Ronald Reagan to figure out how to beat a former Republican like Pat Brown. And like his father in 1966, Jerry tried to reassure his supporters that being adaptable was not a liability but part of an honorable California tradition reaching back to the Gold Rush. Jerry's advisors believed the flip-flop issue would be his number one problem in the general election campaign. For better or for worse, many Californians had come to distrust the Governor when he spoke out on issues. Did he really believe in a balanced budget, limiting nuclear weapons and encouraging technologically-advanced industries or was he only taking politically expedient positions? Would he reverse himself if he sensed a shift in the prevailing political winds? Brown would have to convince his constituency he was sincere.

Early in the year Jerry decided there was little sense in doing any formal campaigning during the primary. He was convinced money and energy would be better spent in the fall, against the Republican nominee. This strategy made sense as long as the competition was an obscure state senator named Paul Carpenter, Fresno Mayor Don Whitehurst and Ku Klux Klan hopeful Tom Metzger. But in March, a surprise threat emerged. The author of *Burr, 1876,* and *Myra Breckenridge,* Gore Vidal.

Californians already mourning the loss of S.I. Hayakawa's hyperbolic utterings were delighted when Vidal announced his candidacy by calling Brown "The Lord of the Flies" and demanding a chance to debate him. Jerry, who had never forgiven Jimmy Carter for ducking out on a debate with him and Kennedy during the 1980 Iowa primary, wasn't about to give this champion of one-liners a chance to reduce the campaign to a TV talk show. "I'm not going to debate my Democratic opponents because I'm preparing for an uphill battle in the general election," Brown explained unconvincingly.

In speeches to his liberal admirers, Vidal was caustic about Brown's last minute support for building the B-1 bomber in California. "He has really, in a curious way, sold out in the last eight years as Governor, as he has gotten to know the defense industry rather too well." Vidal also charged that, just before he entered the governor's race, one of Brown's aides dropped by to talk over other opportunities. "He told me that a Congressional seat in Northern California was becoming vacant as was a place on the Board of Regents of the University of California. He told me also that a chair of English ($80,000 a year) had just been created at a conveniently located university. Of course, it could have been sheer coincidence that they all came up at the same time." Brown didn't respond and the novelist was unable to produce evidence to back up this job offer charge that was featured in newspapers as far away as the London *Times.*

Keeping his eye on the general campaign, and paying as little attention to Vidal as possible, Brown remained confident he could turn voters around. Reagan's declining popularity was likely to hurt the eventual Republican nominee. In addition, Jerry believed once he started campaigning he could again charm the many disparate constituencies that supported him in the past. Noting that even some of his once less popular stands, such as support for a balanced budget amendment, were finding their way into the mainstream, Brown saw the November election as a chance to win a great personal victory.

Jerry was encouraged when political writers like the *San Francisco Chronicle's* Larry Liebert, who had taken a no-nonsense approach toward the Brown administration for years, began to view him more positively. For example, the San Francisco journalist chided Teddy Kennedy and Walter Mondale for living in the past when both made appearances in California in March 1982 and trotted out the traditional liberal Democratic welfare state agenda, adding only a proposal in favor of subsidizing futuristic industry. Even the high technology issue, Liebert added "seems a belated discovery of what Jerry Brown has been saying for several years."

Would any of this matter to the voters? Jacques Barzaghi wasn't sure. "You could take all the Republican candidates, melt them into one and it wouldn't make any difference," he argued. "The person who votes in November doesn't know that much about Wilson or Goldwater or McCloskey. But Brown is the governor. He's made a lot of tough decisions in eight years. Some of them are bound to upset just about everyone. It's impossible to please both sides all the time." Fred Branfman, sitting beside Barzaghi at the Lobby restaurant across from the Capitol, added: "You have to look at it as the earth going around the sun . . . He's in the center of all California and he reconciles all these opposites. What he's created is kind of like the Copernican theory. Every discussion of Jerry Brown ends in confusion and hysteria."

Jacques was one of a handful of survivors from the first days of the administration. Brown, who had gone through seven press secretaries in eight years, hoped many of his alumni would return to help in the fall campaign. Tony Kline now sat on the bench in San Francisco; Jerry Lackner taught at U.C. Davis; Tom Quinn and Llew Werner were back in Los Angeles running City News Service and trying to put together an investor's group to purchase the floundering United Press International News Service; Sim Van Der Ryn now worked on developing a solar community at a former Marin County Air Force Base and Percy Pinkney was Chairman of the California Youth Authority Parole Board. Stewart Brand continued to edit the *Co-Evolution Quarterly* and update his Whole Earth Catalogue. He was also planning to open a school that taught people how to deal with government. Wilson Clark was in Washington D.C. writing books and doing energy policy research, while Robert Batinovich and Dick Silberman resumed business careers. Rose Bird remained Chief Justice of the California Supreme Court, with conservatives continuing to call for her ouster. Preble Stolz weighed into this struggle with a sharp attack on Bird entitled *Judging Judges*. And in Beverly Hills, Gray Davis was campaigning for the Assembly.

Nearby, Pat kept a heavy schedule at his law office. He and Bernice, still sweethearts after more than sixty years, traveled extensively for both business and pleasure, sometimes taking their grandchildren with them. Both looked forward to participating in Jerry's 1982 senatorial campaign. Pat was particularly sensitive to the possibility that Jerry's inconsistencies would handicap him in November. Reflecting on how his own changes of heart in the Chessman case hurt him politically, Pat remarked in February 1982: "I'd just come off one of the most successful first years any politician could ask for. All my programs were going through. I was riding high. Then, when I changed on that one, the public didn't understand. People began saying I was indecisive. It was the sort of erroneous impression that was impossible to shake. I was haunted by it for years afterward. That's the thing about politics. Things can change so fast!"

As the campaign approached, Jerry banked heavily on his family's strong ties with minority groups. In one interesting campaign sidelight, Jerry apointed Mexican-American Cruz Reynoso to the seat on the California Supreme Court vacated by Matthew Tobriner, who retired in February 1982. (Tobriner, a lifelong friend of the Browns, died two months later.) The appointment of Reynoso, a court of appeals judge who once headed the activist California Rural Legal Assistance program, predictably triggered a campaign by conservatives to oppose his confirmation. This pleased Jerry's strategists, who were convinced the controversy would help get out the Spanish-speaking vote in November.

* * * * *

Nearly eight years after becoming governor, Jerry Brown remains an ideological free agent. Like a particle in high energy physics, he always seems to transform himself before he can be identified. In the process of charting sensible alternatives to both the laissez-faire attitude of Reagan and the welfare state approach of most liberal Democrats, he continues to pioneer attractive political ideas. By quickly spotting concepts that hold promise for the future and responding to the needs of Americans outside the traditional mainstream, Brown has earned the respect of diverse constituencies. Unfortunately his personality sometimes undermines his achievements. Too often Jerry starts out in one direction with great fanfare, has second thoughts, and ends up following an entirely different course, all the while pretending he never changed his initial position. And while this sort of zero-based thinking may suit a philosopher, real people with real problems inevitably demand more programmatic clarity' from their political leaders, as well as a greater commitment to following through on last year's good ideas.

273

* * * * * *

Late one night, B.T. Collins looked across the deserted executive suite and suggested: "Jerry's big problem is that he's thinking forty years in the future. He's out on Uranus half the time."

When he heard this, Brown took it as a compliment. For him space represented a vast frontier, offering people many of the same possibilities that inspired his ancestors to come to California a century ago. He believed that in space, where there was no poverty, war or pollution, mankind could make a fresh start. With some luck, he might live to see it. First he had to get to Washington.

EPILOGUE

In mid-May, Gore Vidal remained the maverick underdog in California's Democratic Senatorial primary. Managing to raise only enough money to put a few homemade spots on television, the man of letters confidently predicted victory. "It's been estimated that I would get between 30 to 40 percent of the votes automatically," he told interviewers Dave Phinney and Lois Richtand. "People will see Brown's name and just go straight for the next one. So my task is to pick up one in five voters."

Vidal, of course, had to admit he was having some difficulty identifying his constituency. Comparing this effort with a 1960 run for a New York Congressional seat, he explained: "The difference is in 1960 we still had political parties in the state of New York and I can't find any political parties in California... The Democratic party here is a law office in Century City. Not exactly grass roots."

Jerry Brown had been accused of neglecting gubernatorial duties during his ill-fated 1980 Presidential campaign. No one was making these charges in 1982, however. Certain that Gore Vidal would self-destruct and the general election would probably be decided on Southern California television in the fall, Jerry resisted attempts of his aides to get on the primary stump. Brown believed it was better to quietly raise money and tend to the recession-worsened budget crisis in Sacramento than to contest a primary election he was confident of winning.

When Brown did speak out, he took the high road. Lending his support to the California Bi-Lateral Nuclear Freeze Initiative, he attacked both Soviet President Brezhnev and Ronald Reagan for failing to move

275

ahead on disarmament. Referring to the nuclear overkill capacity of both nations, he pointed out the Robert McNamara-McGeorge Bundy proposal to renounce the "first use" of nuclear weapons in European hostilities even made sense for the American military. Brown was particularly caustic when he poked fun at Reagan's proposal for a $4.2 billion nuclear war civil defense preparedness program. "Los Angeles can't even evacuate itself on a Friday afternoon with no 'sigalerts' in effect," the Governor pointed out.

The other principal issue on Brown's agenda was the economic crisis. He worried that the recession unfairly limited the horizons of millions of Americans. Thus, Frederick Jackson Turner's theories about the effect of the Western frontier on American life turned up in his talks about the necessity for "growth in an era of limits." Jerry still hadn't quite figured out how to combine an increased population with expensive and limited resources to produce expansion. But he remained convinced if there was an answer to this grim equation, it would be found in the expanding electronic technology industries. Among other things, he warned that the failure to train sufficient numbers of American students in the high technologies amounted to "economic unilateral disarmament."

Since 1965 Jerry pointed out public works investment in America had dropped 28 percent. "We face a financial crisis of alarming proportions because of aging facilities and the huge expenditures needed for replacement and expansion of our public structures." The time had come, he argued, for a consensus across political lines to invest $660 billion over the next 15 years to rebuild and expand roads, transit, ports, rail lines, sewage facilities and other parts of the endangered public infrastructure. And while he was talking about improving American facilities, he went on to recommend a Marshall plan for the Third World, which he claimed would incidentally create a strong market for our goods and services.

Brown's prescription to get the nation on its economic feet differed from Vidal's in several significant respects. The Governor believed the "tax code had to be geared to encouraging innovative investment and discouraging unnecessary consumption. Toward this end, California had increased its capital gains tax on antiques, paintings, gold and other collectibles while wiping out capital gains taxes for companies with less than 500 employees. The hope was this would inspire more geniuses like Silicon Valley's Nolan Bushnell, the video game pioneer who created Atari and now seemed ready to levitate his Pizza Time Theater right off the Dow Jones charts. Small scale capitalism, Jerry thought, remained an awesome engine when it came to creating wealth and jobs.

Vidal countered with the Jeffersonian dream. He believed it was time to face up to the realities of a post-industrial economy and turn back toward "a nation of services, agricultural and small entrepreneurs." By breaking up the multinationals and conglomerate merchandisers, there would be room once again for the small family farm, the cottage industry and the neighborhood grocery. While not quite an agrarian call to arms, his suggestions evoke for some images of a turn of the century Main Street minus Walt Disney. In a way, California, the place people came to when they wanted to escape the old American way of life, seemed like a strange place for Vidal to try to sell this idea. While the idea of turning local bedroom suburbs into self-sustaining communities with a strong local economic base appealed to many, Californians as a whole were probably not ready to voluntarily accept the lower standard of living that went with it.

Although Vidal's view was consistent with some of Schumacher's best thinking, it was a bit too nostalgic for Brown. Jerry believed that any major politician had to commit himself to fixing deteriorating freeways and helping employers, especially in new industries, succeed in order to avert a total economic collapse. He was also willing, somewhat reluctantly, to support the construction of the B-1 bomber and other defense oriented projects. The governor believed defense spending was necessary to pay the bills until the high tech era took up the slack. But, asked a listener at one of Brown's talks, didn't that contradict his support of the nuclear freeze initiative. "I didn't say how many B-1's," the Governor replied.

REFERENCES

Prologue

Page

xi   The Governor met: Author present at meeting, Ames Laboratory, July 1977.

And according: See Gerard O'Neill's *The High Frontier* (New York: 1977), Chapter 1.

xii A non-industrial: Ibid.

xiii but soon: Schweickart quoted in *Space Colonies* (San Francisco: 1977), p. 116.

"You want": Remark made in author's presence.

"Would it": Ibid.

"You realize": Ibid.

xiv "This," said: Comment to author at Space Day, 8/11/77.

"Like the": Ibid.

"I don't": Jerry Brown speech, 8/11/77.

"Oh, I": Jerry Brown at press conference, 8/11/77.

Introduction

page

1   "California politics are": Quoted in Carey McWilliams' *California: The Great Exception* (New York: 1949), p. 172.

2   This young progressive: In Walton Bean's *California, An Interpretive History* (New York: 1968), p. 324.

To protect themselves: Ibid., p. 335.

3   Not only did: Pat Brown's oral history, Regional Oral History Project, Bancroft Library, University of California, Berkeley.

4   "The politician who": T. Harry Williams, *Huey Long* (New York: 1969) p. x.

6   "Contradiction is the essence": Author's interview.

Chapter 1

10   "war of extermination": Bean, p. 166.
        who persuaded state: Ibid., p. 214.
        "This is the best": Ibid., p. 411.
        While Pat deliberated: See Pat Brown's *Reagan and Reality* (New York: 1970), p. 224.
        "I'm not going": Ruth Stein in *San Francisco Chronicle,* 12/26/74.

11   Knowland was: Delmatier et al. *The Rumble of California Politics,* p. 308.
        "I had no other choice": Ibid., p. 338.

12   "It's a felony now": *San Francisco Chronicle,* 5/12/57.

13   "I kept my mouth shut": *Omaha World Herald,* 6/22/58.
        "The last man to speak": *The Reporter,* 6/26/58.

14   "The real story of Billy's reason": Open letter, Mrs. William F. Knowland, in Pat Brown papers, Bancroft Library, University of California, Berkeley.

Chapter 2

18   "These German-born hay": Author's interview with Harold Brown.
        When he arrived with: Ibid.
        Although this handsome, cultured: Ibid.

20   One of the newcomers: Author's interview with Pat Brown.
        The new: Pat Brown's oral history, Bancroft Library.

21   But as rebuilding: Author's interview with Pat Brown.

22   Ida always had: Ibid.
        Afterwards the boys: Ibid.

23   "I just said": Author's interview with Bernice Brown.

24   As the young: Author's interview with Matthew Tobriner.

25   "I was": Author's interview with Harold Brown.

26   Then, in 1913: see Bean.

27   This grassroots: see Bean.

28   "to try instant": Quoted in McWilliams.

29   "You run": Author's interview with Harold Brown.

30   "Oh Father": Ibid.

Chapter 3

32   "Crack down": Author's interview with Pat Brown.

      Inside, the: Pat's account of this wager appears in the *San Francisco Chronicle*, 5/12/57, and in his oral history at the Bancroft Library.

33   The first bookie: see Mary Ellen Leary in *San Francisco News*, 11/7/58.

34   Back at the office: Pat Brown oral history, Bancroft Library.

      "That child": Author's interview with Frank Brown.

35   Jerry's behavior: This anecdote is part of a good story on Jerry's early years written by Jerry Flamm in "California Living," The *San Francisco Examiner*, 6/26/77.

      Here in the shadow: Dick Nolan, *Esquire*, 11/74.

36   "As for me": see Pat Brown oral history, Bancroft Library.

      When the new: Delmatier, *The Rumble*, p. 321.

37   Their superiors: Rev. John Leary, "The New Governor of California; Once a Jesuit" in the *Los Angeles Times*, 1/6/75.

39   And while this: *San Francisco Chronicle*, 6/16/49.

      Instead of: Author's interview with Jerry Brown.

40   Like many: see Pat Brown's oral history.

      As they: Author's interview with Pat Brown.

41   At one of his: Ibid.

      His younger sister: Author's interview with Kathleen Brown.

42   "Play your cards": see Pat Brown oral history.

Chapter 4

46   Neighbors often saw: see Flamm.

48   He suggested: Author's interview with Pat Brown.

49   Under the leadership: Author's interview with Matthew Tobriner.

      "Do you know": see Pat Brown oral history.

50   These Santa Clara: Author's interview with Marc Poché.

51   "gave it to Kefauver": see Pat Brown's oral history.

52   Like the Forty: see Charles Fracchia's article in *City Magazine*, San Francisco, 1/20/76.

53   Bernice cringed: Author's interview with Kathleen Brown.

Chapter 5

55   "It was certainly good": Pat Brown papers, Bancroft Library.

56   "Why not": Sign in Governor Jerry Brown's office.

      He saw men of: See Hugh McElwain's *Introduction to Teilhard de Chardin* (Chicago: 1967).

57   "I sit here": This quote qppears in *Thoughts* (San Francisco: 1976), a compendium of Brown quotations.

"I think you": Author's interview with Pat Brown.

59 Opportunistic accounting: Paul Taylor, professor emeritus of economics at the University of California, Berkeley. Also see his article, "California Water Project, Law and Politics" published in *Ecology Law Quarterly*, Vol. 5, No. 1, 1975. He was also interviewed by the author.

"On land": Pat Brown statewide address, 1/20/60.

The only problem: Kuchel's remarks appear in Hearings on S. 178. Before the subcommittee on Irrigation and Reclamation of the Senate Commission on Interior and Insular Affairs, 84th Cong. 2d Sess. 179 (1956).

60 "The hell": see Pat Brown oral history, Bancroft Library.

"When I hand you": see Dick Nolan, *Esquire*, 11/74.

61 "The employers": Quoted in Hal Draper's *Berkeley: The New Student Revolt* (New York: 1965). This book has excellent background on this issue and Clark Kerr.

62 "intellectuals are": Ibid.

63 Pat's vacillation: see *Ramparts*, 10/66.

"You're not going": Author's interview with Pat Brown.

65 Dorothy Day: Author's interview with Jerry Brown.

66 "The Senator and I": Letter, Pat Brown papers, Bancroft Library.

67 "I'd like you": Author's interview with John Vasconcellos.

68 Kathy's hair horrified: Author's interview with Kathleen Brown.

Jerry kept wishing: Author's interview with Jerry Brown.

69 The millionaire: see *San Francisco Examiner*, 7/21/70.

Chapter 6

71 "Dad, you should": Author's interview with Jerry Brown.

72 His first move: see Pat Brown, *Reagan and Reality* p. 9.

73 "has gone": George Orwell in *The Orwell Reader* (New York: 1956).

To help Nixon: John Ehrlichmann, *Witness to Power* (New York: 1982).

75 Then looking: see Pat Brown, *Reagan and Reality* p. 39.

To bolster: see Lou Cannon, *Ronnie & Jessie* (New York: 1969), p. 122.

"What are you": Author's interview with Kathleen Brown.

"Now that": *in Los Angeles Times*, 11/5/62.

76 "I don't like": see Cannon, p. 123.

77 "Hi, my": Author's interview with Jerry Brown.

78 "I think you": see Pat Brown oral history.

"Dear Ross": Letter in Pat Brown papers, 4/10/63.

79 "1,410 grant": see *San Francisco Examiner*, 7/21/70.

"Jerry, is": Author's interview with Kathleen Brown.

80 "After all": Ibid.

After his own: Jack Thomas in *Boston Globe*, 1/18/76.

82   "I just": Author's interview with Paul Halvonik.

83   "I don't think": Author's interview with Jerry Brown.

     "We cannot": see Draper.

     "Thank God": Ibid.

84   "There wasn't any need": Author's interview with Paul Halvonik.

     "I didn't know": Author's interview with confidential source.

Chapter 7

85   "I have some": *San Francisco Examiner*, 6/16/65.

86   "I don't": Author's interview with Matthew Tobriner.

87   "Jerry, please": Author's interview with Ken Hahn.

     "I understand": see *Ramparts*, 10/66.

88   "Si, I've": Ibid.

89   Drew Pearson: see *San Francisco Chronicle*, 6/32/66.

90   "The greatest scientific": see Pat Brown, *California—The Dynamic State*
     (Santa Barbara: 1966), p. 13.

91   "California is": Ibid., p. 15.

     "Either the": see Pat Brown, *Reagan and Reality*, p. 203.

92   "McLuhanesque": Ibid., p. 19.

     "There are": Ibid.

     "Brown could": see *Ramparts*, 10/66.

95   "Reagan's talent": see *Reagan and Reality*, p. 46.

Chapter 8

112 "For many years,": Ibid., p. 4.

     "I'm sorry": see *San Francisco Chronicle*, 2/27/67.

113 "I enjoyed": see Robert Pack's *Jerry Brown The Philosopher Prince*, p. 36.

114 "Jerry wants": Author's interview with Ken Hahn.

     "No one": Author's interview with Pat Brown.

115 "When you": Quoted in *Thoughts*, p. 14.

     "In October": Author's interview with Gerald Hill.

116 "Dad is": see *San Francisco Examiner*, 12/17/67.

     "I think it": see *San Francisco Chronicle*, 6/24/67.

119 "I'm not disillusioned": Author's interview with Gerald Hill.

120 "I want": Ibid.

     "Blacks and": Pat Brown, *Reagan and Reality* p. 18.

121 "I see": see Pat Brown, *Reagan and Reality*.

     "Oh, no": Author's interview with David Roberti.

122 Radio News West: Author's interview with Llew Werner.

123   "The Board": see *Downey Southeast news*, 8/20/69.

"every attempt": see *Los Angeles Times*, 8/10/69.

124   "In Christ's": see *Hollywood Citizen-News*, 6/24/69.

Before either crucial: see *Van Nuys Valley News*, 7/24/69.

125   "Edmund G. Brown": wire service story, 12/28/69 in Los Angeles papers.

126   "We often": see transcript of conference, 1/21/70.

127   "airborne campus": see *Huntington Park Signal*, 10/1/70.

"hard hitting": Ibid.

"That's a fine": Ibid.

Chapter 9

"Years ago": see *The Citizen*, 10/9/70.

Determined to: See *California Journal*, 6/70, p. 168.

132   "Many times": Dick Nolan in *San Francisco Examiner* 9/3/70. Also see *San Francisco Chronicle*, 9/19/70.

"Jerry has": Author's interview with Pat Brown.

Kennedy confessed: Michael Harris in *San Francisco Chronicle*, 9/2/70.

"Campus rules": Ibid.

133   "if I": *California Journal*, 4/70, p. 111.

134   "In politics": see *Town Hall Journal*, 1970.

135   Barzaghi was: Author's interview with Jacques Barzaghi.

136   "I only": see Orville Schell, *Brown* (New York: 1978), p. 133.

137   After an: Author's interview with Jacques Barzaghi.

138   "Compared to": see Schell, p. 136.

140   "Early in": see *San Francisco Examiner*, 1/3/72.

141   "He was": Robert Pack, *Jerry Brown The Philosopher Prince* (New York: 1978), p. 44.

143   "A Tom Quinn-led": see Bollens & Williams *Jerry Brown in a Plain Brown Wrapper* (Pacific Palisades: 1978), p. 68.

While working: Author's interview with Lynn Ludlow.

"The worst": Author's interview with Marc Poché.

144   "You know": Comment by Jeremy Larner to author.

146   Brown ran: For an excellent discussion of this campaign, see Mary Ellen Leary's *Phantom Politics, Campaigning in California* (Washington: 1977).

147   "I've lived": Author's interview with Kathleen Brown.

The only problem: Author's interview with Frank Brown.

148   "I don't know": see Pack.

"And we": see Schell, p. 60.

To help: see Leary.

150   "You almost": Richard Reeves in *New York Times Magazine*, 8/24/74.

Chapter 10

151 The moment: Author's interview with Jacques Barzaghi.

154 The car: Author's interview with Gray Davis.

155 "Remember": Jerry Brown speech, San Francisco, 1/6/75.

157 One who: Author's interview with Tony Kline.

158 "If I": Author's interview with Dr. Jerome Lackner.

"The administration": Author's confidential interview with Brown staff member.

159 "I had": Author's interview with Rose Bird.

Lackner tried: Author's interview with Lackner.

160 The exposition: E.F. Schumacher in *Small is Beautiful* (New York: 1973).

"You look": Speech at University of Santa Clara, 6/8/75.

161 "Have you": Comment to author by Charles Baldwin.

"When are": Author's interview with Batinovich.

162 "It's ready": Speech, 9/23/75.

"There's no": Speech, 11/14/75.

163 "One great": Speech in San Francisco, 4/15/77.

164 "It's a technique": Author's interview with Rose Bird.

"I loved": Author's interview with Preble Stolz.

166 One early: see J.D. Lorenz's *Jerry Brown The Man on the White Horse* (New York: 1978).

167 "If he": Author's confidential interview with Brown staff member.

"I want": Ibid.

"Who are": Ibid.

psycho-historians from: see John J. Fitzpatrick in *New West*, 1/16/78.

Lorenz wrote: see Lorenz.

And the Reverend Robert Ochs: see *New York Times*, 6/4/76.

169 "I'm raising": March 12, 1976 governor's announcement of presidential primary campaign.

170 "It would be a mistake": see *America*, 2/14/76.

"I don't": George Dissinger & John Kern interview in *San Diego Tribune*, 4/5/76.

171 "Jerry Brown: NYC May": see *New York Post*, 4/12/76.

"I represent": see *San Diego Union*, 5/3/76.

172 Instead he moved: Author's interview with Gray Davis.

173 "There is": see *People*, 6/14/76.

according to: see *Parade*, 6/6/78.

Brown took: see *New Age Magazine*, 5/76.

174 Dennis Ghenke: Author's interview with Dennis Ghenke.

175 "he only saw": Author's interview with Gray Davis.

176   "We're consuming": see *Thoughts*, p. 36.

"If you ask": Ibid., p. 11.

177   "I'm not": see *Rolling Stone*, 7/15/76.

"Oh, I": see *New York Review of Books*, 6/10/76.

178   Suspicious of: see Pat Brown's *Reagan and Reality*, Chapter 5.

When Jerry: Author's interview with Matthew Tobriner.

179   "Jerry you've": Ibid.

"I feel": see Nancy Skelton, *Sacramento Bee*, 1/16/77.

Pacing the: For an excellent survey of the state's mental health dilemma, see Michael Harris' series in the *San Francisco Chronicle*, 3/15/79 and 3/16/79.

The controversial: see Szasz's talk with Jerry Brown in *Co-Evolution Quarterly*, No. 18 (Sumer 1978).

180   One of the first: see Bollens & Williams.

181   After work: Author's interview with Percy Pinkney.

"I have": see *Los Angeles Times*, 1/17/77.

"It used": Carol Pogash in *San Francisco Examiner*, 1/16/77.

182   "This is": Author's interview with Percy Pinkney.

"People are": see *Los Angeles Times*, 1/17/77.

183   "Why haven't": Author's interview with Stewart Brand.

184   "Now what": Remark made in author's presence at Ames Laboratory.

185   "It's hard": Ibid.

187   "Intelligent people": Comment by Dr. Leary at Space Day to author.

"the gold rush": Jerry Brown speech, 8/11/77.

190   "What did you think": Remarks made in author's presence, 8/11/77.

191   "In space": Ibid., 8/12/77.

"TV makes it": Ibid.

"This thing": Ibid.

192   "When I saw": Schweickart to press, 8/12/77.

"When I saw it": Brown to press, 8/12/77.

Chapter 12

194   "I think": Speech, 6/9/75.

195   "rehabilitate jails": Ibid.

"This is": Press conference Los Angeles, 9/77.

198   Undiscouraged, Silberman: Pizza Hut story is based on author's interviews with Richard Silberman and Tony Kline.

199   Silberman believed: Author's interview with Richard Silberman.

200   "It's no asset": Author's interview with Robert Batinovich.

"He complained": Comment by Brown to Silberman in author's presence, 10/77.

202   "We in": Brown's remarks to City Mid-Day Club, 10/24/77.

"The state": In *Thoughts,* p. 37.

"The profit motive": Ibid., p. 68.

203   "I learned a lot": Comment by Brown on New York trip in author's notes.

"You have": Brown's remarks to New York business group, Barclay Hotel, 10/27/77.

"The Governor": Ibid.

"You can say": see *Rolling Stone,* 3-10-78.

204   "I think": Brown's remarks to *Time* board of editors in author's presence, 10/25/77.

"Gee, this": Comment to author, 10/25/77.

205   "No one wants": Comment to *Newsweek* editorial board, 10/25/77.

"Maybe I": Comment to Tom Wicker, 10/25/77.

"It's kind": Comment by Silberman at *New York Times* meeting, 10/25/77.

206   "I know": Comment by Brown to Davis in author's presence.

"Oh, just": Comment by Brown in author's presence.

"I'm not so sure": Ibid.

Chapter 13

208   With more: see author's article "Whimper Across the Bay" in *New West,* 11/17/80 for background on Oakland issues.

210   "I was": Author's interview with Tony Kline.

211   Even Gray Davis: Author's interview with Gray Davis.

212   "Truly a": Wilson's remark at Oakland Guard press conference 11/77.

"It has": Brown's remarks at same press conference.

213   "Mr. Reed": Interviewed at Oakland guard press conference.

The once-powerful paper: See Peter Collier's article in *MORE* 1977.

"I had": Brown's comment to *Tribune* editors in author's notes.

In 1972: see Peter Collier's article on the Knowlands in *MORE,* 9-77.

214   "That's a": Ibid.

"Say 'In Oakland' ": Ibid.

215   Instead he: *New West,* 11/17/80.

216   "People say I": Remark made in author's presence.

217   "The media": Ibid.

218   "Here": Comment to Barzaghi in author's notes.

"That would": Comment by Jerry Brown in author's notes.

"Hey," said: Ibid.

"Hey, Dick": Ibid.

219   "I don't": Ibid.

220 Then he: Author present during this discussion, 11/29/77.

"We've created": Brown's remarks at Hambros Bank, 11/29/77.

221 Under the unitary: This information is based on several interviews with members of the governor's staff and state agencies. Also, see Carolyn Street's article in *California Journal*, 11/77, p. 382.

222 "After all": Author was present, 11/30/77.

223 "I came": Press conference, 11/30/77.

Laker had: Author accompanied Brown party on trip, 11/30–12/1/77.

224 "I first": Brown speech, 11/30/77.

225 Here just minutes: Author present.

"all the": see Schumacher.

226 "I've got": see Nancy Skelton, *Sacramento Bee*, 12/4/77.

227 "If people": Comment to author.

"I'm more": Ibid.

Chapter 14

229 "In 1971": see *San Francisco Examiner*, 1/3/72.

"Again in": see Bollens & Williams, p. 71–73.

230 Lowell Darling: Author's interview with Lowell Darling.

231 worst governor: see Richard Bergholz in *Los Angeles Times*, 10/20/78.

"It's not": see *San Francisco Chronicle*, 9/30/78.

232 "Californians": see McWilliams.

Alameda County: Your Alameda County Tax Dollars brochure 1978 by Alameda County Board of Supevisors.

233 SB 154, SB 12 & SB 1: Legislative analyst's studies of these three bills made in 1977. Author has copies.

234 "The Jarvis": see W.E. Barnes article *San Francisco Examiner*, 6/30/78.

"There are": Ibid.

UCLA's graduate: In UCLA news release, 5/11/78.

"If I": see Richard Reeves in *Esquire*, 5/23/78.

235 Its promoters: In Bean, p. 422–23.

"Higher levels": In *California: The Dynamic State*, p. 55.

236 "With the slow": Quoted in McWilliams, p. 171.

"biggest can of": see *San Francisco Examiner*, 6/25/78.

237 In one of: *Los Angeles Times*, 6/7/78, Brown address to legislature, 6/8/78.

"pirouette": *Time*, 6/7/78.

240 "Perhaps you": Comment to author.

"We appreciate": Comment to author.

"Ten years": Dan Mariarz in *New Age Harmonist*, Vol. 1., No. 2.

242 "We have": Author present at luncheon, 10/78.

243 "There are": Author present on this campaign tour 10/78.

Chapter 15

247   "People have asked me": Brown television commercial fall campaign 1978.

248   In Doonesbury: Trudeau strips appeared in 7/79.

249   "destructive programs": *Jerry Brown, the Rhetoric and the Record,* Americans for Democratic Action.

      Screenwriter and: Larner in *New Republic,* 6/24/78.

      Jerry's long-time: Author's interview with John Vasconcellos.

250   For instance: John Fogarty in *San Francisco Chronicle,* 4/3/79.

      In Monrovia: see *San Francisco Chronicle,* 4/9/79.

      Normally: see Larry Liebert in *San Francisco Chronicle,* 4/14/79.

251   "I only": *San Francisco Examiner,* 4/11/79.

      For a while: Author's interview with confidential source.

      Now a: This story came to the author from another confidential source.

252   At one point: Author observed these books on visit to Governor's office.

253   When the public: *San Francisco Examiner,* 5/4/79.

      In Dallas: *Sacramento Bee* article by Lee Fremstad, 9/25/79.

254   "Well if": Linda Breakstone in *Los Angeles Herald Examiner,* 1/9/80.

      "We are": Chuck Buxton in *San Jose Mercury,* 3/14/80.

255   But in New Hampshire: Author's interview with Jacques Barzaghi.

      "I am broke": Roger Simon in *Los Angeles Times,* 2/25/80.

      "Who are": Author's interview with Jacques Barzaghi.

      The group: Author's interview with Fred Branfman.

256   Produced by: Account of the Wisconsin show based on interview with Jacques Barzaghi, Herb Michaelson in *Sacramento Bee* 4/5/80 and Chuck Buxton in *San Jose Mercury* 3/29/80.

257   "The lesson": Chuck Buxton, Susan Cohen in *San Jose Mercury,* 4/2/80.

      "Do not": Brown speech, 8/13/80.

      Partially pre-empted: *San Jose Mercury,* 8/14/80.

      "I don't": Mike Royko in *Chicago Sun Times,* 8/15/80.

260   "There is": *Village Voice,* 7/2/80.

      "By expressing": *Los Angeles Times,* 12/6/81.

      A survey: Neal Pierce in *Los Angeles Times,* 5/11/80.

      Then in 1981: John Fogarty in *San Francisco Chronicle,* 11/22/81.

261   "The first thing": Bella Stumbo in the *Los Angeles Times,* 11/1/81. This utterly candid interview with Collins, quoting the chief-of-staff during an interview at a Sacramento bar, related many stories the right-wing aide told privately for several years. "Hey B.T.," he'll say, "Didja know they make rubbers in colors now? Or he'll want to know in all seriousness, 'What's wrong with beating your wife?'" Discussing staff loyalty, Collins observed: "Pinhead [Jacques Barzaghi] is probably the only real friend Brown's got. Most of the others are just kissing ass." Summing up

his boss's problems, he observed: "He's smart, maybe brilliant. But he's never been in a whorehouse or a war. He's never had to worry about a mortgage or kids at home . . . He doesn't really relate to the everyday problems people have, because everything's come too easy for him . . ." Collins responded to post-interview criticism by offering to resign. But Brown replied that he wasn't offended: "If you haven't been attacked by B.T., you have't arrived in California politics."

"Since 1975": Speech, Sacramento, 2/8/82.

262   During his: *San Jose Mercury,* 6/14/79.

On another: *San Francisco Chronicle,* 7/12/79.

Finally: *San Francisco Examiner,* 5/17/79,

By early: W.E. Barnes in *San Francisco Examiner,* 1/31/82.

264   "I'm probably": Author present at these Los Angeles speeches, 2/12/82.

265   "Jerry Brown is": Jack Germond & Jules Witcover in *San Francisco Chronicle,* 2/10/82.

266   Brown personally: For a good review of the medfly crisis see Tracy Wood's article in the *Los Angeles Times,* 8/3/81.

"It's not": Author's interview with B.T. Collins.

267   Brown vetoed: *San Francisco Chronicle,* 10/2/80.

269   Brown continued: For a good summary of the peripheral canal issue see the *San Francisco Chronicle,* 4/15/82.

271   "I'm not": Larry Liebert in *San Francisco Chronicle,* 3/31/82.

"He told me": *London Times,* 3/29/82.

272   "seems a belated": *San Francisco Chronicle,* 3/25/82.

"You could": Author's interview with Jacques Barzaghi.

"You have to": Author's interview with Fred Branfman.

"I'd just": Pat Brown's comment to author.

274   "Jerry's big problem": Author's interview with B.T. Collins.

Epilogue

275   *"It's been": See interview with Gore Vidal in 4/82* Bayside Magazine, Emeryville, CA.

Lending his support: Brown's speech to World Affairs Council of Los Angeles 4/16/82.

276   Frederick Jackson Turner's: Speech 3/30/82.

BIBLIOGRAPHIC NOTES

Most of this book is based on interviews with participants in the events described or those who have first-hand knowledge of the material. More than two hundred interviews provided the core of this book. In some cases, key subjects were visited several times.

Many of the events described, such as Space Day, Jerry Brown's trips to New York and England, campaign appearances by various Browns, informal talks, and press conferences are based on my own reporting. Jerry and Pat Brown were both interviewed on several occasions. Pat's recollections were supplemented by his oral history that will become available to the public in the near future. Bernice Brown, Frank Brown, Harold Brown, Kathleen Brown, and Cynthia Kelly also contributed their recollections.

The Bancroft Library's Pat Brown papers, its largest collection, provide both his correspondence, campaign memorabilia, and files on many of his opponents over the years. This library's Earl Warren papers and oral history are a useful supplement. I also made use of state records and archives on both governors. In addition, a manuscript provided by Gerald Hill offered insight on Pat and Jerry's role in the California Democratic Council.

Jerry's collected speeches, both in manuscript and on tape, as well as transcripts of his press conferences were similarly useful. His research office maintains detailed subject files which contribute to an understanding of the issues. The Los Angeles Community College Board provided a clipping file detailing the story of Jerry's first political office.

Extensive newspaper scrapbooks maintained by the Bancroft Library and Pat Brown's own office provide useful background on his career. Jerry Brown's daily news summary, retained by his research office, also offers a good running account of the issues. Although much of the magazine literature is uncritical, a number of excellent articles are available on Jerry Brown. They include: "My Life in the Seminary with Jerry Brown," *City Magazine,* San Francisco 1/20/76; "How does the Governor of California differ from a shoemaker?" *New York Times Magazine* 8/24/74; and Dick Nolan's article in *Esquire* 11/74. *Co-Evolution Quarterly*'s fascination with Brown during 1977 and 1978 led to a flurry of interesting articles in that publication. *California Journal,* an excellent statewide magazine, provides good running coverage of political issues.

Basic to any study of California politics is Carey McWilliams' *California: The Great Exception* (New York: 1949). *The Rumble of California Politics* (New York: 1970) by Delmatier, et. al., offers a look at the state's political past. Although Pat Brown has unsuccessfully tried to write his own biography with the help of several collaborators, his book, *Reagan and Reality* (New York: 1970), does provide some background on the 1958-66 period. Unfortunately, from a historical standpoint, the emphasis is more on Reagan than Brown. *California, The Dynamic State* (Santa Barbara: 1966) provides additional perspective on Pat's two terms as governor.

For a long look at Jerry's first gubernatorial campaign, see Mary Ellen Leary's *Phantom Politics: Campaigning in California* (Washington: 1977). *Thoughts* (San Francisco: 1976) is a useful compendium of Jerry Brown's ad libs during his first year in office. Ed Salzman's *Jerry Brown: High Priest and Low Politician* offers the *California Journal* editor's writing on Brown issues during 1975 and 1976. Orville Schell's *Brown* (New York: 1978) is a journalistic account of the Brown phenomenon that includes travels with the Governor's entourage during 1977. Robert Pack's *Jerry Brown The Philosopher Prince* (New York: 1978) focuses on the years since 1970. *Jerry Brown: In a Plain Brown Wrapper* (Pacific Palisades: 1978) by John Bollens and G. Robert Williams analyzes the Governor's performance through 1977. Certainly the most critical book is J.D. Lorenz's *Jerry Brown: The Man on the White Horse* (New York: 1978). Irreverent and at times amusing, this provides an insider's account of Jerry's first year in office.

INDEX

ABOUT THE AUTHOR

Roger Rapoport is the author or co-author of five previous books including *The Superdoctors*, *The Great American Bomb Machine* and *The California Catalogue*. His articles have appeared in many national magazines including *Harper's*, *Science '82*, *Esquire*, and *Saturday Review*. He lives in Berkeley with his wife Margot and their children, Jonathan and Elizabeth.

0380